All I Need to Get By

All I Need to Get By

Sophfronia Scott

St. Martin's Griffin ⚜ New York

www.stmartins.com

Library of Congress Cataloging-in-Publication Data

Scott, Sophfronia.
    All I need to get by : a novel / Sophfronia Scott.—1st ed.
        p. cm.
    ISBN 0-312-31856-1
    1. African American families—Fiction.   2. African American
women—Fiction.   3. Parent and adult child—Fiction.   4. Brothers and
sisters—Fiction.   5. First loves—Fiction.   6. Ohio—Fiction.   I. Title.

PS3619.C684A45 2004
813'.6—dc22

                                                                    2003058547

First Edition: March 2004

10 9 8 7 6 5 4 3 2 1

For my brothers
Vassie and Wayne,
and for my father,
Vassie Scott Sr.

Acknowledgments

I am deeply grateful for the love and support of my husband, Darryl Gregory, my mother, Ruby Scott, and of all my siblings. I would also like to express my appreciation to my editor, Heather Jackson, who believed in my work even in the earliest stages. And to the people at my agency who believed long before that: John Taylor Williams, Jill Kneerim, and especially Brettne Bloom and Lindsay Shaw, who saw me through multiple rewrites. Thanks to my readers: Kevin Buckley, Brooke Bizzell Stachyra, Greg Monfries, Jenny Lumet, Naomi Barr, Sylvester Monroe, Benjamin Busch, Anne Mini, Lisa Harris, Katy Kjellgren, Emily King, Marcy Lovitch, and Donna Michelle Anderson.

Thanks to Marie Pajer and her son Curt for typing out my first poems so I could see my work in print for the first time. To my Harvard writing teachers, Carl Nagin and William Corbett, who made me realize writing could be my life. To Lou Willett Stanek for helping me begin. To the Writers Room in New York City, where most of this book was written. To my personal coach, Kristin Taliaferro, for getting me through the final stages. To Jenny Lumet for being a role model on how to get work done amid chaos. To Keith Hamilton Cobb for being the inspiration for Tree. To Michael Belasco for coming out to play. To Jensen Wheeler for introducing me to yoga. To my cousin Earline Boone for her story. To Peter Krause for suggesting I start telling stories. To Jaron Bourke for being the first to believe in me as a serious writer. To my sister-in-law Mershela Scott, niece Reva Mitchell, and nephews Michael R. Scott and John Whelan Jr. for loving and validating me just as I am. To Richard and Tracey Cooperstein, Michael and Kristina Sheridan, Jenny Busch, Barbara Busch, Derrick Downie, Cathy Castor, and Scott Talcott for ongoing love and support. To Susan Toepfer for her respect and guidance. To Jy Murphy and Amo Gulinello for Kool-Aid, Talking Jazz, visions of flying, and warm summer nights in Washington Square Park filled with magic. I have been awake, aware, and alive ever since.

All I Need to Get By

One

For six years running I've had the dream, and in the dream my brother always dies. He is cowering in a bathroom stall in the basement of some downtown club, the place lit horror blue by a fluorescent light pulsing overhead. There's sweat glistening on his chocolate brown forehead. It drips from the springy curls of his short black natural. He holds his shaking hands, fingers laced close to his mouth and from his throat seeps a mournful high-pitched utterance that pierces my heart when I realize what it is. My brother is whimpering.

Then the drug dealer throws open the main door, the sound of the metal slab exploding through the room as it slams against the wall. His face is an expressionless rock beneath dark sun-glasses, his body a long trunk of black leather. His steely arm totes an Uzi like the gun was built into the appendage. He moves purposefully; he doesn't even look under the doors to see which stall Linc is in. He makes it to the right one in three long strides, kicking the door in with the fourth. And there is Linc, that stupid look on his face a mix of fear and surprise, like a startled squirrel caught in the middle of the road. It's eerily familiar somehow, perhaps because it's the look he wears in so many of the family photos hanging in our house, as though he didn't know how to prepare his face for the onslaught of light. But this time Linc's eyes grow even wider as the man raises his weapon and without a word from his silent thick lips he fires. Fires way too many times. It doesn't take that many bullets to rip a body of its poor shredded soul. My brother gasps, an inhale the force of which I feel as I awaken with the breath caught in my throat. There's no blood, no corpse to set the finality of the act in my brain. So I dream it again and again.

I bolt up from the pillows, gasping to catch my breath. I can't see. My blinds are shut tight, the curtains drawn. If there's daylight outside, it's completely hidden. The dream slips away, as it has so many times, but this time it's left something behind. Inside me. It's like a darkness, a little gray cloud placed quietly within my being. I have felt it coming on for days, but I couldn't tell where it would come from or when it would strike. Now I am floating in the space between sleeping and being awake, and I'm closer than I've ever been to understanding what might come of this darkness. I can feel a knot forming, a kind of twisting of the flesh below my ribs and just above my abdomen. My hand rises to the spot and pulls at the flesh as though it could rip out the cloud and its premonition.

The phone rings.

"Jesus!" I swallow. I pick up the phone. My clock reads 6 A.M.

"Hi, Mama."

"Hello, Crita, this is Mama."

Of course it's Mama. At 6 A.M. it's always Mama. Only she calls this early. She says that way she knows I'll be home and she won't waste a long distance phone call. It doesn't make for coherent conversation, especially when I'm just minutes recovered from a dream.

"How you doing?"

About as fine as I would be, I think, when I'm not supposed to be up for another ninety minutes. She starts every call the exact same way. The meat she drops in later, like beef into soup, with the answer to my question.

"I'm fine, Mama, how are you?"

"Crita, honey, I'm worried." She speaks in hushed whispers and sounds like a child hiding in the closet under a blanket with a flashlight. I wonder if that is indeed what she is doing. It isn't easy to make a call in our house without Daddy hearing it.

"I think there's something wrong with your daddy."

"What is it, Mama?"

"Well, he's had this cough. It's been going on a long time now. We just thought it was a cold he couldn't shake, you know?"

"It's not?"

Her voice drops even lower. "Honey, he started coughing up blood yesterday. I'm trying to get him to see a doctor, but he won't go. He'll listen to you . . ."

Of course he will. Daddy still thinks I'm Marcus Welby, M.D., based on the pronouncements I made years ago when I was a child and thought I wanted to be a physician. And those only came of my fascination with watching *Medical Center* on television, thinking Chad Everett was it, and some vague notion that I could handle a surgical instrument tolerably well. I brought home good grades in science, which fed my father's idea that we would have a doctor in the family. But those dreams had faded with college, when my interests moved more toward math and accounting than science. Still, Daddy has this idea in his head that I know a lot about medicine.

"Mama, put him on the phone." This time I'm glad I have such influence. We can't hesitate, no way. My father is a black man in his seventies with a history of smoking that stretches back to his youth as a sharecropper in Mississippi, picking cotton with a breaktime cigarette tucked behind his ear. I'm certain that such blood seeping up through his lungs isn't benign.

"Yeah, Crita," Daddy's voice sounds strained and more gravelly than usual. "How you doin'?"

"I'm doing fine, Daddy, but Mama tells me you've been coughing up blood?"

"Yeah. Sure have."

"Daddy, you have to go to the doctor. You should make an appointment with Doctor Joyce right after you hang up with me."

"Well, what do you think this is, Crita?" He sounds so unconcerned, so matter of fact, as though he's asking me, "Does that sky look like it's gonna rain or snow to you?" My response has to be pitch perfect, with enough force to make him see a doctor but not enough to alarm him. Fear in someone so massive could be dangerous, like a lion with a thorn in his paw raging through the jungle. There is no telling how he would strike out or where. And it's too soon. If there's something truly wrong with Daddy, there would be time enough for all that fear—time and a whole wide world to inflict it on.

"I don't know, Daddy," I say. "I just know that it can't be a good sign. You should go to the doctor. Mama says you've had that cough for a while and he can check you out and give you some medicine for that at least. A check-up can't hurt."

"Nettie!" I hear him calling my mother, "Find that number for Doctor Joyce. Crita here says I should see him and I'm gonna go down there today."

"Thank you, Daddy," I say when I know I have his attention again. "You'll call and tell me what he said when you get back?"

"All right, girl, I'm out the door already."

I sigh and close my eyes as I hang up the phone. Once upon a time, my mother didn't have to call someone else to get our father to do her bidding. I still remember the story, can see the image of her, standing on the corner in all her 1950s girlish glory with her cat's-eye glasses, silky straight hair, wide red poodle skirt with the frills underneath. Daddy had been in her sights, tall and powerful, his cigar-shaped fingers wrapped around the handle of his lunch box. He was crossing the railroad tracks after putting in an eight-hour shift at the steel mill. She had put on her best doe-eyed pout. "Mister, will you buy me a bottle of pop?" And he, who could resist neither her eyes nor the pout, had taken her into the air-cooled establishment where she, tugging him by the rough green canvas of his work-shirt, led him to the display. "Oh look," she had said, running a finger over the metal teeth of the bottle caps, "here's a whole case of pop on sale." And he had flashed her the look I'd seen so many times in my childhood—the look that showed he was wise to the scheme but willing to play along. He heaved the wooden case upon his shoulder and took it to the cash register. A wife for a case of cherry pop. My daddy, Henry Carter, had thought it was the best bargain he'd ever had.

The jackhammering has not yet begun. The men from Con Edison have been pounding away at the pavement outside my window for the past week, but now my room is filled with a soft silence. I make myself get up. I put on a robe and go downstairs. As I pull the pink terry cloth around my waist my fingers lightly touch the scars on my belly. There are four of them in all—three are raised asterisks, each about the size of a fifty-cent piece. The last is a long scrawl angrily bisecting my torso. I cover them, as I have every morning for the past five years.

I rent a sunny two-bedroom duplex in a Harlem brownstone stuffed with original details like the carved wood mantelpiece. I draw back the curtains to let in the morning light, then I fill a pitcher and water my six house plants. They are placed throughout the living room according to their need for sun, starting with the ivy and ending with the African violet my assistant had given me last Christmas. The violet is finally beginning to bloom, its fat purple buds curling out among the velvety green leaves. I would have loved more plants, but I have decided it is enough to care for these six, and to do it well. I pluck a yellowing leaf off the abutilon.

At my front door I kick aside the pile of mail, about a week's worth, accumulating on the floor. Then I go out to retrieve my copy of the *New York Times* from the stack left by the superintendent on the hall shelf.

I hear a door close and Mr. Pittinsky appears in the hall. He is so hunched over with age that he could almost be a paper clip with legs. I like to think that he has been living here ever since the brownstone was built some hundred years ago. It makes me feel comfortable somehow. Stable. He eyes me as he reaches for his paper. "Early," he says.

"Yes," I reply, hugging the *Times* to my chest and hoping my carelessly tied robe won't fall open. "I'm up early. I hope I didn't disturb you?"

"You don't disturb me," he says, already disappearing behind his door. His voice is flat, dismissive. I stand there wondering what could disturb him when he has probably lived long enough to see it all, hear it all.

As I come in, the bright blinking red light of my answering machine insists on catching my eye, but I ignore it as I head into my tiny kitchen and pour myself a glass of orange juice. The messages must be at least three days old by now, maybe more. I'm thinking Mama's right to call me at the goddamn crack of dawn. All right, then. I better listen to them.

I hit the play button.

"Hey, hon, this is Lisa." She draws out the first syllable just a bit, so it sounds like she's saying LEE-sa. "I know you're busy, 'cause I haven't heard from you in a while, but let's get together, okay, 'cause I miss you. So here's what my calendar looks like: I have production meetings on Wednesday, Friday, and Sunday. Those are downtown and I could meet you for coffee or something before or after. Then on Monday . . ."

I hit the skip button, knowing she could spend up to three or four minutes reciting the details of her schedule in her casually nasal Seattle accent. I'll listen to the whole thing later.

BEEP! The next voice is masculine. "Hi, um, Crita? This is Warren. I really enjoyed having that drink with you the other night. I didn't want to seem pushy, but I thought maybe I'd made a mistake. The way we left it, you were gonna call me, right? I was just wondering—no pressure! I just didn't know because you didn't—you didn't call—and I had a good time."

Of course you did. You spent the whole time talking about yourself. Delete.

"Girlfriend! It's Mari! You got my invitation, right? This party will be kickin'! The birthday of all birthdays, at least until I turn thirty-five! So are you coming? And are you gonna help me set up?"

BEEP! Mari again. "Okay, since when don't you return *my* calls? What's the deal, sugar?"

BEEP! "Hey, sis, it's Hazel. I just wanted to give you a heads up—Mama's gonna call you. Daddy hasn't been feeling well. I've got a class this afternoon, but give me a call if you want the lowdown. Fudge, forget that, call me anyway. By the way, did you read that article in the new *Essence*? It's called "The Ten New Trials of Loving a Black Man." I don't know about you, but I haven't figured out the old ones! At least Ella doesn't have to worry about that, huh?"

BEEP! "Five days and counting!" Mari again. "Now you've done it! I'm coming after your butt! *Where are you?*"

I am in my kitchen, eating breakfast. I have the newspaper spread out on the round black metal patio table that I dine on. I am drinking tea and I have made myself some toast and eggs, soft-scrambled, with Cheddar cheese melted and blended within. The sharp taste fills my mouth and I chew slowly. I count each chew the way they teach you to count breaths in meditation classes. I only want to think about the food. I want to stay perfectly present, right here with my breakfast. I don't want to think about Daddy's cough or Hazel's message or the office or anything that may come to me today.

The twisting is still there—the tiny bit of tightness below my solar plexus that nudges me to be alert. I cannot ignore it. Something is about to happen. I whisper back to it after a long, thoughtful sip of my Ceylon tea.

"I am not ready."

She is sitting on my front steps. Her hair falls down her back in a thick drape of silky blackness, reflecting the morning sun.

"Mari! What are you doing here? I can't believe you're hounding me like this."

"No, no, no, my dear. Hounding is when you go out of your way. Fortunately, you are conveniently located between my place and the train. Therefore, no effort whatsoever!"

I kiss her cheek and she stands, wriggling her toes further into red leather mules with two-inch heels. I met Mari a couple of years ago at the gym after an aerobics class. The exertion had been a little too much for her, and she left the room early. I, recognizing the flushed face of a first-timer, went after her and took her arm just before her body made it clear that the majority of her blood was in her legs and not her head. I kept her from falling over into a dead faint. She's hung on to me ever since.

"So listen . . ." Mari takes my arm now so I have to walk, well, this isn't a walk, it's a more of a stroll, at her pace. The rhythm of walking in New York City had come easily to me. Move forward, not back, don't think about the past. Mari still

walks with the gait of her native Trinidad; it is a walk of
scented evenings and soft warm air, of smoke from clove cigarettes beneath tropical trees and love that aches in slow, exquisite ways. I trip over a raised lip in the sidewalk. This pace
is foreign to me. "Oh, watch it dear. I hear tell that someone
is throwing a birthday party for me. Oh wait! It's me!" She
laughs and the sight of her large white teeth make me smile.
"But I have yet to get an RSVP—no matter how hard I've
tried!—from one Crita Carter."

"No, you haven't."

"Uh huh, and why is that?"

"I've been busy—distracted."

"Too busy for a two-minute call?"

"Calls with you are never two minutes!"

"Well, maybe not, but I'm not the only one you've been
avoiding."

"Mari, I could kick your butt for siccing that sorry excuse
for a man on me! I'll call him back when I want an update on
the Federal Reserve. What were you thinking?"

"Maybe I was trying to kick *you* in the butt. Ever think of
that my dear? I thought experiencing a Warren would inspire
you to seek greener pastures."

"Greener pastures?"

"Yes, maybe even find another guy like the one you used to
talk about. What was his name?"

"Tree. His name was Tree." Tall. Leonine features. I used to
blush at the sound of his name. And I did talk about him all
the time, like an accident victim replaying the scene, trying to
see if anything could've been different, avoided. When enough
time had gone by, I pushed my ex-boyfriend out of my mind
and refused to be sorry about him another day. "Anyway, it
didn't work. I told you, I'll date when I'm ready."

"But you're never ready!"

"Then that's my problem!"

Exasperated, she drops my arm. "Fair enough, honey. But why haven't you called Lisa?"

"I just got her message."

"I don't believe you! Don't you know it's serious business when a single black woman in New York City isn't heard from in days? Any number of things could have happened to you; you had me worried."

"You could have called my office at any time, Mari, and Isabella would have told you I was there."

"Well, perhaps, but it was much more interesting to believe you had run off somewhere with Warren. That is, until he called me and said you had disappeared on him, too."

"Yeah, well."

Mari stops and makes me face her. She scans me from head to toe, her round black eyes taking in all the information.

"Honey, what's wrong? You're pale, like you haven't been outside in ages. What are you doing to yourself? Why are you shutting yourself off like this?"

I don't answer. Doesn't she understand that I am just being cautious, so very, very cautious? I want to live in the present, to *be* in the present, so I cultivate the present like a gardener would a blue rose. With care. With reverence. Friends, like insects in the garden, destroy my hard work. They ask questions, want to make dates, are constantly throwing me into a future I don't want to think about.

"I just don't have time . . ."

"Crita!"

"Okay, okay." I start walking again, but this time at my pace, forcing Mari to skip along in her mules as best she can. "My mother called this morning. My dad might be sick."

"Go on."

"I don't know, Mari, I just have this weird feeling that something is about to happen. I feel it in here." I stab my gut with my fingers. "It's been coming on for days."

"You think you might have to go home, don't you?"

"Yes."

"You haven't been home in, what, like five years or something? You didn't even go to your sister's wedding."

"I had my reasons."

"Yeah, like avoiding your brother."

"What do you know about it?"

"I know you don't know where he is, hon, and you haven't for a long time. That's what happens with junkies. They disappear . . ."

"My brother is *not* a junkie!" My head feels hot and there's a throbbing in my right temple, but my tone has turned icy. "Don't you ever say that to me again."

Mari doesn't know and can't begin to understand what Linc once was—and how I prefer to think of him. When I was in third grade and Linc was a high school senior, he would come over to the elementary school to sell copies of the school newspaper. His classmates were in the halls hawking the paper as well, but my teacher, Mrs. Meade, had stood guard by the door and let them know we would buy only from Linc. We fidgeted madly waiting for him to come, everyone looking at me because I was his sister, a lucky girl, they said. Then, finally, Linc would stroll into the classroom smiling. He seemed so tall I thought I would never be able to reach up high enough to kiss him on the cheek when he came by my desk. "I understand someone in here wants to buy a paper?" he'd announce in that deep voice. We'd raise our hands and squeal "I do! I do!"— even the kids who had no money. But kindly Mrs. Meade would pull out her little blue coin purse and fulfill the needs of the penniless. "Bye bye, Linc!" we'd cheer as he waved and moved onto his next customers. "Bye bye!" We would then settle into the sound of rustling paper and the smell of fresh printer's ink. We'd scan the sports page for mentions of Linc—his latest record broken on the track team, how he flew farther than anyone else in the long jump. Choruses of "wow" would float through the room and we'd look toward the door where this god had appeared fleetingly.

Then later, at home, I would wait in the front yard for Linc's orange Chevy Nova to pull up. As soon as he got out of the car I would jump into his arms and squeal, "Linc, everybody loves you!" He'd lift me up, my hands on the polished steel of his biceps, shiny with sweat underneath his track uniform. He would sweep me into the air and I would laugh. The feeling in me, as unfocused as so many childhood notions are, was that my brother was invincible.

"Crita," Mari is speaking gently to me now. "I'm sorry. You know how I am . . . always saying the wrong things. But you are upset. You'll give me that, right?"

"Yes, okay, you can have that."

"My dear, you've been upset for a very long time. And it's getting worse every day."

I sigh. "Mari, how can you possibly know that?"

"Because it's showing, honey! It's on your skin, in your hair . . ."

"What's wrong with my hair?" I run a hand over the short, dark brown puff of kinkiness that covers my head. Three weeks before there had been a luxurious mane of dreadlocks, shoulder length and thin like pipe cleaners.

"Crita, why did you cut your hair?"

"It was too long."

"Crita . . ."

"It was! You don't understand . . ." I stick my fingers into the cloudlike tufts of afro and I force my voice down to keep it from screaming. "It was so long. So much longer than when I last saw Linc. It was like a clock, always reminding me, always numbering the days . . ." Tears well up in my eyes. "I'm just tired of waiting . . ." Suddenly I can see the face of one Doctor Leeper, pale and ghostly in his white lab coat, floating in front of me and around me, whispering the words "terminal addiction" in my ear so only I can hear it. He never lets me forget how short the time is, or how tenuous Linc's existence is. I try to get away from him by walking faster.

"Crita!" I suddenly feel Mari's fingers around my upper arm, tugging me to her just as I am about to step off a curb against a red light. "I asked you what you think you're doing! Obviously not paying attention!"

I smell the fumes of the cars idling at the light. The day is already too warm for the little red jacket I had thrown on over my white tank top. I take it off now and wonder if Mari can see the perspiration staining my shirt. At the same time I ignore the thought that I could have been mowed down by a minivan just moments ago.

"Mari, I'm just tired, okay? I'm tired and worried about my father. Can we just leave it at that for now?"

"All right." She is still evaluating me, her eyes skeptical. "And what about my party, hmm?" She nudges me. I know she wants me to smile, but at the moment I can't stretch one out of my berry-tinted lips.

"You know I'd love to help you, but at this point I don't even know if I'll be here for the party. Let me see what happens when I hear from my parents again."

"But you will let me know, whatever happens?"

"Yes."

"You'll call me?"

"I promise."

" 'Cause if you don't, I know where you live!" Her solemn look doesn't match the playful notes of her voice. She kisses me on the cheek.

"I know."

It's almost 10 A.M. when I get to my office. I've never liked the idea of working for other people so that's why I'm here, in this little two-room office with a plain sign that says, simply, "Crystal Carter, CPA" on the door outside. A tidy salary in the accounting department of some midtown corporation would've been easy to snag, with benefits to boot. Instead I let myself get seduced by an empty storefront on St. Nicholas Avenue. Actually it wasn't so much the space that had attracted me as much as the little girls who scampered around outside every day. Their hair freshly greased and braided, foreheads shiny, they wore little bright dresses or too long T-shirts out of which hung their coltish limbs. Running down the street in the sun, they reminded me of my sisters and me when we were children, never out of each other's company, always on our way to some mischief, always stuffed with laughter. Now each day as I wait for those girls I pick through shopping bags of receipts from professors at the nearby City College and, with my poorer clients, hand hold their way through 1040 EZs, the main gratification coming from their lit-up faces when they see how much of a refund they're getting.

Isabella has opened the office and is just settling down with her second cup of coffee. She moves slowly for a young woman, like she's in her own weird time warp or something. But she is good at set, mechanical tasks. She can open the office, answer phones, and put someone off if I don't want to talk to them.

"Isabella, I might have to go out of town for a few days," I tell her, pointing to a stack of folders. "I need you to go over the files, make sure there's nothing outstanding, start with that pile there."

"Okay, but what am I looking for?" a reasonable question, she asks as she flips back her mane of blue-black hair. She stands and slides the stack of manila folders to the center of her desk.

"Make sure all the returns are signed, that all supporting documents are there, that the pages are in the correct sequence. Stuff like that."

She opens the first folder with the tip of a long magenta-painted fingernail and eyes the top page, looking it up and down casually, as if she's perusing a fashion magazine. She flips to the next page. Right.

I frown and close the folder, just missing her hand, and I pick up the stack.

"Never mind, Isabella, maybe I should do this myself." I whisk the folders into my inner office and drop them with a thump on my desk. I need air. "I'm going to pick up a muffin," I tell Isabella as I go out again. "Want anything?" She shakes her head.

Outside, three women are herding a group of children down the sidewalk. I step back to let them pass but a little girl, a toddler, brushes against me. I feel like I have been touched by the sun. She runs off, a teeming ball of energy, light glowing from her hair, a newborn supernova. I look at the spot on my arm where she has been and I feel her heat dissipate into the air. I didn't know I had grown so cold.

Two

Mama calls me back that afternoon to say Daddy had a chest X ray taken. The doctor saw spots of some sort on his lungs and suspected pneumonia, so he's put Daddy on a series of antibiotics. I'm satisfied, at least this is what I tell myself. My father's a big man—he can crush a virus like a roach underfoot. Nobody messes with my daddy.

That's not the way I act, though. As the days pass, I notice that in subtle ways, I'm packing up. Getting ready to split. I don't do my grocery shopping—I use up the last of my eggplant, tomatoes, and zucchini and then I eat Chinese dumplings and beef chow fun for three nights straight. I lug two duffle bags of dirty clothes to the laundromat. I return the *Beverly Hills Cop* video to the library. Seven days pass. One night the dark cloud inside keeps me awake, so I stay up all night cleaning the whole apartment from top to bottom. I've just finished dusting the mantel and I'm watching the sun's first light move across my newly polished floor when Mama calls again. She is whispering. My heart sinks.

"This just don't seem right," she says and I can hear her fear. "He's getting worse, Crita, he's so sick. I called the doctor again, but he keeps saying we just need to let the medicine run its course."

"Okay, Mama. All right. I'll get on the road in the morning."

"You'll pick up your sister on the way?"

I hesitate. Ella lives in Alexandria, Virginia, where, fresh out of Spelman, she had moved after marrying a real estate broker two years ago. I'm not sure I can deal with Ella for five minutes much less the eight-hour drive to our home in Lorain, Ohio. "Can't she come on her own?"

"You know they only have the one car, and Forrest needs that for his job."

"Oh, right, I forgot," I lie. "Then yes, of course, I'll get her."

"I'll tell her so. I'm calling her right now."

"Thanks, Mama."

"I'll see you soon, baby doll."

Later that morning I dial Mari's number.

"I'm going. Mama says he's getting worse." I stand there, chewing on a broken nail and trying to organize my thoughts. Outside the jackhammers rattle against the pavement and the sound is jarring my stomach. "I have to pick up Ella first."

"Oh, honey, I hope everything will be all right."

"Yes, so do I."

I watch the sun still bouncing off the yellow wood of the parquet floor. The African violet on the window ledge soaks up the light, its flowers all velvety and purple.

"Mari, do me a favor. Water my plants while I'm gone, okay?"

"Of course, dear."

My sister Ella is an orchid. Lovely and fragile with an elegance that touches you and lingers for hours after she is gone. When I think about when she was born, in mid-July heat, it makes sense to me: a hothouse season for a hothouse flower. At twenty-five, Ella's two years younger than me, and for some reason I never could figure out, she's always thought of herself as a black southern belle. She tries pretty hard to make people forget that she's from the Midwest, an honest mistake. Just a little bit of accent does the trick—she knows not to overdo the twang. Maybe she saw *Gone With the Wind* too many times and didn't get the point, I don't know.

But Ella did get her Ashley, that's for sure. Forrest is a gentleman—a quiet guy and a Yale graduate who, while not necessarily in possession of a green thumb, knows how to shelter Ella, how to encourage and care for her. And with him she has blossomed. That's enough for us. It doesn't matter, my sister Hazel's joking aside, that he's white.

The next morning, I am in Alexandria, in Ella's driveway, staring at two rows of perfectly trimmed boxwood hedges. The lines are so straight, as though they'd been pruned with a guiding leveler. I shake my head. If I had such a lawn, I'd plant flowerbeds, and not shrubbery, with bold perennials lustily flaunting their summer beauty. But then again this neighborhood itself was a study in manicured landscaping with its bluegrass sod and perfect bushes. Not a place where I would fit in.

Forrest, dressed in a crisp white shirt and pressed khaki pants, comes out to greet me. "Hello there, Crita," he says, opening the door of my battered but dependable Ford Taurus sedan. He claims the familiarity of a brother by kissing me on the cheek, a habit I still haven't grown used to. "Sorry to meet under such circumstances." His lips are thin and I feel more bone than flesh as his mouth grazes my skin.

"It's all right."

"I'd drive Ella myself, but my appointment book's full." He puts his hands in his pockets and looks down at the ground. "I'm showing several new houses this week."

"It's okay, Forrest."

He shows me into the living room and waves me over to a couch but I'm afraid to sit on it. The piece of furniture, a pristine white leather sofa, is too clean. I've never seen such a ridiculous sofa before and this one, a sectional anchored in the corner of the room and fanning out on two sides like a snowy stealth bomber, looks like it has yet to be touched by anyone's backside. Forrest understands.

"Go ahead, you won't hurt it. It's really comfortable. You'll love it."

I sit and sink into the cradling cushions. The leather is surprisingly warm. I look around and take in the cool white elegance of the room, which is sparse except for a few pieces of sculpture including an African fertility symbol, carved of polished ebony.

"Isn't it great?" Forrest says, sitting kiddy-corner from me on the sectional. He brushes a boyish forelock of brown hair away from his sea-green eyes. They shine with the excitement of a child with a toy he's not supposed to play with. "Ella picked it out. Pricey, but I think it was worth it. It'll last forever."

Yeah, if you can keep it clean, I think. But Ella is obviously an excellent housekeeper. With me, it is enough if I can keep the dust bunnies from taking over the place.

Sitting here it occurs to me, for something like the millionth time, how different Ella and I are. I prefer old stuff: antique wood, stained glass, and the detail and care of a bygone era when things were made to last. But for Ella old is where we came from, where all the polishing and scraping could not make something new, spotless, untouched, as though it were made just for her. No, this home is hers. No shadings of the past will ever darken her walls.

"So, what kinds of places are you showing these days, Forrest?" I know this is a safe subject. He negotiates real estate with the ease of a fly fisherman. The market, interest rates, trends, all these factors make the waters difficult and he has to cast his line just right, matching the right person with the right property. I've dreamed of having a house of my own enough to appreciate Forrest's enthusiasm for his work.

"I've had the most amazing house fall into my lap," Forrest says, reaching for his maroon leather organizer on the glass-topped coffee table. His eyes focus on me with such empathy and sincerity that I wonder if he's practicing his pitch on me. "I bet you'd like it. Just three years old, but the people who built it were into detail, Victorian stuff."

He hands me a photo and I have to suppress a burst of laughter. It's an oversized dollhouse, but I love it. Gingerbread trim, painted ivory, drips from every eave. An octagonal gazebo forms one part of a wraparound porch that's nice and deep enough for a rocking chair. Okay, it's a bit overdone, but the house's color, a lovely dusty rose, makes me smile.

"Yes, it's gorgeous." I hand the picture back to him.

"Ten acres. And the place is huge. Six bedrooms, cathedral ceilings, a Jacuzzi in the master bath."

What new house didn't have all that these days? "How much?"

He grins. "$775,000. That's just the asking price. I'll have multiple bids by the end of the day, I know it."

"Bids for what?" Ella calls out, and I see her coming down the hall dressed in a cool blue linen skirt and long sleeve shirt with the sleeves tastefully rolled just to the elbow. She embodies the stability of the house's mausoleum-like calm. "Now Forrest, Crita's barely through the front door and you're already talking business."

"She asked!" he protests as I rise to kiss Ella's powdered cheek.

She pauses and gives me this look. I can't quite explain it, but I've seen it before—it's like she's surprised to see me. I try to forget about it right when the moment passes. Ella makes that real easy to do. "Oh, honey!" she says, sucking in air as though she'd just burned herself. "You cut your hair! And I was just getting used to that natural look you had."

Oh, Ella, I think to myself. Not yet.

"Did you want to get it straightened before we see Mama? I think my hairdresser can squeeze you in." She raises her hand to touch my head, but I flinch away. Strangely enough, the moment reminds me of our childhood when she and I shared a bed. In her sleep Ella used to tangle her fingers in my hair and unbraid it. After days of waking up with a head looking like a rat's nest, I started to half-waken and grab her hand whenever she touched my hair. "Cut it out, Ella!" I'd say.

Now I just say, "No, Ella, thanks. I'm going to keep it natural. I'll start growing it out again. I wanted a change for now, that's all."

"Oh." She checks her motion and then, as if on second thought, she returns my kiss on the cheek.

"I am glad to see you, honey chile," she goes on. "This thing with our daddy has got me worried sick." She sinks into the sectional next to Forrest.

"Have you spoken to Mama again?"

"I speak to our Mama *every* day." The comment stings, but I'm not sure if Ella meant it that way. "Well, I don't have to tell you that I don't know what to think about any of this. I spoke to Mama, spoke to Daddy, too, but Crita I didn't even recognize his voice. He sounded like . . ."

"Like what, Ella?"

"Like he was drowning. I have so feared drowning. I used to have nightmares about it when we were children. We would be running along the edge of the pier at Hot Waters and I would fall in. Oh, Crita, it just smelled horrible—of fish and dead plants and the whole muck just sucked me under. And the water, the water is filling me up, like we used to fill those old milk jugs with water and they would just expand and grow heavy with the liquid. I felt just like one of those jugs; like my body was puffing up and crushing my chest and I couldn't breathe." She puts a beautiful, delicate hand to her chest and shakes her head. "Not once! Not once did it ever occur to me that something like that could ever happen to a body without it ever falling into the water—that something could just rise up from inside you and smother you of its own accord."

"Uh-huh." I look at Forrest and he lowers his chin and clears his throat. Again he runs a hand through his hair, brushing it away when it hasn't really fallen. I'm guessing he's heard all this before. Since I haven't, I want to know exactly what she's been cooking up in that silky straight head of hers. "Tell me what else you see."

She looks at me like I'm accusing her of stealing somebody's silverware.

"Ella, I know these things are kicking around in your head, and you gotta tell them to somebody. I think you should tell me here and now. You can't say stuff like that—about drowning and whatever else—around Mama and Daddy. You'd freak the hell out of them."

She looks at Forrest and he nods. "You're right. What is the matter with me?!"

"You're afraid, that's all. It's okay, so am I. But the last thing we need is to let them know it. They're depending on us."

"Yes."

"It's kind of like that time Daddy sent us to get those cats out of the shed, you remember that?"

"Oh, honey, I sure do."

We couldn't have been more than eleven or twelve when, unknown to us, a stray cat had taken up residence in our backyard shed and given birth to a litter there. Daddy discovered them one day when he went to pull out the lawn mower.

"Jesus Christ!" We heard a clash of metal, cans falling from shelves, yardwork implements shoved aside as Daddy fell over his own limbs; he couldn't get out of that shed fast enough. "Goddamn cat in there . . . kittens . . . all over!"

Daddy was afraid of cats. It probably had to do with him being scared of black cats and the legendary bad luck that trailed their little lives. This cat in our shed happened to be orange and white, but it didn't matter; it made no sense to him that all the bad luck should be with black cats simply because of their color. No, the bad luck had to be in a cat's being, in its shifty nature and the way it looked at him, slant-eyed, like it knew all his secrets.

We had witnessed all this, suppressing giggles, but when Daddy yelled for us, we snapped to attention.

"Crystal! Ella! Get back here right now!" Hazel, then six, ran along with us, but she slipped on the grass and I nearly tripped over her. I pulled her up, annoyed. She was always underfoot, and Daddy hadn't even called her. I brushed at the green grass stain on the seat of her white shorts as we went.

"Yes, sir!"

Daddy was breathing hard and mopping his head with his red and white kerchief.

"Damn cat done gone in there and had babies."

"Yes, sir." Sure enough, one of the kittens, a tinier version of its mother, was stumbling out of the shed. I wanted to laugh until I looked Daddy in the face. He looked so scared. I was sorry to see him like that—it was like I had seen him naked. I felt so embarrassed I wanted to turn away. It just didn't seem right to see my father look so *small*. I poked Ella hard with my elbow and frowned at her with a look that said, *This is the face you should make. Be serious. This is serious.* I ran into the shed and pulled out a metal folding chair speckled with peeling blue paint, a chair Daddy often took fishing with him. He would sit in it by the water and monitor the number of poles he had cast. I opened it for him and he sat down slowly, his legs shaking.

"Thank you, Crita." He sat back in the chair, seeming grateful for it, and drew in a deep breath. "You girls think you could round up those cats and put 'em in a box?"

"Yes, sir," we both trilled.

"Have your mama call that animal shelter downtown and see if they're open. I'll take the damn things down there right now."

And Ella, Hazel, and I did box the little critters. I managed to grab the mother even though I was afraid she'd scratch my arms bloody. But the cat seemed weary and glad to see she was going with her babies. She licked each kitten on the head, then curled up and went to sleep.

"Where was Linc then?" Ella asks me now. "We could have used his help."

"I don't know. College, maybe." Or, if my recollection is off by a few years, in high school, at a friend's house, or on a date, or eluding the hands of some hapless defensive back in football practice. I don't like to think of those times when Linc wasn't with us, as though he had outgrown us and had gone off in search of worthier, more challenging adventures. But Ella is right. We could've used his strong shoulders then.

"Did you try calling Linc?" I ask Ella.

"No, did you? Does anyone know how to get in touch with that boy?"

"No. Of course not. Stupid question." Like any of us had any clue as to where our brother lives or how he gets by. Wishful thinking. Big time. "I'm sorry, Ella."

For a moment we all find other places for our eyes to go.

"I guess we'll just have to wait and see," says Ella, getting up to brush away some unseen particle on the fertility sculpture.

Forrest clears his throat. "Well, it's time I got going." He gathers up his book. Ella takes his briefcase from the dining room table and brings it to him, kissing him good-bye and walking him to the door. I am thinking about Forrest's kiss on my cheek and how much it felt like I was being pecked by a chicken. What does Ella feel when she kisses him? But then I look away, my face burning slightly as I remember how long it's been since I kissed anybody. Who am I to judge? Ella comes back and slowly, wearily, sinks into the sofa again, her confident look fading like a sunset. "Honey, I have half a mind not to go," she says in fainter tones. "I'm thinking Daddy has cancer."

"Yes. I think that's highly possible."

"This isn't right." I can see Ella's shoulders beginning to hunch forward. "I feel like I've been waiting so long to hear bad news about Lincoln—that I've been standing in the middle of this road facing one way, in one direction for so long, and then someone went behind my back, driving down a different path and ran Daddy down because I wasn't looking that way. It feels like it's my fault. I know that sounds silly . . ."

"No it doesn't." I don't quite understand her, but nothing in the way any of us process things with Linc can ever feel normal now. It seems like the best way of dealing is to respect our different responses. Still, I know Mama needs Ella, so for the present I've got to persuade her to stick with the notion of coming back with me. If nothing else, it will keep me from getting pissed off at driving three hours out of my way for nothing. "But why does that keep you from wanting to go home?"

"Better to sit here and guess than to go there and be certain."

"Okay, Ella, that's just crazy. You're gonna find out anyway."

"I know! I know! Crita, I just feel like I can't handle it right now."

"But . . ."

"Have you thought about what he's going to look like? What if he's already shrunken into a shadow of himself? How am I supposed to take that when I'm used to that man being as big as a wall? And not just any wall, a wall that held up our lives, Crita, our very lives! What's to hold us together if Daddy can't anymore?"

"Please, Ella, don't go there. Okay?" She's really getting on my nerves now, but I have to say that I do find her response— her way of coping—fascinating. It's like she's running down into the future, trying to see things that aren't there yet and make plans and create motions when in fact all this drama just masks the truth: she isn't moving at all. She's just as stuck as I am, paralyzed with fear, and preferring to do nothing rather than deal with anything to come.

"I will tell you," she goes on, straightening her spine, her voice rising with shaky authority, "I don't know what to expect, but it cannot be good." Her lower lip begins to quiver as she laces her long fingers around her right knee and pulls it toward her as though she were shielding herself with it.

This isn't the first time I've seen my sister behave this way. The first time was the most raw, the most telling, making clear to me how my sister and I were not the same. I was eleven then and she was nine, and Daddy had sent us to the store on our tandem bike for bread and milk. Daddy had bought the bike used because he thought it would make a good errand bike, save for the lack of a basket to carry things. When he brought the bike home he took an old metal basket that used to belong in a chest freezer and attached it to the back of the bike with thin metal bars and nuts and bolts. Then he armed me and my sisters with cans of spray paint and we colored our new ride yellow. The basket contraption was clever, but the rectangular thing was really a little too wide and shallow to be practical. Items had to be strapped down to stay inside it.

We didn't know that, of course, Ella and I, that day as we rode home from the store, faster and faster, drunk with the feeling that we were free and flying. Our neighborhood in Lorain was hilly with gentle rolling slopes that could really get your wheels spinning. West Thirty-fourth Street featured many such formations, but had so few stop signs that Daddy often said people were speeding down the road like they were going down Route 2, our local highway. To get to our street, Oakwood, you go down West Thirty-fourth and make a left just after coming down a slight hill. Ella and I descended and went into the left turn leaning left, letting the bike turn and shift as it would. I remember being impressed that Ella and I were handling the bike so well as one. She, in the backseat, wasn't shifting her weight awkwardly or braking to make us slow down.

The bike leaned over with our weight and the momentum of the turn and I heard the paper bag sliding along the metal bottom of the basket. It must have hit the side and the milk came tumbling out because I heard a sloshing and then a splat as it hit the pavement. Ella gasped as we righted the bike and allowed it to slow as it completed its roll to the top of the next hill. We dismounted and turned back, walking to the spot where the milk carton lay busted, its contents trickling down the hill in a little white river.

I picked up the loaf of bread. It was banged up but salvageable. Ella and I looked at each other. We were in for a whippin', as sure as that milk was running down that street. We knew we had been careless and had committed what Daddy thought were among the most despicable of crimes: wasting money and wasting food. We couldn't gauge how mad he would be, but we knew we were gonna get it.

That was just the way things went at our house. Daddy had been born and raised in that old southern school of thought that said a child is born evil, and the parent is supposed to beat it out of him—or her. Daddy used his belt on us whenever we forgot to wash up the dishes or broke something in the house. The memory of the red welts on our arms and the stinging slap of the strap was enough to drive us to tears at the mere thought or suggestion that we might get a whippin'.

And I had wanted to cry that day with the bike, but for some reason I refused to do it. Watching as the milk trickled down the street, I was suddenly filled with anger. After all, the basket design was flawed, I could see that now, and it was stupid to think that a half-gallon carton, sitting upright, could have made the trip home without tipping over and falling out. Which didn't necessarily mean I thought we shouldn't be held responsible for the mishap—it just seemed inevitable. I felt heat, like a slow-creeping lava moving up through my chest as I picked up the cracked carton and threw it, still dripping, into the basket with the bread.

"Come on!" I ordered Ella, and I started walking up the hill. We were just two blocks from home and I didn't see any reason to get back on the bike; I let Ella push it and I stomped on, empowered, determined to be neither scared nor sorry. I had gone on for a half a block before I noticed Ella was not with me. I looked around and found she had stopped. She was back there staring down at the ground, one of her thick black braids flopping down her forehead and across her face. She didn't bother to brush it away. When she did look up, two big fat tears spilled from her eyes and down her cheeks.

I'd forgotten what it was like to be that afraid. While I was overcome with this strange boldness, surging with anger and defiance, Ella was immobile, frozen solid. It was as if she lacked the resources to take another step. Up until that moment, I had always imagined my sisters and I were exactly the same, and that we would experience life the exact same way. It was so wrong, so untrue. I walked back to Ella, removing the handlebars from her grip and taking her by the hand. "Come on," I said and, pushing the bike with my right hand and squeezing her hand in my left, I navigated us toward home.

Now, years later, as Ella sits stiff and uncertain in the passenger seat of my car, I take her hand. "It will be all right," I tell her. I drive up the on-ramp and merge onto the interstate, navigating us toward home.

Three

"We were born to be beautiful," Ella says. "Just like Grandma Carter."

No, I think to myself, as I set the cruise control on the car. We were born to be fierce like her.

Grandma Carter, Daddy's mother, isn't even a real memory to us. She died long before any of us were born. She's been reconstructed in our minds from the stories Daddy and his brothers and sisters have told to each other, and sometimes to us. Of course, now she has taken on a larger-than-life presence. She was a powerful but gentle being who smoked a corncob pipe and sat by the fire with a switch on her knee. Ever since we were children, we have conjured up her memory whenever we need to feed on her strength, knowing that a part of her lives on in each of us, that her ferocity is our legacy. She's how we know that we're strong. She's also how we know that we were born of the earth.

Vinola Ellis Carter dug a family out of the Mississippi dirt, shaping it with her fingers and her skin and her blood because she knew nothing else in a white man's world would be truly hers except the children that sprang from her womb. And the earth that gave them to her, ten in all, was the earth she worked to feed them. She picked cotton and pulled up turnip greens, all the while singing spirituals with the other women in the fields.

I been rebuked and I been scorned,
I been rebuked and I been scorned,
Chillun, I been rebuked and I been scorned,
I'se had a hard time, sho's you born.
Talk about me much as you please,
Talk about me much as you please,
Chillun, talk about me much as you please,
Gonna talk about you when I get on my knees.

Vinola herself had been born of fire, her head covered in a surprising mass of kinky red hair and her cheeks dotted with dark brown freckles that danced when she laughed, which was often. Perhaps too much, or so her husband, Louis, thought. Her smile of large teeth neither perfectly straight nor perfectly white lit up the yellow beneath her skin so that when she smiled she glowed. When she glowed the moth men came and, claiming to be waiting for her husband, lingered on the porch too long and, when she handed them glasses of lemonade, ached to keep the touch of her fingertips for a few more seconds than they were entitled.

Louis, our grandfather, was once proud of possessing the fiery woman, but he grew resentful, then jealous, and, in the end, deadly. My father and his siblings would later reel out the tale, so carefully coiled up in their childhood memories, of the horrible day their father opened the broken floorboard underneath his bed and pulled out a .22.

As the story goes, that day Mama Vinola was wearing her shiny apple dress, the one she had made out of old curtains. It was light green and covered in apple blossoms. The material had a fancy sheen, but it was sturdy, even rough, so it made a good dress for housework. On the front of the dress she had sewn two big pockets large enough to hold a pair of scissors, her pipe, and the collection of colored stones and bird feathers her children were forever handing her as tokens of their love.

Louis barged into the house after sowing a field, where a man whom Vinola didn't even know had said something about her to Louis in a way that suggested they had become too closely acquainted for Louis's liking. The story about what the man, Morris, said has changed over time, but one version is that Morris claimed to know for certain that pretty copper was Vinola's natural hair color. Before Morris could finish his snide chuckling and turn away, Louis had pulled a knife and slashed Morris across the stomach, who was wild with fright and surprise because he was only teasing. "What's goin' on between you two?" Louis kept asking him as Morris tried in vain to cup in his hands the blood spilling from his wound. "What's goin' on?" But the other men in the field grabbed Louis and disarmed him before he could do further damage. They carried poor Morris like a sack of potatoes, off to get stitched up by his wife. They must not have realized that Louis, still boiling, had decided his own wife would answer what Morris did not.

Louis set on home, his determined feet ignoring his youngest children who were playing in the dirt in the front yard.

Vinola had heard the heavy footfalls thumping through the living room and left the kitchen just in time to meet Louis head on. She must've thought her husband had gone crazy the way he was spewing a battery of completely unintelligible nonsense. She shooed the children out of the way, handing the baby, James, over to her twelve-year-old, William, while she said, calmly, "Louis, what's the matter with you, waving that gun like that around these babies? And who the hell you babbling about? What man? Morris who?" Another wave of words washed over her, but this time Vinola knew that there could be no talking sense into Louis when he was in this state, and she dismissed him. "Louis, you go on out of this house and go find yourself a drink."

When she turned away from him, he grabbed her by the pockets. A piece of cloth pulled away from the apple dress and spilled its treasury: three carbon pebbles from the railroad tracks that Henry and Will were using for marbles; the sky blue shells of a robin's egg that Katie had brought to her that morning; pins she'd forgotten to stick back into the pincushion in her yellow sewing basket. The force of his pull spun Vinola around and she wobbled like a top, but didn't fall.

Her hand, the palm pale and clean from having just rinsed greens in the sink, whipped out like a hot comet and made stinging contact with Louis's cheek. "Now I done told you to get on out of here, you crazy bastard," she said, her voice hard and low. "I said all I'm gonna say. You go and take your damn gun with you."

But Louis's anger was surging anew, starting from the sore spot on his cheek and blossoming red into the whole of his twisted, heartbroken face. "Whore!" he cried, tears now coming to his eyes. "Goddamn whore!" But Vinola was already leaving him, heading back into the kitchen and to her sink of greens. For her this mess was over.

Katie and Mary, two of the younger girls, screamed as they watched their father raise the gun and point it at their mother. Vinola turned just as he fired and the force of the bullet knocked her flat on her back. Louis, wracked with sobs, fell to his knees. Gun still in his hand, he half-crawled, half-dragged himself out of the house and threw himself down the steps before finally forcing his body to stand and run off down a road barely visible through his tears.

It was Henry, our father, who saved Vinola's life.

Henry was the seventh of her children, and everyone thought he was slow because, at age ten, he still had not learned to read or write. His brothers had teased him, but Vinola, hearing the taunts, had come out into the yard and scolded hard. "You boys leave Henry alone. When y'all are grown and your lazy asses is starvin' you go on to Henry's house. There'll always be sumpthin' to eat there." She turned to Henry. "Youse the seventh son," she told him. "You special. You'll always be able to take care of things." The other boys looked on and hung their heads as though they were strands of Esau who had just missed out on his father Isaac's blessing. They put their hands in the pockets of their threadbare overalls and kicked at the dirt as they walked away.

That day Vinola, a hole in her upper left torso, lay flat on her back and still, as still as the possums her children had seen trapped and dead in their father's traps in the woods. The children sobbed, sure their mama's fate was sealed. But Henry, confused and curious over the lack of blood, turned his mother over. A spray of blood from her severed artery shot up and covered the now screaming children. Henry lay Vinola down on her stomach, then pulled up her long skirt. He couldn't tear the tough fabric so he balled up as much of it as he could and pressed it on the gushing hole in his mother's shoulder blade with all the force he could muster. Fortunately, he was tall and heavy for his size, so that force was quite substantial.

"Go get Doctor Delany!" Henry shouted, but his siblings looked at him in shock, hopeless, trying to wipe their mother's blood from their arms. Henry looked at his sister Earline, who was the fastest sprinter of them all, so much so they'd nicknamed her Early. "Run, Early, run!" he cried, a command her legs, if not her mind, could register. Early turned and bolted out the door, her limbs pumping, the fear painting blotches of red on her eleven-year-old face.

Doctor Delany and an assortment of neighbors soon arrived to the shameful scene of Vinola Carter, her undergarments in full view, with her son on top of her, straddling her back and pushing down on her as though he were trying to keep his mother from flying up and floating away.

"All right, son, we've got her," Doctor Delany said, putting his big, careful hands where Henry's were. The boy wouldn't move, wouldn't look at them, focusing only on his mama's wound. One of the neighborhood men finally had to wrap his arms around Henry's torso and pull the boy off Vinola. He picked him up and took him outside where Henry immediately shook himself out of the man's arms. He posted himself in the yard, near the front steps, and stood with his arms crossed and staring down the road. His siblings, newly stuffed with respect for their brave brother, clustered around him like chicks to a hen.

Vinola got out of her sick bed just two days later. Though she listened to Doctor Delany and kept that left arm in a sling, Vinola ignored his talk about rest and used her good arm to clean up her house and set it to rights again. She soothed her children as best she could and the following week Vinola was in the field picking cotton to keep food in her children's mouths. She was calm like a windless ocean, if a little slow from the soreness in her shoulder. No one spoke to her at first, but her friends, all skittish and frightened, cornered her in the field.

"Vinola, honey," they told her, "You know you shouldn't be here."

"I feel just fine, thank you."

"That's not what we're talking about." They went on to say that she should run, she had to take her children and hide because Louis might return and finish the job. "He won't come back," she said with composure so cool it felt like the ice age to anyone within twenty feet of her. "He missed his chance. If anything, he knows he needs to be out there running *from me*."

Louis did not come back and within five years the state of Mississippi was in the fierce grip of the Depression. Vinola and her children began to starve. Without animals to pull the heavy work, they could barely farm the land let out to them, but Vinola was determined to survive. Her older boys worked the plows while she and the girls sowed the seeds. William and Henry took to walking the local roads, asking for day labor and trying to bring home ready cash so they could eat until a crop came in.

One day the two brothers were on their way home after earning two dollars for cleaning out a stable. They passed a farm where they saw a mule in the field chewing on grass. The farmer, a white man in filthy overalls, was closing up his barn.

" 'Cuse me, mister," Henry said, going up to the man but keeping a respectful distance. "You use that mule to pull a plow?"

The man flicked a glance out toward the animal and chuckled. "Naw. I would if I could. That there's the meanest, orneriest beast to walk God's green earth. He'd kick you in the head in two bits. I got him cheap and now I know why. Killed a man before I got him. Damn near killed me when I tried to put a plow on him. Now I just let him wander out there."

Henry and William looked at each other. A mule could make a world of difference to their family. They could plant a variety of crops instead of just one. William nudged his brother and Henry spoke. "Mister, if we can get a bit in his mouth, can we have him?"

The farmer spit out a mouth of tobacco juice. "Yeah, but this ain't no giveaway. I 'spect to be paid for my property."

Henry pulled out one of the two rumpled dollars he had in his pocket. He didn't want to show them both, just in case he needed to bargain with the farmer. But the man quickly snatched the bill from Henry's hand. "All right now. If you can get him, you can have him." He disappeared into the barn and brought back a length of rope and handed it to the two boys. Then he went off into his house so he could enjoy the show from a safe distance.

Elated, Henry and William ran into the field. The mule, the color of railroad soot, munched away and quietly ignored them. "Aw, man, this is gonna be easy!" Will laughed and raised his arms to swing the rope around the mule's head. In an instant the mule turned and kicked his back legs squarely at Will's head. If Henry hadn't jumped on his brother and rolled them both away from the beast there would've been a bloody pulp where his head had been. The mule brayed and bucked furiously.

"Shit!" hissed Will, getting up and backing away. "What are we gonna do?" Henry rose, too, and stood staring at the kicking mule. "Henry, should we go get our dollar back?"

"That man ain't gonna give nobody no money back," Henry said, his face burning as he felt the eyes of the farmer on them. He didn't have to see the man to know he was laughing at them. So Henry started walking. "I'll be right back." He went back to the farmer's barn and looked around. He'd heard enough stories about his great-grandparents being whipped to know there had to be a bullwhip somewhere in that barn, and, after a few minutes, he did find the coil of blackness hanging from a hook in a corner filled with tools.

He went back out in the field and, standing away from the mule, he tried one lash into the air. The snaking whip swung back and bit him on the left hand. A red welt leapt from his skin and Henry bit his tongue. It took a few more lashes for him to figure out how to flick his wrist just right and he was able to make the whip sing "sha-TING!"

He approached the mule with quick, strong strides. He

wanted the animal to know he wasn't afraid of him. Just as the mule began to buck its hind legs, Henry released the whip on it. "Sha-TING!" The mule brayed and backed away, then it turned and tried to get a better aim at Henry. But the boy raised the whip and lashed out again. The whip flew and touched flesh two, three, four, five more times. The mule stopped trying to buck and ran, but Henry ran with it. He cut in front of the animal and lashed out again. The mule stumbled. Then Henry dropped the whip, balled up his right fist, and punched the mule right across the jaw. He connected once, then twice. The mule dropped down on one knee, its head reeling.

"Will, get that rope over here," he said in a voice so calm he had to repeat the order to his stunned older brother. Henry looped the rope into a makeshift bit and got it into its mouth and over the mule's head. Then he pulled. The mule got off its knee and followed. He was wobbly, but he followed. "Come on, Will. Mama's waiting." As they led the mule out of the field the farmer came out of his house and stood speechless. He didn't know what shocked him more: that he let that mule go for only a dollar, or that a boy no more than fifteen was able to take it with him.

As we cross the state line into Ohio, Ella and I are laughing, as we always have over Daddy's mule story. But then my sister bursts into tears. I turn on the radio and I hit the scan button in search of some soothing music. "He was something else, wasn't he?" Ella asks as she takes a tissue from her purse and blows her nose.

"No," I reply quietly. "He *is*."

She takes out her compact and powders her tiny nose. She looks at me, a little embarrassed at her vanity. "He likes it when I look pretty," she says. She looks out the window and sighs.

"God, what will we do without him?" She is silent another moment and then: "Crita, what's that thing you used to say about Daddy? You know, from *Hamlet*, that thing you used to say?"

I find a station of soft jazz and I turn up the sound of Shirley Horn's comforting piano notes so that they fill the car.

"We'll not look upon his like again."

"Yes, that's it. For certain. We'll never know a man like him again."

Four

I've grown accustomed to the strange comfort of skyscrapers. The towers of New York wall me in and I don't have to think about any of the life going on beyond this man-made horizon. I can focus instead on Manhattan's little bit of square mileage and pretend the world is just me, my business, and my house plants. I didn't realize how much I've grown to depend on this security. I guess five years is longer than I thought. Makes more of a difference than a soul can know.

The Appalachian Mountains fall away and as we cross the border into Ohio, I'm struck by the flat, wide-open spaces. They're haunting and lonely. Ella and I drive and drive, the green fields spreading away from the highway, and we don't see a single soul, not even a man on a tractor. But the road itself is filled with cars, with people in them, and none of us looking at each other as we coast through this empty space. We seem to resist making ourselves a part of it.

By the time we arrive in Lorain I know one thing has not changed: I can still smell the desperation. It's in the air with the sulfur that belches hot and red from the steel mill stacks. It weighs down the hearts of those who thought they, or at least their children, would be someplace else by now. My daddy had come there dreaming of a better life, of a family with children.

A lot of people did. But they soon discovered that their dreams lay not in the steel mill or the Ford plant or in the emptying stores of the diminishing downtown. They aged early, lamenting a youthful glory that, for some, ended with being a high school quarterback or a sunny prom queen.

On Oakwood Drive, when the pavement ends and I'm steering the Taurus over pothole-pocked tar and gravel, we know we're almost home.

"Tsk," Ella says under her breath as she shakes her head. I know what she means and I agree. As children we never understood why we couldn't have smooth concrete and sidewalks that we could skate on in front of our house. It had something to do with taxes that my parents and our neighbors in the four small houses around us didn't want to pay, at least that's what Daddy always said.

The formal development, the part with the picture-perfect houses with shutters and rosebushes in the front yards, ended with the pavement. Our area had monster-size high-tension wires running through weedy plots separating us from that part of the neighborhood. The original builders knew no one would want to live near the lines so they only built a few small homes just beyond them.

My parents' house is a small square structure covered with thick green asbestos shingles and, behind it, a gnarled wooded area filled with raccoons and squirrels. Mama and Daddy had bought it unfinished in the early 1960s, and Daddy had built the little front porch himself, pouring the concrete and cutting the posts that held up the roof above it. There are seven rooms in all—three bedrooms (one in the front next to the living room, two in the back), kitchen, bathroom, utility room. "How did you all fit in there?" Mari once asked when I told her of my childhood home.

"I don't know," I had said. "I guess when we were little, we didn't take up much space."

I pull into our gravel driveway and Ella takes a careful look around before opening her door. "If that Mrs. Bitsy comes anywhere near me, I'll scream. I'm not in the mood for her."

She means Geraldine Bitsy, the widow who lives across the street in a long, rectangular white house with a blue-and-white awning overhanging her big front window. On our visits home from college the spry old lady would come running, sometimes with curlers in her gray hair and her purple housecoat flapping open in the wind to reveal ashy brown kneecaps. "Oh you're home! My girls are home!" she would say.

"God, Ella, how old is she now? Eighty-something? Can she even get around on her own anymore?"

"Heavens, I don't know, but she always seems to get around to pinching my cheeks. And loving it, too."

Well, and why shouldn't she, I thought. She thought of us as her own. After Mr. Bitsy, a white-haired man with blue-black skin who used to read meters for the electric company, died of a heart attack in the late 1970s, Daddy took pity on Mrs. Bitsy because she had no children to look after her. He would send all of us, Linc included, to rake up the leaves from her oak trees in the fall and to shovel the snow from her driveway in the winter. She paid us with chocolate fudge brownies fresh from her oven and crisp five-dollar bills that she pulled from her apron pockets.

But that afternoon Mrs. Bitsy is nowhere to be seen. As I get out of the car I find myself examining the catalpa tree, which now commands the postage-stamp plot of our front lawn. Its double-trunk spreads out in a strong V, and the lower perpendicular branch, the one we used to grasp in order to climb into the tree's embrace, has grown well out of reach. *Hot weather won't come for good until the flowers on that tree open up.* How many times had Mama said that? The catalpa's buds are still tight and knobby and green. My palms are already sweating.

Mama, who I imagine has been sitting at the living room

window waiting for us all afternoon, appears on the porch holding open the front door. Her expression is a mess of conflicting emotions all at once, as though she is trying to figure out how she should look. I know she's happy to see us and wants to smile, but worries it would seem out of place since this is no ordinary visit.

"He's sleeping now, in his chair," she says after hugging us both. "He sleeps during the day a lot because the nights are so bad. I'm so tired myself I don't know what to do. I drop off and wake up hearing him walking all over the house. Then in the morning he can barely lift himself out of the bed."

I step into the house behind Mama and see Daddy reclined in his chair. My chest freezes, surprising me so badly I have to move backward onto the porch. Ella gasps. It's just as she feared, but until this moment, I don't think I really had expected Daddy to look so ill. His cheeks are drawn and excess skin sags from his face. Beneath his white undershirt, tinged yellow with sweat, his skin flaps under his arms as though it's exhausted from years of holding together his massive bones and muscle. His breathing is labored, a heavy, slow gurgling moving through his chest. Worst of all is that my daddy, shrunken against the upholstery of the chair, no longer looks big at all. An image flashes in my head of me scratching his back when I was little. He was so huge and his back was so broad, there could have been a map of the world etched across his skin.

"Mama," I breathe.

She just nods and pushes her eyeglasses closer onto her face.

"Mama, where's Hazel?"

She shakes her head. "I was trying to wait until she finished her exams."

"Do you want me to call her?" I ask.

Mama doesn't answer.

Daddy stirs at the sound of my voice and he opens his eyes. "Crita?" He struggles to get up, but his legs cannot press down hard enough to bring the chair out of its reclining position. I put my left hand on the footrest and my right hand behind him, pushing down the one and pushing up the other until he's upright again. "Girl, what you doing here? Wasn't I just talking to you this morning? What, you speeding all the way here?"

"No, Daddy." A long lock of his hair, streaked brown and gray, falls down along his left ear and I swipe it back into place as I kiss his cheek. He tastes salty, his skin a strange mix of hot and cold. "That was a couple days ago, when we spoke. And I had to pick up Ella, remember? She's right here."

My sister had turned away to wipe tears from her eyes but now she gives Daddy her sunniest of smiles. For a split second I'm struck dumb by her sudden beauty. "I most certainly am," she says, kissing him on the forehead. "What's this I hear about you not feeling up to snuff?"

"Oh, girl, it ain't nothing. Nettie . . ." He breaks off, coughing a deep cough that barrels out of the core of his chest and shakes his frame. He gestures to the floor and Mama picks up an empty coffee can and hands it to him. He spits into it and I can see the yellow gobs of phlegm with threads of red running through it.

"I'm tired now, Crita."

"Yes, sir." I help him recline the chair again. He says he will "just rest a moment" but he falls asleep again, the labored breathing going on and on, sounding like a pitched battle complete with miniature explosions, muffled advances, and deathly silence.

We stand there watching him, transfixed. When I finally let my eyes wander about the room I take in the sad state of our house. Cobwebs droop lazily in two ceiling corners. There are three brown clouds, water stains from leaky pipes, floating in the plaster on the ceiling. A floorboard hunches up where the living-room floor meets the kitchen tiles. Daddy had always made us pay attention to our home's condition. "Don't walk past that paper on the floor, pick it up!" he'd say. "Wash that window, I don't have to point that grease out for you. We own this house, we're not renting it." Now that the house requires more than a pluck and a wipe, it is obvious that its primary caretaker, the one who had loved it the most, has been long off duty.

Mama, Ella, and I retreat to the kitchen.

"Mama, what's the doctor saying now?" Ella asks. "Did you talk to him today?"

"Yeah, he just said to keep your father on the antibiotic."

"And he knows how bad Daddy looks?" I want to know.

"He saw him just last week, so yeah, he knows he's weak."

I lean against the sink and cross my arms. "We're just going to have to take care of him as best we can. This must have been hard on you, Mama, but we're here now and we'll just take turns sitting up with Daddy."

"That's right, Mama, we're together now." Ella hugs our mother who then speaks, her voice almost muffled in Ella's sleeve.

"What about your brother? Should I call him, too?"

Ella frowns at me over our Mama's head. "What?"

"Mama, you know how to call Linc?"

"Well, not exactly. I guess I spoke wrong just then. I can't call him, but he calls here. Lincoln calls every day. Won't say where he is or what he's doing. Just says he's fine, he's all right. When he called yesterday, I finally told him your daddy was sick."

I look at Ella and she shrugs. My hand moves to the spot on my abdomen. I'm certain the dark feeling, the awful twisting in my stomach will return any minute now. Goddamn him, I'm thinking over and over. I can't believe Mama talks to him *every day*! How come she never told us? I can't believe how much I'm already wondering whether he's ever asked about me, what he looks like, who he is. It's like I'm an old jilted lover and I can feel the shame blossom on my face in a rush of blood. I can't think about this shit right now.

"Mom, you never said anything."

"Wasn't nothing to say." She pushes her glasses up on her nose. I can see streaks of grease on the lens where she has touched them with dirty fingers.

Ella moves over to me and puts a gentle hand on my arm. "He knows."

"Yes," I respond slowly, taking in her meaning. "If he comes, he comes. If he doesn't, well, like you said, he knows."

"Chandra's been coming by," Mama goes on. "She'll let me know when she's going to the store and she'll come by here with groceries, cranberry juice for your daddy, stuff like that."

"Oh, God bless her heart!" says Ella. It's good to know Linc's ex-wife is still around, still connected to us, even after all that's gone on. But even with Chandra around, we do need Hazel. Ella and I agree on that. I ask Mama to get her home from college right away.

While Ella and Mama call Hazel, I go back into the living room to watch over Daddy. As I sit on the couch in full view of my father's withering body, I wonder how I'll endure this new hole. I can almost feel the prick of an invisible needle making yet another puncture deep within my chest. First Linc, now Daddy. I so want to cry out that when Mama and Ella return, I run outside, gulping breaths of my childhood air.

Standing there in the yard, I take off my shoes. I comb through the grass with my toes and I try to pull together a picture so far recessed in my brain I worry it might be irretrievable. I close my eyes. The first images are dark, shadows that cloud my brain and scare me because of their emptiness. I push these away, knowing that somewhere in this there was sunlight and warmth and the smell of clover and the yard.

Ella comes to the screen door and interrupts my thinking.

"Hazel has an exam on Monday. Since today's only Saturday,

I told her she's better off staying on and coming to us when she's done."

"Okay," I say, stepping back onto the porch and into the house.

I use the pink princess phone in the bedroom I once shared with my sisters. Once Linc went to college, I had taken his room in the front, but most of my life I had slept here, in one of three twin beds positioned against the walls. The beds were still made, with linens covered with butterflies and flowers. Ella's white vanity still had photos of Michael Jackson and Lionel Ritchie taped with yellowing cellophane to the sides of the mirror.

"I'm here," I tell Mari when she answers the phone.

"Thank goodness for that, dear! How is he?"

"Oh God," I sigh, leaning my elbow on the vanity and passing my hand over my eyes. "Mari, he looks so bad. I can't get over it. He's really sick."

"What happens now?"

"Well, the doctor wants us to wait a few days. We'll see if the antibiotics kick in. All we can do right now is nurse him, make sure he feels comfortable."

"Okay, hon, I understand. Keep me posted, all right? Let me know how it goes."

"I will."

"And Crita, take it easy dear. You sound tired already."

"It was a long drive. I'll take a nap soon and I'll be fine."

My first real memory of Linc was when I was three or four. Before that, I was oblivious to everything, sitting on the porch steps engrossed in the powdery scent of dandelions. Then, suddenly, there he was, a boy of twelve or thirteen, wrapping his skinny arms around my waist, pulling me to him and tickling me. The sensation ripples across my stomach as I squeal and hear my voice as though for the very first time. I laugh. I gasp. I breathe.

As I grew I lived to be filled and comforted by the sight of him. When he wasn't around, I asked where he was. And when he was there, I followed him around like a puppy.

My brother was a runner and, believe me, he was always running. He chased us barefoot on summer mornings across the front lawn, slick with dew, Ella and me squealing with delight and tiny Hazel toddling behind us. He ran down our long driveway to get the mail; he ran to the store for milk for our mother. He ran sometimes just because he knew Daddy was watching; he knew how much Daddy loved to watch him run, amazed by the power in his son's long limbs. When Linc entered high school, a coach harnessed this power and taught him to control the flailing limbs of adolescence, to pump his arms and legs with strength and rhythm like the perfect machine he was. Soon Linc's home was on the track, where he would perform the paradoxical magic of crushing cinders beneath his feet while moving with the gracefulness of a gazelle. Only a few could beat him. My brother could run, all right.

Even today the smell of spring to me isn't about fresh flowers, but the pungent smell of soot from the cinder track and the hard splintery wood of a bleacher seat on my rear end as my sisters and I sat with Mama cheering Linc on. Daddy never liked sitting in the bleachers. He would walk up and down by the fence on the track and watch Linc warm up. Sometimes, before Linc went down to the starting blocks, Daddy would motion him to come over, and I could see Linc nod and his mouth make the words "Yes, Daddy."

I never knew exactly what Daddy said, but my bet is that it had something to do with taking charge of situations and believing in your own strength. Daddy always did have a sense of his own power, I'll say that for him. That was something I couldn't fully appreciate until I was an adult and learned how racism causes many black men, quiet and loud, to lead lives of desperation. From the young boys walking around with fingers twisted into gang symbols to the Armani-suited lawyers, I came to understand they all live in a world that daily ate away at their self-esteem. Daddy should have been one of these men; with no education, he was doomed to be poor and stay that way. But he and his brothers took a chance and moved North, where they had heard about factories offering good jobs and good money. Daddy not only got one of those good jobs, working in a steel mill in Cleveland, but he rose to the rank of foreman and supervised a group of men. His success, no doubt, was spurred on by his habit of carefully observing his own supervisors. "If you're pickin' up matchsticks and another man is workin' a machine, you know that man is making more than you are," he always said. "I'm gonna learn what that man is doing so if something happens to him, I can step right into that job." And so he did. And not once did I ever hear him say, "This white man kept me from doing this," or "I can't do this because white people did that." His power, the sheer force of his determination, drove his life and molded his existence, ensuring that he got the things he wanted with mesmerizing certainty—Mama, our house, a good education for his children. To him there wasn't any situation that didn't have a solving action, no problem so hopeless that there was nothing he could do to remedy it.

And it did seem, at least at first, that Linc had these same capabilities. But then again he loomed so large in my world. He was from the start a half-man, half-boy, striding around in our midst. And I wasn't sure what I was. As a child I rarely paid attention to mirrors, so I didn't see my reflection enough to remind myself that I even existed. When I see pictures of myself from that time I see a little girl of regular size—neither small nor tall. Flecks of red streaked my hair. I looked hopeful, as though I knew the ice cream truck might come down our street at any moment. But when I try to recall specific feelings, very few of them had to do with me. If I was excited, it was because of something Linc had done—a race he had won or a game in which he was the star.

Sometimes my excitement was as simple as Linc taking me for a ride. This he did one Saturday morning when I was the only one awake when he came home from delivering his paper route. He had just gotten his driver's license, and Daddy entrusted him with the keys to our prized family station wagon so he could make his rounds. I remember him coming in and I was sitting on the living-room floor, wearing my blue-checked flannel nightgown and watching *Josie & the Pussycats* with the sound turned down low. I was seven years old.

"Hey Crita," Linc said. He scooped me off the rug for a kiss on the cheek and I could smell the cold morning air still clinging to his skin. It made me squeal. He put me down and shushed me with a quick finger to his lips. "You wanna go for a ride?"

"Yeah!" In two seconds I was in the kitchen stuffing my nightgown down into my snowpants and pulling my boots over my sockless feet. I moved as fast as I could knowing that at any moment Mama could appear to make Daddy's coffee and ruin the whole adventure. I scrambled into the front seat of the car and turned on the radio as Linc turned on the ignition. Seeing him in control of a vehicle had been amazing to me. He did everything just like Daddy did, but a little bit slower. Linc gently put the car in gear and was careful to go the 25-mph speed limit in our neighborhood. He pulled to complete stops at each stop sign and looked both ways before we moved again. I blissfully sang along to "Billy Don't Be A Hero" and had no idea where we were going.

We ended up in downtown Lorain with its low strips of stores and office buildings lining Broadway, the main road. None of the structures was over five stories high except for the hospital, St. Joseph's, an orange block of bricks standing against the blue sky. I didn't know it could be so calm on a Saturday morning: no one rushing to or from work, no one carrying bags out of stores, most of which were still closed. The cars cruised lazily down Broadway, stopping at red lights as though they were welcome breaks and not annoying inconveniences. Linc and I cruised in the same way, and eventually we turned into the parking lot of Bob's Donuts. "Yay, Bob's Donuts!" I yelled, jumping out of the car and running into the bakery ahead of my brother.

The smell of confectioner's sugar and yeast enveloped me as soon as I opened the door. I never imagined a bakery could smell so good, and that it only truly smelled that way the first thing in the morning. It was almost too much for my senses to bear. The scent went straight to my stomach, setting off a keen hunger. I wanted every pastry in the shop. I got to the display case just as Mr. Bob himself, a beefy white man with thick forearms, was sliding in a tray of freshly baked glazed donuts. They still had a dull sheen to them and I knew they would be warm and sticky because the glaze had not yet set.

"Hey, I remember you," Mr. Bob said after spotting my eager face on the other side of the glass. "It's the cinnamon girl." He snapped open a white, wax-lined bakery bag and slid open the door to another part of the case. "How many will it be today?" I always ordered the same thing: cinnamon-swirled coffee rolls. I loved pulling them apart, unwinding the sugary spiral and then tearing it into little pieces.

"Three, no, four," I said, leaning forward but careful not to touch the spotless glass. Linc filled out the rest of the order with other kinds: jelly, Boston creme, plain glazed, lemon-filled, until we had a baker's dozen.

Then I tugged on Linc's coat until he lowered his ear. "We have marshmallows at home," I told him. That meant there was cocoa as well and that Mama could be coaxed into making some for us. There wasn't any need for Bob to turn on his machine that spit out a mixture of syrup and water. The concoction wasn't bad, but Mama's was better.

When we got home, Daddy and Mama were up, but they weren't in their usual places. Daddy was in his chair, a tattered brown Barca-lounger, looking out the front window the way he did when he was looking for the mailman to come. Mama was sitting on the couch like she was looking for something, too, but didn't know where to look.

"Look, Daddy, we got donuts!" I offered up the white bags and Daddy pulled my hood back and ran his hand over my hair. He looked at Mama, then at Linc. My arms started to ache so I drew the bag of donuts back into my chest. "Can we have hot chocolate?"

"Nettie," Daddy snapped, "what are you sitting there like that for? Take that girl in there and get that coffee going."

Mama took the donuts and pressed her hand on my back. She told me to take my coat off and go hang it up. I remember she called me "honey."

In our bedroom Hazel was asleep in her crib. I found Ella awake, but hiding under the covers. "Mama was scared," she whispered. "She didn't know where you were."

"We got donuts! Me and Linc went all by ourselves."

Ella immediately jumped out of bed and we tumbled back into the kitchen just in time to hear Daddy's voice, tight and furious, yelling at Linc. "I don't care where the hell you went. I said you don't take any of these children out of this house in that car. You hear me?"

"Yes, sir." Linc sounded tiny.

"Somebody could've taken that child or she could've been lost for all we knew. Now am I right or wrong?"

"You're right, Daddy."

"Now get on out of here."

Our father's voice bounced off the front wall of the house

and Linc carried the echo into the kitchen. He sat down at the table, his head hanging down. He wouldn't look at us.

"Lincoln," I finally said, and offered him one of my cinnamon donuts. But I kept a firm hold on the pastry so that when Linc took it, I pulled and made the donut unswirl until we sat holding a rope of glazed dough between us. I started to giggle and Ella giggled and Hazel giggled. We swung the dough around like a little jump rope and my brother laughed and my sisters laughed and we filled him up with the sound of our voices.

Now, I drive from Mama's house and find Bob's Donuts again. The man with the beefy forearms is gone, and the wispy white woman who stands in his place can't seem to snap open a bag. She unfolds it tediously and tries to give me cinnamon-sugar-coated cake donuts when I ask for my swirls. But I correct her and I get what I came for. I sit in my car pulling them apart and eating the dough end to end, stuffing my face anew when each piece is gone. I drive home dizzy and sickened by the sugar, but I feel a little less hollow, a little less lost.

Five

I used to think our living room wasn't big enough. When I was a child I watched my brother grow out of it, literally; he grew so much during adolescence, his head nearly touched the ceiling. The configuration of the furniture was so cramped, with our two blue corduroy-covered sofas, matching winged armchair, and Daddy's recliner, there wasn't room for a coffee table, only two small end tables. But now, sitting with my father just behind me and to my right, his every breath within earshot as I sit reading or pretending to watch television, I find the size of the room has a purpose, and it somehow feels right. Daddy doesn't want to be fussed over, so Mama and Ella flutter back and forth between the living room and kitchen, feigning busyness. If he wakes up to find the three of us all seated around him, watching him, he becomes agitated, reacting as though we are covered in mourning shrouds and taking up these positions all too soon.

"What are y'all sittin' around for?" he says.

When he needs it, I get up without asking and thump the center of his back with the heel of my hand, forcing the phlegm and mucus up through his lungs. We don't say much.

"Thank you, Crita."

"You're welcome, Daddy."

Mama and Ella move in and out, bringing food, which, for Daddy, doesn't amount to much more than Ella's chicken soup and maybe a soft-poached egg. That he still has an appetite makes me feel hopeful, and each time a ball of yellow, tinged with blood, makes its way up Daddy's throat, I have no doubt he'll be okay. His body continues to fight. Perhaps because of that, my mother and sister are content to be secondary in his care. Our intimacy fills the space as I sit silently with my back to him. There is no room for much more.

Nursing a father is an inevitability, or so we've been taught. A man withers away and, if he's fortunate, he has a loving family to help ease him from this life into the next. No one tells you, though, about how difficult this process of dying is when the man is still so heavy, as if his body is not prepared to relinquish its size, weak though it is.

It's good for him to move around and get a little exercise, even if it's just moving from one room to the next. But, I'm ashamed to say, I dread each time he stirs. Moving Daddy is by far the most challenging of our tasks. Though he sleeps much of the time, he insists on doing his night sleeping where he is supposed to—in his bed, coming out to sit and sleep in his recliner during the day. The weight of my Daddy leaning against one of my sisters and me is enough to break my heart.

Mama and Daddy keep their photo albums wrapped in plastic and rubber bands, stacked on a shelf underneath the television. I am tempted most evenings to open one up, but I can't face the whole production of excavating the books and then wrapping them back up properly so Daddy won't complain. "Who's been messin' with them books?" he'd say. There is one picture in particular I'd like to see. It is a photo of me as a baby, and Daddy is holding me aloft in one hand, the sun shining in my light brown curls. He is smiling and handsome and far younger than I can ever remember him to be. Linc is there, too, his head peeking up in the lower right-hand corner of Mama's Polaroid viewfinder, sticking out his tongue.

I think about this picture because I wonder if it ever occurred to Daddy then that he would have to lean on that baby for support as he leans on me now. Sometimes it seems I am still that small and he will crush me with the effort. I move him twice a day.

"It's gonna take a bit longer tonight, Crita."

"That's okay, Daddy, I'm not going anywhere."

"Let me stand here and rest a moment."

"Yes, sir."

"You doin' all right?"

"Yes, sir, Daddy, I'm fine."

"You're a strong girl. I raised a good, strong girl."

I smile. "Yes, sir."

It is harder for Hazel, and I feel bad about that. She comes home a few days after Ella and I do, arriving on the back of a chrome-wheeled motorcycle ridden by a short, barrel-chested black guy who looks like he could be a running back for the Cleveland Browns.

"Good Lord, wouldn't that child be scared coming all this way on the back of that thing?" Mama, watching with us from the living-room window, is shaking her head at her youngest daughter.

"You forget, Mama," says Ella, holding back the fabric of the curtains. "Our Hazel's not afraid of anything. Not a darn thing."

Our sister takes off a shiny green helmet and shakes loose her long dark braids. Then Hazel unlatches a large brown and red tapestry bag from the back of the bike. Inside I know it contains two, possibly three dolls of varying sizes and ages.

They might be made of porcelain, china, or the old Bakelite plastic. Their cheeks may be cracked or an arm or a leg missing. Hazel is never without a doll. She repairs them.

As a girl of five or six Hazel had been clumsy and rambunctious. She was always crashing into Daddy's card table, tripping over garden hoses, or dropping glasses of milk. Anyone else would have considered this normal childhood behavior, but Daddy had seen something else in it.

"That girl's too strong to be out of control like that," he had said. "It'll only get worse as she gets older. Gotta put a stop to that right now."

His solution, however, was so unexpected. He came home one day with a new doll for Hazel. She was brown-skinned with pitch black curls that perfectly framed her rosy-cheeked face. Her dress, a nineteenth-century ball gown, was burgundy red with black lace at the bodice and layer upon layer of black lace on the petticoat billowing out from underneath the skirt. Daddy had placed her gently in Hazel's hands and she had stared at it with the blush of first love.

"Now you know this ain't like your other dolls, don't you?"

"Yes sir," Hazel said, and it was true. This was no Barbie doll that could be carried around by the legs and used to batter me or Ella, which was what Hazel was wont to do. In fact this doll, made of the most delicate porcelain, would have shattered if she did such a thing.

"That don't mean you can't play with it," Daddy said. "You just have to be careful, you understand?"

"Yes, sir. Thank you, Daddy."

And Hazel had cradled the doll, which she christened Ruby Brett, and carried her to our bedroom. Ella and I had been so surprised by her reaction that we forgot to complain that Daddy had brought nothing home for us.

Hazel would get more of these dolls over the years, for her birthday and for Christmas. But they didn't all stay pristine.

She kept them on top of her dresser and one day, when they numbered five in all, she closed a drawer and a bonneted blonde lady tumbled to the floor, her right leg shattering. I had expected Hazel to start screaming full out, but instead she gathered up the wounded specimen and took her to Daddy. He, as though he had been waiting for such a moment, put Hazel in the car and took her to a doll hospital in Sheffield, about twenty minutes away. From what I understand, they were supposed to leave the doll there, but Hazel had wanted to stay and watch how the repair was done. So Daddy came home without her. He seemed satisfied.

"This will be good for her," he had said. "Maybe she'll learn something."

Indeed, Hazel did. By the time she was a teenager, she had her own drawer in the kitchen stocked with glue, pieces of fabric, and spool upon spool of thread. When she became a teenager she worked at the doll hospital part-time, and the hospital often would refer people to our house to find Hazel when time was short and the client wanted the doll in time for Christmas, their busiest time.

Now, in our driveway, Hazel pulls up the visor on the man's helmet, plants a kiss squarely on his nose, and smiles. She strides up the driveway, unzipping her too-big leather jacket—it must be his—and stepping up onto the porch. The room seems to brighten when she comes in—it's like someone has turned a knob and upped the voltage of the sun a few notches. When she hugs me she feels warm in my arms. Full of life. Full of love. "Hey sis, how you doin'?"

"I'm fine," I say. "Who's Mr. Easy Rider?"

"Oh, that's just Darius. He gave me a lift."

"So I see."

"We'll have to hear more about him later, now won't we, honey?" Ella raises one perfectly arched eyebrow higher than the other.

Hazel is hugging Mama tight. "Uh, right. Much later."

I want to giggle. I feel it right there in the back of my throat, almost in my nose—it's kind of itchy. I smile and it's just about to come out when Daddy's voice, rough but firm, barrels into my ears.

"Girl! What are you doing home? Ain't you got school?"

God, I'd nearly forgotten him there. All this time Daddy has been sitting up asleep, his chin on his chest, head bobbing forward slightly. We must have woken him.

"Yes, sir, but I'm almost done." She kisses him, her brown eyes flashing nervous glances at us. None of us expected him to be so feisty. "I heard you were a little under the weather, Daddy. I wanted to come up and have a look at you."

"Yeah, a look's about all you're gonna get. You see I'm fine and your sisters are here helping out. As long as I can sit up here in this chair, I'm gonna keep on being fine. Didn't nobody pay good money at that school for you to sit your ass here all day looking at me. You visit here with your mama and your sisters, but then you get your ass back down to that college."

"Yes, sir."

In the kitchen Ella puts on water for tea while Hazel sits next to me at the table and dabs at the tears seeping from the corners of her eyes.

"As long as he can still fuss at me like that . . . ," she whispers.

"Yes," I tell her. "As long as he can fuss like that, he's okay."

"Honey, you can stay a while anyway, right?" Ella says, her eyes pleading. I know how she feels. We can already feel the steadiness Hazel provides, as though she is the third leg of a stool. There's less danger of us tipping over. "I'm sure Daddy won't mind as long as you let him know you're not missing any exams."

It's a good idea. I feel for my youngest sister and I don't know if I could've stood being banished from Daddy's presence then.

"Yeah, I've already arranged it with Darius. He'll pick me up in a few days, I'll go take my last two exams, and then I'll be back here so fast you won't have a chance to miss me." She gives me a quick kiss on the cheek and I put an arm around her, burying my face in the space between her throat and her shoulder. She smells spicy, like a fresh pumpkin pie.

I underestimate Hazel. The very next day, I can hear her moving about in the attic, where she takes a caulk gun and seals, if only temporarily, the leaks in the roof. Later she is sweeping away the cobwebs in all the corners of the house. The following evening, after Daddy goes to bed, she is dabbing at the living-room ceiling with a brush full of white paint, and now the brown clouds no longer float above our heads.

One morning, nearly a week after her arrival, I wake up to find Hazel standing on Mama's stepladder in the kitchen. Her braids are tied back in a sprightly high ponytail cascading down her back. She is spraying apple cider vinegar on the windows and rubbing away with newspaper. When she looks down at me, her big brown eyes are shining from the exertion. She blinks and grasps the side of the ladder.

"I'm sorry, Haze, did I startle you?"

"Uh, no, hon. I just didn't think anyone else was up. Hand me some more paper, will you?"

I pick it up from the floor and tear pieces of the newsprint for her. The smell of the ink on my hands tickles my nose.

"Thanks." She spritzes more vinegar from her plastic bottle. "I've been wanting to do this forever."

"What stopped you?"

"School, I guess."

"Too busy?" I pour myself a glass of orange juice from the refrigerator.

"No. Shit, Crita, that's not what I mean. It's more like I had this feeling like it wasn't time. Like, once I came home and started doing this shit, I knew I'd never leave again."

"What are you talking about?"

"This is where I need to be. I know that. I can't explain any more than that. It's like what the chick with the red shoes said, 'There's no place like home.' "

"You're joking, right?" It's not that there's anything wrong with Hazel being at home. But I've always thought Hazel would grow up to be something like a comet, shooting through the universe, gracing many worlds and meeting many people. We would only see her once in a blue moon, or every year or two perhaps. But here all the time? I just didn't see it.

"Crita, think about it. What would I ever want that I couldn't find within a fifty-mile radius of this house? Right here?"

"I don't know. Independence? Freedom?"

"Highly overrated." She finishes wiping and studies the glass. She dabs at a couple of spots. "I have those at school. And it's all no biggie, I'll tell you that right now. From what I can see, independence and freedom just means you're alone and there's nobody to care about what you do. And the people you care about are someplace else. What's so damn great about that?"

I think about Mari and I'm suddenly grateful that I have someone who worries when I carelessly drop out of sight. I should call her. "When you put it that way, nothing much I guess. Hey, but what about Mr. Easy Rider? He looks like somebody worth caring about."

Hazel smiles. "Darius? He's a good guy. A nice guy. I like him, that's all. It's nothing special. Not like what you and Tree had."

"Yeah, and look at what happened to us. This home crap screwed us up."

"No, the Linc crap screwed you up." She's pointing at me

with a big wad of newspaper, her eyes calm and steady. "There's a difference. I'm sorry, hon, but that's a mistake I won't ever make."

I am silent for a moment. "I'm going to check on Daddy."

As Mama said he would, Linc does call on most days, though it isn't like clockwork—he doesn't seem to call at the same time. Even so, we haven't been home a week and Ella, Hazel, and I have already learned when not to pick up the phone.

Whenever it rings my shoulders, tucked into the corners of the wing chair, stiffen; Ella and Hazel's hands suddenly are occupied with washing dishes, arranging newspapers, writing grocery lists, and Daddy's right arm shudders once in his sleep, as though he ought to answer the call himself.

"I'll get it," Mama says, but it's not like anyone else has moved a fingernail toward the phone. Soon after I hear her brief murmurings, gentle and motherly and forgiving. "That's all right, baby. I'm just glad to hear you're all right." I find myself leaning in Mama's direction, straining to hear something of my brother's voice.

On Saturday morning, the phone rings and this time Ella picks it up from our bedroom. She doesn't call out for any of us, so I assume she's talking to Forrest, especially when, twenty minutes later, I walk in to find her still pouring her honey tones into the mouthpiece. "Baby, it's so good to hear your voice." It makes my teeth hurt. She's practically cooing! God, how did she learn to talk like that?

She sees me. Her eyes widen briefly and her left hand rises to cup the mouthpiece. "I'm sorry, it's just not a good time right now. In fact, I really should go. Is that all right, sugar?"

I motion to her that I'll be out of the room in a moment, she doesn't have to hang up on my account. "It's okay," she mouths back.

"All right, hon. Bye now." Ella's hand stays on the phone a few moments longer.

"Trouble on the home front?"

"What?" She seems startled. Ella at a loss for words?

"That was Forrest, wasn't it?"

She's staring at me like she's never heard her husband's name before.

"Yes." She draws the word out so it sounds like she's sipping it through a straw. "Yes. Everything's fine, though. Nothing for you to worry your curly head about. How do you think Daddy's doing?"

"Same. I'm worried about Mama, though. She seems so tired."

"Maybe she needs to get out of here awhile. You do, too. Why don't you take her out tomorrow after church? The House and Garden Show is at the Cuyahoga Mall, she'd love that."

"Okay." I shrug. "Good idea."

Red azaleas crowd the walkway between the stores, gushing their color and competing with the lilacs and King Alfred daffodils for our attention. "Mama, does it bother you that you don't ever get to see Linc?"

"No, honey," Mama says as she pauses to examine the information tag of a small potted pink rose. The mall has been transformed into an English garden, complete with arbors built over the benches and wisteria drooping lazily from the white plastic latticework. Hyacinths—pink, purple, and creamy white—perfume the air and seem to slow the shoppers who drift among the flowers as though in a dream. "I just thank the

Lord that your brother is alive. I can't ask for much more than that, especially when I ain't likely to get it." She breathes in the scent of a lilac bush. "I've always loved these," she says.

I finger the baby soft petal of a rose and sigh. "Mama, you haven't had flowers in front of the house in ages. What if I planted some annuals? Impatiens, and maybe dahlia bulbs?"

"Humph, who's gonna weed it, baby doll? I can't bend down like that anymore. Hazel would pull out the whole bed and call that weeding. She don't know a thing about flowers. You were the only one who ever took to it."

That is true. Many springs Mama would give me egg cartons to fill with soil. We would delicately press seeds into each cell of dirt with our fingertips and then nurse the tender green shoots rising into the sun. The care of seedlings required patience—watchful, diligent patience that involved giving the right amount of light and water. My sisters had no such patience, and Ella herself loathed dirt under her fingernails. But I was good at waiting. The effort always paid off with gorgeous blooms that seemed to smile and thank me even as I clipped their stems and carried them into my room.

Mama and I sit down on a bench flanked by two forsythia bushes bursting with yellow flowers. The hum of the shoppers' voices makes me feel sleepy. I close my eyes and feel my muscles relax.

"Things like this never have a right time to happen, do they?"

"No, they don't."

"You know, Crita, sometimes I try to figure out how we got here."

"Mama, you shouldn't think like that."

"But Lord, honey, I do. All the time. Was there something your daddy and me could have done differently with that boy? And I think Henry might have given him too much freedom. I know he was a boy and all, but maybe he should have had more responsibility, something that would have helped him get a sense of himself instead of all that running he was doing."

"Track helped pay for his college, Mama."

"I know that, but what's it doing for him now? Not one thing."

I say nothing. I pluck a forsythia blossom and I spin the stem of the tiny flower between my thumb and forefinger.

"We could've kept a closer eye on who he socialized with," Mama goes on, shaking her head. "But then he was already grown when he met that son of a gun, Tick, so we couldn't have done anything about that. I knew that boy was trouble the minute I laid eyes on him."

"Oh, Mama." Tick was a friend Linc had met in college. I was never sure if Tick actually attended school, or if he had just been around. Linc said they called him Tick because he was always on time—tick tock. He was a tall, coffee-colored man with sleepy eyes and a swaggering walk. He liked to wear a fatigue shirt with his last name, MICKENS, in black block letters on the front. He used to address me with something along the lines of "Well, little lady, aren't you growing up fast?" And I never could think up a witty response fast enough. I usually ended up smiling shyly with a little half laugh. He was by default okay by me. But Hazel and Ella weren't so easily charmed. Ella ignored him, mostly. Hazel, not even a teenager then, had always accosted him upon arrival with an ironclad stance, arms crossed, eyebrows arched, with an icy look that said "Don't bring that over here." And Tick never did.

But when I try to find an image in my mind of Mama in Tick's presence, it's difficult. I guess I hadn't been paying attention to Mama during those times when Linc and his friends were in the same room with her. I have no memory of her frowning disapproval.

"I believe Tick brought Linc down into that dirt with him.

I knew he would. I knew there was something about that boy I couldn't put a finger on."

"It doesn't matter now."

"No, it don't. Now that he's sittin' up there in Eaton Penitentiary, all's just right with the world. Bad things come back around and get you, and that's what happened to him."

I sit up straight, suddenly washed from my sleepiness. "What?! Mama, Tick's in prison? Since when?"

She crosses her hands over the brown vinyl purse in her lap and nods matter-of-factly. "Ever since he got caught selling drugs out of that house that used to belong to his aunt," she answers. "It's been almost a year now; I thought you knew that."

"No, I totally missed that one."

"Well, it's not all that surprising. Anyone could tell it was only a matter of time before that boy landed behind bars. I just hope they threw away the key."

I don't care what Mama says, I cannot feel such satisfaction. Yes, the last few times I had seen Tick, the blood underneath my skin curdled and my posture, stiff and uninviting, had provided a wall of ice between us. And the times I had feared for Linc's life most had involved him. But I never thought of him in trouble, let alone in jail. I just assumed he would always be out there, like a termite working his way through wood— always surviving, always managing to conjure his brand of slow, inconspicuous devastation. That type of creature didn't get caught.

"Mama, how did it happen? Was Linc involved?"

"Not that I know of. But like I said, they arrested him at his aunt's house up there on Cooper Road. I guess it was one of them police raids. Two people got shot, I believe. It was in the paper."

"Did Tick get shot?"

"No, it was some fools dumb enough to pull guns on the police. Lucky they weren't killed. Time was, you were supposed to run when you saw the police. These young idiots now think they can shoot at everything like they're in a damn cartoon."

I nod, only half listening. When I think of Tick I see him, shovel in hand, digging his portion of the rift that had divided me from my brother. The work is not all his own, as Mama seems to believe, but he has done his part. All the times Linc was the least himself, when his being had shriveled to the point where he cared neither for his safety nor my own, Tick had been either there or nearby. I never saw him place a coke pipe in Linc's hands or carry cocaine into Linc's home, but my suspicions at the time had been strong. I had to squelch them so I could follow my brother anywhere.

It wasn't all Tick's fault, though. I know that for certain. I like to pretend that it was; that way I can shift some of the blame weighing on me onto him. The ruse has allowed me to free up strength for other struggles. It has worked well so far. Maybe that's why I never hated Tick.

When I finally turn to my mother she's looking hard at something or someone across the walkway. "Mama, who are you looking at?"

"A man over there in the doorway of that store looked like Tree. Wasn't him, though."

I follow her sight line over to a man in medium-length dreadlocks and dressed in a green baseball jacket and khakis. He had a complexion similar to Tree's—fair with a sprinkling of freckles, but he wasn't as tall.

"I see what you mean. But why would Tree be here anyway?"

Mama looked at me like I was lying to her. "You know Tree moved back from Akron."

So many things happen in this instant. My mouth goes dry, my heart does a complete 360-degree flip, and my hands gloss over with sweat. I'm saying "What?" to Mama and at the same time I'm scanning the mall because suddenly it's become this great wide and fertile field. It now has the potential to yield at any given moment bounty I didn't even know I hungered so much for: Tree.

"Yeah, he moved back last year and got a job teaching at Admiral King. He lives over there off Meister Road."

I could barely hear her for looking for him, even though there was still no good reason for Tree to be at the mall. How crazy am I? God, it's been five years. Would his skin still smell the same—of sandalwood oil and summer sun?

I remember rising from our bed in the middle of the night to go to the bathroom and afterward passing him in the hallway en route to the same. Even in our dreamlike state, he would wrap his arms around me and hold me, briefly, before going on. Then he smelled of musk and the brininess of our sex. He never encountered me, however briefly, without touching me.

"Didn't you talk to him when he called the other day?"

"What?" Mama has my full attention.

"He was speaking with Ella all that time yesterday. I thought you got to talk to him, too."

Ella. What is she trying to play me for?

The next morning I awake to the smell of Ella frying sausage patties in the kitchen. I lie there and take in the scent, wondering if either of us would ever have a plate of scrambled eggs and sausage on the tables of our own homes. Yet somehow ever since we arrived here, it has been okay to eat such things. The grease has no effect on us, the eggs have no cholesterol, and we can eat as innocently and ravenously as we did as children. I find myself taking one more leg of Mama's fried chicken; another piece of her green pepper cornbread, slathered with butter. It is safe, familiar, and delicious.

But I feel the need to take control over my body again. I have been sleeping in the front bedroom, next to the living room and near the front door, so it is possible for me to dress and slip out of the house without having to face Ella and decline her expertly prepared breakfast. I sit on the porch steps tying my running shoes and mapping out a three-mile route in my head. I haven't gone for a run in weeks. Even before I left New York I had been trying to force myself to exercise again. I consider it a necessity of the Carter line. We are blessed with long strong muscles, but with the slightest provocation our bodies might betray us with obesity, high blood pressure, and, in some cases, diabetes. Reminding myself of these things forces me into action. I remember what Tree has always said, that I will be good to no one if I don't take care of myself first.

Outside it is already warm. I start fast, my feet pounding steadily on the pavement and my thighs raising and lowering, pumping smoothly underneath me. My breath is hard and my lungs burn slightly. My stride seeks equilibrium and eventually finds it as I even out my pace. After some minutes I begin to feel Tree's absence and my heart aches more as I recall the feeling of him running beside me. He moved with more skill and vigor than I did, and I always had to push myself a little bit more so I wouldn't slow him down. I never wanted him to slow down for me.

He took me running with him not long after we started dating. I'd been reluctant to go. I wasn't crazy, I didn't want to embarrass myself. Plus, I didn't know the route he wanted to do, through a wooded area not far from my college campus. I hated running on unfamiliar paths, I still do. It makes the run seem twice as long. But that day I remember wanting to please Tree, and being so happy for having a few hours when I knew that Linc was at home and functioning and I didn't have to worry about him.

We were both wearing shorts. His were red, long, and loose, hanging just above his knees. Mine were orange with blue piping—loose enough to be practical, but short enough to say, "Yeah, I'm a runner, but I'm cute, too." I remember Tree and I both kneeling in the parking lot, tying our shoelaces, and when I looked up he was smiling at me.

"We have the same legs."

"Okay . . ." I wasn't sure if I should be insulted or not, but I was looking at him, this man I knew I loved madly enough to put me out of my mind and thinking, "How gentle do I need to be when I kill his butt?" I told him, "Man, Tree, I'm sooo flattered."

"No, no, Crita, don't be like that. Come here." He motioned me toward a bench and then pulled me down to sit on his knee. He lined his right leg up behind mine so that my foot rested on his. "Look, see what I mean?"

From ankle to knee, our lower legs were long—not the same length, of course, but proportionally very similar. In the back we both had large calf muscles that ballooned out below our knees. I'd always hated that about my legs. I could never wear those sexy knee-high boots like Ella did and now I knew why—I had a guy's legs.

"Do you see what I mean?" Tree asked again.

I sighed. "Yeah, yeah, yeah." I swung myself around on his lap to face him and wrapped my muscle-bound gams around him, hugging Tree to me with my knees. "The better to squeeze you with, my dear."

He laughed then. The sound was deep and rich and when he wrapped his arms around me I felt myself grow moist between my legs. And he kissed me—his thick soft lips were warm on my own and delicious.

"Damn."

"What?"

"Crita, I think we're gonna have to do this run some other time."

"That's fine with me."

I'm proud when I finish my loop in just under thirty minutes. When I get back to Mama's house I enter to the sound of a child's voice singing. Tiptoeing past my father sleeping in his chair, I follow the song into the kitchen and I find Linc's daughter, Savannah, sitting at our kitchen table. The nine-year-old is singing between bites of her waffles soaked in syrup, and coloring a cartoon scene with aliens and various incarnations of Bugs Bunny. She has the same cinnamon-colored skin as her mother, Chandra, and the broad forehead and high cheekbones that distinguish the Carter family. When she sees me she squeals, "Aunt Crita!" and launches herself from her seat into my arms for a full body hug. I have forgotten how lightning-quick she can be. She almost topples me but the contact feels good. She smells of maple syrup and Johnson's Baby Shampoo.

"Careful, honey, I'm all sweaty," I say, placing her back in her chair. "What are you doing here? No school today?"

"Nope. Teacher's in-service day," she says, slightly lisping on her s's. "My mom had to go to work. Grandma's hanging the clothes out back and Aunt Ella's helping her."

"Oh, well, I think we're lucky to have you around. I was in the mood for a Savannah kind of day." I sit down across from her and pour a glass of juice from the pitcher on the table.

"What should we do first?" I ask her.

"I'm coloring right now," she says. "But you could read me a book."

"Did you bring any?" I ask, scanning the table and countertops but finding none. "Or do you already have books here somewhere?"

"Read me a story *without* the book," she says, pointing a pink crayon at me.

"Okay, let me think of one."

"Tell me a story about my daddy. A nice story."

"Okay." I know Savannah misses her father badly. She grieves for him in her private little ways, in moments that are easy to miss if you aren't watching her closely. Savannah looks through Mama's photo albums and lingers over pictures of herself as a baby with Linc and Chandra holding her and grinning. She plays Linc's favorite songs on her plastic tape recorder and asks us to tell old stories about him. I lean over and kiss her on the forehead, happy to oblige.

"Well, did I ever tell you about the time your daddy thought he saw a bear?"

"A bear!" Savannah is pleased with the element of excitement. "No, you didn't tell me! What happened?"

This had been a long time ago, in that brief shining moment when only Linc and I existed for our parents. I was a toddler while my brother was getting old enough to glimpse into the abyss of puberty. I was too young to remember that day at Findlay State Park, too young for the bulk of the details, anyway. Mama, and sometimes Daddy, would tell us the story on our visits there in ensuing summers.

We were there that day for a walk. Daddy loved to get out to the woods from time to time. He especially loved fishing, but I was too young to sit still while my parents and Linc nursed their poles. And Mama was pregnant again and unwilling to be too far from a bathroom. So we were just walking in the woods and not down by Findlay Lake with the other fishermen. Linc and I scampered just ahead of Mama and Daddy, enough to feel free, but not out of their eyesight. I like to think they had walked hand-in-hand.

I don't know the shape of the sound that had scared Linc. Or the color of the form that went swishing past him in the distance, making the dry leaves rustle and the hairs on the back of his neck rise. But I do recall the feeling of my brother's hand, soft and moist with perspiration, when he suddenly grabbed me by the hand and ran. I nearly fell, being too small to keep up with his stride, but then his hands were under my armpits and he was lifting me up into his arms carrying me as his legs pumped up and down. The scenery became a blur and I bounced up and down with his motion. Linc's heart beat fast and hard and I could feel it just under my coat. I don't know how far we went. What seemed like miles was probably just a few hundred feet. That's when Daddy caught up to us.

"Boy, where the hell did you think you were going?"

Linc, out of breath, coughed twice before he answered. "I saw a bear."

"Say what?"

"A bear. Right back there in the woods."

Daddy put his hands on his hips, bent over to catch his breath. I could see a smile fighting to form on his lips. "Boy, you done gone crazy. Ain't no bear in these woods."

Mama caught up with us soon afterward. Unable to restrain herself like Daddy, she was laughing full out. In later years she would always laugh the same way, almost out of breath, as she described this picture of her children. "You should have seen the way Lincoln grabbed Crita. That boy was scared out of his wits, but there was no way in the world he was gonna leave that baby behind. Danger or no danger, he made sure he took Crita with him. That's what you call brotherly love. That's the real stuff."

Savannah giggled. "My daddy was scared of a bear! And there wasn't a bear there!"

"Yup, it was mighty funny." I get up and kiss her again. She screws up her nose.

"You stink!"

"That means it's time for me to take a shower. You finish up those waffles and go play outside where Grandma can see you, okay?"

"Okay." But she continues to sit and color. "Aunt Crita?"

"Yes, honey?"

"That was a good story."

"You're welcome, baby. Ask anytime."

Six

After four years, the cinder of high school transformed to the bouncy red rubbery surface of a state college track and again Linc was a star. I helped Mama paste pictures in a scrapbook filled with newspaper clippings and awards and quietly suffered through puberty while I waited for my brother to come home. I felt completely invisible until the moment he walked through the door.

When Linc graduated from college I waited anxiously to see what my brother would do next. I imagined him having scores of glamorous job offers. If I had thought more about it I probably would have realized that I had never heard my brother say what he wanted to be when he grew up. No utterances about being a doctor or lawyer or even a coach. Back in Lorain, we were all waiting for him to return and fulfill a bright future and instead he came home with Chandra.

When Linc's car pulled into our driveway that summer, I ran out to help with his suitcases only to be stopped in my tracks by the appearance of a tall, lean woman who emerged from the passenger's side and stood over my head by a good eight inches. Walking up to her I felt I had shrunk and disappeared. She smelled of earth and herbs and her skin glowed a warm reddish brown like cinnamon.

I heard Linc introducing us. "Chandra, this is Crita, my old-est baby sister."

She smiled an open-mouthed smile that revealed a tiny gap between her front teeth.

"Oh, Linc, there's no baby here. This is a young lady."

I offered her my hand to shake, but she took it and held on to it much longer than I wanted.

"Crystal," she said as though she were naming me for the very first time.

"Crita," I said quietly and quickly added, "Everybody calls me Crita."

"Now I hope you girls get along," Linc was saying as he slammed the car door. "You'll be seeing a lot of each other."

Before I could answer, Hazel, then nine, and Ella, thirteen, joined us and demanded to know more about our brother's new girlfriend.

"She's tall," Hazel exclaimed, measuring herself against Chandra's long legs. "How'd you get to be so tall?"

"Are you a model?" Ella asked. "Do you know Iman?"

"No and yes," Chandra said, laughing. "But not personally."

"Can you put my hair up like yours?" Ella insisted, admiring her French twist.

"Can we get into the house first?" Linc said. "It's a small chance, but I'm sure Mama and Daddy want to see us, too."

"Yes, let's go inside," said Hazel, pulling Chandra along with her. "I want Mama to see how tall she is."

"You keep pulling her arm like that and she might get even taller before you get there," Linc said. He smiled and winked at me.

I smiled back, but inside I felt wary, as I'd always felt meeting Linc's girlfriends, ever since Angela Robinson. She was his first serious girlfriend in high school. I had followed her around, loved the colors of the granny-square crocheted vests she wore

and her deep-blue blue jeans. I even made a valentine for her
once, cherub colored with pink, blue, and red Magic Marker
and pasted on red construction paper bordered with paper lace.
We had shared Doritos and waited together on the front porch
for Linc to return from track practice. I imagined they would
be together always, but Angela had warned me, "Your brother
is headed for the moon and I am only one of his many stops."
But that information didn't stop her from crying when the
breakup finally came. In the dark outside my window I had
heard it all; Linc saying he needed his freedom, and Angela,
without a choice, giving it to him. I imagined tears on her
pretty young face glistening in the moonlight. I listened and
learned then that love does not last forever.

Would Linc make Chandra cry one day, like Angela had
cried that night? Because she was so tall and so stunning I felt
that it would be terrible if he did. It would be like breaking
the face of a perfect china doll.

"Hazel, stop pulling on that girl and let her sit down," Daddy
was saying when we got into the house.

"Lincoln, where are your bags?" Mama was asking at the
same time.

"We already dropped them off at the apartment, Mama,"
Linc said. "It's not far from here, actually."

Daddy glanced at Linc, then at Mama. Chandra, still carrying
on her conversation with Hazel and Ella, looked at them all.
Daddy sat back in his chair.

"You got that job over there in Cleveland?" he asked.

"Yes, sir, Daddy, I did. I start next week."

"What job?" I asked, sitting down next to Mama.

"Your brother's got himself a job at Sohio, honey," Mama
said.

"At the gas station?" I was incredulous. I'd been to the Sohio
stations with Daddy too many times not to have noticed the

blackened fingers of the men who worked there. They wore greasy clothes, were missing teeth, and spoke with Appalachian accents and poor grammar. My brother did not belong there.

"That boy ain't working at no gas station," Daddy declared in his gravelly voice. "He's working at the headquarters up there in that big building—it's bigger than the Terminal Tower. They used to only let white people work up there in that building."

"You got what you need for your place, honey?" Mama asked, testing the waters. "You got enough towels and sheets?"

"Um, yes," Chandra said, looking cautiously at Linc. He went over and sat next to her.

"Chandra's going to be living with me," Linc said. "She just graduated, too. We were talking about it and we thought we've been hanging around each other long enough to do it." He paused, then added, "And besides, two can live cheaper than one."

Chandra smiled at Linc's butchered explanation and said, "We'll see if we can put up with each other. I'm starting nursing school in the fall so we should be pretty busy."

"Oh, you'll be all right," Mama said, to my surprise, going over and patting Chandra's hands and kissing Linc on the cheek. "The boy's hard-headed and he eats like a mule, but as long as you can feed him, you'll be all right. Can you cook, honey?"

"Yes, ma'am," Chandra answered.

But Mama was leading her into the kitchen anyway. "Let me show you how to make his collard greens with okra, just how he likes them. And you gotta cook them greens with a ham bone, not hamhocks. Them hamhocks are greasy as all hell." Hazel and Ella followed them.

I stayed with Linc and Daddy.

"Let's have a look at that car," Daddy said, getting up. I went and held the door open for them. I could tell Daddy wanted to move the conversation with Linc to an area in which

Daddy would feel more comfortable, which was usually in front of an open car hood or at a barbecue grill. It was under this facade that Daddy found out about us, when he would ask his questions, and voice his concerns. In essence, these were the times when we learned our father loved us, the places where he laid out the coded words that said so and where we picked them up to decipher later on. He did this, I think, because he couldn't find the actual words himself and had to resort to indirect ways to give them to his children. And we had to watch out closely for them, for they were often buried under thorns, under moss. It was like searching for the tiny treasures of an Easter egg hunt.

"When was the last time you got it tuned up?" Daddy asked, raising the hood of the used Dodge Colt he had helped Linc purchase last year. I remember Ella had turned her nose up over the car because it was gray, such a bland color, and I had agreed with her. We wanted him to have a bright-colored car, something impressive, like his old orange Nova.

"Just last month after my exams were over," Linc said, leaning on the car with his elbows which, I noticed, made him seem a lot smaller than Daddy.

"Uh-huh," Daddy said. He went over to the garden hose and filled a plastic bottle for the radiator. I opened the Colt's door and climbed behind the wheel, pretending to drive, and rolled down the window so I could continue to hear my brother and father.

"When you're dealing with all them white people you gotta watch your back," Daddy began as he twisted the cap off the radiator.

"Yes, sir," Linc said.

"Nice as some of them may seem, they might not like seeing a black man messing around in their territory, in their money. They might not *know* they don't like it, but they'll start messing with you just the same. So remember, it doesn't matter what they do. It's what you do that will count in the end. How you respond, how you protect yourself."

"Yes, sir," said Linc.

"And don't you go and get that girl pregnant too soon," Daddy said, pausing to send Linc a stern glance. "Plenty of time for that later. From what I can see, that's a smart girl. She should know that."

"Yes, sir," Linc said.

"Didn't nobody send you to that school so you could go around having babies with no money and no home to raise 'em properly."

"Yes, Daddy," Linc said.

"And make sure you're in that office on time, even earlier if you can. There'll be people watching that. Seeing if you're lazy. Don't even give 'em an inch to go on. Don't give 'em any reason to think you're less than what you are."

"Yes, Daddy."

"You'll be all right. I know you will be. Just look after yourself and you'll do just fine."

"Yes, Daddy."

Linc did wait, but I don't think it was as long as Daddy had hoped. Two years later, Chandra was pregnant, and she and Linc were engaged to be married. After Linc called with the news, my father sat out on the porch looking over the yard, shaking his head. My mother stood with her arms around his shoulders, rubbing his back and whispering words of reassurance in his ear.

Seven

Linc's wedding day dawned a clear bright Saturday in October. I held the skirts of my hunter-green bridesmaid dress above the red fallen leaves as I walked across the yard and up the steps of the house where Chandra's mother lived. The brick-and-stucco home was in Shaker Heights, a far grander and more polished community than our rough-and-tumble neighborhood with its tar and gravel road. Inside the house Chandra's room was a fascination in itself since Ella, Hazel, and I had always shared a bedroom. We were amazed Chandra had had this room all to herself her whole life. Now on her wedding day we all waited on her there: my sisters, her mother, and Shelly, Chandra's best friend and maid of honor. This would be Shelly's third trip down the aisle as an attendant and the nutmeg-colored woman with the turned-up nose had developed a thing for wedding protocol. She refused to let us appear in the ceremony wearing mismatched hair accessories. She'd brought her own supply of clips and bows and sat each of us down to tear out our assorted bobby pins and clips and twist our hair into French braids identical to hers. Hazel was downstairs undergoing the operation while the rest of us sat in Chandra's room as she finished dressing. Yards and yards of satin and chiffon flowed from Chandra's head down her back where she sat at her vanity table. Her dress was white, low-cut, with a relaxed waist that hid the roundness already forming on her belly. Mrs. Templeton, Chandra's mother, tall and elegant like her daughter, stood behind her adjusting the folds, straightening the bow at Chandra's back. Not used to wearing heels, I kicked off my shoes and padded around the room examining the stuffed animals and posters of Michael Jackson, Lionel Ritchie, and Clifton Davis that still decorated the walls, furniture, and shelves. Ella sat on the bed, mesmerized by Chandra's careful application of foundation, eyeliner, and lipstick.

"Mom," Chandra said, glancing at Ella in the mirror, "will you go downstairs and see if my flowers are here yet? I thought I heard the doorbell a little while ago."

"Of course, dear, be right back." Then, as her mother left, Chandra turned her head to us.

"Ella, why don't you go help her bring them up?"

Ella snapped out of her gaze. "Your bouquet? Yes, sure, I'll help," she said, always eager to be useful, and followed Mrs. Templeton out of the room.

Chandra brushed her hair in silence for a moment. "I swear, sometimes it seems that child's eyes will burn right through me."

"Oh, she just reads too many magazines," I said, taking Ella's place on the bed and arranging the folds of my dress around me so they wouldn't wrinkle. Then, trying to sound casual, I said, "So, have you seen Linc yet today?"

"Now, honey, you know it's bad luck for the groom to see the bride before the ceremony. But don't try to be sly, young lady, I know what you mean. Tick probably had him out so late he couldn't see straight this morning."

She laughed, shaking her head, then put her brush down and looked at me in the mirror. "Linc likes talking to you. You know, he talks about you all the time."

"No, I didn't know that. He talks about me? What does he say? What *is* there to say? I'm just a kid."

"Come on, Crita, you're his sister. He's proud of you. He thinks you're becoming quite a young lady."

"Well, I don't see it. It's not like I'm popular or really good in sports or anything like he is. And I'm not as pretty as Ella or as smart as Hazel. I'm just me."

"Yes, but it's the way you go about things. You think about things. You're careful. Careful about everything you do. Look at the way you're sitting, you won't even wrinkle that dress. He admires that in you because he doesn't have it in himself. He doesn't know how to be that way."

I swung my legs out a little and leaned back on my elbows. "Linc doesn't have to be careful. He's good at everything."

"Even being good at things requires a certain amount of care. Just because you do something well doesn't mean you know when to do it or why to do it." She looked down and gently rubbed her abdomen. "If we had been more careful I wouldn't be having a baby right now."

I was worried she might start to cry so I looked away and in another moment she had picked up the brush again and was sweeping her hair away from her face. "Here, help me with this," she said. "Hand me the bobby pins." I got up and gathered a small pile of the brown, vinyl-covered pins and delivered them to Chandra one by one. "Look, it's not that I'm not happy to be having your brother's baby. I just wish the timing had been a little different. I wanted us to have a choice in when we got married, when we had our children. I didn't want Linc to feel pushed into anything."

"Do you think he feels like that? Like he's being pushed into marrying you?"

"Oh, honey, I don't know. Men can be so closed off sometimes it's hard to tell what they are really thinking. Your brother works so hard, when he comes home he only wants to eat. You know it was nearly a whole week before he told me he got promoted?"

"I didn't know he got promoted."

"Well, it's kind of a semi-promotion, I guess. He doesn't have a new title or anything, but he's been put in charge of supervising the research on a big project—something involving South Sea oil leases. He probably didn't want to tell his daddy because it wasn't a full promotion. But I still think it's a big deal, don't you?"

"Yeah, it sounds great."

"My mother says men in general don't like to talk too much. I don't mind that, it's just that I worry about your brother. I love him, I do."

"Why are you worried about him?" I asked, fiddling with the pins in my hands.

"I can't put my finger on it exactly." She frowned as though trying to focus on the thought and secure it. She looked away. The expression had escaped her. "Maybe he's not as sure of himself as he used to be. I don't know."

I laughed a little, hoping to take the edge off a mood that was starting to cause a sour unease in my stomach. "Linc's always sure of himself," I said cheerfully. "Things are just kind of weird now, like you said, with the baby coming and the wedding and all that. But you still have months before the baby's born. That'll give you time to settle down some, won't it?"

Chandra smiled. "Yes, maybe you're right, honey. And here I am sitting here making myself anxious thinking about all these things. It can't be good for the baby, either."

She went on pinning and I returned her smile in the mirror but already my brain was spinning, calculating, trying to shove the pieces of a puzzle into place.

We arrived at the church at 10 A.M. The ceremony would take place at 10:45 because, as everyone knows, it's bad luck to get married when the hands on the clock are going down. They should be on their way up, heading for the twelve. "That's why morning ceremonies are best," Ella once told me when, as children, we were planning our imaginary weddings. But, I had thought, the ceremony, the marriage, the life, it all keeps going after the hands pass that number and go down. *What happens then?*

Inside, my sisters and I set ourselves up with Chandra and Shelly in a small recreational room near the entrance of the sanctuary. It had long tables and a sink and a refrigerator. Chandra's dad was there, too, a thin man wearing thick glasses. He didn't live with Mrs. Templeton, and we didn't know why. Mrs. Templeton seemed glad to see him.

I lied and said I had to go to the bathroom. I wanted to find Linc and see him just once more before the wedding started. I had to know that this was all right, that he was all right. Hurrying down the hallway and holding up the layers of lace on my dress, I saw Tick emerge from a side room, off the main sanctuary. He straightened his bow tie and turned on his jive. "Hey pretty lady, green sure is your color," he said.

For once I didn't have time to think or blush about anything Tick said so I did my best to put on a no-nonsense, Hazelesque face. "Where's my brother?"

He nodded back at the door he had just come through. "He's still in there. The man just needed to be alone for a few minutes before we go in. Tell him to come on out when he's through."

The room was paneled in dark wood, but lit with the colorful rays of the sun filtered through a wide set of stained glass windows. Linc was standing there looking at the glass, and he turned to me as I opened the door and he seemed to glow in the aura of this strange light. Then I saw him and saw what, until then, was inconceivable. He had tears in his eyes. He stood there quietly, not sobbing or brittle and yet the tears were still there, like the remnant of a kiss from an angel long flown away. I stood there and swallowed hard, my arms hanging from my sides, my hands suddenly not feeling the small bouquet that now seemed to float off the tips of my fingers.

I had never seen my brother cry. Never. Not when he got a whipping for pitching a baseball through the living room window, not when he left us for college, not when our grandfather Buford, whom he was closest to, died. But here he cried now and it was as though someone had pulled down a curtain and along with it a god and suddenly he walked the earth. And as if that weren't enough to happen in that one strange moment I realized something extraordinary was happening inside of me. Out of that same ground he had walked and watered with his tears I rose up. I rose and grew. Somehow this moment of weakness in Linc pulled something out of me that made me want to protect him and all at once I was large enough, strong enough, *me* enough to do it.

"Linc," I said once, still standing in place. Then I realized I wasn't moving and went to him. "Linc, what is it? Are you all right?"

I reached into my glove and pulled out the "crying tissue" that Mama had tucked in there earlier that morning. I wiped his tears like Dorothy wiping the tears of the Cowardly Lion, though there was little about Linc at that moment that was either lion or cowardly.

"Linc, Tick says you have to come on out soon. Can you do it?"

"Oh yeah. I want to. I just had to take a minute and breathe a little bit. Everything's fine. I was thinking about Chandra and the baby; you know, and I just want so much for them. And

Chandra, she's like my anchor. I knew that when I first met her, that if I hung on to this woman everything would stay solid and real. That I would always have a home with her."

"But that's good, isn't it? That's why you're marrying her. Why are you crying?"

"Well, I think it's just a mix of things, Crita. It's a little because I'm happy, a little because I'm scared, I guess. I really don't want to mess this up."

"What are you talking about? Mess it up how, Linc?"

He pulled a wooden chair out from under a nearby table and sat on it, leaning on his knees and looking forward like he was staring down a tunnel.

"Whenever I look at my life, I mean really look at it, Crita, I see a pile of dominoes, built up like a pyramid. And those bottom rows were so easy to put together. High school, college, track, it was all a breeze. I lined 'em up so fast. Nothing was gonna fall and I knew it. Put me in the goddamn Army Corps of Engineers, I used to say, because I was building! But it doesn't feel that way anymore. Now every time I put another domino on the pile I wonder if it's the one that could make the whole thing, my whole life, just fall apart. And the thing is, now I'm not the only one who'll get hit on the head when the shit falls. There's Chandra. There's a baby."

"Since when have things been so tough, Linc? What makes you think things will get any harder for you? Your job is going okay, right? Chandra says they even gave you more responsibility. Come on, Linc, they probably think you're the greatest thing since Velveeta. Everybody likes you. It's always been that way. What is there to mess up?"

"Yeah, the world is my basketball, right? I'll just take it to the hoop like Magic Johnson."

I looked at my watch and realized we had to get going.

"Well, you've always been magic to me." I smiled and walked away from him and opened a door leading to a small powder room. I pulled some paper towels from the dispenser above the sink and took them back to Linc. "Here, blow your nose." He did so and took a deep breath and smiled at me. I put my hand under his freshly shaved chin and lifted his head and examined his eyes. Still a bit wet, but not red. I dabbed at them again.

"You love her, right?"

He took another deep breath, a clean one this time, clear of the wet and mucous of his tears.

"Yeah."

"Okay, then we have to go. Chandra's waiting for you. And she loves you, too. She told me so today. You'll be okay."

I took his arm and headed for the sanctuary. We parted when I went to join Chandra. The groomsmen were all lined up, ready to escort the mothers in. Mama scolded me for being late. "Girl, where you been?" But then the processional music started and Mama clamped down on the arm of a startled young man and was off down the aisle. I was left standing with my excuse stuck in my throat.

Shelly lined my sisters and me up with our respective groomsmen. Mine was a skinny opportunist Linc knew from college who, after meeting me at the rehearsal, seemed disappointed that his partner in this was underage, not to mention gawky. As usual, Ella had the prize and I was still seething over it. Her escort was Chandra's brother, whose real name was Demetrius Mark Templeton, but everyone called him Tree. He was nineteen and a college man, with smooth, caramel-colored skin like his sister's and a dimple in his chin. His large, deep eyes were the color of hot fudge.

We had met him for the first time at the rehearsal dinner the night before, and I had willed myself to muster every morsel of maturity and sophistication budding inside my seventeen-year-old body. I was too preoccupied to notice Ella moving in for the kill, extending her hand and putting forth a fifteen-year-old bosom that easily shamed my sad nubs and saying, "Tree! I am so glad to meet you. I hear you're the man on that college campus of yours."

Later at the dinner as I sat waiting for everyone else to sit down so the food could be served, I heard the chair next to me scrape the floor and turned just as Tree dropped himself into it. "That Ella is wise beyond her years, isn't she?"

"Yeah, she's wise all right. Where is she? I'm surprised she let you out of her sight," I said, surprised at my own brazenness.

"I escaped. I think she went to powder her nose or something. She is a good source of information. I think I learned something about everyone—except you. What's your story?"

"My story? I don't think I have one yet."

"Well, I don't believe that," he said, leaning back in his chair and surveying the room. "Let me try something easier. Tell me about something you like."

I looked at him wryly, wondering if this were some college-boy prank Tree was perpetrating on me. But he seemed relaxed and sincere and it made me want to tell him something surprising. Trouble was, I couldn't think of anything to say.

"Oh, I don't know . . ."

"Come on, there must be something you like. Do you like Kool-Aid?"

"Yeah, that's kid stuff." I looked at him still full of doubt, but went on. "Okay, I love Kool-Aid. We make it all the time."

"What's your favorite flavor?"

"Tropical punch."

"Yeah, that's a good one. But I prefer raspberry."

"It's okay," I said, starting to feel the rhythm of our conversation. "It's too tart for me. But I like to mix raspberry with other flavors, like lemonade."

"I've done that. I also like to mix other stuff in, just to weird out Chandra. I've done grape and strawberry and lime and orange."

"Oh gross! What color did that make?"

"Well, as I recall, it was kind of brown. Tasted good, though."

"Did you make it by the pitcher? 'Cause we drank it so fast we had to make it by the gallon, in a cooler jug."

"Naw, we did the pitcher thing. A clear glass one, like you see it on TV. That way I could see the weird colors I made up."

I laughed at him and shook my head. "I can't believe we're sitting here talking about Kool-Aid!"

"Hey, but it's a connection, right? Now we have something in common."

"Yeah," I said, smiling. There was much more to him than hot chocolate eyes. "I guess we do."

Then Ella reappeared to lead Tree off to her part of the table. He humored her, but as the evening wore on I caught him staring at me, perhaps because I couldn't stop watching him. When I looked at him, I could see Kool-Aid.

When it was my turn to go down the aisle I could only see the back of Tree's head as he offered Ella his arm. For the moment I was relieved. I needed to concentrate and I would have found that impossible if his eyes had been on me.

I saw Linc at the end of the aisle, he and Tick looking sharp, hard and clean in their tuxedos. Linc winked at me and I smiled and wobbled slightly on my high heels.

I took my place at the altar with the rest of the party and looked out at all the faces swimming in the pews before me. Then the sea of faces rose as the music trumpeted Chandra's entrance. I think in that brief moment my sisters and I were thinking exactly the same thoughts. *"Will I be that tall? Will I be that pretty? Will I look like her when I grow up?"*

I looked at Linc and what did I see? Astonishment, pride, fear, love, enchantment. I couldn't tell, the mix of his emotions was so strange and yet I was sure of one thing: my brother did want her. She had become a part of his foundation, a necessity for his existence. Whatever was going on with Linc, whatever he was afraid of, it was clear that Chandra was important to him.

During the ceremony I couldn't stop thinking about what Chandra told me Linc admired about me: that I was careful. This became the seed of an idea planted so easily, so quietly, in the soft willing furrows of my young head. As I watched Chandra and my brother pledge their vows I felt the germ spread and the roots reached out into the synapses of my brain and began to whisper, *"What if I could use that part of myself for Linc?"* It was seductive, comforting, and I tilted my head as though into a hand caressing my face and I listened further. *"What if I could help him somehow? Couldn't I be careful for him?"* What that meant exactly I didn't know at the time, but I liked the feeling of it. It presented me with an action, something I could do instead of standing there as life rolled over me. And it seemed simple. The idea was satisfying enough to take hold of my being without further thought to the details. This was something I could do. This was all I had to offer to my brother who seemed to be in need of *something*, however nameless and faceless, and I was willing to give it.

It was then, as if on cue, that the minister's voice cut like a lance through the curtain of my reverie, and I felt the beginning of a tornado spinning in my chest. He was preaching and the energy, the spirit in the room, was starting to surge. I knew it was the Spirit, the Holy Spirit, and every Sunday it would make people screech at the top of their lungs and fall to the ground testifying. Those spectacles sickened me and long ago

I had vowed never to look like that, eyes rolling, tongue spinning, in front of my neighbors and family. But when the minister preached and the energy surged, it was all I could do to hold the seams of my soul intact.

"To all of you here today," the minister was saying as he conjured and cajoled, "TO *AWWLLL OF YOU HERE TO-DAY*. Will you STAND before the Lawd with these two young people? Will you give your PROMISE just as willingly and lovingly as they are promising to each other this morning, setting the example for us? What promise is that you ask? Do you want to *KNOW?*"

"YES FATHER!" "TELL US, FATHER, TELL US WHAT TO DO!" Some of the women in the pews waved their hands back and forth and rocked. "TELL US WHAT THE LAWD WANTS US TO DO!"

"MMM-HMMM!" the minister sang. I could feel a spark like a sizzling jumping bean twitter inside me. I fought the impulse to sing, fought the spark's burning sensation and its crowbar arms prying and widening my soul until I was sure it would rip out my insides and spill them through my mouth and into the world.

The minister was smacking his wide, thick hand on the Bible, rhythmically emphasizing each word. "THE-LAWD-WANTS-YOU-TO-*HELP*-THESE-CHILDREN! Will you do that? I said WILL you do that? Will you help *maintain* this union? Will you help them walk down the path of the Lawd? Will you help Lincoln and Chandra to build their home and build their family so that they can *stand* with the Lawd in glory and righteousness?"

"I will," I said out loud along with the rest of the congregation, which erupted with shouts of "YES LAWD!" and "THANK YOU JESUS!" The choir broke into joyous peals of down-home gospel and I stood there, clutching my bouquet tighter and tighter as I kept on whispering my oath. "I will,"

I said to myself. The minister declared Linc and Chandra man and wife and sent them off as the newly minted Mr. and Mrs. Carter. "AMEN!" shouted the congregation. "God Bless You!"

"Amen," I whispered as Ella nudged me to get moving and I began my unsteady walk back down the aisle. "Amen."

Eight

When Chandra comes to pick up Savannah that evening she doesn't get further than her car. She sees me on the porch and hesitates, unsure which way to go or how she should look. I stand my ground for a moment and pray for the time when once she could see my face and not be startled, when we lived as sisters and basked in our mutual love and respect. Then I go to her and, deciding against a kiss on her cheek, I touch her arm and rub it slightly, hoping she can feel, if only in tiny increments, that I still love her. She is still breathtakingly beautiful.

"Hey Chandra. It's really good to see you again."

"I see your mama's called in the reinforcements," she says, closing the car door and leaning against it. She glances over to the house and yard to see if Savannah is within earshot, but the child has already gone in to collect her belongings. "How's your daddy doing?"

"I don't know. He doesn't look too good. And I think Mama's kind of scared. She doesn't know what to think about what's going on." I pause and lean against the car next to her, aligning my body with hers. "She's glad that you've been around, and so am I," I say gently.

Chandra looks at me, but then she softens and says, "No. I know you probably mean that. But I already stuck my nose in and had it chopped off and handed to me by Hazel in the most ungracious manner. I know where I'm not wanted."

I frown. My littlest sister has been busy. "What did she say?"

"I was just trying to get her to understand that with your daddy sick and all, that Linc might want to come and see him."

Chandra takes a deep breath and her eyes narrow as she looks across the yard as though she is trying to find something to focus on. Whatever Hazel has said to her is bitter, I can see that. Her muscles still struggle to shake loose the sourness the words had left behind. She reaches back and nervously flips the car door handle up and down.

"She—she had the nerve to tell me that I didn't know anything about this family and had no say in it. She said a lot of this was my fault because I didn't have the good sense to deal with Linc the right way before, back when it all started."

I try to interrupt. "Chandra, you know that's not—" but she goes on.

"She told me to mind my own business. And that's exactly what I'm going to do."

She starts to walk toward the house and I feel a tug in my heart that makes me desperate. I am a castaway and she is the solid rock I need to stand on, the place from which I can safely survey this crazy corner of the world. I grab her arm again.

"Chandra, please," I say, afraid of her reaction, but too determined to let go. "I'm scared out of my mind, too. I don't know what to do. I just have this awful feeling that this is it . . ." The tears rise in my chest and, for the first time since I have arrived in Ohio, I don't stop them. I let them spill down my cheeks and drip from my chin, the salty water making round splotches on my shirt. I swipe a hand over them. "Whatever happens here, with Daddy or with Linc, this time it'll be forever. I just know it."

"Crita, it's late," she says quietly. "I've got to get Savannah home."

"Yeah, okay," I say, releasing her arm. "I'm sorry. Really sorry." I think that Chandra will go into the house then, but she stands there a moment longer and shoves her hands into the back pockets of her jeans.

"You know," she says, a painfully forced casualness in her voice, "Tree is around."

"Tree?" I echo. "Yeah, so I've heard."

"Maybe you should call him. Okay?"

"Okay." She goes into the house and I walk the short length of driveway to the road and back, crying the rest of my cry and hoping to feel some relief for the effort. By the time I reach the house again, Chandra and Savannah are coming out. Chandra's back is ramrod straight, her face hard and stony. I realize I should have told her that Hazel was in there. She looks at me and I can't say a thing, even when Savannah yells, "Bye bye, Aunt Crita!" from her backseat window. I only wave and make a feeble attempt to smile.

When I can't see Chandra's car anymore I go to the backyard and sit in the dark under Mama's cherry tree, my knees pulled up to my chin. I have forgotten how dark it gets in Lorain, especially on this night when there is no moon. The sky is black and filled with stars, reminding me of dreams I had as a child where I would walk outside and see the whole solar system hanging in the dark above my head in vivid color, just like in my science textbook. Instead of being in awe I was always frightened by the spectacle, by the heavens being right on my own doorstep. But tonight the stars are a safe distance away. It shouldn't be that dark, not in our yard anyway. Daddy usually has big, bright outdoor lamps lighting our property: one over the back door, one in the backyard, and one on the porch. But the bulbs over the back door and backyard have burned out and no one has bothered to replace them. I'll go to the hardware store tomorrow, I think. I can fix a burned-out light, if nothing else.

Then I think Daddy might have more bulbs in the shed.

"Damn!" When I step in I stub my toe on something thick and hard. I fumble for the light switch and as my hand flails air in search of its pull string, I knock something to the ground that feels light and hollow.

"Love you! Love you! Love you!"

I gasp. The mechanical voice is still singing as I finally grasp the string and light up the room. It has been rearranged. The assortment of boxes filled with stored junk are gone and the lawn mower is placed in a corner. Rakes hang from nails on the walls. The new setup has left the center clear for a work-bench, which I had kicked upon entry, and the shelves are lined with doll parts and dolls. There are babies with big soft bodies, one of which sits with its head in its lap. There are legless torsos colored brown and pink and tan. An armless doll with brown curls and huge green eyes stares at me like I'm an intruder. I pick up the chattering redhead I had knocked to the floor. Hazel's workroom. She is truly at home now. How long is she planning to stay?

When I awake the next morning, I smell water. I have slept with the window open, and the night air has blown the misty scent of fog into my room. The day is heavy with it, so much so that I can't see the road beyond the stop sign down our street. I know it will be raining within the hour.

Ella has again commandeered the kitchen. She must be trying to cook away her nervousness because the table is covered with food way more than three women alone, let alone Daddy, could ever eat. At least a pound of bacon is piled high on a plate covered with paper towels, and there's a platter of freshly scrambled eggs and a ceramic bowl full of grits. A basket of warm blueberry muffins scents the room, and Ella is just pulling a pan of biscuits from the oven.

I stand watching her for a moment and silently wish that she would slow down. She moves with such authority and I want her to be able to savor being in a realm where she knows what she is doing and is obviously in control. It might fortify her for later and feed her soul with confidence. But instead Ella works hastily, like a robot, finding comfort only in her motions and not her mastery.

"This is a serious amount of food, sister dear," I say, picking up a plate and wondering how I can politely eat very little. My stomach feels sour and the smell of the bacon makes me light-headed.

Ella pauses, holding the hot pan with an oven mitt, and surveys the table. "Well, it won't hurt if there are extra," she says before turning out the biscuits into another basket. "I just thought things might go easier if we were all well fed."

I spoon grits onto my plate and stir in some eggs, hoping the bland mixture will soothe my queasy stomach. Ella sits down across from me with a muffin and proceeds to shred it to pieces while alternately nibbling at the resulting crumbs.

"So, El, what did Tree have to say when he called the other day?"

She doesn't look away from her muffin shreds. "Tree? Well, hon, how would I . . ."

"Cut it out, I know he's the one you were cooing at."

"Crita, don't be mad, honey. I just thought with all that was going on with Daddy, you didn't need to bother with your ex right now."

"Very sweet of you to think so. It took you twenty minutes to get him off the phone?"

"I didn't want to be rude, of course."

If this were ten years earlier, I'd probably jump on Ella and shove her pretty face into the linoleum until she apologized. "Ella, for you he was a crush. It was high school. Get over it."

"You don't need to be that way about it."

"Maybe I do. What would Forrest think?"

"Crita, stop teasing, that's mean."

"All right, you two, break it up." Hazel comes in and takes a strip of bacon from the plate and leans against the sink while she chews on it. "Whoever he is, he ain't worth it! Isn't that what Mama used to say?" Hazel wears a black T-shirt and, to my surprise, a bit of makeup: foundation, eyeliner, and a touch of a brick-red lipstick. Compared to my sisters, I look like a construction worker in my faded jeans, T-shirt, and blue plaid flannel shirt with the sleeves rolled up to my elbows.

"Yeah, well this time Mama would be wrong," I say.

"Are they still asleep?"

"Yeah, thank goodness," I say and I mean it. Our parents need the rest.

"You shouldn't eat standing up," Ella tells Hazel.

A smile creeps into the left corner of my mouth and I look at my youngest sister, hoping silently that she isn't so distracted she can't pick up the cue.

"Humph," Hazel grunts before popping the remainder of her bacon in her mouth. She wipes her hands together, then pulls a chair out from under the table and drops herself into it. "That's right," she growls, imitating our father. "You're sup-posed to sit down when you eat. Your ass won't fill up standing there like some damn mule, and I ain't got the money to feed your ass all day. You sit *down* and fill your stomach up right!"

"Yes, sir!" I reply and the three of us fall into a comfortable laughter. Hazel always was the best at impersonating Daddy. She can mimic his inflection, his accent, and the gravel in his throat even though she can't force her own voice down low enough to match his deep pitch. We thrill to hear her and feel the exquisite ache in our hearts from laughing and loving Daddy so much in the same instant.

"What else did he used to say?" asks Ella, her expression

suffused with nostalgia. I can tell she wants to float a little longer in this protective bubble.

"He said," replies Hazel, taking another piece of bacon, "that a woman in a kitchen can throw out more with a teaspoon than she can with a shovel."

"And whenever you asked him what time it was," I added, "he'd say, 'Why, what time you got to be there?' " We laugh again and suddenly I am ravenous. I pick up one of Ella's biscuits and it is still warm. I break it open and slather the insides with a knifeful of butter just like Daddy used to do. "God, I haven't made biscuits in ages."

"Neither have I," Hazel says. "Isn't that weird considering how long it took us to learn how to make them?"

"I know, Daddy must have thought we were retarded. Remember that one time I forgot those biscuits were in the oven?"

"Oh, girl," says Ella. "They were so black and flat and hard we could've used them for coasters!"

"And Daddy made me make another batch all over again. Dough just wasn't my thing."

"We all had our specialties," Ella reminds me. "Yours was muffins, Hazel's was pancakes, and mine, well, mine of course was biscuits!" She holds one of her fluffy creations aloft.

"Daddy never made Linc learn to bake, did he?" Hazel says, a touch of bitterness in her voice.

"No," Ella replies quietly. "Daddy said he was a boy and he didn't have to do these things. He made him wash dishes, that was about all."

We are silent then and I am no longer hungry. I push the cold eggs around on my plate.

"We can do this on our own, can't we?" Hazel asks. Ella and I look at each other and nod because we know what she means: without Linc.

"Honey, it looks like we don't have a choice," Ella tells her.

"But I want it to be our choice. We don't need him. We have each other. And what good would he be if he were here?"

"None," I whisper, but I feel I am lying. Still, I want to believe in this warmth, this bond that now holds me so strongly to my sisters. At the moment I will say anything to maintain it.

"All right then, honey girls," Ella says. "Give me your hands."

We grasp each other's hands in a circle and there, with the eggs and the biscuits and grits and bacon fragrant between us, we make a promise to each other. "This is our goddamn family," Hazel says.

Adds Ella, "And we will stand together."

"Yes," I say. "God willing."

"We don't need a brother," says Hazel.

I squeeze her hand and say nothing.

I intended to keep our promise. I wanted it with my whole being. I knew why they needed it: they found the weight of we three as a force comforting, the substance they would need to take us through whatever we had to face in the future.

But we have never quite worked well together—our hands clasped as we had them made it seem like we would run around in a circle, like we did playing ring-around-the-rosie as girls. Something tells me we are in danger of running around in the same fruitless circles once more. I don't believe we know enough to comfort each other in the necessary ways. We have not truly been in cahoots since we were girls. I know I cannot depend on this dream, this prospect of we three.

They would not have asked me for this promise if they knew or understood what challenges would befall us next, when Daddy gets so that he can't sleep in his and Mama's bed. It is too hard for him to breathe, so he spends the night now in his recliner. My sisters do not, or, I should say, Daddy does not allow them to sit up with him at night the way that I do. With the emptiness of the sleeping house around me, the only sound I hear is Daddy's breathing, the only sensation is that of his spirit slowly seeping out into space.

No, I am not aware that I will soon betray them. The next night Daddy mumbles a string of incoherent words, which, thinking he is dreaming, I try to ignore. But then he forces my name from his lips.

"Crita, girl, you hear me talking to you?"

"Yes, sir," I say, getting up to stand over him. "What is it, Daddy?"

"I asked you where did that little boy go?"

"What little boy?"

The stream of mumbling goes on, but then I understand Daddy to say, "That boy been coming in here every day now, talking about death and wanting a cookie. I keep telling him I put one in that bottom drawer for him, that one in the kitchen."

I take Daddy's hand and rub it while I look around, worried that this puckish spirit might actually be in the room now. I have listened to enough of Daddy's dreams over the years to know whether they are the dumping ground from a day of rubbish or they are foretelling something. He does, too. The thought frightens me. "It's okay, Daddy," I reassure him. "He's not here anymore."

Later, after Daddy is calm and sleeping soundly, I wake my mother. The bedroom is stuffy and warm because Mama sleeps with the windows closed. Her body, curled beneath the sheets, is small and round and soft to my touch as I press my hand gently against her hip to rouse her. Her eyes look tiny and weak without her glasses.

"Huh? What is it, baby?"

"Mama, the next time Linc calls, tell him to come home."

"All right. How's your daddy doing?"

"He's restless. I don't think we can wait until the end of the week, we might have to take him back to Dr. Joyce tomorrow or the day after. We're gonna need Linc to help us do that."

"All right, if you say so, baby, I'll tell him to come straight home."

"Okay, you go on back to sleep now. You need your rest." She settles back into her pillows, but as I leave I find myself pausing at the door.

"Mama, before Ella and I got here, was Daddy able to walk around much?"

"Yeah, honey, a little. He wasn't sleeping too good then, either. I'd hear him walking around the house, but since he didn't ask me for anything, I paid it no mind. After a while he'd come back in here and get back in bed. Why you ask?"

"Oh, it's nothing, Mama. I'll see you in the morning."

"Good night, baby."

In the kitchen there is a bottom drawer, just left of the sink and near the floor. It used to hold small pots, the kind Mama used for making sauces. But the drawer has been empty for years because, after my parents reached a certain age, they thought it was impractical to have to bend down every time you wanted to get something. Now, Daddy's words still on my mind, I go into the kitchen to open it. I leap back and suppress a scream. The drawer, stuffed with unwrapped cookies, is crawling with roaches.

"Come out with me."

"Hazel, I can't." I'm whispering. I'm in my usual seat, pretending to watch *Little House on the Prairie*, but the sound is turned so low that I couldn't tell you for the life of me what Laura and that little bitch Nellie Olsen are arguing about. I'm listening to Daddy's breathing as he sleeps just behind me in his chair. I'm also waiting to hear the phone ring—waiting to hear how Mama will tell Linc that he's needed here. I'm wondering if and when he'll come. It's not a given that he will. I'm starting to feel stupid for ever asking Mama for him. As if I haven't learned.

Now here's Hazel wanting me to go Lord knows where, probably so she can kick my ass because she knows what I've done. I can't take that right now. And I can't leave Daddy, so I'm keeping my butt right where it is.

"Crita, you've been up all night and you didn't go out yesterday either."

"So?"

"So? You need air, honey."

"I'm fine. Be quiet, you'll wake Daddy." He stirs a little when I say that. I hold my breath as his body releases again into sleep.

Ella appears at the kitchen doorway and crosses her arms like she's waiting for something. She has a little frown furrowed deep between her pretty eyebrows. Hazel puts a finger to her lips, silencing our sister before she can speak. "See," she tells me, "Ella's here. She'll watch Daddy. Come on, we won't be gone long." She has me by the arm now and I can't struggle with her because I don't want to disturb Daddy. "You're driving," she says as she ushers me out the door.

I roll down the window. The warm air feels good on my naked arms, but the light makes me squint. I need sunglasses. Hazel pulls off her sandals and props her bare feet up on the dashboard. She's wearing a red tie-dyed tank top and cut-off jean shorts; her braids are braided into two fat pigtails and hanging down to her chest.

"Where to, madam?" I ask.

"Lakeview Beach!" she announces. "Time to take the crazy people to the water!"

"Right." I can't help but laugh a little. Daddy always said that you have to take crazy people over water, over bridges, because it eases their minds. On a whim he would, when we were children, take a different route driving home, crossing the Black River Bridge and justifying it with a playful, "You kids are out of your minds! I gotta take you over this water!"

"Look, Haze, you're not gonna give me a hard time about Linc, are you? Because I'm not up to it."

"Crita . . ."

"I'll even beat you to the punch—I'm already on my own ass because I'm sorry as hell I did it, all right?"

"Fuck it, Crita, it was inevitable. If he's within shouting distance, there's no way you'd ever shut him out. We both know that. Now if he had dropped his butt off the face of this earth, that'd be different."

"Hazel!"

"Well, hon, it would be! He doesn't let us forget about him and he doesn't join in. What is that crap about him calling Mama every day? Ego crap, that's all that is. He can't live if he doesn't think somebody's worrying about his ass."

"Maybe so."

"Honey, more driving, less flapping. We're gonna be late."

"Late for what?"

"I'm meeting up with some of my posse."

"Oh, great! And what am I supposed to do? Wait in the car?"

"No. Tree will be waiting there for you."

I've lost the steering wheel in my hands. I'm gripping it, but the matter seems to have disappeared, first becoming like a sponge, then foam, then nothing. Suddenly the knot in my stomach has unloosed and now it feels like a ribbon flailing about in a breeze. "Hazel, I . . ."

She wiggles a big toe at me. "Don't worry about it, sis. You can thank me later."

"But I don't know if I'm ready to see him yet."

"Well, you have a few miles to get yourself ready, don't you? Use 'em well, sis, use 'em well!"

How do I do that? Prepare a speech? A smile? I run a hand through my hair. It feels dry, like I've got a tuft of tumbleweed growing from my head. At a stoplight, I look in the rearview mirror and I want to cry. My skin is pale, like coffee with too much milk, and my eyes seem to disappear into the blotchy brew.

"Here." Hazel offers me a lipstick—sheer, with just a hint of reddish brown pigment. When I put it on my face comes to life a little—but just enough.

I can already see Hazel's friends as we pull into the park. They are Hispanic, black, white, all fresh and funky like they just stepped out of a Mountain Dew ad. They're on and in a black convertible Ford Mustang that's blasting rap music from monstrous speakers. "Don't worry about me," Hazel says as we both get out. "I'll catch a ride home. Tell Mama I'll be back in a few hours." She smiles. "And tell Tree I said hi."

"Thanks, Hazel." I have a powerful urge to hug her, but she's already gone, enveloped in the group.

As I stand waiting for Tree, I try to steel myself against the wave of emotion that I know will sweep over me when I see him—the deep, intoxicating sensation the heart reserves for first passion. I stare out over Lake Erie. The shore and the lake still glitter in the sun as they did when I was a child. But time has marred the lifeguards' shelter and chairs with peeling paint and dull colors.

I see Tree before he sees me. He wears leather boots, blue jeans, and a black leather jacket and he travels across the park path in long, determined strides. I have forgotten how tall he is, a full six foot four. Everything else is familiar—the shape of his lips, thick and sensuous, the hollow between his Adam's apple and his chest where my snuggling face had once fit so perfectly. Only now his hair is locked in long pipe-cleaner-thin strands cascading away from his forehead and down his back, a dramatic change from the close-cropped style he'd worn before. The sight of him, powerful and majestic, makes me catch my breath.

When we lock eyes for the first time I realize I don't know how to greet him. I used to think I could feel him approaching from miles away. I could sense his mood from an even greater distance. And because I could feel him everywhere and touch him when I touched myself, I called it love and felt protected and cherished in his existence. I thought we would never be far from each other. I certainly never thought I would be the one to break us in two.

But Tree does the work for me, smiling and caressing the left side of my face. My head leans into his touch. I wrap my arms around his waist and bury my face in his coat. He smells the same, of sandalwood oil and soap. And there is a familiar smell, one of sweet herbs, and I realize he uses the same oil on his locks that I once used on mine. The reminder of my own hair, now shorn, embarrasses me and I'm loath to emerge from the folds of his jacket.

"Hey," he says.

"I didn't realize . . ." My voice trails off. I don't want to cry. But again he does the work and finishes the sentence for me.

"I didn't either. It's really good to see you again. I knew it would be. I just didn't know how much."

"Me neither."

He takes my hand and leads me to a bench overlooking the lake and we sit and I wonder what I should tell him.

"I don't know where to begin."

"Start where we always have, Crita," he says, sitting sideways on the bench so he can face me. He takes both of my hands, slightly sweaty, in his. "Tell me who you are and where you are. Tell me and make me understand."

"I'm fine." God, it's a lie and I know it because it tastes sour in my mouth. I'm sure Tree can see it in my face, too. "No, wait, that's not right. Let me try that again. I'm doing the best that I can with Daddy the way he is. It's been hard on us all."

"I know, Ella told me."

"Yeah, and what was that about? Did you even ask to speak with me?" I push my thigh against his in a way that I mean to be playful, but the feeling of his thigh and its band of hard muscles shocks me. My face burns with embarrassment.

"Sure I did. But I didn't get past the Ella at the gate. It felt like old times again." He laughs.

"Yeah, same old Ella. I told her she had to get over her goddamn high-school crush."

"Why? Did you?" He's smiling, but his eyes, those gorgeous chocolate brown eyes, aren't doing the same and because of that I won't answer. Finally he sits back against the bench—a sort of retreat. "I'm sorry. Dumb question."

There's a seagull on the sand out in front of us. It's lighted onto a brown paper bag and the bird's claws hold the bag down while it tears back the sides with its beak to get at the remnants of someone's lunch. I'm thinking the bird better hurry. Soon others will come and fight him for the food.

"Tell me about school, Tree. You still like teaching?"

"Of course. The kids are something else, though. Seems like they try to grow up faster every year. The clothes they wear . . . The girls especially—they'll be wearing this tight, low-cut crap and they don't know what it means, they don't know what it could lead to. And they don't know enough to protect themselves."

"Daddy would never have let us out of the house like that.

But then, the girls you're talking about probably don't have fathers at home, do they?"

"No, most don't. And if I call a mother in to discuss her daughter's wardrobe . . ." His voice trails off with a laugh.

"What?"

"Nine times out of ten, Crita, the mom is dressed the same damn way! How do you talk to someone like that?"

"I don't know, Tree."

It feels good, this talking to him. It feels solid. But if that's true, then why do I have that Barry Manilow song in my head? *And it seems you and I are like strangers a wide ways apart as we drift on through time. We say love's easier when it's far away.*

Maybe it's because I know it can't stay this way for long— us chatting with safe words on safe subjects. It's not about who we are and I'm afraid of what we really are: hungry for us and afraid all at the same time. I have missed him like I would miss the sun, I'll admit that now. But I don't see a way of lassoing it all in—of setting things back to what they were, or if I should even try. I decide to try.

"Tree, Daddy's really sick. It's like I'm standing here in front of a batch of quicksand. There's no way around it—no going left, no going right. I can't jump over it. I know Linc has to come back into this picture, for better or worse. I have to go through that, even if I don't know what it means for me. Linc deserves his part in this, whatever that may be. I can give him that."

"Haven't you done enough for Linc already? Come on, Crita, since when has he deserved anything, especially from you? You've already made your share of the sacrificing."

"But it didn't do anybody good, did it?"

He sighs and sits up again to look at me. "Crita, you oughta know. You had the worst of it. I don't know why you're not talking about that instead of what you can give Linc. Girl, where is your anger? When and if that crackhead shows up, you should just let him have it. Tell him, 'Look asshole, you were shitty as hell to me. You owe me big time.' Maybe it'll make you feel better." He takes my hand and my fingers seem to dissolve right into his. I want to take his hand up to my face and feel its shape against my skin. "Look, I know when he's firing on all cylinders, Linc is charming as all hell. Even the pope would forgive him for spitting in a cathedral. That's why I'm gonna be paying attention. If he messes with my sister, I'm gonna rip his throat out."

"I can't hear this."

"You never can, can you?" His voice is calmer now in a way that tugs at my chest. You could hit me with a sledgehammer right now and I wouldn't feel it. "I don't see you for five years, Crita! Five years! And this is what I get from you. You left the hospital without even calling me. Do you know how long I waited for you?"

I won't answer. I had promised myself a long time ago that I would never apologize for it. I thought that if he really loved me, he would understand how I couldn't face him. And if he didn't, well . . . I never let myself finish that thought. But I know now, at this moment, that if I open my mouth Tree would get enough "I'm sorry's" to overflow into Lake Erie.

"Demetrius."

Her voice is thin, high-pitched. I don't even respond to it at first—that's how much I'm not used to hearing Tree called by his proper name. It's only when I see he's not looking at me anymore, but upwards and behind me, that I realize someone else has joined us. Suddenly Tree is no longer holding my hand.

"Oh, hey, baby, you're here already? I didn't know."

Baby???

She has stick-straight brown hair and white-spotted light blue eyes that look like they'd been colored in hastily with a child's crayon. Her nose is long, her lips thin, and if I were to encounter this horse-faced woman again, even in another hour, I wouldn't recognize her. She has no features stark enough to stay imprinted on my mind.

"Yeah," she says, "I ran my errand and I drove around a little, then I came back. I've just been parked over there waiting." She nods in the direction of the parking lot and she smiles. Her lips curl back way above her teeth to show bright pink gums.

Tree stays seated next to me and I'm thinking, "well, that's something" even as he's speaking her name to me.

"Crita, this is Talane."

That's not a name, that's a major appliance. "Hi."

"We work together. Talane teaches art."

Of course she teaches with him. She would have to be someone he saw every day—she would have to have been reconsidered by him again and again because he would not have loved her (DOES HE LOVE HER??) at first encounter.

"Hi, Crita. I've heard a lot about you." Why do they always say that? Is it even true? She offers me her cool, pale hand and I take it, but I don't get up. I can't get up. "Tree said your dad is sick. I'm sorry. I hope he gets better soon."

"Me, too. We all do."

She steps back and places her hand on Tree's shoulder. His eyes stay fixated on me as though he's waiting for something. She lifts an unmanicured index finger and lightly brings it down in a single tap. "Honey, we have to go."

"Uh, yeah," he says, still looking at me.

"That's okay, I have to make a phone call." I stand up and turn away, pretending to look around for the phones, but my eyes aren't seeing anything. "I want to check on my father."

"Hey, Crita," he says, making me turn to him again. "What happened to you? What happened between you and Linc?"

I can't believe he's asking me this in front of her. I run my hands through my hair and squint into the sun because I can't look at him anymore. I have to get out of here. I want to throw rocks. Break windows. I will do anything rather than stand here and feel what I'm feeling. I was so sure—so sure that we could never really replace each other. "Let's just say you were right about a lot of things."

"What did you mean by that?" Mari's voice over the phone is reedy and eager.

"I can't explain it." Hell, I can barely stand up right now. I'm holding on to the receiver like it's the one thing keeping me vertical. I've walked away from Tree and Talane and called Mari, so it would look like I'm doing something other than kicking the sand or driving away in disappointment. I asked Mari to keep talking as I watched them get into her boxy Chevy Cavalier (I never did like that car) and drive off. "He knows what I mean."

"Are they gone now?"

"Yes." And I know this is true because now I can feel the tears coming on—huge, hot and weighted tears that want to take me down to the ground. "Mari, how the hell am I going to make it through this shit?"

"Dear, only you have the answer to that. But you're not alone, okay? Just remember that. You're not doing anything by yourself."

She doesn't understand. By myself has always been the best way for me to do things.

Nine

After Linc got married he bought a house not far from where we
lived. It was right on my way to and from school. The house
was small, three bedrooms, with beige aluminum siding and
dark green shutters on the windows. A concrete porch jutted
out from the front with black metal supports made to look like
ivy vines. In the back there was a postage-stamp backyard and
a metal swing and slide set waiting patiently for Chandra's baby
to be born. In style and substance it was not unlike any of the
other houses on the street and yet this house was special to me;
it was the first house I'd been in other than my parents' house
where I felt I could truly "make myself at home" and move
from room to room, touching walls and opening doors, without feeling like an intruder. This was a family house and I was
part of that family.

I was there a lot. I stopped by before and after school. When
they first moved in I was there to help Chandra unpack the
boxes. After they had settled in I would still come by and ask
if she needed anything from the grocery store and if she did I
would pick it up and take it to her on the way home from
school. I would linger there in the afternoons, trying to stay
until Linc came home. That plot didn't always succeed since
he often worked late and Mama would call Chandra and tell

her to send me home for dinner. Mama wouldn't let me stay no matter how I pleaded. "I don't understand why you're always running over there," she'd say. "Those two are newlyweds, Crita. They want to be left alone." She didn't understand that Linc needed me.

One morning as I was leaving Chandra, Shelly called. "Hey, girl, how you doing?" Chandra said. As I quietly lingered over my book bag, pretending to dig out a stray stick of lip-gloss, I heard Chandra say, "Yeah, I have an appointment today. They're doing the sonogram and the doctor says we'll actually be able to see the baby. Oh, Shelly, I can't wait to see what it looks like." I heard a pause, then a tug of hesitancy from Chandra's throat.

"Linc's supposed to be there. But to tell you the truth, I don't know if he will be. I'm tired of reminding him about my appointments, and he can't make a lot of them anyway because he's working." I tilted my head in the phone's direction. Linc's missing Chandra's medical visits? He's just forgetting, I was sure.

Shelly said something that made Chandra laugh and I zipped up my book bag. "Well, he *does* know about it. I did my part, now he'll have to do his and show up."

I waved to Chandra, but said nothing as I slipped out the kitchen door. I ran all the way to school, already calculating. I had to contact Linc, I had to warn him. I just needed enough time before the homeroom bell to make the call. I entered the building and rushed passed the slamming locker doors, cutting a way through the chaos and down to the pay phone across from the high school office. I put my hand on the receiver and paused, suddenly thinking. A phone call would not be enough. Another thing he would mark down and forget, or that his secretary would scribble onto one of those pink message pads and he would not notice until much later in the day when it would be too late.

I left the phone and rushed back to the hall where the senior lockers were. They were in alphabetical order and I had to go farther than usual, up some steps and into another hall, down where the Ws were. I was looking for Malcolm Warfield. He was my age and had been in every class of mine since kindergarten. He'd made me believe I was talented just because one day our third-grade teacher was having trouble drawing straight lines on the blackboard. "Crita Carter can do it," he had said. "She can do lots of stuff." I have no idea what made him say so, but I had believed him.

Malcolm was leaning against his locker. His big sienna-brown biceps seemed to spring from the holes of the Cleveland Browns jersey that he had cut the sleeves off of. His jeans were likewise ripped and loose, but on his feet he wore gleaming white Nike basketball shoes.

"Hey, Malcolm!"

"What?" Like so many high-school boys, Malcolm couldn't be bothered to string two sentences together. But last year Mr. Belfiore, the choral director, had coaxed him into choir and we were all surprised to learn Malcolm had a gorgeous voice, a velvety baritone that would go buzzing through the risers as we rehearsed. I could feel it in my feet.

"Can I borrow your car?"

"Girl, you're out of your mind!" Malcolm drove a battered Dodge Omni that used to belong to his mother. "Can you even drive?"

"We took drivers' ed at the same time, remember? And I got my license. Come on, I need it, I won't be gone more than a hour. I'll be back before *lunch*." I wanted him to understand that he could still skip out on the rest of the school day if he wanted to. "I'll even put gas in it."

His eyes lit up then. "You'll fill the tank, right?"

"Yeah, sure." I thought, *Just give me the damn keys.*

"Cool." He tossed me a leather key fob decorated with a

horse's head. I recognized it as one of the design projects from the industrial arts classes.

"Thanks."

I went to my homeroom. I knew there was a right way to skip school; I knew kids who did it all the time. You had to go to homeroom first. That was where teachers took the main attendance rolls, the ones reported to the office. You had to be there to be counted and if you weren't, that meant an immediate call to your parents from the school secretary asking for your excuse and whereabouts. But if you went to homeroom and left afterward, then you would only be missed in your individual classes and those teachers would wait until later in the day to ask questions. I would be back by then. At that moment anything was possible. I walked into the room and planted myself in a chair and, while the class announcements droned out from the P.A. system, I mentally ran through a checklist. How much gas was in Malcolm's car already? Would it be enough to get me to downtown Cleveland? Would Linc even be in the office?

When homeroom ended we all filed out and I walked casually toward an exit. If I looked like I was supposed to be leaving, a teacher or hall monitor might assume I was one of the seniors allowed to work half-days in offices and stores. I kept my eyes focused straight ahead and just kept walking a long, purposeful stride. I reached the doors, putting my hands out in front of me to push them open, and I was once again out in the morning sun. I stood there for a moment staring at the parking lot. I took two deep breaths and my nostrils tingled. The air was different, different from when I had arrived at school that morning. I tried to feel it out, to sense it on my skin, so I stood very still. As my hands retreated instinctively into the pockets of my jacket, I felt the hair on my arms, raised, brushing against the inside of my sleeves and I realized what was in the air. Danger. Just a hint of it. It wafted beneath my nose and made me feel all the insecurity of being in this unfamiliar place, this dimension where I wasn't supposed to be. It suspended me there on the stoop for I don't know how long. Then suddenly the air was in me and around me, rising above my head, clarifying my thoughts and I began to move. I ran around to the student parking lot at the back of the building. The trim on Malcolm's Omni was rusty and there was a big dent in the blue metal of the rear door on the driver's side. Inside, the car smelled of body odor and Big Macs, the floor littered with empty McDonald's bags and burger containers. I put the key into the ignition. Behind me, sinking away into the distance, I heard a bell ringing.

I had been to Linc's office only once before, just as he had started working there. We all had gone down on a Saturday and he had shown us the conference rooms, the walls of maps, the canteen, which my sisters and I had found fascinating because it was stocked with snacks and all flavors of pop that you didn't have to pay for. In my mind I was replaying that day, retracing Daddy's path to the building's parking garage and entrance. The building itself was difficult to miss: a true skyscraper made from salmon-colored brick rising to a point like a freshly sharpened pencil.

I pushed my way through the revolving doors and headed for the elevator. "Excuse me, miss!" The deep voice knocked my insides and I froze. I turned to the guard's desk where my eyes fell over a sign that read VISITORS MUST BE ANNOUNCED and a uniformed man was motioning me to come over.

"Who are you here to see?"

"Lincoln Carter," I said. Then, realizing I couldn't look as though I had business there, I added, "I'm his sister."

But the guard just nodded and picked up the phone, murmuring into it while at the same time scribbling on a piece of paper. He ripped it from the pad and handed it to me. It was a visitor's pass. "Go on up," the guard said. "Twenty-first floor."

When I got off the elevator Linc was there, standing in front of the Sohio Corporation sign on the wall. He had on the same dark blue suit I had seen him wear a thousand times, but somehow he looked different. Or the suit looked different here in this place. Its lines seemed to mimic those of the walls, the office doors, the windows. Suddenly Linc was a block plugged into this network of straight lines. He still moved with the stride that was so familiar to me, but in this world he was a stranger.

I followed him down the hall, past secretaries clicking keyboards, listening to the crisp notes they spoke into their telephones. At one desk he told a dark-haired woman with a frizzy ponytail to hold his calls for a few minutes. Then, almost as an afterthought, he said, "This is my sister." I waved and she put her hand up to return the gesture.

He shared an office with another man, their desks on opposite sides of the windowless room. A wastebasket stood on the floor between them, strategically placed, for pitching balls of discarded memos. On their desks, the computers glowed with bright orange numbers on the screens. His office mate wasn't there and Linc rolled over the guy's empty seat and motioned for me to sit down. He picked up a mug of coffee, still steaming, from his desk.

"All right, Crita, what's going on here? Why aren't you in school?"

"Well, I started to go. I mean I went to homeroom and everything, but I was worried about something so I had to come talk to you."

"Worried about what?" He took a careful sip from his coffee and eyed me strangely. "I saw you this morning and you didn't say anything then. Is there something going on with Mama and Daddy I don't know about?"

I twisted the handles of my book bag. "No, they're fine. It's Chandra. Is she okay? Is the baby all right?"

I could see I was testing his patience. "Crita, what are you talking about?"

"Well, okay, I wasn't eavesdropping, but I heard her on the phone this morning talking about some kind of test she had to have today and it sounded scary."

"Shit!" He sat up straight and too quickly, making the chair rock and spilling his coffee. "Shit!" he said again as he flipped through the pages of the calendar on his desk. I sat back in my chair and pulled my book bag up further on my lap. Finally, I thought. Action.

He picked up the phone and started dialing before he glanced at me and realized he hadn't responded to what I'd said.

"Everything's fine," he said, with the phone still to his ear. "It's just an ultrasound, a kind of picture they take of the baby." Then, into the phone, he said, "Hello, Chandra? Can you tell me just one more time, honey, what time we have to be at the doctor's today?" He wrote something down and said, "Okay, I'll see you there" and hung up.

I rocked silently in my chair as Linc sat back and passed a hand over his eyes and forehead. He closed his eyes for a moment, but when he opened them he leveled them at me.

"You knew, didn't you?"

"Knew what?"

"You knew I had forgotten about Chandra's appointment."

I wanted to say no, to slip that lie to him so casually and harmlessly so he wouldn't have to know. But in that room, surrounded by an unfamiliarity that included the cold look in Linc's eyes, I couldn't get the word to come out of my mouth.

"Yeah, I did. I mean I thought you might have, but I wasn't sure."

He got up and walked over to the wall bearing the maps and stood there. I couldn't tell if he was staring at the lines in front of him or just staring into space. He stuffed his hands in his pockets and turned around.

"You're here to warn me, aren't you?"

"What?" Whatever I had expected to come out of his mouth, it certainly wasn't that and I sat there, thoroughly confused.

"That I'm not doing it. Not handling things, that I'm not in control. I can see it happening, I can feel it coming on." He was tugging at his tie. I sat up quickly, my book bag falling on the floor.

I really didn't know what he was talking about. In fact, he was sounding kind of freaky to me—too dramatic, even for my tastes. I figured he'd snap out of it once he got back to work. All the more reason for me to get my butt out of there.

"Linc, I think I should go back to school. If I leave now I'll only miss a couple of classes."

He looked at me and frowned. "What?"

Come on, big brother, get with the program.

Then, shaking his head, "Right, right. Yeah, you've got to get going." He went back to his desk and started writing something. "Here, here's an excuse for the office so you won't get nailed for skipping. I'll tell them I had to take you to the dentist. Mama and Daddy won't have to know about this."

"Okay," I said, taking the paper and feeling a little relieved. I hadn't thought about how to explain my absence. I gathered my things and started to leave.

"Hey, Crita. I'm all right, okay? Everything's going to be all right."

"Okay," I said again. It seemed to be the only word I knew. "Bye, Linc."

When I got to Linc's house that afternoon I heard voices already bubbling in the living room. One sounded lower, the other higher. I thought it was Linc, somehow home early, but as I bounded into the living room I found Chandra was sitting with Tree. We hadn't spoken since the night of the wedding rehearsal.

"Crita, come see," Chandra was saying. "I'm having a boy, a beautiful little boy."

She handed me the black and white photo, a mass of light and dark squiggles bent in the form of a semicircle. In the center was a bean-shaped figure, curled into itself. It took me a moment to figure out the lines and see that the thing actually did look like a baby.

"That's it, huh? It's hard to see."

"Well, of course it's not all that clear," said Chandra. "But that's my baby."

"Yeah, I think he looks just like his uncle," said Tree. "Always ready for a nap."

"Where's Linc?" I asked, wondering if my plan had somehow faltered after all. "He did see these already, right?"

"Yes, but he had to go back to work," said Chandra, still gazing lovingly at the picture. "That man never ceases to amaze me. I thought for sure he'd miss this appointment today."

"That's just like you women," teased Tree, stretching out his legs from the sofa like a pair of Sugar Daddy caramel sticks. "Never giving us the benefit of the doubt."

"Oh, we try," said Chandra, getting up to go to the bathroom, as she seemed to do with increasing frequency then. "Lord knows how we try!"

Tree watched her negotiate her rising from the sofa. Once safely on her feet, she left the room.

"She looks happy, doesn't she?" he asked.

"Yeah, I think things are going well," I said. "We're almost done with the nursery. We put the crib together yesterday and I put that wallpaper border with the teddy bears up. It looks good."

"We? You sound like you're having this baby, too."

I plopped myself down into a chair and crossed my legs.

"Yeah, well, it's a family thing, right? We're all having this baby."

"Yeah," he said slowly. "Yeah, I guess you're right."

I sat back in my chair and made myself comfortable. "And what are you doing here away from college? Playing hooky?" And then, suddenly feeling playful, I added, "Looking for some Kool-Aid?"

"Well," he laughed, "sure, that and my mama's meatloaf. A guy can't eat cafeteria food forever and still have a sound stomach."

"Well, there's no meatloaf here. I don't like it and Chandra doesn't make it."

"My sister can't make my mama's meatloaf? Humph, now that's a tragedy."

"I don't see anything tragic about meatloaf. That's silly."

"Well, you don't like it so you don't know anything about it."

"Yup, and I'm proud of it, too."

I giggled. I hardly knew what I was saying. I think I had a bit of my sister Ella in me at that moment. This was a new feeling, a burst of light inside me. It was brilliant and white, like a bolt of lightning, and it made me bold. *Was this what it was like to be Ella?* I was so caught up in the sensation that I was unprepared for the straightforward tone of Tree's next question.

"So what are you doing here, really?" I looked at him, but he had his hands behind his head and he seemed relaxed.

"I'm just visiting," I replied. "You know, hanging out."

"When I was your age I could think of a hundred other places I'd rather be than hanging out with my sister or brother."

"Yeah, well, we're a very close-knit family." I slung my legs over the chair's arms as though to drive home the point that I was *very* much at home there.

"What?" He laughed. "Look, Crita, it's great that you're

helping Chandra out and all. I just think it's strange that you're so interested."

"I love my brother, okay?" He was starting to get on my nerves. "What are you on my case for?"

"What are you so touchy for?"

Before I could answer the phone rang.

"Crita!" Chandra called out from the kitchen. "It's your mama on the phone. She says you better get your butt home ASAP. You're gonna be late for dinner."

I sighed and heaved myself out of the chair. "All right, I'm going!" I gathered my things. In a few minutes Chandra came out and kissed me on the cheek. "It's too bad you can't stay for dinner, honey. I've got a meatloaf in the oven." Tree clapped his hands and laughed and I flashed him a scowl. Maybe he wasn't so cute after all.

"Thanks anyway," I told Chandra.

"Hey, I'll catch you later," Tree said.

"Yeah, right." I waved. "See you."

When I got home that night, Daddy, Mama, Ella, and Hazel were just sitting down at the table. I threw my book bag on the living-room couch and went into the kitchen talking, thinking I could head off a scolding if I got Mama and Daddy to discuss something else. "Hey everyone, guess what? Chandra had an ultrasound picture today and she's having a boy! Is that cool or what?" I sat down and Mama dropped a napkin in my lap as she put a plate of biscuits on the table.

"We already know that, little missy," she said, taking her own seat, "without you nosing around that boy's place. Chandra told me that on the phone."

"Humph," said Daddy as he spread butter over one of the biscuits, still warm from the oven. "I still say that baby will be whatever God intends it to be. Don't care how much science and how many sound waves they throw at that girl's belly. Nobody can know what that child will be until it comes out."

"But Daddy, it looked like a boy, I saw the picture."

"I *said* nobody can know." Daddy stopped his buttering and looked at me sternly over his glasses. "Now don't talk back to me, Crita. Especially when you drag your butt in here late without greeting us like you should. You know that's not right."

"Yes, sir. I'm sorry."

A moment of silence passed as we chewed our food and then Mama spoke up. "Oh, Crita, you got mail today. Some more pamphlets and catalogs from different colleges. You know you have to start thinking about applying."

"Can I have the ones you don't want?" Ella asked me. "I want the one from Spelman."

"How do you know there's one from Spelman?" I glowered at her. "Stay out of my mail!"

"All right, she will, but if you don't want that book please give it to your sister," Mama said. "Be nice to each other."

"I will, Mama." I moved the meat around on my plate. Recently, I hadn't really thought about college. The glossy photos on the brochures depicted rolling green lawns and quiet libraries and seemed inviting enough, but it all still seemed like it was a lifetime away and not worth my immediate attention. Not like Linc.

Ten

As it turned out, Daddy was right about God and Chandra's baby. But that shouldn't have surprised us. When it came to the mystery of Mother Nature, Daddy knew what could and couldn't be counted on. Leaves falling in autumn, robins returning in spring, sunrise, sunset, the cycles of the moon, when a child will teethe. He could be sure of all those things. But with anything others wanted so much to depend on, Daddy knew it would change. With a shifting of the wind he could sense a storm that was supposed to pass us turning back into our path. He would notice the number of grasshoppers in our backyard and know how wet or dry the summer would be. His being flowed in sync with the world and it was evident in the way he smelled the sun and greeted the morning with wonder and satisfaction: this was the way things were supposed to happen. I felt all this when my sisters and I had to salt the driveway because he had sensed a late-season snow; when he took us fishing and coaxed the bluegill out of the water, all the while singing old spirituals. These are the magical memories of our fathers, the ones children seek to drive away in adolescence because we think we no longer need to believe in them.

I was no different. In the heightened sense of empowerment that I felt after Linc's wedding I wanted to feel wise, not realizing I hadn't yet gained the wisdom I needed. I wanted to know better than Daddy, specially when it came to something I had seen with my own eyes, like Chandra's ultrasound picture. His terse correction of me at the dinner table had stung and if I had an ounce of the backbone I thought I had that evening I would've argued with him. But all I had was attitude and nothing to back it up. I could only keep quiet and believe in my head that I was right until circumstances would prove otherwise.

It all happened just after dark on a frigid early March day that refused to give in to spring. I was coming out of school, buttoning my coat and hunching my shoulders against the cold air, thinking I would catch the bus with Ella instead of walking. But then I saw them, my parents parked in the semicircle in front of the building in our red Ford station wagon. Hazel was inside and Ella, waving to me to hurry as she slid into the backseat. I ran down the sidewalk and jumped in.

"Hi, Mama. Hi, Daddy. What's going on?"

"Chandra's having the baby!" Hazel said, cheered at being so informative. "We're going to the hospital!"

"That's right," said Mama, who eyed Daddy because he was giving the car a little more gas than usual. "The child went into labor an hour ago."

The hospital was mysterious territory to me. None of us had ever been sick enough to be hospitalized, except for the time Linc broke his arm in a baseball game when he was eleven. And I had a vague memory of Mama being there after having Hazel, and throwing gum down to us from a window five or six stories above because Ella and I had been too young to visit her. Now my sisters and I kept a respectful distance as Daddy and Mama approached the desk nurse. "Maternity ward is on the fifth floor," she said in crisp tones. "Elevator is right around the corner."

People were milling about in various levels of quiet excitement and anxiety. There was a square space with a wall of windows looking out over the park, and a television on a shelf screwed into the wall played Bugs Bunny cartoons but no one seemed to be watching. A man wearing an Ohio State sweat-shirt chain-smoked and stared silently out the window. Down the hall a woman with salt-and-pepper hair chatted happily into a pay phone. Mama and Daddy left Ella, Hazel, and me in this way station while they found Chandra's room. Ella flipped through her *Seventeen* magazine while Hazel switched channels on the TV and sat down to await the five o'clock news. I pretended to watch the screen, but I was listening, searching for a familiar voice or to hear a nurse mention Chandra's name.

"So, what do you think it'll be like?" Ella asked, breaking my concentration. She had put her magazine down and was leaning towards me.

"What?"

"Having a baby, silly, what else?"

"It'll be gross," Hazel responded in my stead. "Not like they make it out on TV. There's all sorts of blood and stuff. And the baby comes out looking all gooey."

"How do you know?" I asked.

"I saw it in a book at the library."

"Jeez, Hazel," I said. "Why do you always have to dig up the dirty details?"

"That's not what I was talking about anyway, Miss Smarty-Pants," said Ella. "I'm talking about the deep stuff. Like Linc's gonna be a daddy after today. Is that weird or what? What's that gonna be like?"

"And we're gonna be aunts," added Hazel.

"That's right," I said.

"I was thinking about Tamara Jackson," said Ella, referring to a girl in my class who had gotten pregnant last year. "Re-member when she brought her baby to the football game, at homecoming? She had the baby right there, blue booties and all, but I couldn't see her as that baby's mama. It just didn't seem real. It was like she was carrying around a doll. Is it gonna feel that way with Linc's baby? Like it's not real, like this little baby just dropped out of the sky or something?"

I looked at Ella sitting there, legs crossed, her big hair feathered perfectly into layers. She was wearing one of those man-tailored shirts, popular at the time, with the big poufy sleeves and wing-tipped collar. She also had on her fake designer blue jeans and a skinny necktie made of imitation red leather. It surprised me to hear Ella thinking this way. I wasn't giving Ella any credit. I should have been marveling with her over the imminent change in our lives, but instead I was the know-it-all and wanted to tell Ella that I was sure we would love the baby and it wouldn't be as weird as she feared.

"No," I began, but then there was Daddy, shrugging off his heavy red plaid hunting coat and pulling a chair closer to the television near Hazel.

"It's gonna be a while," he said, settling in his seat. "Chandra's mama is in there with her. Your brother's on his way."

"Can we see her?" we all asked. I had already jumped out of my seat.

"Yeah, but you're not all gonna run up into that girl's room. Let Crita go first and you take turns. She's in room five nineteen. Ella, I want you to go down that hall there to that kitchen, it's on your left, and bring me a cup of coffee."

"Yes, Daddy."

Chandra labored in a space dominated by white, pink, and beige: white walls, pink blankets, white sheets, and beige trays and water pitchers. She lay back in her bed, a thin film of sweat on her forehead and nose. Mama was sitting in a pink vinyl armchair with a high back, her ankles crossed. She was knitting, finishing up the second baby blanket she'd made in a month.

Every so often she looked up and around the room as though she were waiting for a bus or a train.

Mrs. Templeton was pouring ice chips from one of the water pitchers into a plastic cup. Dressed comfortably in sneakers, jeans, and T-shirt with a sweater tied around her shoulders, she looked prepared to be in for a long haul. I could see through her motions of caring for Chandra that she had the mom thing down cold—had practiced it forever, like maybe when Chandra had chicken pox or the flu when she was a kid. But what I didn't know at the time was that Elizabeth Templeton, this coolly elegant woman who spoke in low sophisticated tones, housed a fierce maternal instinct, especially where her daughter was concerned. Or how frighteningly quick that ferocity could manifest itself in her hazel eyes. The version of her I saw then was subdued in comparison. "Here, baby, chew on some more of this ice," she was saying as I came in. "Oh, hey, Crita."

"Come on in, honey," said Chandra, lifting her head a little from the pillow. "You don't have to stand over there."

"How are you doing?"

"I'm tired," she said, then exhaled loudly before taking the ice her mother offered.

"She's doing just fine," said Mrs. Templeton. "The contractions are getting closer and they're just taking a lot out of her."

"Is your daddy down there drinking coffee?" Mama looked up over her eyeglasses. "I told him he wouldn't be able to sleep tonight if he did."

"Yes, Mama, but he's only had one cup so far." I went over and gingerly sat on the edge of Chandra's bed. The four of us said nothing for a while and I wished I had something to do. Instead I watched Mrs. Templeton and wondered how she managed to stay in motion while doing what seemed to me was so little: moving Chandra's pillows around, filling the cup with ice, going into the bathroom for wet paper towels, adjusting the blinds on the windows. I sighed, smiled at Chandra, and wondered whether I should pick up the newspaper on the table near Mama and find something I could read out loud.

Then Chandra cried out.

Mrs. Templeton was at the bed in an instant, putting her arms around her daughter's shoulders and exhorting her to breathe. "Shoosh! Shoosh! Shoosh!" went Chandra, then she opened her mouth wide and cried out again. This time the sound was deep, broad, and raw as she pushed it out from the bottom of her being and arched it into a high wail that made me jump up from the bed. I looked at the monitor attached to Chandra by colored wires and saw the glowing red numbers racing upward. Then the wail again. I crossed my arms and took one step backward. A great stone rolled around in my abdomen and I wanted to put my hands over my ears and turn away. I looked at Mama and her fingers had stopped working the needle and yarn. She sat perfectly still for a moment, then glanced at her watch, glanced at Chandra, picked up a pencil, and wrote down the time on a pad of paper on the table next to her. Chandra wailed again and I tried to find a safe place to look away, feeling guilty for seeing her so vulnerable. Two minutes later she fell back on the pillows, breathing heavily.

"Did you get the time on that, Nettie?" Mrs. Templeton asked Mama.

"Yes, twenty minutes since the last one." Mama picked up her needle again and the scene was as before. Chandra weakly smiled at me.

"Hey, you okay over there?"

"Uh-huh. But I should be asking you that."

"Oh, honey, I wish I could tell you it's not as bad as it sounds, but I love you too much to lie to you like that."

"Chandra, stop that, you're going to scare that poor girl," said Mrs. Templeton. "There's nothing happening in this room that hasn't been happening since the dawn of time."

"Mom, that *doesn't* make me feel any better."

"I'm okay," I said. But what Mrs. Templeton had said only made me feel worse. Yes, women had been having babies since the dawn of time, and yet I felt so woefully out of place in this scene in which my mother and Mrs. Templeton seemed so capable. This time I couldn't help Chandra by climbing a step-ladder or lugging a bag of groceries. All I could do was sit, so I sat on the bed again. In a few minutes I felt I could reach out and stroke Chandra's shin underneath the sheets and this I did. In that space of time I felt calmer.

It didn't last. When the next contraction flowed over her I kept my hand on her leg and willed myself to sit still. Only Chandra wasn't still. She shifted and kicked away from my touch as another cry rose to the surface and she panted and groaned and wailed. My fingers gripped the sheets and then Chandra screamed and what she screamed ripped into my brain.

"MOMMY, *WHERE IS HE?*"

I blinked and for some reason turned and looked at the door as though expecting my brother to walk through it. Linc. Yes, where was he? I thought. *God damn it.* I didn't dare swear out loud in front of Mama, but in my thoughts I took hold of the words and felt grateful for their strength. Where the hell was my brother?

Wherever he was, I knew one thing at that moment. I couldn't stay in that room. Chandra's voluble cries were dig-ging fingers into me, embedding themselves into the fiber of my nerves and pulling with every ounce of their might. I felt as though I were the one being torn open and her pain was being poured into me. But with Chandra's energy racing through my blood, I also knew I couldn't go back to that wait-ing area and sit with Daddy and my sisters.

"I'll go downstairs and look for Linc," I said, backing out of the room. "I'll bring him up as soon as he gets here. I promise." Mrs. Templeton just nodded and Mama wrote on her notepad. I turned and fled.

I went back to the waiting room and motioned to Ella so she could take her turn with Chandra, then I took the elevator down to the lobby. It had grown dark and the place was empty save for the nurse sitting at the reception desk. I went over to one of the large-paned windows where I had to cup my hands around my face against the reflections so I could see outside. I closed my eyes for a moment and held my forehead against the cool glass. The quiet was comforting. I took a deep breath and focused again.

The parking lot was an island of light pools cast down from the tall street lamps. Beyond it I could see the bright headlights and red taillights of the cars in the surrounding streets. Then my eyes fell over the cars in the lot and, right there, a shiny black Pontiac parked very close to the hospital doors caught my eye. I frowned and walked outside to get a better look. It was Linc's car. He'd recently bought it for himself, a racy Grand Am with two doors. I had been surprised because it just seemed to be a weird thing to do, buying a car like that out of the blue. No one else seemed to think so, so I had let the thought go. Besides that, it was a cool car and I had been hoping he might let me drive it sometime. But here was the car now, right there in the hospital parking lot. I couldn't believe it. Where was Linc?

I went over to the car and looked into the windows. I could see his briefcase on the floor of the passenger side, but otherwise the car was empty and locked, no sign of Linc. I started to walk back into the hospital when I heard voices coming from another part of the parking lot. There was something familiar in the tones, so I followed the sound further back into the lot. I felt swallowed up each time I stepped out of a pool of light and into the darkness and each time the level of my fear turned up a notch. Then, quite suddenly it seemed, I made out their figures in the shadows: Tick and Linc, just outside one of the circles of light. Tick was leaning against his blue Trans Am and Linc was sitting on the hood. My nose twitched and I detected a strong tobacco and herbal scent. As I got closer I saw that Tick and Linc were smoking cigars—thick brown rolls of tobacco that they held between their thumbs and the tips of their fingers.

My chest burned.

"Linc!"

"Hey, Crita . . ." He smiled, actually *smiled* at me. No, I thought to myself. I didn't want his smile, didn't want his pat on my arm. I pulled away when he reached out to me. I felt a belt of tension cinch tightly around my body and it froze me in the spot as I stood there and stared at them. How could he look at me like that? My muscles twitched and my throat went dry as my being went in search of the voice, the sound, the nerve that would allow me to speak to my brother in true anger for the first time in my life. My hands rolled into fists, the fingernails cutting into my palms, and when the voice finally came I couldn't recognize it.

"What the *hell* are you doing out here?" I looked at him so hard I was seeing spots before my eyes. I let the words come. "Chandra has been screaming for you and screaming for you. She's in pain and she's yelling her head off and I can't do anything but sit there like a total idiot and act like you're on your way because that's what I'm stupid enough to think! And the whole time you're down here being an asshole! What *are* you doing?"

Linc's face slowly screwed up into a frown. He slid off the Trans Am and handed his cigar to Tick. He stuffed his hands in his jacket pockets and took a step my way.

"Hey, it's okay, Crita. We're just celebrating a little early. You know the tradition. Cigars and babies."

"Yeah," Tick grinned in a sleepy way. "Something like that."

"What kind of jerk are you?" Linc wasn't reacting to me, at least not the way I wanted him to. I swung my arm out and smacked him on the arm and the contact felt good so I kept hitting him and hitting him. "There's no baby yet! But Chandra's up there screaming like crazy trying to have it and you're down here fooling around. I-can't-believe-you!" I punctuated each syllable with a smack on his arm. "Come on! You can smoke your stupid cigars later."

"All right, all right," Linc said. "I'm coming in. You coming, man?"

Tick waved him off as he carefully stubbed out Linc's cigar. "Naw, I'll stay out here a little bit. I'll be in later, man."

On the elevator Linc grinned at me, but I crossed my arms and stared only at the numbers as they counted away the distance between us and Chandra. What was with him? My body still shook with anger and I didn't understand why Linc wasn't feeling it, why he didn't seem to care. When we reached the maternity floor I breezed out of the elevator ahead of him and walked quickly down the hall. He had to liven his step to keep up and that gave me a morsel of satisfaction.

I pushed open the door to Chandra's room where the women were as I had left them, only now Daddy was sitting in a chair next to Mama. "I found him," I said quietly. Linc went over to the bed and wrapped his arms around his wife and held her close, his chin on the back of her neck, as though he would melt into her. Chandra was laughing and crying at the same time. "Oh, God! I thought you'd never get here! What took you so long?"

"Traffic," he said. "I thought I was being smart, taking 480 instead of I-90, but I forgot about the construction going on over there."

Daddy looked at Linc. "They haven't finished that yet?"

"No, sir, not yet," replied Linc, taking Chandra's hand.

"Humph," Daddy said. He sat back in his chair. "Crita, you go on back there with your sisters and eat some dinner."

I gave my brother another grim glance. "Yes, sir."

Daddy had ordered pizza and pop for us and Hazel and Ella were still working on their first pieces when I got there. "Linc's finally here," I told them.

"It's about time," said Ella, using her polished fingernails to pluck the pepperoni off her pizza. "Where's he been anyway?"

I took a bite of pizza and mumbled through the crust, hoping it would keep Ella from asking more questions. "Traffic," I said and went on eating.

"That's funny, I saw the traffic report on the news," said Hazel. "They didn't say anything about any backups."

"Well, that's what Linc said." I opened a can of orange pop and took a long drink. "I saw Tick downstairs."

Hazel rolled her eyes to the ceiling. "Oh, now *there's* your traffic! What's he doing down there?"

"He was sitting on his car when I left."

"Let's invite him up and give him some pizza," said Ella, already wiping her hands and fluffing her hair.

"Hey, it's a free country and he can go where he wants, but he's not getting any of this pizza!" said Hazel. "Let him get his own."

But Ella was heading for the elevator. I flipped the pizza box closed and grabbed my pop. "Come on," I told Hazel.

The parking lot was just as it was before. I led my sisters in the direction of Tick's car but the Trans Am was gone.

"It's dark out here, maybe you got the wrong spot," said Ella. We walked around the lot, to the edge of it and back, returning to the spot where I thought Linc and I had left Tick. I sipped my pop and was about to suggest we go back in when Hazel started.

"Ugh, I stepped on something."

She nudged something with her toe and Ella and I came over to inspect. It was hard to see in the dark, but we could make out that it was something shredded, like paper. It was scattered densely all over the ground. Ella kneeled, picked up a bit of the stuff, and sniffed. "Yuck, it's tobacco," she said, flicking it from her fingers and wiping her hands on her butt. "Somebody's been making blunts."

"What's that?" I asked.

"You know, those things the Washington boys were smoking when they got suspended last semester. They take a cigar and hollow out the tobacco, then they stuff it with marijuana."

"Humph!" Hazel said in a very Daddylike way. She crossed her arms. "Maybe our boy Tick needed something to eat after all."

Coming out of the elevator upstairs, we saw Daddy and Linc standing together down the hall. Daddy was talking to him and I thought the sight of the two of them looked strangely like the one of Linc and Daddy speaking before Linc's track events in high school. Once again, I couldn't tell what Daddy was saying to him, but this time there was a difference. Linc couldn't seem to focus on Daddy in the same way he couldn't seem to register me in the parking lot. Now I knew why. *Goddamn idiot!* But would Daddy be able to tell that Linc was high? I tried to read our father's face. It was calm and his lips weren't moving in the quick, staccato beats as they did when he spoke out of anger. After a few minutes Daddy put his arm around Linc and they went back to Chandra's room together. My sisters and I looked at each other and went back to our pizza. "Looks like our bro dodged a bullet," Hazel said.

By eleven o'clock Hazel was dozing, her head in my lap, and Ella and I were listlessly watching the end of an old movie on the television in the waiting room. Mama and Daddy came in just as the evening news was starting. "You girls come on and see your brother's baby," Mama said, gently shaking Hazel. "It's a girl."

I looked at Daddy but he was already heading back down the hallway and we were helping Hazel get up and gathering ourselves to follow him. I lingered behind a few moments and took a deep breath. A girl. Daddy had been right. He knew, he knew all along what Chandra's baby doctors with all their education only thought they knew. In that tiny space of time that bridged the old part of my life with the new, all I wanted to do was be very quiet, very still, and appreciate the wonder that was my daddy.

Eleven

The amount of love in our hearts isn't infinite. We've been duped into believing the reservoir is always full, no matter how much we give out, because there's always such a constant influx. Children, our families, friends, all are continually pouring their love into us, into the wellspring that makes up our hearts. But the beloved take even as they give and as our heart is filled it's also emptied. Most people are unaware of this balance, I think. It's what makes it possible for someone to take too much and when the deficit cannot be overcome, even with love from others, a part of us dies inside.

I didn't know on the night of Savannah's birth that Linc had punctured the part of my heart that held my love for him. The hole was tiny, so very tiny. I couldn't even tell it was there. So I didn't, couldn't, know that it would slowly drain away my life.

Perhaps all this wasn't noticeable because we had Savannah, a perfect cherub of an infant who, to me, unraveled the mysteries of life on a daily basis. In the year after Linc's daughter was born, and of course forever after that, my sisters and I were enthralled with her. I found it fascinating to be so completely *there* as she sampled each bite of her existence for the very first time: the indignant look of shock in feeling the cold air on her naked body when we changed her; her laughter when water first touched her skin; hearing her happy gurgling vocalizations and seeing her look of recognition when we came running in response to them.

And there was a definite *we* because all of us—Mama, Daddy, Mrs. Templeton, Ella, Hazel, and I became a regular presence in Linc's house. (I thought it odd that we never saw Mr. Templeton, though I would hear Chandra talk to him sometimes on the phone.) There was always something to do. Mama cooked, either in Chandra's kitchen or heating up dishes she had made at home. Ella and I loaded and unloaded the washer and dryer, folding piles of diapers and baby clothes that seemed never-ending. Hazel helped Daddy out in Linc's yard, raking or weeding while Daddy mowed the lawn. Even Tree popped in, when his schedule allowed, but I always kept my distance. Something about him just made me feel awkward and uncomfortable. I found myself wondering how Mama had handled all of this, especially when Hazel was born and Ella and I were still small. I didn't remember anyone coming back and forth to our house to help her.

Those first few weeks Chandra, still attended by her mother, only had to lactate and heal. She padded around the house in a fluffy pink terry-cloth robe Linc had bought for her and smiled gamely whenever she came upon one of us doing a household chore for her. Linc moved in and out among the chaos. He took two weeks off from work but seemed to be on the phone constantly. Other times I saw him in Chandra's rocking chair, holding Savannah and communicating with her in a low cooing voice that I would learn was the language used universally between fathers and their daughters.

Years later I would look at the photos taken right after Savannah's birth and see Linc's red eyes and think about the lies I had told myself that night. But they were necessary, assembled with desperation. Otherwise, I wouldn't have known what to do with the anger, hot and unfamiliar to me; I wouldn't have known how to forgive him, especially since he didn't even seem to be in a mind to ask for it or even realize he needed forgiving.

It was Mama who rescued me. She had surprised me. I knew she would soon be reminding me that I had to start preparing for life after high school. I knew these words would come, but I expected them to be sharp and brief, like the quick smack on the rear end she used to give us when we were small. I thought she'd say, "Girl, you better get your butt moving and fill out those college applications." But that's not what happened. Instead the push, the motion, was gentle, as though she were putting Savannah on her feet for the first time and helping her to walk; as though she were a bird easing her young out of the nest because she knew they were afraid to fly.

We were in the kitchen that night after dinner. She had poured out a bag of pinto beans onto the table and she was picking out the bad ones and the stones. She moved the beans methodically, one by one with the tip of her index finger, into piles of good and poor. I used to think all her effort was futile before I realized she found the mundane task somehow relaxing.

I was going through the newspaper, clipping articles for my civics class, stopping to watch Mama's hands, rough and slightly knobby, slide the beans across the table's surface. These were the same hands I had felt on my scalp as a child when she braided my hair. They smoothed, twisted, and pulled, sometimes a little too hard. I was tenderheaded and the tug of the comb often made me cry. I remember resting my head on her knee, my eyes shut, hoping she would be finished soon. And then there was the strange brew of feelings afterward—the relief of having a clean head and tight braids, as though in pulling together the unruly kinky lengths of hair, Mama had somehow pulled me together again.

I think she'd been waiting for one of these moments, when she had my full attention. My eyes rose from her hands to her face and I saw her dark brown eyes looking over the top of her glasses, holding me in a soft but unrelenting gaze.

"Baby doll," she said, suddenly giving me the feeling of being very small and dressed in pink, with ribbons in my hair, but I didn't mind. She never called my sisters this and it had always been a touchstone between us. "You know I'm not a caretaker, don't you?"

"What do you mean, Mama?"

She continued to move the beans as she spoke. "Well, the people in this world are basically of two types, just like these beans here. But it's not that some are good and some are bad, the way most people make it out to be. It's more in the way of there's people who take care of things, and there are people who have to be taken care of.

"Now your daddy's a good man—he's a caretaker. I always knew that about him. You see we don't want for anything in this house. I knew he'd be like that, that's why I grabbed him right off like I did. Because I'm one of those people who needs to be taken care of."

I put down my scissors and scratched my head. "That's not true, Mama. You take care of all of us. Of me and Ella and Hazel."

"Oh, I could do the hands-on things pretty well, especially when you and your sisters were little. It wasn't nothing to put clothes on you, braid your hair, and fix you something to eat. That ain't much different from playing dress up with a doll."

"You never treated us like dolls!" I protested, feeling at once that I had to defend her nickname for me.

"I know, honey, I know. I'm just trying to show you something. How much use have you girls had for me since you got older?" I opened my mouth to object, but she raised a hand, silencing me. "When was the last time you came in here and told me anything? Now I'm not complaining, it's nothing like that. I'm just saying that somewhere along the line, you figured out you could take care of your problems better yourself. Either that or you got better advice from your daddy. Now am I right or wrong?"

I thought about it. The memories were there: of conversations where her expressions had turned vague and I knew she wasn't listening to me; of hearing her say, "Honey, these things tend to work themselves out" and leaving me empty when I hungered for help and guidance. I didn't realize that I had learned, on some unconscious level, to counteract her. To think something over, I would go to Mama and talk forever. But to actually *do* something, I went to Daddy. His advice came down like a commandment.

Like the time when Mr. Belfiore, our choir director at school, had decided to make part of our grade based on how many candles we sold to finance our annual field trip to the Cincinnati Playhouse. I had been mortified. Unlike my brother, I was no salesman. I couldn't imagine anyone wanting anything I had to sell, let alone a stupid vanilla-scented candle with a teddy bear on it. I was prepared to watch my grade point average go south with dignity and told my parents as much. Mama sat there, her legs crossed at the ankles, crocheting and saying nothing. But Daddy lowered his chin, leaned forward in his chair, looked me dead in the eye, and, shaking a forefinger at me, told me exactly what to do.

"You go on up to that school and tell that teacher that you're going to sell ten of those things. No more and no less. You can do that and that's good enough for you to get the grade you're supposed to have. You tell him and then you come back here and tell me what he said and I'll be damned if it isn't, 'That's all right, Crita, you do that.' "

And I would carry out the commandment, mimicking Daddy's words in a shaky voice that sounded like it was coming from a broken tape recorder. But to my astonishment, an agreement followed, as it always did. Daddy was just better at those kinds of things.

Sitting across from Mama at the table, I looked down and shuffled my newspaper clips. I felt a small lump forming in my throat.

"Yes, Mama. You're right, I guess."

"You know I'm right. A person's got to know what they are and I know what I am and that's all right. I learned that a long time ago. Now it's time for you to understand what you are."

I looked up, wondering, almost hoping, this would be some magical moment when all of life would be explained and everything else made fantastically easy from that point on. "What am I, Mama?"

She picked up a big plastic blue bowl and held it at the edge of the table and began sliding the good beans into it. "You have so much of your daddy in you, Crita," she said quietly. "You're a caretaker. I see it in you a little bit more every day, growing all the time. Trouble is, you're already taking things on and you're a little young to be doing that. Especially when you don't know much of anything about yourself."

I suddenly felt embarrassed and Mama must have sensed it because she paused, put her bowl down, sat back, and looked at me steadily.

"I understand you want to help out with your brother and his family. We all do. But there's something more of you tied up in this and it's the caretaker part of you doing it. You don't need that right now. Crita, honey, the way that you are— you're gonna be taking care of people for a long time, the rest of your life. But you don't have to start doing it now. Not when you have to go away from here and learn to take care of yourself first."

"Go away," I said, almost to myself. I put an elbow on the table and rested my forehead in the heel of my hand. "Mama, I want to go to college, I really do. It's just that, I don't know, it's like I can't see myself there, wherever *there* is. I can't picture myself away from here."

"Well, honey, you're gonna have to make that picture up as you go along. That's all life is anyway. Making that picture and making that picture. You just keep doing it. Maybe sometimes you get to step away and have a look at the thing, see if you can see what your life looks like. But you gotta get on with it. Nothing happens if you stand around looking."

"I know." I put away my homework, closed my notebook, and sat for a moment staring at the table. Then I asked her a question I knew I had not asked her in a very long time. "What do I do, Mama?"

"Oh, it'll be all right. Just pick a place. Think of how the Lord has blessed you. You're young, you're smart, and at this moment in your life you can go anywhere you want to go and just start . . . well, honey, just start *being*."

"But Mama, what about—"

"Crita, this world here, with your daddy and me and all the rest—it'll keep going on, with or without you." She got up, wiped her hands on her apron, and went over to the low white metal kitchen cabinet on which my college mailings had been piling up for months. She gathered the collection of envelopes and glossiness and placed them on the table in front of me. Her face, round and benevolent, gazed on me as though she would pour hot cocoa into my soul. "It's time to find a world of your own."

"Yes, Mama."

She ran her hand over my hair and kissed my forehead. "You should put some oil on your scalp, baby doll."

I finally smiled. "Thank you, Mama." She took the bowl of beans to the sink and continued her work. I picked up the pile and went to my room and tossed it on the bed where the brochures landed with a satisfying splat and spread out across the sheets.

I hadn't noticed Ella sitting in front of my dresser. She had broken yet another curling iron and was using mine without asking, as usual. She was rolling her hair for the night with her big green curlers. We had figured out long ago that the curls stayed better and our hair straighter if we curled each lock with a hot iron before rolling it up. But we could only afford cheap curling irons that sold for as little as $6.99 and eventually fell apart with our frequent use. Of course Ella went through twice the hair supplies that Hazel and I did.

She had just released a perfect black ringlet that bounced down from the side of her head when she turned around to face me.

"Uh-huh. You finally got yelled at for not filling out those applications, didn't you?"

"Sort of," I replied, plopping myself down stomach first on the bed. "But not really. Mama just said I should be thinking about doing it. I have to figure out where I want to go."

"I don't know why you keep putting it off," said Ella, moving on to her next lock of hair. "I can't wait to get out of here."

"How come?"

"Because nothing ever happens here," she said, turning around and pointing at me with the curling iron. "Not to us anyway. Everything happens to Linc and we have to wait for everything. Nothing can happen to us until we get older. I can't even be eligible to run for homecoming queen for another year. At least now you can get started."

I grinned. "But I don't want to be homecoming queen."

She zinged a green plastic curler at me. "Don't be such a nerd! You know what I'm talking about."

"Yeah, you're right. Everything does happen to Linc."

The things Mama had said did make sense. It would be so different for something to happen to me. But what did I want to have happen to me? How could I want something if I didn't know what to want? Or even where to go?

The brochures were large and small, the accompanying applications both short and long. Some required pages while some wanted only one. The stack was big: Wittenberg, Mount Union, Case Western, Miami U., Denison, Baldwin-Wallace, Oberlin. But these were all in Ohio and if I were to fully follow Mama's advice, I assumed I should look further afield. There was Grinnell in Iowa. Mount Holyoke, Emerson, Williams, and Boston University in Massachusetts. Spelman, Morehouse, and Emory in Georgia. Berkeley and Pepperdine in California. East, west, north, south. How does one choose when you can go anywhere in the world?

I pulled out another—wide, thick, and heavy with photos. New York University. I thought it was unusual because there were just as many pictures of New York City views as there were pictures of students going about their scholarly endeavors. But it was these pictures, of soaring skyscrapers against too-perfect blue skies and the great Brooklyn Bridge spanning the East River, that caught my eye. So this was the storied city, one I had only seen depicted on TV and in movies. Where the kids from *Fame* leapt in the streets to a never-ending soundtrack. If there was a place where I could find or even re-create myself it seemed to me New York would be that place.

I turned through more pages and discovered a photo of Times Square at night and it made me laugh and think of Daddy because it reminded me of his Christmas lights. He decorated the house every year, stringing up bulbs on the house and in all the trees in the front yard. On the lawn glowed Santa in his sleigh pulled by two plastic brown reindeer suspended in mid-takeoff by wire stands. Another Santa with a bag of toys stood watch on the porch flanked by two red candles, each topped with a yellow plastic flame. On Christmas Eve Daddy would leave the display on all night long. Sometimes, especially if there was snow on the ground, I would go out after everyone else was asleep and stand in the middle of the yard. It felt magical, bathing in the reddish-yellow-orange tones given off by the bulbs and wondering if, in this energy field, I would catch a glimpse of the real Santa streaking across the night sky. I was always sad when the lights came down after the holidays. The yard seemed so much darker than in the days before we had lit it.

But here was a place called Manhattan where the lights were always on at night, and that excited me. Where there was no darkness, there was no loneliness. And yet with seven million people there would be more than enough solitude in which to sculpt my new existence. Yes, I decided. This is the place. I will go to New York. I flipped to the back page and began filling in the little white spaces of the application with the letters of my name.

I wanted Linc to be the first to know what I had decided, so the next day I went to his house and sat in the backyard on Daddy's freshly mown grass while I watched Linc trim the hedges. He had, after some persistent prodding, convinced Daddy to go home and let him finish his own yard work. I laughed and picked flying leaves out of my hair throughout the whole process because Linc's technique was so different from Daddy's. Daddy cut carefully and judiciously, pausing at regular intervals to examine the results to see that the shrubs were taking their proper form. With Linc the pruning was so obviously a chore and not art as he squeezed the shears again and again and hacked away at the hedges in a businesslike manner, knowing only in general how straight he was cutting.

"So," he said, pausing to swipe his elbow over his sweaty brow, "is this your shift?"

"What?"

"Mama just left with Daddy. I think she deposited a mess of collard greens in the refrigerator and some fried chicken in the oven. I gotta get her to stop doing that. It's gone on long enough. She acts like nobody here can cook."

"Too late. She's in her groove now. You're gonna have to wean her off it real slow. And it's not my shift. I'm not here to do anything."

"Oh, you're not, are you?"

"Uh, no," I said, sitting up, "not unless you have something you need me to do."

"Chill out, Crita, I'm joking. There's enough people running around here doing stuff for us as it is."

"You don't like it, you can lump it," I teased, using one of our childhood expressions. "You're the prince. Nobody's going to let you lift a finger."

He laughed as he brushed leaves off the front of his sweat-shirt. "It ain't all that bad. It means something to have everyone here around me. Without family, a person's all alone in the world."

All alone in the world. I turned the words over and over in my head, blending them with the ones Mama had given me and trying to compare their significance. But instead they only formed more questions and these I poured out to my brother.

"Linc, what was college like? I don't mean classes and stuff like that, but the life? What's it like being in a totally new place where you don't have any family and no one knows you?"

He looked at me and stopped cutting. "You know, I don't think you're ever in a place where no one knows you." He put the shears down and joined me on the grass, leaning back on his elbows and stretching out his legs in front of him. I noticed for the first time that he had gained some weight that took the shape of a water balloon laid out on his belly. "It's funny, Crita, I mean people are funny. Sometimes what you are is all over your face and people pick up on that. I felt like that in college, like people already knew what I was by the way I dressed, the way I walked around. Then things get sort of mixed up and turned around because after a while you don't know if you're being yourself or if you're just acting out the image they have of you. Sometimes it *still* seems that way to me."

I didn't quite understand him, but I pressed on. "But you can still find yourself, right? Or become something you want to be, because no one knows you?"

"Well, in theory, I guess so," he said. "But it doesn't always work that way. And when you're a black man it never does."

"And why is that?" I inquired, smiling wryly. "You're not special."

"No, not special. Dangerous. Crita, for most people a black man is the deadliest being there is, someone you can't turn your back on. One is no different than the next, no matter what you look like. You can't make yourself up, because people have already made their decision about you. And I know this because I have to live it every day. I can't tell you how many people look at me with fear or mistrust in their eyes. Even when I'm wearing a suit, even when I'm smiling and trying to be polite."

"Yeah, but that's only in the beginning when you first meet someone, isn't it? Linc, come on, you've always charmed people. You gotta admit that."

"Yeah, people like me, but I see in their eyes what they're holding back. It's like a little part of their world, a little corner of their precious lives that they'd never let me into. Sometimes it seems the only kind looks I'm gonna get in a day come from my family.

"They don't look at a black woman like that, you'll see. You can be pretty and nonthreatening so you're safe where you are. People at work are always looking at me like I'm gonna take something from them."

Something in Linc's tone, perhaps the self-pitying nature of the notes he struck, prodded me to challenge him. I was not naive about racism. Indeed, I had already begun to question things I had seen in school. Why was it always the same black guys in trouble and why did they have the lowest grades? At times I'd wonder, looking back on our elementary-school experiences, whether they'd been singled out, labeled as trash, and ignored early on. But it had seemed those boys' lives were different, often fatherless, and lacking in someone who would stand up for them. Linc certainly never had their problems.

I also knew part of what he was saying was true. I had never been in trouble, never felt that a teacher ever looked at me as something lesser. Still, I wasn't sure I would have behaved any differently if they had, and I wanted Linc to see that.

"Why let it get to you?" I wanted to know. "Do you really have to care about what all these white people, what all these strangers think?"

"If they were just strangers, no. But I'm not talking about strangers. I'm talking about the people I work with. I'm talking about the security guard I pass when I go into the office. People I see every damn day." He sat up abruptly, crossed his legs, Indian-style, and pointed a finger at me as though to drive home his urgent point.

"You've been to my office, you know I share that space with another guy, right? He's a white guy. Name's Chad Pilgrim. He's a couple of years older than I am, but basically we're in the same trough: just a couple of hot shots, trying to hit it big, make a name for ourselves with the managers. We're in that office together every single day, working so late sometimes it seems one of us is daring the other to go home first. Sometimes we laugh over some ass-kissing vice president, or we kick back and toss paper balls into the wastebasket. But you know what, Crita? That asshole has never once gone out for a beer with me, or even asked me out to lunch."

I shrugged. "Why don't you just ask him?"

Linc shot me a hard, accusing look that almost knocked me backward when I recognized flashes of Daddy in his eyes. "You don't think I have? I used to do it every other day. Then I let it drop off to once a week. He always has an excuse. I quit asking. I figured he'll ask me when his ass thaws out." Linc got up, shears in hand, and attacked the shrubs once more. I got up, too.

"When he does leave for lunch I see him clearing his desk, putting all his papers in folders and locking them up in the filing cabinet. I mean he does it every time he leaves, even when he's just going down for a smoke. Asshole doesn't trust me. Thinks I'm gonna steal some deal from him. That's what I have to put up with every day."

"Okay, come on, Linc, this is stupid. What's so bad? Huh? The guy is an asshole, you just said so. What is so bad about all this?"

"*Because I am not a fuckin' thief!*" he barked, chopping hard into the branches. "*I am not a goddamned janitor! I am not a fuckin' boy!*" He hacked a hole deep into the hedge and finally threw the shears into the abyss he had created. He walked away, striding just six steps before falling to his knees in the grass where he sat, eyes closed, with his clenched fists pressed to his temples.

I had wanted him to soothe me, to be my older sibling and explain things to me and tell me everything would be all right. Why was he flipping out on me? "Linc, what's going on?"

When he finally spoke his voice was quiet again and even. "A person needs to have family, strong people around them. When I have strong people around me, I feel strong. Then it's easier for me to fight them."

"Okay," I said to him. Okay, I thought to myself. *Okay*. I still didn't fully understand what Linc was saying, but my brain was processing the words, kneading them, punching them, pushing them into some chain of meaning I could use to pull my brother up from the grass. At the same time I was, in this new light, redeveloping past pictures of Daddy and Linc. So this was what Daddy had always wanted to prepare Linc for. Yet for all his vigilant oversight, somehow Linc was not ready. I felt pissed at him for not being ready, but I also felt anger for a world that didn't seem to acknowledge the magic of my brother. I began to realize the world was so much wider than the narrow strip of life where Linc's magic had always held sway.

And here I was, ready to play the part I knew so well—to remind him always of that magic, to help him negotiate the minefields in any way my love would give him. Okay. I could do that. Maybe I had to do it even better. Give him my singular attention and relentless love.

Linc stood and mumbled, "I should check on Savannah . . . give Chandra a break."

As he turned to leave, I reached out and grasped a piece of his sweatshirt at the waist and tugged it like I was once again a little girl demanding his attention. But when he turned back to me the arms I threw around his neck felt strong and sure as I kissed him on the cheek and, though he couldn't hear it, whispered a promise and a prayer for us both that buried the idea of New York City deep in the dirt beneath the hedges.

I will not go far.

Twelve

I changed my life to the sound of tearing paper. The scowling, schussing noise hissed from every page and scolded me in advance for everything I was about to do. I was trying to be as quiet as possible so Mama, with her finely tuned maternal senses, wouldn't hear and yet I wondered how she couldn't because it seemed for those minutes that the ripping filled my world and that the noise would go on long after I had torn my New York college application into snowy fine pieces of trash. It hissed on as I searched Ella's drawers, rummaging through perfumed magazines and badly written notes from boys to find and take back what I had given: the brochure and application for Belden College. The school was just thirty-five miles away. Tree was there, too, but that wasn't an influence on my calculations. I had to be close to home and this was it.

I knew I couldn't tell Mama right away. I wanted to apply to Belden first, get accepted, and then argue my point from there. I thought I was being pragmatic, but looking back I know I really feared the look of surprise and disappointment that would bloom from Mama's eyes. I wanted to put it off for as long as possible. But I did have one idea that had to be told to Linc and Chandra, because it involved them.

I waited until just before the day when I knew Belden would

be mailing its acceptance letters. Then I found the moment, a quiet one, when Chandra and I were peeling potatoes in her kitchen. We had different styles when it came to peeling. I sat perched on the edge of my chair, a trash can between my legs, as I carefully cut through the potato's skin, skimming it off in one, sometimes two, perfect curls. This was the way Daddy had taught me to do it. Chandra sat bellied up to the table with rectangles of paper towels laid out in front of her. She held the potatoes close to her and used fast, short scrapes to strip the tuber of its skin. My method required me to sit away from the table a few inches, a good thing for this conversation since I could look down at my work and away from Chandra's face if I needed to do so.

"I think I'm going to go to Belden," I began. "I'm pretty sure I'll get in."

"Really? Well I'm sure your mama will be glad to have you so close. And you know Tree can show you the ropes and give you advice about classes."

"Yeah, I know. But the thing about living close? I don't wanna do that," I said, shaking my head. "I mean, I don't want to live at home anymore."

"Oh? How come?" she asked, getting up to retrieve a cutting board from a hook on the wall.

"I just think I'll feel like a kid if I stay at home. I want to do my own thing, keep my own hours."

"So you're gonna live in one of the dorms then, like Tree?"

"I don't know. I was thinking . . . Can I live here?"

Chandra looked up from her work and gave me a wry smile. "Okay, Lady Day, I know you didn't dream that up this very moment. You have a plan in that thick head of yours already. Let's hear it."

"You're gonna need help with Savannah because you'll want to go back to school at some point yourself, right? When you do, we can split the time. I'll schedule my classes for the morning and then I can take care of Savannah while you go to afternoon classes. If you're running late I can start dinner. I'd just have to get a car, but I think Daddy would help me with that if I asked, and—"

"All right, all right. You're right, it makes sense. I do want to get my nursing certification and Linc and I have been talking about how we're not too psyched to stick Savannah in daycare. She's too young, I don't care how many infants they have up there. I want my baby to stay at home." She paused. "Your being here would be a big help, honey, but you know I have to ask your brother first."

"Yeah, I know, that's okay. I'll do whatever he says." But I said that fully aware of the fact that the cards were stacked in my favor. Linc loved me and I had never asked anything of him before. No way would he turn me down in this.

The next morning Linc came by the house to see Mama and Daddy just as my sisters and I were leaving for school. He stepped aside as we bounded out the door, but he pinched me on the arm and whispered, "Hey, little sis. *Mi casa es su casa.*" I smiled, kissed him on the cheek, and ran down the driveway to catch up with Ella and Hazel.

As it turned out, I had timed it all perfectly. The Belden envelope, fat and wide, was waiting on the kitchen table when I got home. Mama was stirring something on the stove, but I could see a thundercloud, heavy and black, sitting on her forehead just over her brow. I could barely see her face for the darkness so I treaded carefully, unsure which step would bring me to her unwanted attention.

"Crita, what is that?" I had hoped to scoop up the package and go straight to my room, but Mama's tone was cold and it froze me in my tracks.

"It's my acceptance material, I think."

"You think? I think you better sit down and tell me exactly when you decided to apply to Belden."

I did what she said, but I didn't give her an answer. Instead I picked up a butter knife from the table and ran it under the envelope's seam and slit it open. I found forms and booklets stuffed inside and I had to rummage through them before I found the piece of paper with the letter that actually said "Congratulations on your admission to Belden College . . ." The ink on it still smelled fresh. The odor tweaked my senses and I began to rally and formulate a response for my mother's stern visage.

But Daddy came into the kitchen and the room's dynamic changed. His person and presence were so big that whenever he moved through the house it seemed the building shook with trying to contain both him and the energy wave that followed him from room to room. I always wanted to sit up straighter when Daddy came in the room. When I was with my sisters we immediately tried to look like we weren't doing anything even if we were already not doing anything. It just seemed you had to be ready for whatever Daddy might say or tell you to do. I shifted in my chair until my shoulder blades just touched the back rungs.

After glancing at Mama, Daddy sat down at the table across from me. He slid the ashtray that Mama always kept from him on the table closer and he shook a cigarette from the red Pall Mall pack he'd brought in with him. He lit it and blew a plume of smoke in the air. "Is that the school where you're gonna go?"

"Yes, sir," I replied. "I'm getting scholarship money from them." I didn't know why I added that. When Linc had gone to college Daddy seemed to think he was entitled to scholarship money because he, Henry Carter, had worked hard for thirty-four years and shouldn't have to pay to put his children through school. To him, me getting financial aid, whether academic or need-based (and this was a combination of both), was a given.

"Ain't that the one out there off of Route Ten?"

"Yes, sir."

"Lord knows I don't know nothing about sending no girl to school. My sisters all stayed home until they found a man to take care of them. Now I didn't want to keep you from getting an education, but I've been worrying about you going away to school. Your mama doesn't know it, but I ain't got no sleep over it."

Mama looked puzzled. "But Henry—"

"No buts. If that child is going to be here close to home, then I'm glad of it."

I glanced at Mama, knowing every word from my mouth would be a betrayal, but Daddy had emboldened me.

"Daddy, Linc and Chandra said it was okay if I lived with them. I can help take care of Savannah and I'll sort of be on my own. I just need to get a car so I can drive myself back and forth to school."

Mama had heard enough. She pushed herself off of the stove she'd been leaning against and planted a hand on her hip. "Now you listen to me little girl. Linc and Chandra do not need you up there in their business every day. You wanna go to that school, fine. You live in a dormitory with all the other students."

"I can be a day student, Mama."

Daddy stubbed out his cigarette. "Nettie, if that girl wants to help her brother out, let her go on over there. She's almost eighteen now. She's grown. She can do what she wants." He got up and took his car keys from the nail he kept by the kitchen door. "I'm going up to True Value Hardware to get some new spark plugs for that mower." He walked out and the house exhaled as Daddy took his energy with him.

But Mama was still standing there. And she still had her hand on her hip. And she still wanted an answer. "Will somebody tell me please just *what* you think you're doing?"

"Mama—"

"No, I don't wanna hear it," she said, shaking her head. "Girl, you have no idea what you're getting yourself into. I already warned you. I'm not coming anymore!"

"Who says you had to?" I got up and as I rose I felt the voice coming out of me was different. It seemed deeper, more powerful than I'd ever sounded before. I would later come to recognize it as my woman's voice.

Mama must have heard it, too, because she said, "Oh, you think you're grown now, is that it? It ain't right, it just ain't right. Girl can barely take care of herself let alone someone else. You're not big enough. It just ain't right."

"I don't know, maybe I am. But that's for me to find out, isn't it? How can you know what I can and cannot do! I can definitely take care of myself."

"Little missy, I've seen way more than you have. And I'll be damned if I let you think that don't count for nothing."

"What's wrong with me doing this, Mama, that's what I want to know. What's so bad?" I gathered my Belden materials from the table. "To tell you the truth, I don't why I should listen to you. You said yourself you don't know how to do anything!"

That hit home and Mama, suddenly small and unsure, backed down. My sight was colored with the exhilaration fed from my newfound strength, but through the field of clarity I saw Mama shrinking from me. I had stuffed her back down into the corner of being a timid, cared-for creature. I wouldn't have thought I could do such a thing, but I'd done it. I wanted badly to undo it, but I was at a loss as to how. I walked out of the kitchen and left her there in her tiny, tiny space of the world.

When I left Mama I walked out on the porch to find Hazel standing there blocking the way down the steps. Her hands

were balled up into fists at her side and her face beneath long
fat bangs glowed with ferocity and was drawn up tight with
determination. I took a step backward. I had never seen Hazel
look like that before, not even when she stared down Tick.
She must have heard every word Mama and I had said. I considered jumping over the porch railing into the yard and running for my life. Then Hazel spoke and the voice that
emerged from her throat was unfamiliar. It was low and
rough, almost growling in the undertones. It was like her
voice was flowing over a riverbed picking up gravel and debris
that would spew out at me in her words. She sounded just like
Daddy.

"You don't talk to Mama like that," Hazel said, taking a step
toward me.

"You had no right to be listening," I replied, thinking it best
to remain firm and not let her smell my fear.

"You had no right to talk to Mama like that. She doesn't
deserve to have your sorry ass treat her like a piece of dirt."

"I did not!"

"You did, too." Hazel's voice stayed even and threatening.
"Worst of all, you know you did. It was written all over your
face when you came out here just now."

"You don't know anything. You're just a kid, and an eavesdropping kid at that."

"I'm old enough to see you feel like shit and you should."

I slumped. My stance wasn't working. She was right, of
course. I had carried the weight of the argument out of the
house with the motive of finding a place to dump it. I wanted
to revel instead in how Daddy had been on my side and how
things were going to happen the way I wanted them to. But
Hazel was determined to make me feel every ounce of the
heaviness. She pushed the invisible anvil into my arms and the
weight pushed me down into a porch chair. I covered my face
with my hands.

"Look, Haze, you're making a big deal out of nothing. We're just disagreeing on the school thing, that's all."

"All I know is that you were in there disrespecting her, making her feel like nothing. Making her feel bad. She doesn't deserve that."

"I know. I'm sorry Hazel, I really am. I'm just trying to do what I want to do. She doesn't understand that."

Hazel didn't give an inch. "You get out of here," she said, her voice dropping even lower. "Go live on the moon for all I care, but you don't come back here." With that she yanked open the storm door and went back into the house, leaving me feeling utterly miserable.

Thirteen

Tree has a girlfriend and I can't sleep. Daddy is asleep in his chair and I stand staring at my reflection in the darkened glass of the living-room windows. I should close the curtains—we're on full display for anyone who happens to be outside—but I don't want to. It's late, almost midnight, and whoever would be there shouldn't be out there in the first place. The television's been off for over an hour so it's quiet when Ella comes out of her bedroom and steps back, startled, when she sees me. Honestly, I'm getting tired of this. I know she and I haven't seen a lot of each other these past five years, but we've been home for days now.

"Ella," I whisper, so I don't disturb Daddy. "What the hell is your problem? Why do you keep jumping out of your skin like you're seeing a ghost or something?"

"I don't mean anything by it. I just didn't expect anyone to be up so late." She puts her hands in the pockets of her thin, blue cotton bathrobe and perches herself on the arm of the sofa. I can smell the lavender scent of her night cream from where I stand. "I'm going to make some chamomile tea, do you want some? I just got off the phone with Forrest and . . ."

"Tell me."

"Tell you what, honey?"

"Tell me about Tree. How long have you known he was seeing someone?"

"Crita, it's been so long. You didn't expect that boy to be a monk all this time, did you?"

"Well, no. Maybe! I don't know. Maybe I didn't think he'd be single all this time, but I thought—hell, I wished he would be right now. I guess I was hoping hard and didn't even realize it."

"What exactly were you hoping for?"

"A chance to explain myself—to change some things. I just wanted to connect with him, again, you know? To be like we were before. But then there she was."

"Yes, I've seen her. Not a very pretty thing is she? I saw them at the post office the day I went to mail those bills for Mama."

"You told him I was home?"

"Of course I did. Whatever you may think of me, high school crush or no, I do play fairly. But honey, I didn't think under the circumstances that you were ready to deal with finding out he was taken. That's why I didn't put you on the phone with him."

I leaned my forehead against the glass, thinking that if Daddy could he would yell at me for getting the window all greasy. He'd make me get the paper towels and clean it right then and there. "I'm sorry, Ella. I'm sorry about the crack about the crush and being such a bitch."

She comes over and wraps her arms around me from behind. She feels warm and soft, like a light blanket. "It's all right, hon, I forgive you! And I know it's hard, but it's not like you haven't had someone special in your life in all this time, right?"

I laugh. "Yeah, I know a guy who has his mom buy him stolen suits from petty thieves on Seventh Avenue. That's pretty special, wouldn't you say?"

Ella's arms stiffen and it's probably all she can do to keep herself from spinning me around so she can look me squarely in the face. "Crita Carter, do you mean to tell me you haven't been dating in all this time?"

"No. No, not much. It's not like I've had time, with moving and starting my business and all."

"I don't buy that! What is the matter with you?"

"Ella, why does there have to be something wrong with me? Just because I don't have some man laying all up in my house means there's something wrong with me? You're starting to sound like Mari."

"Baby, we just want you to be happy. Forrest was just saying how you're such a sweet young woman and how it's a wonder some nice guy hasn't snatched you up."

"That's nice of him to say so." I put my hands up to the glass so I can peer outside. My palms are tingling. Under the streetlight at the end of our front yard I can see that the area is empty. No lights on. No cars going by. Suddenly I want to see Linc more than ever.

"Crita, what are you looking for?"

"In a man?"

"No, I mean right now, what are you looking for outside there?"

I wait a moment before I answer. "Linc."

"What? Is he out there?" Ella squints her eyes at the glass.

"No, but in another day or so he will be. I don't want him slinking his butt up to this house without someone seeing him. And when I do see him I'm going to go out and put my hands around his throat and give it a good squeeze."

"Crita!"

"What?"

Hazel, Ella, Mama—all three of them—they probably think I'm crazy and I don't care. All the next day I'm pacing around the front yard. I don't care because there's nothing keeping my feet on the ground anymore. I know I'm going to be there. And I am there. I'm standing in the yard when he comes. Way back when Linc was a student visiting home from college, I used to wait for him like a kid awaiting Santa Claus—stuffed with love, anticipation, aching greed. I wanted to be the first person he saw when he drove up the road, the person who would make that warm and gooey feeling form and drop into his stomach like chocolate pudding—the feeling that assured him he was home and beloved.

But now I stand uneasily, my head stiff and alert like a collie sniffing out a storm in the wind. Will I really feel the urge to kill him?

When I see the little car, a sad rusted-out Pontiac, slowly make its way up our bumpy street, I know instinctively that Linc is inside. I cross my arms and stamp my feet as though I'm cold, but in truth it is seventy-five degrees in late May, and I'm trying to arrange the features of my face. I have no idea how I should look. I don't know what it will feel like to have Linc's eyes on me. So much has passed between us. So much has been left unsaid. I feel as though his sight will burn me and a surge of pure panic, warm and electric, washes over my feet and I run. By the time the car stops in front of the house I am back inside, behind the safety of Mama's blue rose curtains and good plate glass windows. From there I can take in the sight of my brother for the first time in what seems like an eternity.

A stranger steps from the car. The vehicle moves away and the man is left at the edge of our yard. This man looks heavy and tired. Dark patches hang like blue-black crescent moons beneath his eyes, his face bloated into unrecognizable roundness. He tugs down on an ugly green sweatshirt that, with another inch of girth, would be too small for his stocky frame.

His chunky face and broad waist look like those of a man ten years his senior.

As he walks toward the house at last, the loping long stride is suddenly familiar to me. He is no longer graceful, his movement no longer effortless. I squelch the urge to lock the door. I don't want this sad and alien version of my brother to come in because I'm sure he'll break what's not yet broken of our hearts.

Mama opens the door for him. He wears his hair in a short flattop afro that is mussed from being shmushed under the Cleveland Indians baseball cap he removes upon entering the house. As I look at Linc, my heart bounces on the floor of its chamber as though he's dribbling it down a basketball court. Suddenly I want very much for him to see me, to give some hint that he knows me, that we are still connected. But he looks at none of us. His eyes stay fixed on Daddy the whole time as Mama relates the details of his decline. Daddy sleeps on, his breaths now burbling and noisy like a brook alive and intent on drowning him.

"Mama, we should get him to the doctor." When Linc speaks I can feel the collective softening of my sisters' stiff spines. His voice, deep and rich, if a little ragged, sounds the same. And we can't help but react as we had as children to the tones that made all seem right with the world. Hazel twitches beside me and I see her frown. She seems angry at her body for this betrayal.

"Yeah, no shit, Sherlock." Her words spark an acrid taste on my tongue. "Now tell us something we don't know."

"Don't talk to your brother that way," Mama says.

Daddy shudders.

"Nettie," he whispers and coughs. Then, "I thought I heard that boy . . ."

"He's here, Daddy," I say.

"What?" He struggles to rise and I move to help him, but Linc—still lightning-quick in his heaviness, reaches Daddy first. He has Daddy up so fast that I wonder what had been our difficulty before I remember that my brother is a good sixty to eighty pounds bigger than the rest of us, and stronger. I already resent him for it.

"I'm here to help you," Linc is telling Daddy. "It's time for us to go see the doctor."

Daddy nods, not having the strength for much else. I am sure he has grown rooted to the chair, and don't know how we will move him. But Linc lifts him. He puts an arm around Daddy's waist and suddenly it seems Linc has taken on half his weight.

The journey to the station wagon is divided out in my brother's steps. He drags our father's feet along to match the stilted lengths.

I follow. My sisters follow. Mama opens the car door and Daddy murmurs words to Linc that I can't hear and my brother pauses in the driveway. Daddy takes a tortured inhale and when he releases it, Linc folds him, helping Daddy bend and maneuver until he is stowed inside on the passenger side. Linc reclines the seat to make him comfortable, and Mama and Hazel get in the back.

"I'll follow with Ella in my car," I say, but Linc is already in the driver's seat, and my voice is lost in the roar of the station wagon's engine coming to life.

"He's looking all right, isn't he?" Ella sounds hopeful as I pull into the street, my fingers tight on the steering wheel. "A little chubby, perhaps, but that's healthy, isn't it? He's got some meat on his bones?" I can't answer her. I have no words, and the rhythm of my thumping heart fills my head.

———

The brick house where Dr. Timothy Joyce practices internal medicine in a basement office sits on a tidy block where each residence has pink azaleas blooming in the front yard. "Nothing bad ever happens here," seems to sing from every neatly trimmed blade of grass. I believe it and so can walk with some confidence through the door into the waiting room. Hazel is there, sitting on a sofa. Her arms are crossed, her frown deeper than before.

"Bastard won't let me in," she says. " *'We have to examine him, you understand,'* he said. Goddamnit, I have every right to be in there!"

"Honey, Linc is a *boy*," Ella says, sitting next to our sister and patting her tensed-up arms. "Now you've got to understand that, for decorum's sake and all." Hazel only grunts. I sit down across from them and say nothing because I know what Hazel's feeling and can only wonder how I will sit still without breaking down the door.

After some twenty minutes we hear it: a siren low but insistent, pressing itself upon our senses. My sisters and I look at each other and in the same instant, Dr. Joyce steps out of his office. He is tall and younger than I would expect a physician of Daddy's to be, perhaps in his early forties. He has small blue eyes on either side of a long nose, and brown hair that curls at the nape of his neck. He explains in haste, with one eye fixed on the window, that a second X ray has shown that Daddy's pneumonia isn't improving and, worse yet, the spots on his lungs have grown.

"They appear to be spreading, spreading fast," he says, but his attention is so obviously not with us. "I am shocked by the progression." The siren grows louder and I jump to my feet, realizing the source, an ambulance, is coming our way. "We have to get him to the hospital," Dr. Joyce is saying. "Now."

As if on cue, the door springs open and an EMS team surges into the space.

Daddy's body on the gurney looks heavy and thick, like a slab of bedrock. When they pull him out of the room and away from us, it feels as though the very foundation has been cut out from beneath our feet. Ella's knees buckle and as I catch her in my arms, Linc runs past us and out the door. He is in the ambulance and gone before Mama emerges from Dr. Joyce's office. I have never seen her look so small and alone. She pushes her sliding eyeglasses back up on her nose. Behind them I can see a tear just beginning to spill from her lower left eyelid.

I whisper to Ella to compose herself. Hazel takes Mama by the hand. "Let's go," she says.

Cancer.

I haven't thought of the word—I pushed it far back and out of mind right after Ella talked about it in Virginia. Yes, in the beginning I knew very well it was a possibility, but when Mama told me they thought it was pneumonia, I hung on to that. I hung on to it and it helped me hold on to Daddy because I knew he would be coming out on the other side of this. I just had to weather this with him and everything would be all right. I had tossed the word cancer out of my thoughts. I didn't want it in my head.

"There will be more doctors, an oncologist," Dr. Joyce explains. "But right now my main concern is the infection in his lungs. It's beginning to affect his kidney function. We can't do anything else until we get that under control."

"And then what?" I don't want the doctor to leave us until he has told us something more concrete. What he's saying is another set of instructions for us to just wait, and I feel like I've been waiting for days. I can't do that anymore.

But he only looks at me and pats my mother on the shoulder. "We'll do our best, Mrs. Carter."

"That's all we or the Lord can ask of you," she says.

Those first few hours we stand in the hall outside Daddy's room. A waiting room with soft blue cushions and views of the early summer light is located at the end of the long passageway, but just then it seems too far away from Daddy. We position ourselves with two of us on either side of the hall. Linc stands to my right, closest to the door, and does not speak to me. Ella speaks intermittently, as if to break the silence. "This is a good place," she says at one point. At another, "It seems very clean." Hazel stares at Linc. He doesn't look at her, but if he did I believe her stare would break him into little pieces—it's that hard. Only Mama is allowed in the room itself as a parade of doctors and nurses move in and out of Daddy's presence. A few make brief reports to us on exiting, and words like "biopsy" and "MRIs" and "antibiotics" float, simple and elegant, in the air. The medics who speak them focus mainly on Linc as though he is the one who matters here. The fact irritates me and I want to tug on someone's sleeve and force them to tell me something, only I don't know what it is I want to hear. Not, that is, until I hear it.

"Crita?" Daddy's voice sounds weak and watery.

I step past Linc without looking at him and go into our father's room.

"Yes, sir, Daddy?"

"There's a noise bothering me . . ." He moves an arm as though he would swipe the sound away and his voice trails off. I look around at all the instruments now hooked up to Daddy. The computer monitoring his intravenous fluids emits a steady monotonal beep.

"It's this machine here, Daddy." I'm looking at all the buttons and little red lights and glowing green numbers. I'm sure the thing is supposed to beep, but isn't there a simple volume button to turn the thing down? I'm afraid to touch it. I don't want to mess with any of the medicine the tubes are delivering into Daddy's veins.

"Excuse me, miss, could you help us out here?" Linc's voice has changed. He has smoothed out the gravel in his throat and he's talking in velvety tones I haven't heard in years to a sienna-skinned nurse. "This beeping is really bothering my father and he needs to rest."

She smiles. "Oh, it's just a timer thing. It needs to be reset. I'll do it." Her eyes linger on Linc a few seconds more before she turns and flips a toggle switch on the monitor and presses a blue button on the side. The beeping stops. "There you go. My name is Tammy and my shift just started. Let me know if you need anything else."

"Thank you, Tammy and, oh, just a minute." Linc touches her lightly on the arm just as she's about to walk out. "You could help us out in another way."

Right. He always has to ask for something more. My brother has never asked for only one thing, it always has to be two or more. Give him an inch . . . Whatever it is, I know she'll give it to him. I can tell by the way she cocks her head toward him, as though she's offering up her neck and a sniff of her perfume. Linc moves closer to her as well.

"I know you probably have a lot of people to watch over here. It might be easier on you, Tammy—by the way is that your name? Or are you Tamara?"

Her eyes open wide as if she's suddenly recognized a friend who knows her intimately. "Actually, I am Tamara. I do prefer it."

"All right then, Tamara," Linc smiles and his cheeks glow. I can tell he's enjoying this. "It might be easier on you if we could do a few things without having to bother you."

"Oh, it's my job and no bother."

"Yeah, I bet you're really good at your job, too! But you can see there's a lot of us here—my mom and my sisters. It would help my sisters a lot if they could feel useful."

My head snaps around and it's a wonder it hasn't rolled right off my shoulders. How dare he speak for us like that? I look at Hazel in the doorway and she crosses her arms and flips her braids back over her shoulder. She's not believing what she's seeing either.

"For instance, if you could show Crita here how you did what you did with the machine to stop it from beeping, we could start with that. If it's okay with you, of course."

"I'm not sure you should touch the equipment."

"Please?" His hand is on her shoulder now and I wonder if she feels the tiniest of pushes. But her brown eyes are soft and she actually pats Linc's hand before she moves back to the monitor.

"Here, sweetie," she says to me. "Come see."

She points and speaks slowly. "This silver switch stops the cycle, and this blue button on the side here, see?"

"Yes, I see it." *I'm not blind.*

"That resets it. Got it?"

"Yeah, I think I can remember that."

"If you have any questions, just ask."

"Sure." *Now get out of my face.*

I seat myself on Daddy's bed and he stirs.

"Girl, you doin' all right?" He turns his head toward me, but Daddy's eyes are barely open.

A tear squeezes out of the corner of my left eye and I wipe it away in one swift motion. "Yes, Daddy, I'm fine. Everyone's here and they're all right. You will be, too. I'm not going anywhere, Daddy." I hear the nurse say "Excuse me" on her way out. Linc is standing not far behind me. We say nothing to each other.

I can't accept this—the nothingness. Linc can't ignore me. I won't let him. I latch onto him like a vicious small dog and I won't let go.

That first night of Daddy's at the hospital, Mama sends me and my sisters home ahead of her. She motions to me with a curved index finger. "I want you to move your things, honey, so Linc can stay in his room," she whispers.

I hold my breath for ten seconds. "Okay, Mama."

"You and your sisters will have to make do in the back bedroom, but I want your brother to feel at home, so you try to have it done before he gets there, all right?"

"Yes, Mama." I kiss my sleeping father on the cheek before leaving the room.

I figure it's enough to have my suitcase and most of my clothes gone when Linc comes in. I am sitting on the bed quietly folding my T-shirts. He's looking around like he's walked into a women's bathroom and doesn't know how to back himself out.

"Yes, Linc?" I look at him expectantly. This is our first moment alone. I'm thinking, "What does he have to say to me?" I'm making it easy. We're not in public and since I have no idea what will satisfy me, I'm thinking he has at least a fifty-fifty shot of saying something I'd find helpful, acceptable— something that will tell me he knows and regrets all that has gone on between us.

"Um, hey, Crita." He stands there and shifts from one foot to the other.

"Hey."

"Um, Mama said I could stay here."

"Yeah, so?"

"So? I'm ready to go to bed, that's all."

I keep staring at him and I can't make my hands move. He hasn't even tried to hug any of us. "You'll have to wait. I'm almost done getting my stuff out of here. You're not going to drop this very moment. Or are you?"

He frowns. "Naw, I ain't gonna drop."

I'm thinking he will stand there until I finish and there will be another moment for him to say something—I mean really say something to me. I take a deep breath and I turn away from him to take the last of my clothing from a drawer, but when I turn around again he's gone.

When Linc does speak, he is giving orders. The next morning I find him in the hospital waiting room, sitting cross-legged on the floor at the wide white coffee table made of resin. He is scribbling on a crude crooked-line chart that he has drawn on a piece of paper.

"What are you doing?"

He looks up and stares at me for a moment and I feel like he wants to cover the paper with his hands. "It's a schedule," he says. I sit near him. He's wearing the same clothes from the day before, and I can smell the sourness that tells me Linc hasn't brushed his teeth.

"Let me see."

"I've got it all figured out, Crita, all figured out."

"Can I see?" I reach out to touch the paper, but he flinches and moves it away from my fingertips.

"I'm not done yet." His hand shakes, just a little, as it moves across the page. He erases something with more ferocity than seems necessary.

I want him to ask me how I am and yet part of me feels I don't know this dirty, smelly fool well enough for him to get so personal. *Who are you?* I want to know. *Where have you been?*

"Give me a minute," he says.

"No, I want to see it now." I reach out again and he puts an arm up to block me. My forearm bangs against his and I wince from the pain. He is still hard and muscular there.

"Crita, back off now! I said give me a minute! Damn! I'm not playing with you!"

I'm not playing either. There's energy between us that's so

familiar, that makes me feel as though I could trace the lines of his fingerprints blindfolded. When he says my name, a part of my heart erases these last years and we are as we were before, when I first lived with him and Chandra. But when I look at Linc now the picture doesn't match the one my brain wants to play back to me. The disparity jangles like out-of-tune bells within me.

"Like I said, it's a schedule. For all of us—you, me, Hazel, and Ella. This way we can take turns being here with Mama and Daddy and not wear ourselves out."

"I'm not doing it. You can't tell me when I can and can't see Daddy. I can be here all day and all night if I want. I did it before you showed up and I'll keep doing it if I want to."

"And what good will that do? Don't you see how crazy that is?"

"You're talking to me about crazy?" I can feel my cheeks starting to burn.

"We don't know how long this is going to go on. We have to pace ourselves."

"Yeah, well, screw you." I get up and walk as fast as I can back to Daddy's room, and I'm damn sure I'm out of Linc's sight before I rub the painful spot on my arm.

"Mama?" She looks up from her Bible and glances at Daddy before coming to me in the hall.

"What's wrong, baby?"

"Mama, Linc's over here trying to give us orders. He wants to schedule when we can all see Daddy, and I don't think that's fair."

"Baby, you can see your Daddy anytime you want, you know that."

"I know that, Mama, but Linc—"

"Linc what?" He's behind me now, waving his piece of paper in the air like a truce flag, throwing his arms up like he's saying, "Who, me?"

I'm saying, "Mama, listen to me—"

"No," says Linc, "Listen to me!" He doesn't have to push me out of the way or take Mama by the shoulders to get her to look at him, to command her attention. It all happens automatically. Her eyes move and now her focus is on him. "Mama, I'm thinking we should come to the hospital in shifts. You can come and go as you please, of course, but I thought if all of us kids took turns Daddy would always have someone here, around the clock. And we wouldn't wear ourselves out doing it because we'd be taking turns."

"And I say, Mama, that we can do this on our own without his stupid schedule. We're upset enough about Daddy without having to think about being on a damn time clock."

"It's not a damn time clock!"

"What is it, then?"

"You two cut this out, right now!" Mama's voice is high-pitched and when I open my mouth to protest, she raises a hand to stop me. "You're gonna make my nerves bad with all this fighting. Crita, the boy is trying to help and it's not gonna hurt you and your sisters to make do with this for now. And, baby, you need to rest! You haven't slept right in weeks. Maybe you'll have a chance to do that now."

I'm thinking she looks like the one who needs to sleep, but then I haven't really looked in a mirror lately. "Fine," I say. "Anything you say, Mama." I head back to the waiting room, but I turn to Linc before I go. "I'll be down here awaiting your orders, captain."

None of us ever gets to hold that piece of paper in our hands, but the very next day, to please Mama, we begin to act out the unseen instructions Linc has printed in the little boxes. We fall into it so easily. I am at the hospital in the early mornings, when Daddy is most likely to be awake and active. On my watch I help the nurses and one male orderly bathe my father. He coughs hard when they turn him on his side and I brush his hair to settle him as they go about their work.

Hazel covers the afternoons. She reads the front page of that day's newspaper to Daddy while he sleeps. She folds it up neatly, kisses him on the cheek, and asks Mama if she needs anything before she leaves. She misses Linc's arrival by minutes, on purpose, daily. Linc comes in time to meet with the doctors on their afternoon rounds. Ella and Mama sit in the evening and pray over Daddy's bed. Sometimes Linc tells them what he has learned and they pass it on to us when they get home. Sometimes, perhaps in defiance of Linc, I go back and sit with Ella and Mama, or I'll sleep on the blue vinyl recliner in Daddy's room until just after midnight. Then I go home to sleep a few more hours before returning in the morning. I grow used to the smell of antiseptic and industrial-strength soap and sickness, which I swear has its own color—yellow. They've inserted a catheter into Daddy's bladder and now his urine flows directly into a bladder hanging down from the side of his bed. Everything coming out of him seems to be yellow: sweat, phlegm, urine. The sickness is draining Daddy.

One day. Two days. Five days. Seven. I realize I am counting the days—but not the ones that tell me how long our father's been ill. I count the days in anticipation of Linc screwing up. That's what I'm used to. I just have to wait, I tell myself, and everything will be as I have known it to be and I'll know what to do. Eight. Nine. Ten. But the opposite is occurring. Linc is growing, even thriving in this crisis. I can see it. He stays faithful to the chart, is never late. His appearance changes. He leaves the house clean-shaven, dressed in new jeans and one of Daddy's good white shirts. I notice his shoulder blades shifting—he stands a little taller.

I'm not the only one who sees it. I go looking for Hazel one evening and I find her in the backyard shed, working on a doll. The smell of the glue she's using makes me a little

lightheaded, but I sit with her because I want to feel calm—
I'm tired of the static electricity that comes of me being watch-
ful of Linc and wondering whether his eyes are ever on me.
"I'm tired of him," I tell her.

"You and me both." Her braids are piled high on her head
and she's wrapped them in a floral print scarf to keep them out
of the way. "I swear Mama and Ella think that asshole walks
on water."

"Yeah, well, we all did once. But for them old habits die
hard, you know that."

"Don't worry, big sis. I'm thinking about the situation."

"What are you talking about?"

She's gluing a piece of porcelain back into a doll's leg. The
little patient has straight black hair braided into two pigtails.
"Things can be fixed," Hazel says. "Repaired." Her hands are
so steady. "It's a matter of feeling the life, like there is within
Bessie here. It's not the kind of life you'd expect, but you have
to try to look at it like it's supposed to be, and help guide
things in that direction."

I'm shaking my head. "I don't understand."

"It takes a certain kind of thought—out of the box, so to
speak. Creativity." At this moment she looks like Daddy. It's
the face he would have when he was planting tomatoes or
fishing—a thoughtful look where he'd be considering how best
to work with nature to bring about his will. "The boy is a
crackhead," Hazel says quietly. "What would be the natural
progression for him?"

I don't want to say. I've considered what could happen to
Linc too many times.

Hazel seems to know what I'm thinking. "No, Crita, he
doesn't have to die. But he could get caught up in other things.
Kind of like you did with Tree."

I lean back in my chair and sigh. "Yeah, Haze, but you
couldn't have known what would happen at the park that day."

She looks up from her work. "Couldn't I?"

"You what?"

"Well, I didn't expect the little white girl to show up, but man it sure made things interesting, didn't it?"

I don't know whether to slap her or rebreak her damn doll. "How could you do that to me?"

"Do what? What did I do that was so bad? I put you back in touch with the love of your life. No pussy-footin' around. You know me—take it to the hoop!" She smiles and lifts a hand into the air like she's making a hook shot with a basketball.

"But did you see what happened? Did you see how hurt and embarrassed I was?"

"No, but I know what would *not* have happened if you guys didn't meet up. There would've been no chance for you to get back together."

"Come on, you know he has a girlfriend."

"Girlfriend!" She points a finger at me. "There's the operative word, honey. She's not a wife, not even a fiancée! Which means there's opportunity all over the damn place. Now what are you going to do about it?"

I prop my elbows on her table and cover my face with my hands. "What can I do now, Hazel? I can't think even straight for worrying about Daddy."

"Multi-task, Crita, multi-task! That's the only thing that'll keep us from going out of our minds with all of this. Follow my example if you have to, honey. I have a lot of work to do on my own."

I'm thinking she's talking about her dolls, but then the next day Hazel doesn't come to the hospital at her appointed time. When I call home, Ella says she isn't there. "She left over an hour ago, honey, she didn't get there?"

"No, and I haven't heard from her."

"Maybe she had to go back to her apartment for something."

"Then why didn't she tell somebody that?"

"Look, Mama's already ready to go, we'll be up there soon to spell you."

"Okay."

"Who's that?" Daddy's voice, so seldom heard now, startles me.

I stroke his arm, the one without all the tubes, as I hang up the phone. "Oh, it's nothing Daddy. Just Ella telling me Mama will be here soon." I'm not sure he's heard me. He's moved his arm up to his forehead and something akin to a sigh comes out of his mouth.

I'm wondering where my youngest sister is. I'm wondering what she's up to.

Linc doesn't move like he used to, and I don't understand that. He's not graceful. He is noisy in the house. I hear him when he comes home in the evening. He makes the floorboards groan with his plodding steps, and he crashes dishes into the sink. Looking for a fork, he rummages through drawers as though he's never been in the house before and doesn't know where anything is.

One night Linc is slamming the cupboard doors and I can't sleep for all his stupid banging around. When I step into the kitchen I smell the meatloaf Ella had made the day before. Linc has two thick slices covered with gravy on a plate on the table.

"Linc, what the hell are you looking for?"

I startle him. He jumps a bit and his eyes widen as though he hadn't expected to see me again in this life. He turns away, but only partially. I can't tell if he is afraid or ashamed.

"Salt," he says. He tugs down on his gray sweatshirt. It has climbed high on his waist from his reaching up and for a brief moment I can see the hair on his belly.

"It's behind you on the counter." I sit down.

Linc takes the shaker in his hand and stands there.

"Hungry, huh?" I nod toward the plate, trying to let him know that it's okay for him to sit with me.

"Yeah." He hesitates a moment longer before finally settling down to his meal, but he stabs at the meat halfheartedly.

"Linc, how did you eat before? I mean, if you don't mind my asking." I'm thinking of the food I used to prepare for him—lunches left in paper bags in the doorways of certain houses; plates of chicken left out on Chandra's counter after I knew she had gone to bed. I used to think my brother would starve if I didn't make these efforts. Linc grunts. "Food stamps, mostly." Then he laughs. "Government cheese!" I cannot see his eyes. They are lowered and focused on his food. I notice a patch of dry skin on his cheek just below his left eyelid. Suddenly he pops his head up and Linc's talking, the most he's said to me in over a week.

"You have to line up for the shit. Man, these people behind the counter, they keep track of how long you been comin' in," Linc says. "And there's this old dude, Willie, must be in his fifties or sixties or somethin'. Willie gets up there at the head of the line and they say, 'Now Mr. Frisbee, do you need food stamps this month?' And he goes, 'Blaaaaah!' " (Linc sticks out his tongue.) " 'Gimme my damn coupons!!' That cracks me up! And of course the woman doesn't know what to make of Willie, him standing there all drunk and all. She just forks over the goods. I laugh my ass off."

There is an ugliness about it, a rudeness in the way Linc forces out his tongue and lets it flail in mockery of these people. I'm thinking he's going on as though he's above them, a prince among addicts and swine. "And what about you?" I want to ask him. The question burns in my mouth like an exotic spice I never wanted to taste. But Linc is spooning it out, and I am powerless to ask for something else.

"There's this other guy . . ." Linc begins. "This dude. We'd pair up to use one set of food stamps for us and we'd sell the other set and split the proceeds. It's weird though. I barely know the dude and we do this every damn month. Sometimes I'm looking at him across the street, doing a deal and I'll be damned if I'm not wondering, 'What's he doing? Is he talking about me?' "

I think that is what hurts the most, that Linc would care what mere strangers thought of him, more so than us, the ones who love him. Linc nods again and asks, "You know?" but I'm silent and he goes back to picking at his meatloaf.

"Linc, when was the last time you saw Savannah?"

"Easter." The answer comes quickly, as if he's been waiting for the question and has had the word sitting on a spring in his brain so he can pop it out on a moment's notice. "Happy now?"

I place my hands on the table and focus on them for a few seconds before backing myself away. "Why don't I let you eat? I'll see you tomorrow."

In my bed I still can't sleep. I listen to the bright sound of Linc's fork tines striking the plate again and again.

Fourteen

My sisters and I share our old bedroom, amazed to find ourselves once again huddled in this space. We sit in there as we did then, trying to make sense of the world. But the plaster walls seem closer now, so that our problems seem humongous—too big for the room. Too big for us.

"I feel like a puppet," Hazel says late one night as she lies on her back in the trundle bed still painted with blue stars and cows jumping over yellow moons. "I have never felt so helpless in my whole goddamn life."

"Sugar, don't we all?" Ella responds. "I had a hunch about all this, didn't I, Crita? I knew it was gonna be this bad."

I am sitting on the floor and I reach up to the desk and push an ashtray toward her. She is perched on the other side of the desk, at the open window, smoking and blowing blue clouds out into the warm night. With a yellow silk scarf tied like a headband around her hair, the long end pieces of the bow trailing over her left shoulder, Ella reminds me of a photo I once saw of Dorothy Dandridge. "Yes, you did," I say. "And I'm sorry. Why don't we come out and say that while we're on the subject?"

"Humph, the less said about that the better," Hazel says and I wince. "The issue here is what do we fucking do now?"

"About what?"

"What are we going to do about big brother?"

"Oh, hon, what's he doing that's so wrong other than eating us out of house and home?" With delicate fingers, Ella taps her cigarette in the ashtray. She's right about that, too. Linc does seem to be eating his way through something, like he's trying to stave off his demons, or whatever the hell is crawling around his psyche, with food. He devours hamburgers in twos or threes, donuts by the half dozen. At this moment I'm craving the comfort of the apple muffins baked that morning but I know they are all gone. Linc has eaten every last one. "Of course I don't *mind*. Cooking to keep up with him gives me and Mama something to do other than worry ourselves into craziness, but to tell you the truth, I'm downright grateful that he's here. One less thing to worry about."

"All right, enlighten us, Ella. What the hell are *you* talking about?"

"He's not in the streets facedown in a ditch somewhere, that's what I mean. With things the way they are, we've got to count our blessings."

"Those bastard doctors only talk to him."

"Oh, who wants to talk to some dumb old doctors anyway? They don't even speak English half the time."

"I asked Mama for her fucking checkbook." Hazel pauses, but Ella and I are startled. "Not that way, of course, I mean I didn't swear at her, but I have it just the same. I told her to make sure there's no money in the house, and I have this." She pulls down on the collar of her berry red T-shirt and shows us a key on a thin silver chain. "It's the key to the drawer where Daddy keeps his guns."

"Honey, did you count the silverware while you were at it?"

"Shut up, Ella," I say. She is forgetting, as she always conveniently forgets. We can't afford to be so naive. I'm startled and struck by Hazel. I should be thinking this way, acting more this way. "She's right to do all this. We all know what can happen if we aren't careful."

Ella stubs out her cigarette now, her face tight and agitated. "I want my Forrest here. I'm calling him now."

"That's good, that's fucking good," Hazel says when Ella has gone and we have the room to ourselves. "Someone else can listen to her whining." She flips forward onto her elbows and confronts me with hard, brown eyes. "I can only put up with so much of him," she says. "Only so fucking much."

"I know. God knows, I know, but Hazel you gotta be cool. Daddy is all that matters right now."

"Everything matters right now. Every word, every movement. That's why we have to make the most of whatever we say or do. Can't waste a single opportunity."

"Was that what you were doing when you went MIA the other day? Where were you, for real?"

"Taking care of some business. It didn't work out, though. I'm gonna have to keep trying."

"Trying to do what?"

"Trying to straighten out a few things. You'll see. I'm takin' it to the hoop. Only next time I'll be slammin'. Big brother won't even see it coming."

"Hazel, be careful, okay? Do whatever it is you think you have to do, but don't disappear again, all right? I need you here. You're probably the sanest out of all of us and somebody has to be normal and on top of things." But I can see what's upsetting her. As Linc takes back his position in our family with all the force of a conquering warrior, my own vexation grows. Daddy worsens over those days and Linc grows stronger to the point where I suspect he is somehow feeding off our father's strength. And even if this has to happen, if by some law of the earth Daddy has to decrease for one of us to increase, I don't believe that Linc is the one who deserves such a feast. But he's already like a parasite to me, chewing away quietly and businesslike, without a touch of remorse. I'm sure Hazel notices this as well and feels, as I do, small and obscure. I can sense myself shrinking further still.

I get up to close the window. The night air is damp and I can smell the dirt eager to push out new life. I want to grab chunks of it and sniff all its essence into my soul. I wish I could have its optimism. I leave the room to Hazel, intending to go outside, but I find Mama asleep in the recliner, bathed in the blue light emanating from the telecast of the eleven o'clock news. I cover her with one of her granny square afghans and sit on the sofa staring at the weathered visage of the anchorman Judd Hendricks who had come to that TV station when I was in junior high and he was a young man. He tells me of that day's lotto numbers, about the impending strike by the Ford autoworkers, and of the robbery of a downtown state liquor store, but not one word of how he had grown so old.

Seven days pass. I am asleep in the chair by Daddy's bed when Tree lays a hand upon my shoulder and wakens me with the scent of fresh coffee in a cup he holds under my nose. I rub the bleariness from my eyes as he whispers, "Come on, take a break." He is close enough for me to smell the fragrant oils in his hair. Without thinking, I take his hand, because that is what I was once used to, and he leads me down to the waiting room. He holds my hand as though this is what he always does.

"Is school out for the summer?"

"Almost. Exams are going on now, so I don't have to go in right away."

"That's cool."

"How's he doing?"

"He hasn't been conscious this morning. But I haven't spoken to him yet. That usually helps. And Hazel and I will rub down his legs later on." My hand flies up to my mouth and I'm surprised to find myself stifling a sob. "There are still things we can do."

Tree reaches out to me and I cringe.

"No, don't do that." I am embarrassed. I haven't showered and I can't fathom what I must look or smell like. His hair is neatly tied back and his black T-shirt is perfect and lint-free. I'm wearing the same gray, long-sleeved top that I wore yesterday and it has a butter stain on the left elbow. I sink down and away from him into one of the waiting-room chairs. But he pulls over another chair and puts it directly in front of mine. Then he sits and takes my hands and holds them in both his own.

I want to pull away from him. I can't accept his touch too readily, as though I'm entitled to it. I'd be stealing. It's stealing because he's not mine and no matter how bland and angled and icy Talane looks, this is the truth I have to remember. I don't like this feeling, this very proprietary feeling I have about Tree, but I can only explain it as something that I see as common sense screwing with my mind. I know too well what we've been to each other. Hell, the smell of him used to seep through my pores and my hair grew through his head. You don't forget something like that. You leave none of it behind.

Then why did you?

I extract my hands from him and pretend I'm doing it so I can rub my eyes. *No stealing*, I tell myself. *No stealing*.

"Crita, you understand, don't you, that you can't control what's happening here? This isn't like it was with Linc back then. This isn't a train wreck waitin' to happen, and you're not a little girl trying to pull the brake."

"Yes, but I can't not do anything. Tree, I have to take care of him."

"And you're doing that, baby, you're doing just that. But whatever the end result is, none of it is about you."

"Oh, God," I say, staring at his hands, now empty without mine entwined. "Tree, I'm so scared."

He leans forward and touches his lips, full and warm, to my forehead. "Remember, you were scared with Linc, too."

"Pulling a brake, you said. That's what I was doing for Linc?"

Tree laughs and something in the sound relaxes me. It's as though I know every word that falls from his sweet mouth will be safe and soft. I have nothing in the world to fear from him. "Yeah! You looked like you coulda been Little Orphan Annie in one of those comic strips, seeing that cliff comin' up ahead and she's pulling on that lever with all her might. Only the thing is bigger than she is, and it's too heavy. But that doesn't matter. She just keeps trying."

"And then what happened?"

"Well, a tree fell in front of the train, now didn't it? Annie didn't have to pull that brake after all."

"But maybe that wasn't such a great thing."

"Why not?"

"Because it feels like the train's still in gear." I'm looking at him, trying to look deep. I'm wondering if he understands what I'm saying.

"Chandra will come by later, after she drops Savannah off at school."

"Okay," I say. I'm thinking of heading back to Daddy's room. He might be awake, if he's going to awaken, by now. "Tree, do you want to see him?"

"Yeah, I'd like that a lot."

"They put a tube down into his stomach yesterday." I stop and sigh deeply, hoping the breath will tamp down the tears in my throat. Tree's left hand rests on the top of my right thigh. I don't move and I don't move it away. But I say, "No, I'm okay." I sigh once more. The breath feels lame, probably because what I really want to do is scream both my lungs out at someone. "It's just that the stuff that came out of him. . . . Blackness, Tree, they were these pieces of blackness. Dr. Joyce said it was old blood, all dried up and black. 'How long has it been in there?' I asked him. He said he didn't know."

Tree is silent for a few minutes. "And your family?"

"I'm worried about Hazel. She hasn't been saying much. She won't sit in the same room with Linc unless it's Daddy's room and then she just ignores him completely."

"Well, you can't exactly blame her."

"No, but I can't shake this feeling . . ."

"What feeling?"

"That she's up to something. She's being secretive, disappearing in bits and pieces and then it doesn't seem like she's being truthful about where's she's been."

Actually, Hazel has been very good about covering for herself. She gives Mama half-mumbled excuses about papers to finish and one last exam to write, but Ella and I know that she finished the semester weeks ago. Plus, she is not gone long enough to be doing anything at school. At most she is gone for an evening, or a few hours in the afternoon. It's as though she is out hunting, looking for something.

"Daddy, Tree's here."

My father lies flat on his back. He is awake. I can tell by the way he responds to my voice, the way his arm, now just a bone with the skin hanging from it like it's on a clothesline, comes up from the bed just slightly and moves toward me. I place my hand on his until it relaxes down to the sheet again. When he speaks his throat is raw. He gurgles something I can't understand. "Daddy, what is it?"

Tree grasps me by the shoulders and I step aside. "Let me try. I think he's talking to me." He leans over the bed and places his ear right next to Daddy's lips. Again Daddy gurgles, but this time I can pick up consonants, the shape of a few words.

"Yes, sir." Tree finally says and he nods. "I'll do my best, you know that, sir. I'll always do my best." When he moves away I see tears in Tree's eyes. I step in and begin to adjust Daddy's blankets, words spilling from my mouth like water from a full open faucet.

"He's just the best, isn't he, Daddy? I love him so much. And he'll do whatever you ask, he's good like that, he's a good man. Right, Daddy?" I don't know what I'm saying. I just want to keep the sounds coming so that he will rest and I won't break into little tiny pieces on the floor.

"Come on, Crita," Tree finally whispers. "I think he's asleep again now." He takes me out into the hall and I stand there and cross my arms. I can't see beyond Daddy's door.

"What did he say?"

Tree puts his hands on the tops of my shoulders and I'm staring at the fabric of his shirt covering his chest. It rises as he takes a deep breath. "He said, 'Make that child grow her hair out again.' "

We laugh and I put my hands on my hips and shake my head. "God, that man is something else."

"What about what you said?"

"What?"

"The part where you told him you loved me."

I said that out loud? Oh God. I wave a hand in the air and it lands over my mouth and I'm mumbling. "Tree, I . . . I . . . ."

Now he's holding me and I'm crying and dissolving like sand overcome by the tide.

"Yo, man, what's up?" Linc's voice, sudden and unexpected, knocks my heart hard like a hammer hitting a bell. It's too early. He's not supposed to be there yet. I separate myself from Tree but I'm still standing close enough to feel the hair on his arms stand up and sway against the back of my right hand.

"Hey." Tree crosses his arms and throws down that one word for Linc. Nothing more.

"Can I talk to you for a minute?" Linc glances at me and shoves his hands into the back pockets of his jeans. "In private?"

"Sure, but just for a minute, gotta get to work." Tree drops a light kiss on my forehead. "Catch you later, Crita."

They stay on opposite sides of the hall as they walk away. If I were in my right mind I would've been more concerned about who was going to throw the first punch and who would be there to pull them apart before their little weather system blew out the waiting room. But I still have sobs heaving up from my chest and I have to find some Kleenex.

I can't stay like this. It is four hours before my sister Hazel will arrive. Two hours before I must call Mama. I plan to ask a nurse for cream with which to massage my father's feet. All the while I am thinking about the machinery that makes up a train, and how one goes about stopping one.

Fifteen

When Linc left for college Daddy began to treat him differently. He was less critical, more deferential, prone to addressing Linc as an equal, as he would another man. I thought this was what happened between boys and their fathers when the boys came of age and the overwhelming amount of testosterone had to be controlled so the newly competing men would not tear the house apart with their bigness. It never occurred to me that this adult treatment, this emotional largesse on my father's part, would ever extend to me.

I suppose there were glimmers of it when Daddy took my part over Mama's when he learned I was going to Belden. I was too stirred up with Mama's upset to truly appreciate it then. But I felt it again, deeply, unmistakably, when Daddy took me to buy my first car. We drove out to the used car lot of Mike Bass Ford out on Route 254. Ella came with us and the morning was sunny and cool with hints of autumn in the air.

I was excited about getting the car, but knew enough not to have too many expectations in terms of color or make and model. It was a used car lot, after all, and my dreams would be limited to availability and price. Of course, Daddy would insist of the salesman, the car had to run well and be in good condition. "I don't want her breaking down some night on a highway," he said. Not that such a thing would be too disastrous. The minute we earned our drivers licenses when we were sixteen, Daddy enrolled us in the Automobile Association of America. Triple-A stickers were fixtures on our family car as well as Linc's, promising expeditious tow service and "roadside assistance," meaning they'd come even to change a tire, twenty-four hours a day. Still, Daddy would have my car examined by his own mechanic before he'd agree to buy.

I only wanted it to be blue—navy—my favorite color, and for it to be not so old that it smelled of another time, like the '62 Cadillac Daddy had when we were little. We walked in and out between the rows of cars. Daddy was dressed up in one of his crisp white shirts and he had his gold retirement pin from the steel mill on his tie. He even wore his special belt buckle, the one with the mass of silver dollars that he'd put together with a soldering iron. In matters like this, Daddy said, "You got to look like you have money, even if you don't got a dime in your pocket. You look like you got money, people will treat you that way." I stayed close by his side listening to his recommendations and denunciations of every car.

"That there's a Buick. Goddamn Buick stalled on me on my way to St. Louis in 1959. Couldn't get it started again for nothing."

Then, "A Cadillac will pull the weight of two of them trucks over there. It's a pretty car, too."

We looked at a Dodge Omni. Daddy favored the Chrysler brand in general, but he thought the Omni too small to be safe for me.

"Who can see you on the road in that damn little thing? Eighteen-wheeler will roll right over your ass. That's a toy, that's all that car is."

I winced. He didn't know, of course, of my trip to Cleveland in Malcolm Warfield's Omni. "Yes, sir. I think I'd be scared driving it, too, Daddy."

He glanced at me as though the word *scared* had reminded him of something.

"You know, Crita, if you ever get scared, if something don't seem right to you up at that school or at Lincoln's house, you can come right back home. No reason for you to be anywhere else."

"Yes, Daddy."

He popped open the hood of another car. "Now that's a V-8 engine. A lot of power. You won't need all that. But four would be too little. I want a V-6 for you."

Just then Ella, who had been in a different row, came running up. "Daddy, Daddy, I just saw the nicest one! It's called a Sunbird! It's red and . . ."

"Girl, stop that yelling like you ain't got no sense. Ain't nobody buying a goddamn Pontiac. That car will freeze up in the middle of June. Now hush talking. You see I'm speaking to your sister."

Ella looked like Daddy had backhanded her across the face with an open hand. He was a rough speaker, but never spoke like that to Ella before. I always figured he just understood the flower that she was, and was careful not to deal with her too harshly so she wouldn't wilt. Hazel and I, he must have assumed, were made of different materials, more raw than refined, and could withstand the hurricane force of his speech patterns. And it looked like he was right because at that moment Ella, in fact, did seem to shrink. "Yes, sir," she mumbled. Subdued, she stayed close to us for the rest of the search, her chin low and her bottom lip just this side of slipping out into a pout.

A Jeep Wrangler caught Daddy's eye. He liked that it was small, but not too small, and high off the ground so I could see. Plus it was made "by the Chrysler people." I climbed behind the wheel and felt I could see the world and not just the road. I thought the vehicle was cute and unusual. And it was blue, with a black hardtop. Daddy kept talking as he examined the car.

"Four-wheel drive," he said. "That's good if you're stuck in snow. I'll have to teach you how to use it."

"That's okay, Daddy, I can learn."

He nodded, then said without looking at me, "I shoulda taught you more about not gettin' mixed up with the wrong kind of men. I know you got good sense, though. You better use it."

"Yes, sir, Daddy, I will."

He paused. Then he came around and climbed into the passenger seat next to me. He leaned back into the seat and I thought he was about to tell me to drive him somewhere. Instead he asked, "You know my daddy shot my momma?"

"Yes, sir."

He kept looking around and out the windows as though he were on a ride and enjoying the view. He didn't look at me. "Men can be crazy. Love can make 'em crazy. You make sure a man's right in the head before you get with 'em."

"Yes, sir."

"You like this Jeep here, Crita?"

"Yes, sir, Daddy, I like it a lot."

"Let's see about gettin' it checked out then."

"Yes, sir."

We both got out then, and he put an arm around my shoulders and we walked into the sales office together with Ella trailing behind. I never felt so big, so loved, and so full of my father than I did on that morning. I may as well have been sitting on top of his shoulders, unafraid of the world because I knew nothing could reach me at that height.

When we got home Ella ran into the house ahead of us. I was in no hurry. I knew the moment we went inside, the chemistry between me and Daddy would change. Something else might command his attention and that something else could be as trivial as a baseball game. I knew I shouldn't be hurt by it, Daddy was just like that after all. He's said what he needed to say and would move on. But because I had felt so special I knew I could be hurt if he didn't give me the same attention the rest of the day. I lingered outside on the porch until I felt disconnected enough from unrealistic expectations.

When I did make my way inside, into my bedroom, I was annoyed to find Ella's sweater and sunglasses on my bed. She was sprawled on her bed on her stomach reading *Seventeen*. "Ella, come on, what's up with this? Get your junk off my bed."

She wrinkled her nose and shrugged as she got up. "Doesn't matter anyway," she said as she gathered her belongings and hung them in the closet. "It'll be my bed soon enough."

"Yeah, well, today it's still mine. Besides, Mama and Daddy aren't gonna let you jump all over my stuff when I start school."

"You wait and see." She tossed her hair over her shoulder. "I'll be the oldest and Daddy will like me best. I'm the one he'll pamper next."

I looked at my sister and wondered just when and where in her brain a screw had popped loose. This wasn't a competition. If she went in to Daddy right now and said she needed another dress for the prom because she needed to wear blue instead of pink, Daddy would scold her for being ridiculous but then he wouldn't be able to sit restful in his chair until he'd gotten it for her. "Nettie, let's go on downtown and see about that dress for Ella," he'd say. "That girl's got to have it." And he'd find a way to get it. Ella didn't need to have me out of the house to get Daddy's attention and I told her so.

"He pampers you anyway, you spoiled brat."

"He didn't have to talk to me like that today. He did that because of you."

"He did it because you were acting like an idiot."

"He never thought so before."

"Yeah, well, I'm positive he will again."

She threw her magazine at me, then picked up the phone to whine on to one of her useless boyfriends. I pulled a pillow over my head and turned my face to the wall, trying to ignore her. I hardly needed another source of friction in the house. The imbalance was already overwhelming. Mama barely looked at me and Hazel carried a frost that left crystals on my skin whenever she passed. I looked forward to the relief of a new existence in my brother's home.

To be in a house not entirely your own, you have to learn a new rhythm of life. By the fall I was ensconced in Linc's home. Even though I'd spent so much time in Linc's house before, I found that once inside the house, I had to learn to dance again, this time to this house's sounds. There was the sound of Savannah crying in the night, and seeing Linc move with those male assertions that men need to make that say, "This is *my* house." Like the way he would leave his coffee cup in the sink in the mornings instead of rinsing it out and leaving it in the drainboard the way Daddy did. Or how he watched television with his body slumped into the sofa, feet propped up on the coffee table. But this he was more likely to do when Chandra wasn't around.

Perhaps because I wanted so much to know this new music I learned quickly and fell into Linc and Chandra's rhythms and mingled my life easily into theirs. Our routine formed just as I had pictured it. I took my classes in the morning, setting off in my Jeep just about the same time as Linc for my drive out to Belden. When I came home in the afternoon I looked after Savannah while Chandra ran errands or shopped for dinner. Sometimes we even cooked together, me chopping onions or snapping green beans while she fried the chicken or peeled shrimp. We chatted and gossiped like sisters.

In the spring Chandra felt confident enough to go back to nursing school. Within days I could see the wisdom in that decision. She was happier, more confident. Soon the expression Chandra would get sometimes, the faraway one where it seemed she was pining for something she had lost, had faded from her pretty face. She looked like she did when I first met her: bright, open, and full of possibilities.

Linc must have seen this, too. One evening I sat with him watching television while Chandra put Savannah to bed. I was folding laundry, stacks of diapers, towels, T-shirts, and sweat suits accumulating around me. "It's cold in here," he said. It was not yet summer so the nights were still chilly.

"Here, put this on." I threw his favorite Ohio State hooded sweatshirt at him, landing it on his head. He started to yank it on.

"Damn, the drawstring came out. I hate when that happens. Shit's ruined."

I rummaged through the remains of the laundry until I found the red cord. "Give it to me, I'll put it back in."

"How are you going to do that?"

"The way Mama always does it. Didn't you ever notice you didn't lose drawstrings when you lived at home?" I found a safety pin in a kitchen drawer. I attached it to one end of the drawstring, then used the pin to thread it through the hood, feeling the pin and using it to pull the string along. When I had pulled it out through the other hole, I tossed the shirt back to Linc.

"Hey, you do good work," he said as he put it on.

"Thanks."

He stared at the TV screen blankly for a few minutes longer. "I should be the one saying thanks," he said.

"You're welcome," I said, giving him a wry smile.

"No, I'm serious, Crita. Your help means a lot to Chandra and me. You've made things a lot easier for us. I'm just trying to say I'm glad you're here."

"Think nothing of it, big brother," I said. I stopped folding and smiled at him, that time a real one, warm and generous. "I'm glad to be here."

Just before my junior year, Linc got promoted. Fully. Finally. He and Chandra threw a huge backyard barbecue to celebrate. The night was warm, the air infused with hickory smoke and beer. We set Linc's stereo speakers in two of the back windows of the house and pumped Rick James into the atmosphere. Linc manned the grill, tending the ribs and calling out to Tick to brag about his sauce recipe. At one point in the evening I saw Chandra, Savannah on her hip, go up to him so Savannah could kiss him good-night. He kissed Chandra, too, and I felt their heat radiate all the way over the table where I sat with Mama and Daddy. If I didn't know it before, I knew it then. I'd done the right thing in moving in with them.

The night progressed and dancing commenced. Mama and Daddy begged off. I was disappointed at first. I remembered dancing with Daddy at parties in our house when I was a child. His hair slicked back like Muddy Waters, Daddy moved with a rhythmic shoe shuffling, the way you danced to the blues. His motion and cadence were small, but his dance seemed very big like he was swimming in the music. I would have loved to see him dance that way again. But as he smiled and waved good-night I noticed the tired lines in his face and felt a twinge of ache in my stomach as I realized for the first time that my father was no longer young.

Mama and Daddy took Hazel with them, but allowed Ella to stay. She was newly graduated and headed for Spelman in the fall. I'm sure she wanted to see how many hearts she would take with her when the summer was over. She had flirted with a number of guys throughout the evening, but when our parents left she must have thought it safe to hone in on her real prize, Tree.

I must admit I found it hard to keep my eyes off him myself. He wore a black V-neck T-shirt that set off the brown in his skin and made it glow. I wished I could run my hand over the muscles of his arm and the very thought made my fingers tingle. I had dated off and on since starting Belden, but none of the men I dated spoke words that told the story of how they knew me. None was as strong as Daddy or as charming as Linc. It seemed a losing proposition to bring a man into my world who would pale in comparison to the other men in it.

But Tree paled to no one and Ella knew this as well. I watched as she brought him a beer he hadn't asked for, her hips moving under her summer dress in the slow Southern style she'd culled from watching Lena Horne movies. I had to admire the way she could place herself right in front of a man in a way where he had to look at her, even if he was talking to someone else. There was no speaking over Ella's head or tactfully turning away from her.

Tree seemed determined to do both. He accepted the bottle from her, but continued his conversation with one of Linc's friends. He did put an arm around her shoulders, though, and she smiled and nodded as though she was really interested in what they were saying. Then Tree must have introduced her because Ella offered her hand to the other guy and smiled her gazillion-watt smile. Once the guy took hold of Ella's hand, Tree excused himself. A smooth hand-off. A flash of a frown crossed Ella's face, but her own sense of decorum kept her from brushing the guy off and going after Tree again. I smiled and took a sip of my Dr. Pepper.

Someone started up an Electric Slide and I joined in until

my feet tangled up my legs and I could no longer keep up with the steps. I sat down and within a few minutes Tree was in the folding chair next to me.

"God, I hate line dancing!" he laughed.

"Me, too. There's just something too unoriginal about it." I smiled at him and offered my cup of Dr. Pepper. He took a drink and handed it back. I felt too good to be nervous. The night was hot and summery, and I was warm and delicious like a piece of fruit. Now I had the most beautiful man sitting next to me. "I love nights like this," I said.

"Yeah, so do I. I could stay up all night on nights like this."

"Tonight's the night to be in a place like New York. The city that never sleeps. I almost went to school there."

"What happened?"

"I just changed my mind. No big deal. Maybe I'll go for grad school." I didn't say more. I wanted to talk about something else. In a few minutes he seemed to pick up the cue.

"Yeah, but what do we do about tonight?"

"Well this party's not going anywhere. I'm sure we can dance until dawn if the neighbors don't call the police."

"But I'm dying for some ice cream."

I laughed.

"What? Don't you want any?"

I leaned forward, resting my elbows on my knees, and closed my eyes to better absorb the Al Green music drifting through the night air. When I opened them again I smiled at Tree and answered the question he didn't ask.

"Yes," I said calmly. "I will go with you."

He put a hand on my knee and looked into my eyes. "I'll go get my keys," he said finally.

When he had gone, Ella came by and sat in his place, fanning herself with her hand. "Lord, it's so hot! Aren't you warm in those jeans?"

"I'm fine." I wore a blue tank T-shirt so my arms were bare and I could catch just a hint of a breeze on my skin.

"Still, you look like you just walked in off the streets. I don't know why you couldn't have dressed up more for Linc's party."

I didn't answer her. It was a barbecue after all. I wore what made me comfortable as I helped Linc and Chandra lug bags of charcoal and tables and chairs into the yard. It didn't occur to me to change.

"It wouldn't kill you to wear a skirt sometimes."

I looked at Ella, the floral print cotton gently clinging to her curves. No matter what skirt or dress I wore, I would never look like her. My morale dipped and I realized that if I were going to preserve my present mood, I had to get away from my sister. Besides, tonight I was the one walking away with the prize. I stood and put my cup on the table.

"Tell Tree I'll meet him out by his car."

There were no ice cream places open. Tree and I drove around for a while looking before we ended up buying Drumstick cones from the freezer case of a Dairy Mart and driving out to Lakeview Beach. We stood in the sand and watched the beacon of the old lighthouse blink in the distance. We talked about school, his pending graduation, and politics, working our way back around to Linc's barbecue.

"You looked so beautiful tonight," he said and I laughed softly.

"Demetrius Templeton, what are you saying to me? I know what I look like tonight and I know what Ella looked like and the one thing I was not was beautiful."

He smoothed a blowing lock of hair away from my face. "Crita, you looked so happy tonight. Happy for your brother, happy to see people, happy to just be there. It was so natural."

"It's summer." I put a hand on his arm, no longer able to resist touching him. "My family's doing well. My brother's doing well. It's just the way I feel."

He drew me closer and kissed my temples and then my cheeks and then my mouth. My body rose into his and I felt off-balance and floating in the breeze off the lake. I touched his arms lightly, content to float as long as I stayed in contact with his skin. He held me tightly and I sighed, a deep satisfying breath that felt as though my lungs were taking air for the very first time. I relaxed and nuzzled into his neck. Whatever happened in the coming hours, months, years, I knew I would be forever grateful for those first moments when I was so close to Tree.

I remember his hand on my stomach. That's what I think about first when I recall that night. I walked into his apartment, draped in that blue-black darkness that comes of being lit only from the fluorescent streetlights outside. Then Tree was there, holding me from behind, his arms wrapped around me so firmly I felt as though a cocoon had closed in around me. His right arm lay across my collarbone and held me by the left shoulder. I lowered my head to kiss his forearm, my lips tickled by the curly dark strands that rose from his skin, and I smiled. Then his left hand slid across my belly and stayed there, just over my naval. He pressed into my skin and I held my breath because I wanted to feel his fingers on every contour of my abdomen.

His fingers curved into my side and he spun me around. I turned quick and tight like a ballroom dancer and I wanted to bend backward over his arms until my head reached the floor. I wanted to feel the strength of my own body then, to be lean and long and stretch over just like that down to the floor, just so he could lift me up again and I could feel the air zing around me and the light zip me into dizziness, the blood lost from my head.

He wasn't the first for me and I'm glad of that. There was a stupidity to my first time that I suspect is common of most everyone's initiation to intimacy. It can't be helped. The blind groping, shaky hands, outsized expectations, and the need to be liked and satisfactory. It's all-consuming, and desire—if there was really any true desire at all instead of intense curiosity— gets lost in the cesspool.

Because he wasn't my first, my desire for Tree could be a sapphire crushed within me and the jeweled dust and heat radiated from every pore of my skin. And everything else was easy—from the way he lifted me, sliding against him skin to skin, and lay me on his lemon-scented sheets, to the way he fit inside me. It lasted longer, too. No abrupt endings, no awkward pulling on of clothes. We would lay, arranging ourselves in different positions on the bed, and talk. Then, once revived, we would start again. Our eyes were always open, our gazes constantly shifting. At times I thought he didn't recognize me. In the dark Tree spoke in soft low tones that drilled up a moistness inside me without any effort.

Afterward, when I was back home and in my own bed, my sleep was strange. My arms moved across the sheets numerous times in search of his body. At the same time I felt sticky and light and delicious like cotton candy. I dreamed dreams I couldn't remember. Nothing seemed real.

The next morning I feared it wasn't. I stared out the kitchen window, stunned to see the world illuminated again with sun and blue sky. Just hours before it had seemed night would go on forever and everything would always be soft and warm and low tones. Maybe there was something to the night owl way of life and why people thought vampires romantic. Would Tree come back today?

"If he hurts my sister, I'll kill him."

"Linc, shut up!" Chandra laughed at him as she scrambled eggs.

"I'm just saying . . . !" He had his hands raised in a "don't blame me" fashion and only lowered them to pour himself a cup of coffee.

I went out and sat on Linc's porch. I couldn't think in there with them. It all had to have been real. Even though the sun still shone like fresh orange juice and the porch's concrete still felt smooth and solid beneath my feet, my body was different. I leaned on my side, putting my feet up on the bench next to me. I was aware of my curves as my arm draped over my hips; I sat into a confidence and comfort with my body that I had never felt before.

But then there was Tree's car. He pulled up right in front of the house and that didn't seem real either. He got out, and I sat up straight, and I was thinking that the next few moments would be everything. Either he was going to make a stupid joke and try to treat me again like the teenager he once knew or . . . or things were really, truly, different and my heart might explode.

He stepped onto the porch. I stood up, and before I could say anything he reached for me and kissed me long and deep like he was giving up the last of his power.

"Crita, what is this about?" he said, finally.

"I don't know." I shook my head, my eyes still closed. "Right now, I guess, it's about spending time together, as much as possible. Then we'll go from there."

"Okay. We'll start tonight. Let's have a date, a real one."

I laughed. It sounded so backward, especially considering the night before. "I don't need you to date me, Tree."

"No, not right now, but someday you might. And I don't want to skip any steps."

That evening he was driving me to an Italian restaurant, a little family place in a strip mall on the west side of Cleveland. We were quiet on the way there. I sunk down into the car seat like I was nesting. I felt like we were in this perfect space just floating down the road. We said nothing until Tree felt the need to comment.

"This is what I want."

"What?"

"This. This silence. I like knowing that we don't have to talk. It's deep. Solid."

I looked at him and then out at the road ahead of us and nodded. "Yes."

All the next day I savored Tree and the new sweetness in my life. Maybe too much so to notice that Linc carried his celebrating into the next night, a Sunday, when he went out with Tick and some other guys. He wasn't home when Chandra and I went to bed. That Monday morning Chandra left for school early so it was I, padding around in my slippers and robe, who heard my brother snoring and found him still in bed.

"Linc!" I shook him and he started awake, but I could see by the way he looked around and had a hard time focusing on me that he was in bad shape. His eyes were veiled in red and his tongue was thick and uncommunicative. I looked at the clock. There was no way he would make it to work on time anyway. "It's nothing, Linc, go back to sleep," I said, pressing him back into the pillows. He went obligingly and soon was unconscious again.

I called the office for him and, with an ease that surprised me, I lied and said Linc was ill, that he'd gone to see a doctor and I was calling in for him. I hung up the phone and went to fix breakfast for Savannah. I was humming. I was happy. I thought nothing of it, especially later when Linc learned what I had done and praised the way I had covered for him. If my eyes and ears and heart had not been so full of Tree I might have realized the enormity of what I had done.

Sixteen

I had to talk about Tree with someone. I would have short-circuited my brain otherwise. That's how full it was of all the sensations and colors and smells I was accumulating from Tree. I chose Hazel because she wasn't too close to him, like Chandra, and wouldn't constantly remind me to be careful, like Mama would. I definitely didn't want that—no censorship, no advice—just a pure appreciation for romance as I saw it and my happiness. Just the type of validation I would get only from a high-school girl—granted Hazel had a little more maturity going for her than others her age, which made her all the more invaluable in this. She even gave me clothing advice, would loan me the cute top I would never think to buy for myself.

"You should think about locking this mess," she said to me one night as she teased my unruly brown hair with her fingers. This 'fro is out of control."

Hazel had come through that night with a navy blue turtle-neck with flared sleeves and black jeans and ankle boots.

"Maybe I will. It just seems like it would be forever. I'd have to shave my head if I ever wanted to get rid of them. And bald just ain't my style!" I laughed as I stood and checked my-self out in the bedroom mirror. "I don't know why I get like this; it isn't like Tree hasn't seen me wear a zillion horrible things before now."

"As if Tree would care!"

"You're right, he probably wouldn't."

"Where are you guys going tonight?"

"Probably downtown Cleveland, to the Flats. He wants to hear some live music."

"But tell the truth," Hazel said, her hands in my hair again and making me turn my head back and forth. "You don't care what you're listening to as long as they include sweet nothings from Tree!" She stuck her tongue out like she would stick it in my ear.

"Ugh! Cut it out!" I pushed her away, but I was laughing. I didn't hear Ella come in.

"Can't you girls manage to put together one ladylike moment between the two of you? And Hazel, you better not be handing out my clothes."

"These are not your clothes," I stated.

"Well, not technically, anyway." I shot Hazel a look and she shrugged. "She didn't pack them! I consider that fair game."

"I'm sorry, Ella"

"Quite all right. In this case, the clothes do not make the woman."

"Gee, who pulled your hair too tight this morning?"

"Going out on the town tonight, are we?"

"Uh, oh, I see where this is headed."

"You are not all that!" Ella was sticking a pointy manicured fingertip into my chest and I was thinking that if she didn't quit, I'd pull her little fake nails off myself.

"I never said I was. Nobody did. Neither did Tree. Besides, Ella, do you have to have all the guys?"

"Be patient," Hazel chimed in. "Maybe he's making his way through the family. We just have to wait our turn!"

Then we were laughing, laughing so hard I had to go to the

bathroom. So did Ella and Hazel. We ran down the hall, knocking each other down to get there.

And Daddy yelled at us, too. His voice came booming from the living room, "What you girls doing back there? Tearing up the house?"

We answered in concert, "No, sir!"

But of course, in our own way, we were.

The next eighteen months or so with Tree I grew into this feeling of being a real woman. I felt it so much I wanted to scream—a terrific raw, throat-cleansing scream that would let the world know—this is truly the sound of happiness. It would outgrow the house. Linc's house. There were times when I spent more nights with Tree than at Linc's and I was glad I was in a position where my parents didn't have to know about it. My real life—this was the distraction. So I wasn't looking. I wasn't watching. Children can slip away, be taken when you aren't watching. Adults can too. I know that now.

The beginning of my senior year at Belden my brother bought a new house in a new neighborhood, Oberlin Hills. It is this place I still see in my dreams, and in those dreams the road to Linc's house is connected to my Harlem home and I can see my brother and transverse five hundred miles in just a few blocks' steps. As though we were still that close, as though we were still that connected. It is a place of class, with street names such as Red Hill Drive, Amherst Terrace, and Wellington Avenue, which was Linc's. The lawns in this neighborhood are large and rolling, cut unlike most developments with postage-stamp yards and weakling trees. The trees here reached up over the rooftops, left untouched because of some thoughtful builder's foresight.

Daddy had been so proud of him, so amazed at himself for even getting to be in such a house. He said the Lord blessed him in that. They even stayed a few days, at Linc's insistence, and it was cool to be in a house with all of us, that fit all of us. Daddy was also impressed that Linc would be keeping the old house and using it for rental income.

I remember driving through Oberlin Hills with Linc and him teasing me, unwilling to say outright which house he had bought. We cruised through the neighborhood at twenty-five miles per hour, the magical speed limit, the one that assured all would be safe and well if everyone came to full stops and moved their cars this slowly.

"What do you think of that one?" Linc asked, pointing out a house with smooth white round columns and white aluminum siding.

"It's nice, I guess," I replied, just in case that was the one. I hoped hard he hadn't purchased that monstrosity. "It's a little sterile."

But Linc drove on, under shady elms and past rows of manicured roses. Every garage had a basketball hoop in the driveway. Every door had a rustic wreath greeting visitors. "There's a beauty," he said. We slowed in front of a fancy split-level painted burgundy with black shutters and a blue-gray door.

"Yeah, that's kind of cool," I offered.

We pulled up in front of a Tudor-style house. It was big but understated, not needing to make its presence known like its gaudier neighbors. It looked like an English cottage, charming in its curves and flowerbeds. It looked like it should have been in the woods, tucked away in some faraway fairy tale. I actually knew this house, the outside anyway, very well. When I ran cross-country in high school our three-mile training route went through this neighborhood. My coach, Mr. Nicholoff, would drive up behind me, scolding me for lagging behind mid-run. In fact the houses, this one in particular, had distracted me. Even though it was no great size, it seemed a mansion to me. It was my Manderly, my Thornfield Hall.

"This is a dream house," I told Linc, with a touch of sadness. "It's gorgeous. The only people who get to live in a house like that are people we'll never know."

"That's not true," Linc said smiling, very pleased with himself. "We live here."

My mouth dropped open so far I thought my jaw would hit the sidewalk. "No! You do not!"

"Yes I do. And now so do you."

I stared at Linc and I could feel a new awe for him being born inside me, bright and childlike. At that moment he glowed like an icon to me, one that had reached into my dreams, old dreams I had long ago put away, and pulled out something I didn't even know I had wanted. "But . . . how? Why?"

"It's my kind of house, don't you think?" Linc turned the car into the drive and parked it in front of the two-car garage with the door painted brown to match the house's rustic coloring.

"I don't know what your kind of house is," I said, jumping out before he shut off the engine. Then, half-whispering to myself, "I know it's always been mine."

Inside the house was in move-in condition: no awkward color schemes or grimy carpeting to pull up. In fact some of it, like the kitchen with its sparkling marble counters, polished wood cabinets, and island cooktop, looked newly renovated. There were four bedrooms upstairs of generous size and a separate dining room. At Daddy's and Linc's old house we'd always eaten in the kitchen.

But the room Linc was eager to show me, the one that would come to mean the most to him, was the finished basement. It wasn't dark and dank like other cellar rooms. It was carpeted, with recessed lights and its own bathroom and shower. As the house took shape it became Linc's recreational room, his personal haven. He furnished it into a plush den with a huge black leather sectional sofa that could seat at least eight people, and a lush recliner covered in black corduroy. There were mirrored tiles on the walls and lamps that were always turned low.

The routine began some months after we moved in. On the weekends Linc and Tick and their friends would disappear downstairs into this room, never to be seen again by the clear-eyed world. Everything else about our lives was the same except for these parties. I never hung with Linc and his friends. The room was perpetually filled with smoke and the men liked to tease me with jokes I didn't understand. They were more interested in sports than my latest math class. Besides, I was often out with Tree, who by then had graduated from Belden and was teaching history at Milton High School, one county over in Erie.

Linc's friends would come in twos or threes or, at times, trickling in one by one. He would greet them, but once he had stowed himself downstairs, Chandra or I had to answer the door for the stragglers. On one night I opened the door wide for Tick so I could stand back as far as I could. The smell of alcohol on him was so strong it hit me just as I turned the handle on the door. "Good evening, good evening!" he said. "Will the lovely Miss Crita be partying with us on this fine, fine night?"

"I don't think so." I opened the basement door for him and the sound of James Brown strutted up the stairs. "I'm going out tonight."

He eyed my low-cut sweater and leaned forward. "You look so good, maybe I should be going with you."

I stared at him, speechless, but Chandra came into the kitchen to fill Savannah's juice cup.

"Tick, you better get your smelly butt down those stairs and out of my kitchen," she said, opening the refrigerator. "Leave Crita alone, or Linc will kick your butt down there for you."

He nodded slowly. "Right on, sister," he drawled before descending the steps.

"Thanks for the save," I said, sitting down at the table. "Tick's always trying to put the moves on somebody. I just wish I wasn't so tongue-tied when he does it to me."

"It's not your fault, honey." She poured apple juice into Savannah's big Winnie-the-Pooh cup. "His momma should have taught him better than that."

"Awwww!" A roar of disappointment swept up the stairs and through the basement door.

"What are they watching?"

"Some dumb college football game," Chandra replied. "I don't know who."

She went back to Savannah and I sat listening for Tree's car in the drive. A cheer, then the sound of palms high-fiving erupted from below. Linc would sleep until noon the next day, at least. But he was happy—happy to be at home and, I assumed, happy in his work. Since we'd moved to Oberlin Hills Linc seemed more relaxed. The haunted look I'd seen in his eyes after Savannah's birth receded. He'd hit his stride, it seemed, and things were coming easy to him again.

"Crita! Hey Crita!" Linc's voice leapt over the crowd noise to reach me in the kitchen. I responded with my presence, walking downstairs just far enough so I could see him by sticking my head down over the stair rail.

"Yeah, Linc, what's up?"

Back then I marked those times by what I saw when I looked in Linc's eyes. That night they were red watery balls of jelly that made his face look soft and affectionate. "Crita, sis, we're staaaarving! Will you pleeease fry up some of that chicken you do so well?" My heart fluttered, wanting immediately to feed him. I looked at my watch. No time for chicken, but maybe there were leftovers I could throw together. Then I heard Tree blowing his car horn outside.

"I'm sorry, Linc, I can't. Tree's outside waiting for me."

"Aw, man, you're cold!" he teased.

"I'll cook for you another time, I promise." I rushed up the stairs and out to Tree.

Outside, as I scrambled into Tree's car, I smiled but couldn't unknit the tiny knot of frown on my forehead.

"What's wrong?" Tree asked, kissing me lightly on the lips.

"Nothing. Linc just asked me to cook him some food, but I had to go."

"Okay, no biggie," he said, touching the palm of his hand to my forehead. "So why are you frowning?"

"I guess I just wished I could have done it for him."

There were other opportunities to cook for Linc. In fact, they increased in the ensuing months. The little parties that once happened only on the weekends began to bleed into the week. First for *Monday Night Football,* then weeknight NBA games. Sometimes Linc and his friends were still up and partying long after Chandra, Savannah, and I had gone to bed.

Frying chicken for him, I would powder the meat in flour that I had seasoned, just as Mama had taught me, with salt and black and red pepper until I could smell the spices. He lingered nearby, leaning against the kitchen counter and already drinking his second beer.

"Linc, you should try to make an early night of it tonight. Stop that!" I playfully slapped his hand as he swiped a drumstick from the chicken I had draining in a bowl of paper towels.

"What makes you say that?"

"I say that because you need to get some sleep. You'll make yourself sick staying up as late as you do. I'm not the only one. I know Chandra's probably already said something to you."

"Yeah, she did," he said, wiping his greasy fingers on his

jeans. "But as long as I get up and go to work, there's no problem. And my boys have been helping me with that."

"What are you talking about?"

"You know, they help me be up when I need to be up."

"Right," I said slowly, not sure if I wanted to hear any more. "Like I said, Linc, try to make it an early night, okay?"

"Okay, sis," he said, planting a sloppy kiss on my cheek as the doorbell rang. "Gotta go."

This scene, of me and Linc in the kitchen alone and joking around, began to repeat itself. Sometimes it varied when Linc sat at the table feeding Savannah or reading to her. But those variations occurred less frequently until one night I finally raised my head from the cloud of flour to wonder where Chandra was in these parts of the early evening. I assumed she was studying or reading to Savannah. One night I caught a glimpse of her going upstairs to her room and found a look I interpreted as disgust written across her face. If she came down later, after Linc's friends were all downstairs and the door closed, she would be quiet or stingy with her words. I felt as though she and I were tiptoeing around each other.

One day I came home from school to find Chandra sitting on the sofa, her legs and arms crossed, staring blankly into the space in front of her.

"Hey," I said in greeting and was headed for my room to dump my books before she stopped me.

"Crita, could you come sit with me a minute, please?" she said. Her tone made me nervous. She sounded like a principal, or one of my elementary school teachers, calling me into the office for discipline. I sat down next to her, putting my bag and coat down on the floor in front of me.

"Honey, would you mind not helping out so much when Linc's friends are here?" she said, not looking at me.

"It's all right, Chandra, I don't mind. I know you have a

lot of studying to do and you're tired from taking care of Savannah."

"That's not what I'm talking about. Linc knows I don't like them being in the house and I don't want to encourage them."

"It's no big deal. Linc will get tired of them after a while." I laughed. "He'll figure out he's not Superman. He's gotta sleep sometime."

But Chandra remained stiff and resolute. "I already told him I refuse to clean up down there anymore. The place is a pigsty. I won't put up with it."

"Don't worry, Chandra, I'll do it."

"Crita, don't argue with me, please," she said, getting up and leaving the room. "Just do as I say."

I sat there some minutes, my mind registering only the ticking of Chandra's mother's clock on the mantel. I didn't understand what was going on. But before too long the sting of Chandra's scolding faded and I shot up from the couch, went into the kitchen, and pulled a garbage bag from its box underneath the sink. Then I stepped downstairs into Linc's basement.

There was no air in the room. I pried open the small rectangular windows that lined one wall and flipped on the ceiling fan. It circulated dust and stale odors of beer, pizza, and marijuana before capturing a breath of fresh air from the outside. When I felt I could breathe I started my work, emptying half-finished bottles and glasses in the bathroom sink and bagging the soiled pizza boxes, newspapers, and potato chip bags. A forgotten jar of salsa, left open, had a furry ring of mold forming around its rim.

I found the mirrors on the coffee table, underneath some papers. There were two of them, each rectangular and about a foot long, standing on half-inch nubs. They were placed on either end of the table. A white residue stuck to the surfaces of each glass. I held my breath for ten seconds, not sure why I was doing so. Then I dropped my garbage bag, picked up the mirrors, and scrubbed them off in the sink with bar soap and a washcloth. I dried and buffed them with a towel until they sparkled. I separated them, placing one on the end table near the sectional and the other on the bookshelf near the wide-screen television. They looked innocuous enough that way. Chandra wouldn't think they were anything other than deco-ration. In fact, I secretly prayed they were accessories she had bought herself, but that was a long shot. I had shopped with her for most of the items in the house and I had never seen these mirrors before.

I stood in the room and surveyed it again, slowly this time, my eyes now adjusted to seek signs of trouble. That's when I saw the little plastic packet, empty and flat, peeking out from under the sectional. I got down on my knees and pulled it out, then ran my hand underneath the furniture to see if there were more. I found two others. Each packet had the same white residue caked inside its corners.

I threw them away, careful to put them in the bag's very bottom. Then I stood there, unsure of what to do next, but sure that I had to do something to keep myself moving so my brain wouldn't have the chance to ask the questions that were now shooting through its circuitry. I didn't want to face so many questions when I knew I had no answers.

I heard a door close upstairs. "Hey-ho! Anybody home?"

"Tree!" I called up to him. "I'm down here."

I gathered up my garbage bag and met him at the foot of the stairs. "Chandra's upstairs. But that's good because I have to show you something." I dug out the packets for him to see and pointed out the mirrors on the shelf and table. "I couldn't believe it. It's like something out of a movie. The only thing I didn't find was rolled-up dollar bills. I don't know how they're snorting the stuff, but obviously it's Linc's friends and he has to do something about it."

Tree sat down on the ottoman and stuffed his hands in his

jacket pockets. "Crita, what makes you think Linc isn't doing coke with his friends?"

"Because!" I said with a little laugh, "Linc doesn't do that kind of thing. I'm sure he smokes weed or something like that, but he wouldn't do coke."

"So where did those mirrors come from?"

"I don't know. One of those guys brought them here. Probably Tick with his silly self."

"And Linc would just sit back and let his homeys do drugs in his house?"

"Well, he shouldn't be doing that. But I'll talk to him about it. Chandra is already on edge and if she finds out about this she'll totally freak."

"If Chandra's edgy, I'm willing to bet she's already on to him."

"I doubt it, but if I throw this stuff away she won't have to know."

"Crita," Tree took my arm as I was closing up the garbage bag. "You don't think my sister has a right to know if her husband is doing drugs in her house?"

I pulled my arm away and held Tree firmly with my eyes. "There's nothing to know yet," I said calmly, slowly. "There's nothing to tell her. Please Tree, let me handle this. Let me talk to Linc first."

"This isn't right. You know this isn't right."

"It will be. For now it has to be." I walked away from him, taking my bag upstairs and into the garage. I stuffed it into a green plastic garbage can and fastened the lid, resolving to find some time alone so I could talk to my brother.

I waited two whole days. They were quiet ones, with no parties. I wondered whether Linc was already tired of them, in which case there would be no reason to bring up the drugs, or whether he simply felt guilty that I had to clean up his mess. Either way, I saw signs that our lives could be normal again and in a world where I didn't have to ask Linc about drugs. But Tree was on my mind and I knew he would be angry if I backed away from my resolution.

I found my chance on a Saturday morning. Linc and I were raking leaves in the backyard. Our progress was slow because I stayed nearby, sometimes raking areas he'd already raked because I wanted to be close and within conversational earshot when I got up the nerve to speak to him. But he surprised me by giving me an opening.

"Hey, thanks for cleaning up the basement for me. I know Chandra was getting pretty pissed about it."

"Yeah, she sort of let me know that. You're welcome." A moment almost slipped by, but I seized it. "Linc, I threw away some packets I found in there. They looked like they had cocaine in them."

Linc paused and looked up at me. "Oh yeah," he said, making a wan attempt at embarrassed laughter. "Those guys make a mess, don't they?"

"So they weren't yours?"

"Nah, Crita! How can you even ask me that? I smoke a little weed every now and then, but that's it." He started raking again. "Now Tick and some of those other guys . . . they're a different story."

"Well, that's okay," I said, relieved and surprised by how light I suddenly felt. "But Chandra won't stand for that stuff being in the house, Linc. You've gotta put your foot down with those assholes."

"Now don't you worry, little sis. I know how to handle my buddies."

"Cool." I smiled at him.

"Hey, but thanks for covering for me. I mean, with Chandra and all. It would've been a whole different thing if she had found those packets."

"That's why I was so careful."

He laughed. "And that's what you do best."

Seventeen

I wasn't careful. Not really, not as I should have been. I should have been more like my father who, smelling the scent of danger in the air, would no longer trust such air, even if the tang seemed to dissipate after a while. I would have noticed that Daddy began to look at Linc differently, with an oblique, inquisitive stare with one eyebrow partially raised. He looked like a dog that had sniffed something out of the ordinary, but the warning, the message that the scent delivered, fell just outside the range of his understanding, so he didn't know what to make of it.

I trusted the surfaces of things. And on the surface I believed things were clear, wiped smooth, just as I had done with the mirrors in Linc's basement. It all happened so fast. I didn't know a person could slip out of a life so easily, like one slipped out of a shirt. I used to think during that time that I had been distracted by routine, the way our lives moved on in brisk, industrious fashion with my growing love for Tree casting a luxurious pink-colored hue over all. But what I'd really done was wrap our lives into a perfect plasticine bubble, and conveyed this world and its precarious existence into my brother's hands. I trusted him that much.

The signs that some tension was stressing the walls of the

bubble must have reached me at some point, must have brushed against my skin when the indentation intruded. The fact that I missed it then makes me hypersensitive now. If someone bumps into me on a crowded subway train I try to see if the assault is an indication that my sky is falling.

So I was unprepared, woefully so, when I came home one evening to find a mad energy zipping about the living room. My head swung about, bewildered by the noise, sharp and painful, that went shooting through my being. When my senses had adjusted to the atmosphere I realized what I was hearing: the sound of Linc and Chandra arguing.

Chandra was hot, her face blotched with rage and her eyes big and unrecognizable. Linc had drawn himself up large and defiant, his voice deep and Daddylike, as he pointed fingers at Chandra, himself, and some invisible entity on the outside of his house.

"WHO IS PAYING THE BILLS AROUND HERE?! AN-SWER ME THAT, HUH? ANSWER ME THAT!"

"YEAH, YOU'D BE PAYING THE BILL AT THE GOD-DAMN RITZ HOTEL AND THEY'D STILL KICK YOUR ASS OUT IF THEY FOUND OUT YOU WERE DOING LINES!"

"WOMAN, WHO DO YOU THINK YOU ARE?"

"I'M THE ONE WHO'D HAVE TO TAKE OUR CHILD TO THE EMERGENCY ROOM AND WATCH HER DIE JUST BECAUSE SHE ATE SOME DAMN COCAINE THAT YOU LEFT LYING AROUND IN OUR BEDROOM!"

They paused and in looking around the room in search of energy for their next burst they saw me standing there in the doorway.

"Shall I tell her?" Chandra challenged. "Does she deserve to know her precious brother loves getting high at home?"

Linc looked at me and said nothing, and I returned the glance with a face that pleaded with him to tell Chandra the truth. She nodded toward a bag, the kind you'd pack a sandwich in, wrapped with a green rubber band and filled with about a quarter cup of white powder.

"I found that on the floor of our bedroom this morning," Chandra said, folding her arms. "It must have fallen out of his jacket pocket when he left for work."

My eyes prodded Linc again and when he still failed to move or speak I pushed myself forward. "Chandra, come on," I said, trying to sound soothing. "You know that stuff isn't Linc's. He doesn't do that, he told me himself. It probably belongs to one of those idiot friends of his."

Chandra shot me a glance so deadly I felt a wash of acid rocket through my stomach.

"Girl, if you're going to be *that* stupid, then GET OUT OF MY HOUSE! There's enough stupidity going on here as it is!"

I didn't hear what came next. I think it was Linc's voice, but I don't know what he was saying, only that it was supersonic loud and my ears, heart, and brain hurt too much to grasp the sound. I was running, running out of the room and up the stairs, away from the field where I'd so miserably performed. I had just reached my room when I heard, filtered through her door, Savannah crying in tiny mewlish sounds. I went in and found her sitting on the carpet, a coloring book in front of her and crayons scattered on the floor. I sat down next to her and picked her up in my arms, her curly brown hair tickling the skin underneath my jaw. When her breathing quieted and her tears subsided she looked up at me.

"Mommy's mad, isn't she?" Savannah inquired. I nodded. "And Daddy, too?"

"Yes, he's mad, too."

"Is it bad?" Her brown eyes widened.

"No," I lied, holding her close to my chest. "Everything's going to be all right. Savannah, why don't I help you finish coloring your pictures, okay?"

I put a Barney tape into Savannah's toy cassette player and we listened and sang as we filled in the browns, blues, and purples of a princess and her horse. In a while I noticed Savannah's head nodding over the paper and the crayon falling slack in her hand. I put her to bed, all the time listening for voices downstairs.

I heard nothing. When I went to investigate I discovered Chandra sitting alone at the kitchen table with her head down in her arms. The quiet stung my ears.

"Chandra," I whispered, afraid to break the silence. "Where's Linc?"

She sighed heavily. "He's gone out," she said, lifting her head and attempting to focus on me. "I told him if he wanted to do that stuff, he'd have to do it elsewhere. I won't have it in the house anymore. I have Savannah to think about."

Before I could respond the phone rang. Chandra moved as though she'd just eaten a bag of rocks, sliding herself out of her chair and lifting her weighted body. She picked up the receiver and spoke a few short "mm-hmm's" and a "Yes, Momma" before I realized she was talking to her mother, Mrs. Templeton.

"I did it. Just like you said I should."

Chandra turned away from me and lowered her voice so I couldn't hear. I sat down at the table and waited. In a few minutes she hung up the phone.

"My mother says in times like this you have to make him aware of his choices. This will get worse before it gets better, but Linc has to be aware of how many times he doesn't choose me and Savannah."

I didn't say anything. I looked at my hands in front of me on the table and laced my fingers together. Chandra continued.

"When Tree and I were babies, our daddy used to take a lot of pills, drop acid, stuff like that. He scared the shit out of my mother. She fought him for so long."

"What happened?"

"She left him. She said she left because he was more inter-ested in the drugs than us. But one of my aunts told me later what really happened. How he went crazy one day and nearly strangled her to death. She left and my granddaddy supported us for I don't know how long."

"Chandra," I said quietly, but determined to take advantage of this soft spot in her. "Do you think it's a good idea to push Linc out of the house? At least downstairs in the basement, you know where he is. He's at home. You can keep an eye on things and make him stop. If he starts hanging out in the streets, you won't be able to do anything."

She put her head down on the table again and as her voice faded I could tell I was disappearing to her. "This is my house," she said, barely audible. "And I have to do what's right."

Yeah, right for you, I thought to myself. *But what about Linc?*

That evening I got into my Jeep and drove, slamming the car into gear with each shift and yanking on the gearshift as though I would pull it out of the floor. If I had known where to find Linc I would have sought him out. Part of me must have tried, because I zigzagged aimlessly up and down the local streets trying to pick out Linc's car in a driveway or the parking lot of an apartment building. I finally came to a highway and I revved the Jeep up into fifth and pushed my foot on the gas. It felt good to put my weight onto a solid object and I let the car speed along for about ten miles before I coasted the car back down to the speed limit.

In another two miles I knew where I was going. To see Tree. He must have told Chandra something; this all had to be his fault. Anger steamed underneath my skin and I had to swing my arms, yell, do something to keep it from burning me to nothing but red ashes. This was the heat to which Tree opened his door, which poured into his apartment and started beating him about the chest as I proclaimed him a cheating, lying bastard.

I don't know how he did it—how he took hold of me, that is, I have no freakin' idea. I just know that all of a sudden he had me enclosed in the steel bands of his biceps and my steam had turned to tears and I was crying. He held me while I cried and after a while he whispered in my ear, "I didn't tell Chandra anything." But I already knew that, of course I did, and I told him so. It wasn't his fault Chandra had found the cocaine.

"Oh," I sighed heavy and long, "I know, I know. I'm sorry."

"But you are angry. Why don't you tell me what you're really mad about."

I sighed again and tried to control my crying. "I hate this being caught in the middle," I hiccuped between my sobs.

"Then don't be."

"You don't understand." I pulled away a little so I could look into his leonine eyes. "I have to help him. He's my brother and I love him. This is as much about me as it is about him."

"Okay, baby, you're gonna have to learn to leave this alone. Starting here, starting now."

I stared at him blankly. How could I explain that I would not run and leave behind a brother who would not leave me behind to a bear? I could only muster, "This is what I do best."

"Come on, Crita. You can only do so much for Linc. He's gonna have to do the heavy lifting with this shit. All you can do is pray he's strong enough."

I sniffed and smeared the tears from my face with the palm of my hands. "I can do a lot more than that." I broke away from his arms and headed for the door. "A helluva lot more."

By midnight I was back at Linc and Chandra's. Linc's car wasn't in the driveway and the house was dark. I slipped in, made myself a cup of tea, and sat up in the living room to wait for Linc. By 2 A.M. I was awake from the caffeine, but my brain, tired and numb from the evening's workings, felt heavy in my head. Linc still had not come home. I wanted to lie down on the couch, but I knew the moment I did I would be senseless.

In another hour I couldn't resist the soft cushions any longer. I stretched out on the sofa and fell fast asleep. In the morning Linc had already come home and left for work again. The next few days went the same way, as though Linc was still having his basement party, only elsewhere. We were lucky if we saw him at dinner. I stopped waiting up for him.

But one night when I was up finishing a paper, I heard Linc outside fumbling with his keys. I didn't get up to help him with the door. When he finally shuffled into the room he moved slowly, as though his muscles, now stiff, had been cut and shortened in the hours since I last saw him. His eyes, red and glassy, slid over the room without taking me in. I'm sure he would have gone on upstairs if I hadn't spoken to him.

"Linc, you lied to me."

He seemed surprised and searched the room again. "Crita! Damn, girl, where did you come from?"

"Linc, did you hear me? Why did you lie to me?"

"Uh-huh. Oh. Yeah." He shuffled over to the sofa and let his body fall back into it. He leaned his head back against it and didn't look at me. "I'm sorry."

"Do you realize what you did?" I hissed, not wanting to wake Chandra or Savannah. "You made me look stupid to Chandra. You knocked whatever respect she had for me and I don't know if I can look her straight in the face again."

He put his hands over his face and I could hear him beginning to cry.

"Linc, what are you doing? Cocaine? Are you crazy? How long have you been hooked on it?"

Suddenly Linc jerked his hands away from his eyes. "Who said I was hooked? Do I look like a junkie to you?"

"How am I supposed to answer that? Do I look like I would know what a junkie looks like?"

He sat up and wiped his eyes. "Look, I'm under a lot of pressure at work, okay? The job wipes me out. But I've got to keep pushing it, playing for that next step on the corporate ladder. How else can I keep my family properly if I don't?"

"Yeah, but Linc, what's the coke got to do with any of that?"

"When I hang with the guys is the only time I can unwind and feel good about myself. I can handle the stuff. I still go to work, I still get things done around the house." I didn't think it was a good time to point out how neglected Chandra felt. I figured she would tell him that herself.

"So is this how it's going to go? You staying out until all hours of the night? Driving home in this condition? I give your butt a few more days before you get picked up for driving under the influence."

"Yeah, well, maybe you should police me."

"Somebody should police your dumb ass."

Suddenly Linc looked dead at me like he was honing in on a target. He sat up and leaned toward me.

"You can do that."

"What?"

"You can do that, Crita, you can police me. What I need is damage control and you can do that better than anybody." He laughed and leaned back against the sofa again. "Why didn't I think of this before?"

"Because it's crazy, Linc. And it's stupid. And I don't have time to follow you all over town in places where I don't want to go."

"Crita," he went on eagerly, "you don't have to! Here's what we'll do. If I need to go out, then I'll go out. Go right after work. But I don't have to stay out that late, I'll get my kicks in a couple of hours and then I'll call you. I'll tell you where I am and you'll come and pick me up."

"I can't believe you're serious about this."

"I'm dead serious, little sis. You've got to give me a hand here."

"Linc, wouldn't it be easier for you to just chill out until Chandra calms down?"

"Crita, let's just try this a couple of times, okay? If it doesn't work or if it's too hard for you, I'll figure out something else. Come on, do this for me. Please."

I sighed and couldn't think of a good enough excuse to deny him. Maybe I should have tried harder. "Okay."

I had no belief whatsoever that Linc's plan was going to work, but then it seemed to do just that. It didn't start right away. I think Linc wanted to burnish his image with Chandra, let her see how he was polishing up his act. The first night he didn't come home after work I stayed in my room trying to concentrate on math, but the whole time I was staring at the phone. I wanted to be the one to pick it up when it rang. Chandra's voice might somehow scare or discourage Linc.

When the phone did ring, I snatched it up from my desk. It was 8 P.M.

"Okay, little sis, you're on." Linc's voice sounded blurry. "I'm at a phone booth on the corner of West Eighteenth and Broadway."

"I'll be right there."

I sped out of the house without saying a word to Chandra. What if Linc wasn't there when I arrived? It was better to say as little as possible.

He was there and his eyes were bright and not glassy. He slid into the Jeep and said in a deep, high-falutin voice, "Home, James!" I took him home. He kissed his wife. Chandra looked a little confused and wary, but said nothing. I figured that meant this was okay. The next morning I drove Linc out to pick up his car and he went to work.

Once again I was lulled by routine. I allowed it to happen; part of me actually felt good about policing Linc. I was helping my brother, I was in control. There was a buzz, so small, but evident, in my driving to his rescue. It required all of my being, all of my concentration, the very best of myself. But, sadly, I had no room in this new world for Tree. Sometimes I wouldn't see him unless I was certain my brother was home for the night. And it was difficult to be certain. I stepped away from Tree in tiny stealing steps, hoping he wouldn't notice.

He did notice. He corralled me one day on campus after one of my classes, falling into step with me and walking me toward a stone bench in a quiet corner of the yard.

"What's going on with us, Crita?" He sat down and pulled me next to him. "I've barely seen you in weeks. I have to call my sister to find out where you are."

"I know, I'm sorry. There's been a lot going on with Linc, you know?"

"Yeah, I know. What's that got to do with you?"

"I'm sort of helping him. He's going through a tough time."

"That's what my sister is supposed to be there for."

"I know, but she gets really mad at him sometimes. I'm just helping him stay straight up with her. I make sure he's around when he's supposed to be around."

"Come on, Crita, what are you talking about? All that stuff is none of your business! Chandra is my sister and you don't see me all up in there checking out what Linc is doing with her."

"Yeah, well, maybe you should. That's what siblings do, they look out for each other. I'm just being a good sister to Linc, especially since I'm fortunate enough to be in a position to help him."

"At what cost? When do you have time for yourself, for us? What am I supposed to do, wait around until whatever is happening between them is over?"

"You're supposed to understand that family comes first. That's the way it is, that's the way our daddy brought us up. We take care of each other. Maybe you don't know anything about that."

"No, Crita, I don't know anything about it. Not like you do."

I looked at him and felt a nervous thrill begin to circulate through my body. If he was asking me to choose, I had to let him know there would be no way I'd choose him over my brother. He should know that, I thought. I didn't understand why he was giving me such a hassle, but I did know I wouldn't put up with it.

Then suddenly he had me in his arms, he ran his hands over the twisted strands of hair, just beginning to lock. I had begun twisting it, almost absentmindedly, as I read my homework and waited for Linc to call.

"Crita, what can I do for you?"

The question was so strange, so unexpected. It made me feel naked—not physically, as if I could be—but naked in my soul. And I hated that. I could feel myself forming a darkness and throwing it over my heart like a shroud so Tree wouldn't see. See what? I didn't want to think about it.

"For me?" I responded. "You don't have to do anything for me. I'm fine."

"Then let me do something for me. Wait, let me put it this way—let me do something for us."

I shrugged. "Well, okay. Whatever."

"For the next two hours, we're not going to mention Linc or Chandra."

"Why not?" He placed a finger to my lips to silence me.

"Because there is more to the world—our world—than them. Tell me what you did in class today. Or look . . ." He stood up and reached into the branches of the crabapple tree hanging over us and pulled a twig covered in fat pink blossoms toward me. "Look, Crita, it's spring. Let's talk about that. Walk with me, let's look at the sky." He pulled at my arms until I stood with him.

"Tree, I can't."

He shook his head. "No, don't say that to me."

Then he was behind me, his hands on my shoulders and kneading his fingers into muscles that I knew to him would feel like stone. "Okay," I said, thinking he would move his hands elsewhere, but he didn't.

"Jesus, Crita."

I was silent.

"What the hell have you been carrying around? I'd bet you any money even Atlas didn't have shoulders this tight."

"Okay," I said again. This time I turned around and took hold of his hands. "I give in. Take me for a walk, take me anywhere."

He smiled at last. "Come on."

We started walking through the yards and for the first time in I don't know how long I became aware of the people around me. Guys who knew Tree when he was at Belden called out to us. Someone from my economics class came up and nudged my shoulder and grimaced.

"That quiz today sucked, right?" I don't remember her name, but she was dressed in the same navy blue sweatpants she had worn to class that morning and her blonde hair was pulled back in a tight ponytail. She seemed to be carrying the same paper cup of coffee as well, but I'm sure this was a refill.

"I know, didn't it, though? And it's not even two weeks before finals!"

"Who dropped a quiz on your butts?" Tree wanted to know. He was teaching now himself, and I was sure he loved being on the other end of such assignments.

"Professor Laibson. Blew us all out of the water, but he really got us. Everyone was thinking he was all cool, because he's not that old, you know?"

"Yeah, but you guys weren't giving the dude his props, were you? You gotta respect him now."

"You're right about that. But I would have been much happier about learning to respect him if he had made his point earlier in the year."

Tree laughed. "I don't know how you do that numbers thing anyway. I've never been a math guy."

"Leave the numbers to me," I said. I loved them. They were clean, they were clear. Numbers didn't hurt and they didn't lie.

"Wait, here are numbers I understand." We had come upon the athletic field and its baseball diamonds. One of them was occupied, a pickup softball game. "See? One, two, three strikes you're out! Those are the only numbers that matter here. I can count that high!"

We stood there watching the handful of guys and about two women standing in the grass and chasing balls in the late April sun. The dust kicked up in the infield floated in the light and made the air seem to glow.

"Templeton!" Someone yelled at Tree. "Grab a glove, man, can't you see we need some help out here?"

Tree took my bag and tossed it into the bleachers and in another moment he shoved a frayed leather mitt into my hands. "Let's go, Crita, you heard the man!"

"Tree, no!" I hadn't caught a ball since high-school phys ed class and I wasn't that good at it then.

"Come on, what's there to be afraid of? It's not like there's a championship at stake—only general embarrassment."

"Gee, that helps. Thanks a lot." But I was trotting out on the field after him, giving a quick smile and a wave to the people already there.

They threw the ball around in quick succession before re-

turning it to the pitcher. When it came to me I held the glove
out in front of me, more for protection than to catch the damn
ball, but that's what did happen: it burrowed right into the
hollow of the glove and I felt the sting of the contact at the
base of my fingers.

I batted before Tree, and though it was just a grounder, skit-
ting along between the first and second basemen, it was enough
to get me on base because I was fast enough to beat the throw.
Then Tree, of course, hit a home run. He came right up on
me on the bases and I screamed because I thought he'd run
right over me with his long legs. We high-fived everyone at
home plate. I was laughing. I remember Tree hugging me.
"Uh-huh, I knew she was around here someplace."

"Who?"

"This girl. Big smile. Lots of teeth. Fearless. I knew she was
around here somewhere. My girl."

Standing out in the field again, I found myself watching
everything. I stepped out of the scene like that, like I had taken
off some clothing. I watched the second baseman reach his left
arm up, long and straight, so that his whole body stretched out.
He caught the ball. I was remembering Linc stretching out the
same way in our front yard, reaching out for a ball one of his
high-school friends had tossed him. The throw was too high.
Linc had reached but the ball floated just beyond his fingertips
and crashed through the living-room window. I remember the
look on his face. I remember Daddy's face when he got home.
I thought the yelling would never end. I turned and looked at
Tree. "I gotta go." I walked back toward the bleachers. "Thank
you for this, but I gotta go."

It began with Chandra standing in the kitchen, a puzzled look
on her face and her purse on the counter.

"What's wrong?"

She looked at me like she was looking through a fog. "Oh, nothing, Crita, I'm just trying to remember what I did with the money I took out of the ATM yesterday. I know I didn't spend it all. Maybe I left it in my other jacket."

She went upstairs and I waited and stared at the empty purse as though it would tell me its secret. When Chandra returned I could tell by the darkness swept over her face that we were thinking the same thing. But she picked up her bag and left the house in silence. That night after I had gone to bed I could hear Linc and Chandra in their room whispering and hissing at each other, arguing as quietly as they could.

As the weather got warmer, Linc began staying out later and later. There were times when I sat at my desk trying to do homework and fighting sleep, waiting for his call. He began to lose touch with the future. He had to be in the present, firmly planted in the moment, and that was all that mattered. I couldn't discuss a date just three weeks away with him. "I can't think about that now," he would say. "Touch base with me later." Linc was no longer bright-eyed when I picked him up. He was sluggish, a string of saliva suspended from the corner of his mouth. Slowly my brother was starting to disgust me.

One night Linc's voice was barely recognizable as his thick tongue slurred out an address I didn't know. It was on the south side of town, where the houses were decrepit. The house where Linc was had a lopsided porch and peeling paint. I could see lights on inside, but the porch light was broken and I walked up to the door in darkness. I held my breath and went in.

The place stank of alcohol and stale incense. It was another dimension and I was in it, but not of it. I could tell because the people in the room didn't seem to register my presence. They shifted about dancing, but unaware of the music blaring from the speakers on the floor. The room was stifling with their body heat, and all the windows were closed.

I found Linc sitting on a dilapidated couch, a black woman with a greasy jheri curl on his lap. I put out my hand past the woman and tugged on Linc's arm. "Come on, Linc, it's time to go home." The woman looked at me like I was crazy and smacked my arm so hard it stung.

"Honey, you better get your ass out of here. This one's mine."

"Damn!" I backed off, rubbing my arm.

Linc looked up and smiled in recognition. "Hey, Pepper, it's just my sister. I gotta go home."

Pepper and I glared at each other as I followed Linc out. I wouldn't speak to him on the drive back.

A few weeks later Linc summoned me to another address in South Lorain. This one took me past empty storefronts with broken windows and newspaper blowing about in the street. Just at the end of West Twenty-eighth Street, where it veered off to the right and became Pearl Avenue, was a gray square building that looked like a gigantic concrete block dropped in the middle of a parking lot. A sign over the door had been spray painted over in black. Goldberg's Warehouse, it once said. Now "Sugar Hill Social Club" was scrawled out in crude letters with the street number 56 beneath it. This was the place. The only windows were covered in thick glass brick and didn't look like they could be opened. The front door seemed to be the only entrance. I gathered from the lot filled with cars (some had fluid women draped over them and men rubbing up against them) that the hall must be packed. I couldn't imagine the hellhole it would become if it caught fire.

Inside I felt many heads turn toward me and eyes scan my form. I couldn't see any faces. Most of the men, covered in leather or black coats, some emblazoned with the Raiders NFL logo, languished in packs along the walls and laid out on sofas, their eyes covered with dark sunglasses. Their chests and necks glowed with gold chains. Gold and diamond rings, encrusted thick with the stones, flickered on their hands.

"Hey, welcome to the joint." I thought I heard my name lost in the insistent rap rhythms and I turned and saw Tick smiling and mouthing words in my direction. His hair was freshly cut and his Van Dyck beard trimmed. His shiny blue shirt, rolled up at the sleeves, was stained with sweat. I put my hand on his arm and moved closer so I could hear. He breathed a stink of cigarettes and malt liquor into my ear.

"I said I sure am glad to see you, baby! We never get to hang, if you know what I mean!"

"Tick, where's Linc?" I shouted, ignoring his come-on. "I'm here to pick him up."

"I'm sure he's here somewhere. Let me show you around and we'll find him."

He clasped an arm around my waist and drew me into the bodies on the dance floor. I held myself stiffly, trying to keep my torso from touching his as we moved past the people.

"What you have here," Tick shouted in my ear, "are the real leaders of our community. These are the badasses, the homeys with the power. Shit, power ain't nothing but a pocketful of Benjamins."

"Of what?"

"Benjamins. You know, C-notes. Hundred-dollar bills."

As I looked around me I began to notice that although the men in the room, covered in logos and oversized clothes, looked like little boys who had never learned to update their wardrobes, their threads were all new and spotless. Their white sneakers gleamed. Some of the men still had tags hanging from their caps or the sleeves of their jackets. The women, though trashy in tight skirts and shorts, looked the same, decked out in expensive leather and diamonds, their hair in elaborate braids or weaves sewn into their hair.

"Your brother and I only hang with the best," Tick was saying. "The cream of the crop."

I shuddered. "Where does the money come from?" I already had an idea, but I wanted to hear Tick say it, to see if there would be any embarrassment or remorse in his answer.

His response was practically jubilant. "Girl, I know you ain't that dumb! They move the commerce that runs the machine! The toy of the white man's playground! Nose candy, smack, crack. They run it all, my sister!"

My head snapped toward Tick, then out toward the men draped over the room. I realized then that some of the flashes I thought were jewels were actually metal; in truth, weaponry: guns fierce and battle-ready. I no longer had to hold my body stiff. Fear raced through me and froze my limbs to the point where it seemed Tick was moving me about like a doll. What was Linc doing in this death trap, and why had he brought me into it?

Tick went on pointing out factions: the Comptons, the Raiders, the Niggaz, the Green Circle. He gave me names I didn't want to know: Boney-T, Sainted Ice, Daddy Big, and the Prince.

Suddenly, a man pushed past us, his eyes wild black marbles ricocheting about in his head. He didn't seem to know where he was going. Why else would he have run smack dab into the 350-pound wall of flesh that blocked his escape? The wall's big hands grabbed the man by the shoulders and carried him off. Two men grinning with gold teeth, one of them dressed in a purple suit, followed nonchalantly.

"Uh-huh," Tick said, nodding and laughing. "They finally caught Leroy's dumb ass. Dude owes them money big time."

My head soon filled up with an image of the man Tick had called Leroy, his body full of bloody holes lying in a ditch along Pearl Avenue. I had to get Linc out of there.

"Do you see Linc yet?" I yelled, tugging on Tick's shirt.

"Yeah, just over here. I think he's in this room."

He led me into a windowless space where Linc was dancing. The woman named Pepper had a thigh wrapped around his waist. I started to rush toward him, but Tick wouldn't let me go.

"Chill out, Crita, you just got here." Before I could say anything, his hands were on me. I was bewildered. I moved my hands as quickly as I could but when I had pried one of his hands off me another had taken hold.

"Stop it, get away," I said, not loud enough to be convincing. Tick pushed his face toward mine and clamped his mouth down over my lips. I cried out and stomped my heel into his foot and ground it into his toes.

"Fuckin' bitch!" he yelled. He leaned over his foot and when he came up he had a knife in his hand. I screamed and suddenly Linc was awake and at my side.

"Nigger, have you lost your mind? You pull a knife on my sister, what kind of shit is that?"

"Oh man, I'm sorry. I'm sorry. Shit makes you crazy, you know?"

I heard a ratcheting sound and swung myself around to find the man Tick had called Sainted Ice staring down Tick and my brother. Just peeking out the end of the overlong sleeve he held down at his side was the barrel of a gun. His voice was steady and calm.

"This here's my lair, man. I don't want no shit in here."

I moved toward Linc, my hand fluttering wildly at my side as I sought Linc's touch but I was unable to find it. Then, in a moment that nearly shorted out my brain because I could not comprehend it, I saw my brother moving toward the armed man. He embraced Sainted Ice in a large, chest-thumping hug.

"It's cool, man." Linc told him. "Hey, everything is cool."

Linc turned to Tick.

"Catch you later, man."

When he came to me at last my brother took my hand and

walked me back through the moving bodies again. I couldn't speak to him. Once we got outside in the cold night air I ran. I held Linc's hand tightly and pulled him through the rows of cars to my Jeep. I dove my shaking hands into my purse, struggling to come up with the keys.

"Come on, come on, come on," I spoke to myself, trying to calm down. To Linc I said, "It's okay, it's okay. I'll get us out of here."

"No, no, no, sis." He laughed and patted the side of my face. "It's all right, you go on home. I gotta check on my man, Tick, and make sure he's okay."

"What?? I'm sure he's *just fine*. If that guy loaded up and pumped a couple of bullets in his head, Tick would probably be *just fine*. Linc, he could have killed me."

"But he didn't. You know I wouldn't let anything happen to you." Linc held open my car door and prodded me into the car. "We're family. We protect each other."

I screeched out of the parking lot and stepped on the gas. I drove blindly, my face hot and flooded with tears. I knew I was safe when I saw our old high school again. I parked around back, by the football field. The loose part of the fence was still there and I slipped under it and ran underneath the bleachers where I vomited up my fear and disgust. The spasms kept rippling through my stomach and my insides heaved up its contents again and again until there was nothing left. And then I kept retching as though I could turn myself inside out with the effort. And why not? Anything would feel the hell better than this. The thought I had in my head was poison to me and it was past two in the morning before I could let myself think it and not feel the sickest I'd ever felt in my life: I couldn't live with Linc anymore.

Eighteen

After Forrest comes, he and Ella get a hotel room nearby. I am left to stay in the house with Linc and Mama. Hazel moves back to her apartment on campus, and sometimes sleeps in a recliner in Daddy's hospital room when she doesn't want to make the half-hour drive back to her place.

It all doesn't really matter anymore, though, because somewhere near the end of June, Linc's hospital schedule for Daddy breaks down. We can't help ourselves. Mama begins first, staying longer, coming earlier. We come back and forth as our hearts tug us in that direction. That's how Hazel and I end up coming to Daddy's room together one day. We have our arms around each other's waists and it feels like we're holding each other up just a bit higher.

"When this is over, you have to invite me to New York sometime, sis."

"Screw the invitation, silly, you can come anytime you want, you know that."

"Yeah, but I'll need reminding from time to time. Depending on how things are, I might get distracted. Might forget."

I smile. "Okay, I'll do that. I'll remind you to come see me." That's when I feel her body freeze.

The door to Daddy's room is closed. That's not right. It's

never closed. Never. There is always someone coming in and out and even when we sponge-bathe him, we just pull the green and white pinstriped curtain around him. No one ever shuts the door.

Hazel and I look at each other and she pushes against the wooden slab until it gives way and swings back. At first I don't understand what I'm seeing. Daddy is there in his bed and looks pretty much the same, with his tubes and his monitors and the sound of his breathing. There is Linc, Ella, Mama, and Forrest. At least that's who I think they are. Their mouths and noses are hidden behind surgical masks, sky blue ones.

"Hey, what the fuck?" Hazel's words come out in a hissed whisper, but I stick my elbow into the side of her ribs just the same. Doesn't matter that I'm asking the same damn question in my head. Mama's in the room and Haze can't talk like this.

"The doctors are concerned about the infection," Ella says from her seat next to Mama.

"What?" I asked. "Do they think we can catch what Daddy has, or that we might make him sicker?"

Their sets of cocoa-brown eyes, and Forrest's blue ones, start shooting around looking at each other like they're marbles rolling around on playground asphalt. Linc comes toward us, crossing his arms. "Um, I'm not sure. Both, I guess."

Hazel throws up her arms and pushes a finger into Linc's shoulder. "Yo bro, that's the stupidest thing I've heard yet. If we were gonna catch anything, we'd long have it by now, don't you think? And look at Daddy—look at him, you fuckin' idiot! He can't get any sicker than this."

"We have to do what the doctors say." Now Linc is shoving a cardboard box of the masks toward Hazel. She knocks them to the floor and the box bursts like a broken piñata, spewing the blueness around her feet.

"If Daddy has to leave this world, he's going to be able to see my face when it happens, not some goddamn mask."

"She's right, Linc." I feel like I'm teetering on a plate on a stick because Hazel has introduced, with unflinching clarity, the possibility of Daddy dying, but I'm determined to keep my balance so I can back her up. "Has Daddy seen you all like this? He'll freak out if he hasn't already. Don't you see this doesn't make any sense?"

Linc takes my arm and starts pulling and pushing me toward the door. "Crita, if you'll just listen."

"Stop it!" I don't want him touching me. I slap at his hands and then at his shoulders. I can't stop because the feeling of making this contact energizes me. Suddenly it seems like if I keep hitting him something will become familiar—and not this weird world I've been living in for over two months. If I keep hitting him I'll get used to it and will come back to myself. The next thing I know, that nurse Tammy is back and in my face.

"Please!" she's hissing, "We can't have this upset in the hospital and certainly not in your father's room."

I look around and can't find Hazel. She's gone and so I leave, too. I can't believe this shit.

I walk down the hall, back to the waiting area. There's a woman there. I glance at her, but ignore her as I go to the window and try to quiet the nerves zinging back and forth in me like a rubber band.

"Excuse me, Crita?"

I turn. The woman is talking to me and I don't know why. I don't know her.

"I'm Talane?"

Oh, God. Right. What does she want from me?

"I wanted to talk to you about Demetrius. Um, I mean Tree."

"I'm sorry, I can't do this right now."

"He's told me about you." She acts like I haven't spoken and I wonder if this is a speech she's prepared just for little old me. "He's like that, but of course you would know. He doesn't hide anything."

"Well, it's not like there's much to hide, is there? We were together once. Now it's over."

"Oh, I don't see it that way at all." She's shaking her head in a way that relates she knows this to be an absolute truth. "You were very special to him." (My heart thuds at her use of the word *were*.) "And I can see that in his concern for you and your family now."

"What are you getting at?"

"I don't want anything to be misconstrued."

"By whom?"

"Crita, I know that if you need to lean on Tree, he would be here for you in an instant. I also see how you could read more into it than there is."

"More than what?"

"More than his natural concern, of course."

I want to sit down. My legs feel tired, but I refuse to place myself in a position where she is above me, talking down to me. "Talane, the way I see it, if Tree only had 'natural concern' for me, we wouldn't be having this conversation. Like you said, he hides nothing."

I could see her jaw tighten, her lips draw together, pursing so hard they take on a purplish tint. "Please, Crita."

"Please what?" Hazel is still in the back of my mind and I don't see where this is going. "Let's cut the crap and tell me what you really want. I don't have time for this."

She puts a hand to her chin, then crosses her arms. "Don't take him from me. Please don't take him from me."

God, how crazy is this woman? "Excuse me?"

"I know that's a lot to ask."

"For Crissakes, look at me! This is the first time I've changed clothes in two days. I haven't seen the business end of a makeup brush in two months and—oh yeah, one more thing—my father is critically ill. Maybe I had a seduction scheduled for this month, but gee, I just can't fit it in. I'm not up for it. You've got nothing to worry about from me!"

She's the one who sits now. She clasps her hands in front of her and rests them on her knees. "If Tree were all about looks and seduction, I think we both know he wouldn't be with me," she says quietly.

She swipes a stray lock of hair behind her ear and I find myself staring at it. How can her hair do that? What combination of length, straightness, and thinness allows it to stay there so perfectly, right where she put it? I can never do that with my hair. I do feel sorry for her, I do know that. How much did she have to humble herself to do what she is doing? Damn it, one woman to another, I have to admit that. But at the same time, I can't make her feel better because I can't make her any promises. And because I won't say anything, she has to create the bargain that only she knows she can live with.

"If he's going to leave me, I want him to go on his own. Don't take him from me."

I know what she means—no stealing. That I can agree with.

"Right," I say. "Whatever you say." I wish I could tell her to have faith—to believe more in Tree than she believes in herself. I feel something coming on, though, something that tells me if I say anything akin to that now, I will turn myself into a liar soon afterward. I lost him as sure as if I had dropped him from my pocket and into the street. Now I feel like I want to run Talane over with a Mack truck because I can see she is about to retrieve him.

She stands and for a moment I think she's going to offer me her hand to shake. I back away as though I want to move aside for her. She doesn't know who I am. A handshake may make her believe things I didn't say. But instead she touches her hair again and says "Thank you." I don't have to go any further because Ella and Forrest interrupt us.

"Talane, this is my sister, Ella, and her husband Forrest."

"How do you do? I'll leave you now, Crita, I know you must have family things to discuss. Thank you for your time."

Ella's eyes follow Talane as she disappears down the hall. "Crita, honey, what was that about?"

"Nothing. She's just looking for her boyfriend. So is Mama pissed at us or what?"

"She knows this is hard on all of us."

"Yeah, well, Linc should know that, too. She should tell him that."

"I'm sorry, Crita," Forrest has his hands in his pants pockets and it makes his shoulders slope down and gives him the look of a scolded puppy. "We did feel kind of ridiculous. We should have listened to our own common sense, but you know your brother has a way of putting things . . ."

"I know."

"Okay." I have a hand to my forehead, trying to massage out the thoughts. "Ella, did you talk to him about looking into Mama's finances?"

"Oh, yes! Honey, Crita thinks we need to do an evaluation of Mama's finances." She sighed. "We have to be prepared for the worst and frankly we don't know what kind of money, if any, they have."

"I understand."

"Forrest, I was actually thinking that you could do some research into the market here. Find out how much the house is worth and all. You know, in case we have to sell." I'm leaving, walking down the hall.

"Where are you going?"

"I have to find Hazel."

Hazel's apartment on the Oberlin campus is decorated with old family photos. Some of them are decaying Polaroid snapshots from Mama's photo album, and I wonder if Mama realizes they have ended up there. There's a black-and-white picture of Daddy in his hard hat and workshirt, an employee photo taken at work for the steel mill's anniversary. There's an old photograph of Daddy and his brothers taken after they had moved north and found work in the mills and factories of the cities. They are dressed to kill in sharp tailored suits, with hats cocked on their heads just so. Daddy has his chin raised to the camera, as though he were challenging the photographer to a fight, daring him to release the shutter.

But there are no pictures of Linc in Hazel's rooms. No clips from his athletic days. No shots of him with his family. There is Chandra standing under a tree in her wedding gown, and Savannah in her playpen with an oversized teddy bear; then Chandra and Savannah waving in front of a yellow bus on Savannah's first day of school. It was not as though Hazel had to cut Linc out of the pictures. She simply had chosen ones in which he wasn't there.

She had opened the door without a word, motioning for me to come in. She had a cordless phone pressed to her ear and she was listening intently to someone I couldn't hear. Her crisp responses make me assume the call has to do with a class, so I stand in her living room and stare at the fifth-grade version of myself, grinning buck-toothed at me from a wooden frame.

In the photo I am wearing a light blue-and-white checked dress. It is trimmed in white lace and at the time it was one of my favorite dresses because I felt like a lady when I wore it. When Ella, Hazel, and I staged tea parties with our toys I wore the dress and we would sit with our little plastic teacups filled with Kool-Aid and chatter away as though we owned the world.

I didn't want to fight Hazel. I just wanted to talk to her and share the grief that must have been taxing her the same way it was taxing me. Then I thought a pot of tea might help. We could drink it like civilized adults, and maybe Hazel would remember our tea parties and soften to my queries.

In her kitchen I find a white ceramic teapot in the cupboard. The teakettle is already on the stove. I fill it and set it to boil and turn to the counter for the blue ceramic canisters with rubber seals and metal latches. I open the second tallest one in search of sugar, but when I pop open the latch and lift the lid I find a white powder wrapped in plastic. Confectioner's sugar, I think, but as I start to refasten the lid I notice the green rubber band enclosing the plastic.

Suddenly I am accessing information in my head that had seeped into it back when Linc was at his worst and I was learning things I had no desire to learn. Drug dealers wrap their wares with colored rubber bands, each hue signifying the source and rate of purity. This bag in Hazel's kitchen contained cocaine, a cheap kind, roughly cut, sold in a certain neighborhood in South Lorain. I pull it out of the canister. The amount is about the size of two golf balls and I can just hold it all in one hand.

My fingers clench over the bag and I feel my heartbeat quicken. For some moments I cannot move and then I am taking the cocaine into the living room just as Hazel emerges from her bedroom. "What is this? No." I stop and put a hand over my eyes until my thoughts clear. I begin again slowly. "I already know what this is. What I wanna know is what you're doing with it."

Hazel narrows her eyes and lowers her chin. "You put that back. It's none of your business. And you damn well better stop snooping around in my things."

I laugh, can't help but laugh. The tension is too high and her response too ridiculous. "All I wanted was some sugar! You know, for tea? But I guess for a real high this beats caffeine and sugar any day, doesn't it?!"

She crosses her arms. "I wouldn't know about that."

"Hazel, how can you have this stuff in your house? Come on, honey, after all we've been through with Linc . . . What are you doing?"

Suddenly Hazel snatches at the bag, but I am too fast, whipping my arm away and stepping out of her reach. "You idiot!" she seethes, "Linc's the reason I have it. I went down to Southie, all by myself, and got this for him!"

"I don't believe you."

"Well, no, big sister, he didn't ask me for it straight out. But I know he wants it. He needs it. I was gonna drop it off at the house in some not too inconspicuous place."

"Hazel—"

"Then I was gonna drop a dime to the cops and tip them off to a little deal that might go down sometime in the next day or so."

My ears burn. I can't believe what I am hearing. "Are you nuts? That would get Linc sent—"

"*To prison??*" Hazel practically screams the words. "Yes! That's where he belongs! We've been nuts because we didn't send him there sooner! Can't you see how brilliant this is? He'll be safe from himself and we'll be safe from him."

I open my mouth and hope that of all the reasons I could give my sister to not pursue such an outlandish plan, the one that would convince her most would come out. But then something else dawns on me with the pretty pinkness and clarity of a newfound day. "Hazel, you just bought this yourself?"

"I just said so."

"Don't you see? If you had to go out and buy this stuff yourself, that means he's doesn't have any. And you know that! If he had drugs over there you could have picked up the phone and had him busted any day of the week. But you couldn't so you knew you had to plant it yourself."

"I don't know that it means anything and I'm tired of waiting and trying to figure it out. I'm putting him out of com-
mission, and none of us will have to worry about him again."

"You're not gonna do this."

Hazel grabs the shoulder of my shirt and holds it balled up
in her fist. Her words come slow and even, but she spits them
out like rotten seeds. "He will not make Mama cry again." She
holds me close to her face and a drop of sweat rolls down my
temple. We stay that way for a slice of eternity, until the teakettle begins to whistle.

Hazel relaxes her grip and goes into the kitchen to take the
pot from the stove. I shove the cocaine in my pants pocket and
head for the door. But just as I touch the knob, Hazel's fingers,
hard and desperate, lock onto my shoulder and swing me
around. I gasp. She grips the teakettle in her other hand.

"Gimme back the bag!"

I focus on the kettle and its boiling contents. "No. I'm not
gonna let you do this."

"Bitch, I said gimme back the bag!"

Hazel pulls at my shirt and I kick at her, hard, in the direction
of the kettle. My big toe makes direct contact and pain blossoms into my whole foot. The kettle flies from her hand and
hits the floor, spraying hot drops over our legs. Hazel screams
and grabs me by both shoulders, shoving me to the floor. Her
hands lash at face and arms as I struggle to protect my head. I
am beginning to suffocate under her weight and her madness
when I shut my eyes and see flashes of us wrestling as kids.
Back then I always won, and I realized I could again. A voice
inside me says, *You know how to do this.*

I draw up my legs so that my knees are almost touching
Hazel's back. My right hand flies out and claws at the side of
her face, and at the same time I rear up my lower body so
Hazel has to ride up like I am a bucking steer. But my hand
in her face has thrown her off balance, and I use the switch in

momentum to throw her off my body. I scramble to my knees, grab Hazel by her shirt, and punch her square across the jaw with all the force I can muster. She falls back, her head banging against the floor.

"Goddammit!" She sits up, holding the back of her head, and I crawl to the door. I pull myself up by the doorknob and let myself out into the hallway. Once on the carpet, I run. My heart pounds in my throat and the throbbing blood vessels in my temple feel as though they will pop at any second. I move automatically. I am seeing but not registering what I see when I get into my car and drive away. I remember stopping at a Dairy Mart somewhere and throwing the cocaine into a dumpster behind the store.

I do not know what I look like when I arrive at Chandra's apartment. But there must be something in my being—a certain brightness in my eyes, a certain weariness in my stance— that tells her I have survived an ordeal. If I had not been so battered, so much in a state of shock, I might have sensed that Tree was following us into her kitchen.

"God, Crita, what happened? You're bleeding . . ." Chandra is wetting a paper towel and the next thing I know I am sitting in a chair in her kitchen and feeling a cool sensation against my collarbone. "Your shirt is torn! Honey, what happened?"

"Hazel . . ."

"She did this to you?"

"We were fighting. . . . She's crazy."

"Tell me."

"It was an accident. I found this cocaine in her kitchen. She had this stupid idea of using it to frame Linc. I took it from her and she tried to get it back and we fought . . ." I try to swallow, but my throat feels closed and dry. "I need some water."

"I'll get it." Tree's deep voice startles me as he moves toward the sink. He fills a glass and offers it to me.

Tree leans against the counter. "So what happened, Crita?" He sounds punchy, almost playful. "I know you, girl. I know you didn't let your baby sister get the best of you, even if she is crazy."

"Well, I got the stuff away from her." The water tastes metallic and warm. I want to spit it back into the glass, but I know Tree and Chandra's eyes are all on me. "I threw it out on my way over here."

"That's my girl."

"I never thought I'd say this, but poor Hazel," Chandra says. "She must be out of her mind."

"Oh, I don't think she's crazy. Do you, Crita? If anything, I think her being pissed off has been a little misplaced this whole time. It might be a good thing that she got to jump on you. You're the one she's pissed with."

"Stop it, Tree."

"Crita, you should know what she's feeling," says Tree. "If anything, she's mad because she's having to carry around this stuff that should be yours. You should have that anger. Why are you acting like the world's gone crazy when you're the lopsided piece in this here puzzle?"

"What is he talking about?"

I stare wide-eyed and stupefied at Tree. Why isn't this obvious to him? He had seen me shredded—laid low and as close to death as any human being could be. To live, to walk away from that place, step-by-step, day-by-day, so that I could piece a life back together and go on was hard enough. Why do I have to put it into words, and for someone who wasn't there, for whom I would have to remember every single detail?

I see what he is doing and I want to tell, no, *scream* at him that I am not ready. It is too much. I know he wants to help, that he believes with all the heart beneath his perfect skin that this will be good for me. But I have never been good at taking medicine; even less so when it is forced upon me.

I change tactics on him. "What did Linc want to talk to you about?"

Chandra looks away. "I can tell you that. It was about me. He wanted to see me and cleared it with Tree."

"Did you do it?"

"The boy had some messed-up idea in his head that if I was going to be hanging around you and have him not kicking my butt about it, then he should be able to see Chandra. I told him it was totally up to her."

"What's the big deal?" I ask Chandra. "He told me he saw Savannah at Easter. Don't you talk to him when he visits her?"

"My mother supervises Linc's visits. He and I hadn't spoken in a very long time."

"So you have seen him now?"

She is silent and I can see Tree looking at her expectantly. "Tree, honey, please leave us alone. I'd like to speak with Crita in private."

"Sure, sis, I understand." He is moving toward her, kissing her on the forehead, and now my heart is banging in my chest like an impatient child. I want him to touch me before he goes. I'm starving for it, even as I continue to hold the cold, wet paper towels against my bruised shoulder. I'm thinking, *Show me that you know me. Say my name.* I want him to call me Crystal and I know I must be insane because there's absolutely no reason to believe that he will. It's like I've quickly built this little sandcastle and placed my heart inside, and in a moment the tide is about to come up and wash it away and I'll be left sitting here wondering, *Now why in hell did I just go and do that to myself?*

"Later, Crita," he says. All I can feel of him is the air as he whisks past me and is gone.

"Damn."

"Did you say something?" Chandra is leaning down over me. Her eyes feel heavy and I'm sinking down further into the hardness of the chair.

"No. Yes. I think I have a headache. Can I have some aspirin?"

"Yes, of course." She takes a bottle of generic white tablets from one of the kitchen drawers. Her cabinets are made of a white veneer over plywood and I can see it curling up over one corner of the drawer. It's hard for me to swallow the chalky little pills and I cough a couple of times. I have to drink a whole glass of water to get them down.

"Crita, why did you come here?"

I open my mouth because I'm feeling that the answer should be right there, instant and obvious, because it's not like I did any thinking or decision-making. I could also make a joke— she is a nurse, after all! But the words that do come to me— "I've missed you"—sound all wrong. I have seen Chandra at regular intervals as she's visited Daddy at the hospital and we have spoken; we are more than civil to each other. So she might hear these words and not understand them, but I do—I miss coming to her, I miss talking to her. I also remember why I don't do either anymore.

I move the wet paper towel to dab at the cut on my head and I examine the soft edges on the red spots that my blood makes on the paper. "Maybe because I remember how you bled like this once. But then that's not a good answer, is it? Because I sure as hell was no help to you then."

She sighs as she goes back to the drawer where the aspirin had been and removes a box of Band-Aids. "That was a long time ago. I've had a lot of time to think."

"How has it been for you? Please tell me, Chandra, I want to know."

"Crita, it's been months of overcoming so much, I'm not

sure you can even tell where I'm coming from. Especially since you don't know where I started."

"Why don't you tell me?"

"You know," she says, sitting down next to me and brushing away some invisible object on her thigh, "back then I could smell the other women on Linc when he came home. I guess I started thinking Linc's problem was all my fault."

"Yours?"

"Try to see it how I saw it, Crita. Linc seemed to be able to enjoy himself in the company of every other woman but me. And that includes you. You didn't know, did you? But then how could you have known, you were so young then. It hurt me to hear you in the kitchen together laughing and teasing. Linc could do no wrong in your eyes and he knew it. He preferred yours to mine. There was no room for me. And I thought it was my fault because I thought if I wasn't so critical of him, if I could be more fun or sexier or more understanding, Linc wouldn't have to be running away from me all the time.

"Then there was the arrogance—my arrogance, and Linc's. I thought because we knew more, were better educated than my parents, that we were smart enough to lick this together. But then I ended up doing things even my mother couldn't conceive of doing. I would threaten to leave him. I'd dress Savannah up in her little coat and hat and take her hand and a bag and say I was walking out, but I never went." Chandra's right hand floats up and covers her eyes. She laughs a miserable, regretful laugh. "I even told him I'd kill myself. But addicts learn pretty quickly which threats are idle."

I try to imagine what that scene must have looked like, how desperate Chandra must have been to threaten suicide. How wild was her demeanor? And how calm was Linc? He surely must have been sedated if he didn't believe her or react to her.

"One time," Chandra goes on, "I found him sobbing and

we went through this whole ritual where we forgave each other and promised to recommit ourselves to our family. He gave me this bag of coke and we flushed it down the toilet together. Later on I heard him on the phone in the middle of the night ordering more from his dealer.

"After a while it wasn't a matter of me leaving, because he was the one who left. He went out one night and just didn't come home. You already know how I sold the house when I couldn't keep up with the mortgage by myself."

"So when did you hook up with him again?"

"I didn't, really, not until he came by after he spoke to Tree that day at the hospital. He told me things were weird between all of you. I told him if he kept doing like he was doing, he could only expect more of the same from you, Ella, and Hazel. I told him he had to rebuild his foundation, prove he could be responsible. He wanted me and Savannah to get back with him then, but I told him he would just be using us to make you all think he was okay when he wasn't yet. On top of that, he has things to prove to me, too."

"But Chandra, you were the one who told me he doesn't know how to be careful."

"But we never let him learn how, did we? That's what we have to do right now. Learn and keep learning it. He'll never be careful if he doesn't have something to care about, something he knows won't be cared for by anyone else."

Chandra sweeps a lock of hair from her forehead back into her ponytail. She had been so distant back then, like a princess on a cloud, and I had assumed she just let herself float away from us. Now here is the truth: that I, along with the dust and detritus of Linc's addiction, had been in the wind that had blown her away.

"I'm sorry," I say. The words feel slight so I know their worth is even less.

But Chandra smiles her benevolent smile, the warm one that I had not felt shining on me for such a long time.

"Crita, we all have I'm sorry's to add onto this pile—you, me, Linc, our families. We could touch the sky with such a hoard and it still wouldn't be enough to fill the space we've put between ourselves."

"Then what do we do about the space?"

"We close it up with ourselves. I'm open to Linc becoming a presence in my life again. Because I love him. In spite of everything I still think he deserves every chance. But this time he has to make the most of this chance."

I want to smile, I'm so tempted to fall into that happy familiarity we once had. The germ of it is there, fertile as a pumpkin seed, and I know all I have to do is give it a little bit of water for it to sprout fiercely and grow into the oldness of our ways. Instead I close my eyes and form a resolution within myself. I shake my head. "Maybe for you . . ." I begin.

The doorbell rings and Chandra's eyes look down before she rises. "Crita," she says quietly. "That might be Linc."

She goes to let him in. I hear their voices and in the next moment he is in the room. When he sees me, his face flashes with anger, but it's not new and hot, like the heat that would have been bred from the fight we'd just had at the hospital. I recognize it as a very old anger, grown through with resentment. I know immediately Chandra is wrong. I shake my head again. "No," I tell her. "I have to do this my way." I ask Chandra to leave.

She is ready to defend, ready to be the wife. Linc's wife. She wears it well with her fierce cinnamon beauty.

"Crita, I don't think you should deal with this with a chip on your shoulder . . ."

"Chandra, I'm asking you to go. Linc doesn't need you to defend him right now. You can have the rest of your life to stand up for him and I will listen to you then, but right now you have to listen to me and go away. I don't have to do this the way you did it. I need more."

She looks at Linc and when she sees he won't protest, she picks up her purse and keys from a coffee table and vacates the premises. When she is gone I sit up straight in my seat and wait for Linc's words.

"We're not gonna talk about what just happened in Daddy's room right now," he says. "We're gonna talk about me first. Stuff I should've told you a long time ago."

I'm amazed to see how clear Linc's eyes are. I didn't notice that before and I'm almost not listening to him for staring into his eyes. But I can hear him, can hear the weaving of words that confess the lies Linc once told and tell the story of how he first took cocaine. He talks about how Tick first brought the powder into his house, and how he was too drunk at the time to consider the ramifications. He says it started at Tick's place, long before we moved to Oberlin Hills. Long before he'd ever been promoted.

"Tick showed me how to rub a little coke on my gums with my finger," Linc said. I feel like we're sitting together, watching a movie of these events and Linc is narrating. I see it all with horror and fascination. "Then he gave me a rolled-up dollar bill and showed me how to snort it up my nose. And I just did it."

"What happened?"

"Well, at first, nothing. Then, Crita, a few minutes later it was like, BAM!, light! It was like the whole world opened up to me. Everything seemed great. I had so much energy. I could do anything, anything I wanted to. I sensed everything, I mean everything, in such a big way. I was a raw nerve. I was alive. I was on."

"You liked it?"

Linc shakes his head. "No, you don't get it. You don't just

like coke, nobody just *likes* coke. It's like an attraction and you gotta go there. It becomes center stage. It's the total reason you go someplace, the goal, the reason you have a party.

"My world just got so small. And I'm not saying this to blame you, but Crita, you made me believe I could get away with anything. I took advantage of that. I didn't have to be interested in anything else. I only had to look forward to the time when I could do more cocaine. I thought, a gram here, a gram there, I wasn't harming anybody. But when you're doing enough coke the downside gets to be shitty. It's unbearable. So I had to do more. And more. Pretty soon it got to the point where the only thing that mattered, the only thing that could pick me up and get me out of bed, the only thing that gave me any pleasure at all, was the goddamn cocaine."

I am restless, my hands fidgeting in my lap. This is all well and good, but so far I'm not hearing what I need so badly to hear from Linc, what he hasn't said for these many years. But I let him go on, telling me the things that he thinks he needs to tell me first.

"You don't believe me, do you?"

"In this instant, no," I reply quietly before turning around to face him. "But you're going to help me do that."

"How?" He rises, throwing his hands in the air. "How can we find our way back, Crita, when you can't trust me when I say such a simple thing?"

I feel my cheeks light up with blood. What about any of this is simple? How dare he use such a clean and perfect word to fit the sloppy mess of pain and regret that littered our lives?

"There will be no forgiveness or trust given out here!" I say, moving toward him and pointing a finger into his chest. "You have no idea what I have lost because of you. You get nothing for free here. You want trust, you have to earn it. You give this to me! You give it to me because I've earned it. I deserve it! You say we're supposed to believe in you? No, brother dear, *you* are supposed to believe in *me!* You do that and pray that I do the thing that you want, and don't tell me you don't—to help you back into this family again."

Linc crosses his arms, draws himself up to his full height, and looks down on me as though he would summon the smallness that once was his little sister out of me again. "You just think you can make it all okay, like you tried before."

"I'm not doing anything. This time you're doing it all and proving that you're being up front about it. If it's real, all I'm gonna do is back you up in front of Mama. I don't trust you, Linc. God damn it, you gotta give me something to work with. I want to trust you. My whole life is depending on it. Do you know how I live? Day to day. I'm always waiting for the other shoe to drop. I'm waiting to hear that someone blew your brains out, or that you overdosed in some ditch somewhere. Yeah, you've been through hell, but that's all it's been—your hell, seeping into our lives like sewage, keeping us all from growing, from being happy. We live in your hell. God, I couldn't make my own hell even if I wanted to—there's no room for it because you've taken it all!"

"There are no more shoes to drop, Crita. That's it. I'm done."

"I'm done, too, Linc."

Nineteen

Seven days pass. By the end of the month Daddy is barely conscious for two hours out of each day.

"Listen." Dr. Joyce takes me by the arm and walks me down the hall, out of earshot of Daddy's room. "Ms. Carter, I think you should know. I just got another set of lab tests on your father back." He runs his long white fingers through his hair. "The numbers aren't good."

"What does that mean?"

He is looking past me, over my head. We stand like huge rocks in a stream and doctors and nurses flow past us. "His kidneys are failing. He's not responding to the antibiotics."

"Why are you telling me this?"

"Ms. Carter, I'm concerned that a cascade effect is happening here. This is only the start of it."

This man has barely spoken two sentences to me in three weeks. "Why are you telling *me* this?"

"Other systems will begin to shut down, other organs." Dr. Joyce's close-set blue eyes scan the hall as though he is looking for someone to help him. "Ms. Carter, we can't reverse the effects. You should prepare your family."

I stare at him. He shrugs.

"I just know—from experience, of course—daughters seem to be better at this sort of thing."

In my mind I am still damning Dr. Joyce as I return to Daddy's room.

As he wakens once more Daddy is frustrated and restless, tired of the battle his body is waging. "Crita," he insists, his forearm covering his eyes. I can barely understand him, his voice now a jagged whisper. *"These people don't say I'm getting any better?"* I lean over him and fashion a lie, small and gentle, to pour into his ear. "They do, Daddy, they do. They say it will take time." His kidneys are failing, but I will not say such a thing to my father, I don't care what Dr. Joyce says. Not when I know in my heart that Daddy would be so afraid. It is better for him to sleep and, when conscious, to know that we are there.

Daddy has been in the hospital for ten weeks when he loses all awareness. His skin grows a paler brown and it is thin and stretched over his tired bones like a veil. His hands are still and no longer reach or grasp or swipe the air. Now I don't want the doctors to speak to me. I don't need them to tell me my father is dying. I find I cannot sit quietly by his side. I move throughout the space of his room, adjusting tubes, adjusting the blinds, straightening the sheets. The spirits will come soon for him and I think I can keep them at bay with my motion, sweeping the room with my body, waving my soul throughout the air.

I lay my hands on him even more than before. I fear the moment when Daddy's body will go cold and hard. I know I could not bring myself to touch him then. So while there is still a hint of his warmth in the air, I massage his hands and rub fragrant oils into his wrists and temples.

"Mama," I say one afternoon when she arrives with her bag of yarn and needles. I have put off this conversation long enough.

"Just a minute, baby doll." She puts the bag down on a table by Daddy's bed and leans over him, as she has every time she has returned to this room. "Henry, honey, I'm back. I'm here." She kisses his ashen face and rubs his hands. "Everything's gonna be all right."

"Mama," I whisper and she turns to me. "It's not, Mama." I reach out for her; I take her hands. "He's not gonna be all right."

"Hush, baby. Don't you worry about a thing." She reaches into her bag and pulls out her Bible. I bring a chair to the bedside and she sits, opening the worn brown leather cover. "The Lord is my shepherd," she reads. "I shall not want."

I leave so she will not hear me crying. I go to Lakeview Beach. The air holds the scent of dead fish from the entrails that a careless fisherman has left rotting on the pavement. A couple, a short bearded black man in a football jersey and a Hispanic woman in sandals with a red sweater tied around her shoulders, stride along the boardwalk. A blonde-haired woman in a brown suede jacket pulls up in a blue Ford Escort. She parks a few feet from me and gets out to use a nearby pay phone. My heart and mind race while the lake, spread out in front of us like a placid blue quilt, is so windless and serene I think it might be mocking me.

I end up crawling into the backseat of the car and locking all the doors. I lie down, my face pressed into the crevice of space where the top and bottom of the seat meet. I have to sleep. The present moment is too painful for me to linger there. I want to move forward, if only by thirty minutes or an hour, to a slice of the future where my heart would hurt just a little, little less. The sensation is too huge, too overwhelming. It seems to fill Lake Erie and threatens to spill over the shoreline and crawl up the dunes to grasp me with cold and roughened fingers. But I can't run away. I have no more energy to will me to such strength. I huddle into the seat,

squeeze my eyes shut, and cry quietly until I fall into the soft-
ness of a sleep.

I awake just as the sun is inching itself below the horizon and
behind the lake. A cloud of slumber hovers over my brain and
I sit up and wait for it to clear. As it does, I begin to take hold
of my senses.

My first thought is "I am alone." The sentence tolls again
in my head, *I am alone,* and I hear the notes of self-pity in it
and it fills me with disgust. I will not feel sorry for myself. The
words give rise to my anger and I begin to resist them.

Where am I, I think. I am in a place where people lead with
their mouths and their hearts and their hands, but not their
heads; where they crash into each other and strike carelessly at
each other's souls without a thought as to how the damage will
be repaired. This is a place where, if one did not hold onto
the essence of one's being, it would melt and mold itself into
the form of what everyone else is.

I climb into the car's front seat and I drive. I end up at a
supermarket in Sheffield Center where I find the lights and the
presence of people so comforting that I stay and stroll up and
down the aisles. I try to gauge if I am hungry, if I should buy
myself some food. In one lane I find a young man unpacking
boxes of paper towel rolls. His head is covered with thick black
hair, worn high and spiky on his skull, and I stare at him long
and hard on the chance that he might morph into someone
that I love. I feel cavernous, empty. I miss Tree like I would
miss the spring, with a rabid hunger for warmth and newness
and love. When the stock boy raises his face, one so wide-eyed
and freckled and unlike Tree's, I want to cry.

"Can I help you?" he asks, pausing the rhythm in which he
tosses the rolls onto the shelves.

I swallow. "Yes. Are those the paper towels with the recipe print? Can I have one of those?"

He plucks a roll from the box and hands it to me jauntily, as though presenting me with a dozen roses.

"There you go, pretty lady," he says, not realizing what aid he has given.

"Thank you."

I buy the towels and I leave the store, hugging them to my chest and pretending the roll is a missive from Tree and that he has written love letters on every single sheet. The feeling lasts about as long as it takes me to reach my car. I throw the towels into a garbage can in the parking lot.

I try not to think at all during my drive to Tree's place. To think might produce a shade of the shame and hurt and doubt connected with what my body wants to do. I am not ashamed to say I took myself this far: to a room out of notice of my family and friends, to an emotional edge I have never before seen in my life, to an emptiness with a bed, with a man who belongs to someone else. To say I don't care would seem callous and yet there's no instance where any notion of sense comes forward to reel me back from this precipice.

Walking into Tree's room, infused by candles and incense with the scent of his skin, only soothes me. I wrap myself in the sound of a Lena Horne tape playing on his stereo and settle myself on the cushions of his sofa.

He gives me tea, and treats me with care and just enough attention to keep from frightening me into flight, as though I am a strange bird that has alighted from nowhere. He smiles when I say I don't feel like talking.

"Well," he says, "we could always have one of our special discussions—we can talk about Kool-Aid."

I laugh, warming to the memory he has conjured. Nostalgia will be my ally in this, I decide, and I have no qualms about using it to my favor. "No, we don't have to talk about Kool-Aid. But if you have to be a chatterbox you can tell me how you've been occupying yourself holed up in this bunker."

"It isn't a bunker."

"It is, too." I nod toward the bed made with Tree's down comforter, encased in a deep golden duvet. He always makes the spaces he occupies a version of his mom's home and this room is no exception. A row of his books neatly line the desk and two sun catchers, which he and Chandra had constructed of colored tissue paper as children, hang by plastic suction cups attached to his windows. He carries them everywhere, he once said, to remind him of who he was and to show him the way home.

He laughs. "Come on, I just like my stuff the way I like it, you know that."

"Of course, I remember very well."

"The prince must have his kingdom about him." I lean against him and my arm slides along the skin of his left bicep. The heat of his body feels like the sun. "Tell me about this music," I say, closing my eyes.

"It's just my jazz ladies. A compilation tape I put together to keep in my car. There's some Lena, some Ella Fitzgerald. Shirley Horn will come on in a few minutes to smooth it all out."

"It's nice."

We listen longer without saying anything and soon Shirley Horn's piano begins a melancholy song. The notes tinkle out of the speakers and drift above us like stars on the ceiling. Leaning back in the sofa with Tree, I think I can almost see them.

"Shirley Horn makes me think of my mother," he says, "especially this song. I think about her breaking up with my father and trying to untangle her life from his."

Shirley croons—*I don't know how, I don't know when, I find myself in love again* . . .

"Did she?"

"What?"

"Did your mother ever find herself in love again?"

"I'm not sure. I think she's dated some, but when you've been through what she went through, trust is a big issue. It's kind of hard to feel, you know, safe with someone when you trusted big time and struck out the first time around."

"I can understand that."

Tree doesn't move and he makes no motion to send me away or separate me from his skin. I don't move, either. The ease with which we stay so close tells me there is a whisper of a chance I can persuade him. I match his demeanor, his calm, his breaths.

When I kiss his shoulder, the skin is so warm and alive beneath my lips, but I can taste his resistance. When I look into his eyes I read the word "no" but he remains silent. I react as though he has spoken.

"Why not, Tree? This feels right, for us to be here like this."

I run my hand along his thigh and, leaning forward, I rest my head on his chest. "Tell me that you don't want me," I whisper.

Tree's fingers glide along my back and come to rest on my shoulders. I hold my breath and wait for them to push me away. They do not do so, and I sigh when I feel his hands caress the back of my head. When he speaks he matches my tone in depth and gentleness.

"You know it's not like that."

"Then what is it? Tell me."

"Crita." He says it in a way that says "You know why," but

I will not make this easy for either of us. I want everything on the table. I want us to be fully aware of who we are and what we are doing so afterwards there will be no excuses—no way of pretending that we have lied to ourselves and in the process sully what is most beautiful between us. If he is going to say "because of Talane" then I want to hear it and feel all the pain that will accompany his statement of the fact. Once it is out there, I can proceed with putting it away and making the cold statement to myself, "I choose to do this in spite of that."

"You don't want to do this, Crita," he whispers.

"Yes, I do! I want it back, I want it all back, everything I lost because of Linc, everything he took from me." Tree doesn't respond and my anger rises. "I don't owe anybody anything. And that's okay because now I just want to be here with you in the closest way possible, in the way that you and I know each other best. Please, Tree. Be this way for me."

"I don't want you like this."

"Then why are we here like this?"

"You're right." This time his fingers do press on the tops of my shoulders and I am obliged to move back as he pushes me away and rises from the sofa.

"Who would know besides us?" I argue. "I would trust you with my life, you know that."

"No, 'are.' The operative word is 'are' here, Crita. You are trusting me with your life. You're laying it all right there. Your life, in my hands. Yeah, you're trusting me to do the right thing here, to look after you when for one reason or another, you don't care to do that right now. I don't even know if you know what you're doing. That means I gotta take care of you here, though you've never let me do that before, have you?"

"You think I don't know what I'm doing?" I say as I stand up to challenge him head on, "You think I don't know what my life is, to feel it in my own hands? I know my life well enough to have felt it drip through my fingers like water with me grasping at it like a woman dying of thirst! I have been to a place where the only thing that mattered was whether I would have one breath to follow the next. I was there and I was there alone! I took care of myself then and I'll do it now. I don't need you to do that."

"Don't get mad at me, here." Tree moves closer, trying to repair the space between us, but I won't let him. I move away, riding on the tide of my anger. "Crita, you should ask yourself, what did Linc take and what did you give up all on your own?"

"You know, I'm surprised at you, Tree. I thought you would at least be interested in seeing me naked. Isn't this what you're all hot about? My scars? You think I did this to myself? That I chose this?" I unbutton my shirt as I speak, tugging at the threads in bitter impatience, pulling at the waist of my pants. I hear Tree's breath catch in his throat.

"Jesus, Crita." Tree sits down in a chair and runs his hands over his face. He looks at me, his eyes full and deep with their sadness. "Come on, Crita. I didn't have to see this. I see them in your face every single day."

"No!" Suddenly I am sobbing and embarrassed, but I hold tight to my anger because I know I won't get out of the room without it. "Shut up!" I pull my shirt closed around my torso. "I will not have you feel sorry for me! You don't know any-thing about it!" I head for the door, but he is up and he catches me in two strides. He wraps his arms around me from behind and I am thankful I can't see his face.

"I'm not gonna let you go like this."

The sobs in my chest feel heavy and I want to let them topple me. Instead I force my spine to straighten.

"What I want and what I need right now is for you to take me to bed. If you're not gonna do that, then let me go because you're wasting my time."

Tree pauses. I am tired, my voice bloodless, and I can tell

he doesn't recognize it. I feel a twitch in his muscles as they tighten around me.

"I said let go."

When he loosens his arms I don't turn around. I make straight for the door and as I turn the knob I hear him find his words again.

"I'm sorry."

I shut the door before they can follow me into the air.

Twenty

On the night that Linc failed to protect me from Tick, I couldn't sleep. Instead I packed all of my things, moving as silently as I could, determined to extract myself from the house in the morning. At 7 A.M. I called home. Mama answered the phone. The sound of her voice made my heart leap into my throat and suddenly I wanted to cry. I forced out a cough, hoping to clear the clogging emotions. I didn't want her to feel the tightness inside me, and I could not let Daddy hear me cry.

"Mama, may I speak to Daddy, please?"

"Yeah, baby, sure."

I heard him in the background saying "What?" with the annoyed tone that he used whenever he had to talk on the phone. He hated it, hated being unable to see a person, to take in all the information he needed to assess a situation. He growled with discontent and I heard my mother telling him it was me. I could picture the quizzical expression I'm sure he gave her in the moment before he took the receiver.

"Yeah, Crita? Good morning?"

"Good morning, Daddy," I said, responding with the manners he'd taught us. We always had to greet someone early in the day like that. "Daddy, if it's all right with you, is it okay if I come home and live there for a while again?"

"Hell, yeah. I thought you were already over here." I smiled at the joke he made whenever we asked his permission to go somewhere. "This is your home. You don't have to stay over there if you don't want to."

"Thank you, Daddy. I'll be over soon."

Chandra was standing by the kitchen sink when I came down. She was finishing a cup of coffee and looking out the window. A wave of red flashed through me. I was angry. She had driven Linc out of the house, had made it necessary for him to go to places like Sugar Hill.

"Where's Linc?" I asked, but I already knew.

"Upstairs, still sleeping it off. He won't make it into the office today, I already left a message there. I couldn't face speaking to someone directly and lying in their ear like that."

I cringed at how easily I had done just that on a number of occasions. "Chandra, I think it would be a good idea if I went back home for a while. You and Linc probably need your space."

She put her cup down in the sink and sighed. "I think you're right. Crita, honey, it's not your fault. You love Linc and you've been trying to help him in your own way, but you don't understand something like this. Maybe you're too young to understand, I don't know . . ." Her voice trailed off.

"I'm going to load up the Jeep," I said quietly, and walked outside to prepare my car.

Being at home again was comforting. I graduated that spring, as did Hazel, and Ella was home from Spelman for the summer. Though our old easiness wasn't quite there, I was glad to be in the company of my sisters again. After living at Linc's house, everything at home seemed so small, but small was what I needed. Each night I crawled into my old twin bed like a butterfly squeezing back into its cocoon, welcoming the safety of the tight darkness. I didn't care that I didn't fit in the space anymore.

For several days afterwards I kept feeling the need to look over my shoulder. I would look, see nothing, and then look again, wondering if something or some sound had made me turn in the first place. Eventually I realized I wasn't just looking for something, I was waiting—waiting for a message, a phone call, a sign. I heard nothing from Linc. He hadn't called to see how I was after that night or even to ask me why I had left his house. I couldn't explain it.

Chandra I did see, but only because some weeks later she started dropping Savannah off with us. She had gotten a job at Fairview Hospital. When Daddy asked her about Linc, she only said he was working a lot. In these moments I was silent. I didn't want Mama and Daddy to know anything, either, but I was sure they sensed the coolness between me and Chandra and already suspected something. Whenever I came into the room and sat down, Daddy looked like he was waiting for me to speak. Instead I picked up a book, or turned on the television.

I could tell Tree thought it was a good thing I was back at home. Hazel definitely did, too. I think she was glad to have a front-row seat to . . . I don't know, me and Tree. Sometimes I thought I could feel her eyes on us when I kissed him good-night—kinda like the way I used to watch Linc with his girlfriends all those years ago.

Now Tree and I really had no reason to talk about Linc and Chandra, but that was fine with me. I wasn't willing, wasn't telling. But then it seemed to me that the things Tree did want to discuss were no easier for me. I would feel this most in his bed, after making love. I would try to stifle the urge to get up and leave right when we were done. Part of me thought it was a girl thing. I didn't want to go home afterwards feeling like Daddy could tell what I had just done. Another part of me felt a kind of shame because I knew I wasn't fully present with Tree and I thought he could tell. Everything he did, everything he said, I could tell he was trying to draw me closer to him and I was resisting like a child turning her limbs to rubber so I could pour myself out of his arms.

"So how do you see us in the next twenty years or so?" he asked me one night as we lay in the dark. I was trying to see the numbers on the alarm clock, which he kept clear on the other side of the room so he had to get out of bed and walk toward it in the mornings to shut it off.

"I don't know," I lied. I lied because the picture was so clear—so very clear that I thought it would scare him. It certainly scared the shit out of me. I am sitting at a patio table with another woman, maybe Hazel, and Tree is splashing around the pool with our daughter. She has curly brown hair that flops over her eyes which are light brown in the sun. She looks so much like him. She has his lips—soft, red, plump, and Cupid-like.

I am looking at them and laughing and smiling. There are roses and red bougainvillea in bloom all around the pool. This is our home. I think it must be on the west coast, maybe Southern California. I tell Hazel I have to join them in the pool and I do, making a big cannonball splash into the water. It is warm. I am laughing. Tree catches me, our little girl on his back. Hazel is smiling, then she hears the baby monitor. "Baby's calling!" she says.

"I'll get him," Tree says and he gets out of the water, dries himself off, and goes into the house.

"It's time for his feeding. He's hungry all the time, just like his father," I tell Hazel.

I pull myself out of the water and I sit on the side of the pool and take my top off. Tree comes out cuddling our newborn son, and he hands him to me and gets back into the pool. He's teaching our little girl how to swim while I nurse our baby. Hazel comes and sits next to me. "God," I tell her. "I never thought it could be like this. I never thought it could be this beautiful. That man sears my soul."

"Sis," she says, "I knew." And she is smiling and I'm smiling. I'm at home.

I didn't tell Tree about this. God, how could I live that kind of life with him when I had failed so badly at helping Linc have it? I was no good at this, no good at all. So I lived this pretend life. I focused on my present. What was practical. I took my first full-time job, keeping books for the Fligner grocery stores. I could have done better: a job at a company in Cleveland and an apartment of my own, but I wasn't ready for that yet. I wasn't ready because I didn't know that when I left Linc's house I had packed a nightmare along with my belongings. I wasn't sleeping well. I was back at Sugar Hill, and the image I dreamed I would see in my sleep so many times over the next few years: Linc, looking like the man Leroy they had dragged off, sitting in a bathroom stall sweating and scared, hunted by one of the sunglass-covered faces I had seen that night. A drug dealer, armed with a shiny automatic weapon, finds Linc, shoots him, kills him.

Fortunately I slept in the front of the house, in Linc's old room. My parents and my sisters couldn't hear me when I awoke in the night crying out. I should have known, though, that Daddy wouldn't let me get away with this for long. That he would notice I wasn't myself. I wasn't free. One morning I emerged from my room to find Daddy already in his chair and studying me hard.

"Good morning, Daddy."

"Good morning," he mumbled. Then, "Crita, what you got sittin' so heavy on your soul that you can't sleep right?"

I rubbed my eyes with both hands so that Daddy couldn't look inside them and see the lie. "Nothing, Daddy. It was just a bad dream. I can't even remember what it was." I walked past him into the kitchen and tore off a paper towel to wipe and hide my face.

In time Chandra started working long hours as well. Mrs. Templeton would periodically pick Savannah up and take her home. One day, when I walked Savannah out to her car, Mrs. Templeton was fluttering, sweeping her hands in the air and preaching to someone I didn't see. She was talking to herself.

"I did not raise my baby for this," she said heatedly. "I walked out on a man already because I would not have her live under such circumstances. She doesn't deserve this. She is a queen. A queen!"

When she saw us, Mrs. Templeton broke into childspeak, asking Savannah about her day. She barely glanced at me and I think somewhere in her flow of verbiage the words "thank you" came out, but I wasn't sure. She packed her grandchild in and was gone.

I still waited. At times I peeked out the curtains and down the road, scanning the sky and earth as though in search of a cyclone. I felt the whirlwind that Linc was spinning could only turn in this direction. It had to find it's way to our door. I cannot tell how long I waited. But I do remember the night it finally arrived.

It was very late. Mama and Daddy had already gone to bed, but my sisters and I were awake in our room in the back of the house. Ella was recounting the details of that evening's date. We all heard Linc's car in the driveway. We heard Daddy, moving swiftly, putting on his red terry-cloth robe, and his feet pounding the floor toward the door. Hazel, Ella, and I looked at each other and then scrambled to the window in time to see Linc standing out by the back door underneath the porch light swaying like he was dancing to music I couldn't hear.

I rushed to pull on my jeans and sneakers. The sight of Linc, long gone from me, thrilled me. I was almost glad to have him here in front of Daddy who would be able to see what he was and talk some sense into him at last. By the time I got to the door, I could hear Daddy outside yelling at him. I ran out into the yard, a nervous silly giggle in my throat, the kind I had as a girl and went with the sing-song "Linc is in trouble, Linc is in trouble . . ." When I got to them, I saw Linc with his arm slung around Daddy's shoulders, his face close in, and I thought, *Oh, he's gonna talk his way out of this.* I was worried he would somehow charm Daddy into thinking nothing was wrong with him. Then I heard the silky whispers of Linc's sentence. "Come on, Daddy, *give me a gun.* This man owes me money and I just need to make him give it to me."

Daddy had guns from a time when black men carried guns for protection, not the way they carry guns today, automatic toys that spew waves of death like a garden hose, used only for naked aggression. I had never known any of Daddy's guns to be fired except on New Year's Eve, when Daddy stuck his arm out the back door and blasted the two pistols and three shotguns into the air while we stood in the kitchen, our hands over our ears, giggling with excitement. How could Linc want to use one of those guns on someone?

I froze, watching in horror as Daddy threw Linc off of him. Linc had a crazy look in his eye and for the first time I feared for Daddy's life. But Daddy shook his head, his whole body shook as he shouted, "BOY, I TOLD YOU NO! You're not taking any guns out of this house!" Daddy walked back toward the house, shouting out for my mother. "NETTIE, CALL THE POLICE!"

Linc was waving his arms and sloppily stomping his foot like a child in a toy store who'd been told he couldn't have the BB gun. "Aw, come on!" he whined. *"Come on!"* I was shocked. Whatever Linc was on, it did not allow him to quake at the sound of his father's fury. But his flight instinct seemed well intact. He stomped back to his car and screeched away down the street. He didn't stop at the stop sign at the corner. He never noticed I was in the yard.

I looked down at my hands and realized I had my keys in them. I could go after him, I thought, but my legs seemed riveted to the grass. I was afraid of what I might find if I went to Linc alone. I went back into the house, by then filled to the ceiling with my mother on the phone to Chandra and Daddy still scolding a stream of words, some of them to Linc, but most only to the air. ". . . thinks he can take a gun from me! That boy was on dope, did you see that? A gun! And if he were to take that gun out of here and kill someone, I'd be the one they'd come after!"

I opened the door of our room to find Hazel sitting up in bed and Ella standing by the window. She was dressed. "Come, on, we have to go after him. He'll get in trouble if he's caught driving in that condition."

"And what condition is that?" Hazel crossed her arms and arched an eyebrow at me. Ella looked at me like I was about to tell her there was no Santa Claus.

"He's high, okay?" I didn't say on what. There was no need to drive stakes in hearts at this point. "Will you come on?"

"I'm not going anywhere," Hazel said flatly.

I looked at her dumbfounded, but then grabbed Ella's hand and dragged her out to my car. "I'm not sure where he'll be, but I have an idea," I said as I pulled her. But just as I was about to open the car door, she wrenched her hand away from mine.

"No, I'm not going." She brushed a hand through her hair and yanked her sweater, which I had nearly pulled off her shoulder, back onto her body.

"Ella, please, we have to. He needs our help."

"No he doesn't. You're making a mountain out of a molehill. He's probably just drunk and I bet you any money he's at home sleeping it off by now."

Tears sprang to my eyes and I felt the sour tinge of desperation creep up from my stomach. I stepped between her and the house. "Ella, he is not drunk." I spoke slowly. "It's as bad as you think and possibly worse. That's why we have to help him."

"I said I'm not going anywhere. Now, Crita, you stop this. It's silliness and you're scaring me." She walked around me, jerked open the screen door, and went back into the house. I sat down on the steps and cried because I could not make myself go alone. I knew I needed to move. When I looked up again, it seemed I found the answer in the sky. I could go to his house. Chandra had to be there; Mama had just been talking to her. Somehow that seemed safer, and I would be doing something, although I didn't know what. I got in my car and drove.

Chandra opened the door.

Her lower lip was thick and purple like a plum split when it fell from the tree.

"Where is he?"

"He left. Tree called the police. If he's out there, they'll pick his ass up."

"How could you?" I'm attacking Tree. "How could you do this to me?"

"To you? What about what he did to Chandra?"

"He wasn't in his right mind! You knew that!"

I turned back to Chandra. "What are you going to do? You can't press charges."

"Honey, I can't think straight right now."

"I said," speaking firmly and slowly. "You can't press charges. Like you said, you're not thinking straight. You can't do something like that when you're all messed up."

Tree said, "What do you expect me to do?"

"Nothing, I expect you to do nothing."

"And why is that?"

"It's none of your business."

"And it's yours? Explain that to me, Crita, because I totally missed the bus on that one."

"Stop it, Tree, we can't talk like this right now."

"Damn straight."

Chandra's face was tired and faded like an old rose and she looked at me with inevitability, like she knew I would appear. "Before tonight, Linc hadn't been here in weeks."

"What?" I looked around the room, scanning for signs of Linc's presence—a carelessly tossed copy of *Sports Illustrated* or his sneakers left by the back door. There was nothing. "Why didn't you tell us?"

"Tell you what?" Chandra asked, throwing herself on the sofa and hugging one of the cushions. "That I found cocaine in his car? That I've given him the same goddamn ultimatum that I've given him a zillion times?" She leaned back and put her hand over her eyes. "He never chooses me and Savannah. Never. I have to accept that."

I sat down next to her. Now wasn't the time for her to wallow in her self-pity or sadness or guilt or whatever was bothering her. "You spoke to Mama, right? You know what happened tonight?"

"Yes. I told her everything, told her we're nearly broke. Linc's gone through our savings accounts. He took huge loans out of his retirement fund. I didn't know about any of it. I still can't believe it, that all that money just disappeared up his nose." She looked around the room wearily. "I don't know if we can keep this house."

"Chandra, we have to find out if Linc is all right. He was trying to get a gun from Daddy, he has to be desperate. Desperate or nuts."

"Well, whatever, he's nobody's priority at the moment," Tree said. "Chandra, you should go to the hospital and get checked out. If you want to be so helpful, Crita, why don't you stay here with Savannah?"

"Yeah, I'll do that." I'm looking at him like we're staring at each other from opposite sides of a fence. There would be no going back to his side, or his coming over to mine.

They left and I sat on the sofa, my legs pulled up under me and covered with a blanket. The night stretched on, but I couldn't sleep for knowing I had wronged Chandra. Around 2 A.M. I heard a scraping sound coming from the family room. I gasped and clapped a hand over my mouth. I crept from the couch, moving as silently as I could, and picked up the fireplace poker. I gripped the weapon in my fingers as tightly as I could. I walked in just as Linc succeeded in jimmying the door open and he was in the house. I caught my breath and still raised the poker because I barely recognized my brother. He looked awful, like someone had made a bad photocopy of him and put it out on the street. His eyes were watery marbles floating in red and he smiled a smile that seemed to say he was exhilarated and dead tired at the same time. His skin was ashy and gray, and his bones seemed to want to jump through to the surface.

"Hey, Linc." I spoke to him quietly, as though he were a stray cat I wanted to coax in for care and feeding. I leaned down and put the poker on the floor. "What is it? What do you need? Are you hungry?"

He looked around as though checking for someone else in the house. "Yeah, I'm starving."

"Come on." I motioned him into the kitchen. "I'll make you a sandwich."

He went in and sat down, still kind of skittish, his eyes scattering about the room. He talked to me in a hurried whisper. "Man, Daddy's pissed off at me, huh?"

"Daddy's worried about you, Linc." I found a can of tuna

in the cupboard and set an egg to boil on the stove. I put two pieces of wheat bread into the toaster. "But Linc, Tree took Chandra to the hospital. You hit her . . ." I wanted to drop my hands into the toaster with the bread just so I could feel something other than the words I just said. "How could you do that?"

"Oh, Crita, it hurts so much." Linc laid his head on the table. "This thing's like a monkey. A goddamn monkey on my back. This is huge." He sighed heavily. "I can't see my way out of this, Crita."

I didn't want to touch him. Instead I wiped my eyes and kept on making that sandwich. I drained the tuna, chopped up the egg, and mixed it with the fish. I added Miracle Whip and a touch of relish, spread the mixture on the bread, cut the sandwich in half and gave it to Linc. He took a bite and cried.

"This is so good." Then Linc covered his face with his hands and sobs shook his body. The table beneath him shivered. "Look what I've done. I hate myself. I hate how I messed it all up."

For the first time I wasn't afraid to touch him. I put my arms around him from behind and buried my face into his neck. "It's going to be all right. We'll help you."

"I'm shit. Oh, God, I had it all, didn't I? I'm shit, look at me. I can't work. Crita, this is the first food I've had in I don't know how long."

I went to my bag and pulled out thirty dollars. It was all I had. "Linc, take this. But we have to do something. You need to be in a program in a place where doctors can look after you."

"I miss you so much. I miss Mama and Daddy—"

"Linc, listen to me. We're here for you, but you have to help yourself." He was eating again and I didn't think he could hear me. Suddenly he got up and starting going through the cupboards. He found a bag of chocolate chip cookies and a large bag of Doritos. He grabbed both and started to leave.

I snatched at his arm and held it tight, fighting him and my tears. "You should be in a hospital. We gotta go. Come on, Linc, we'll find one for you right now." He pulled away from me and headed for the door.

"Linc, at least tell me where you're living!" He mumbled an address I recognized as the ramshackle house I had found him in before, and was gone.

From that night on I quashed my fear. I deemed it useless and put it away. If I was going to help Linc I needed to be focused and unafraid to follow him into the depths of his living nightmare. I saw no other way to show him the way out. I went to the house again and again. It smelled of things dead and wanting to be dead. Linc wasn't always there. Sometimes I had to drive around and pick him out from a crowd on a playground or sitting on a doorstep. My instinct told me Linc needed to remain connected to our family at all costs. He obviously missed us, regretted us. If he wanted us, we would be his road back to sobriety. I was determined to be his go-between between his world and us so that we would remain in his thoughts, in his sights. I brought him food and money when I had it. There were days when he was more like himself, when he would meet me at Lakeview Park and we'd talk and I would tell him about Savannah. Those times gave me hope. But I didn't see what the effort was costing me. My own life drained away as I tried to maintain Linc's. I wondered where he was in every waking moment.

I didn't call Tree. He didn't come in when he brought Chandra home again that morning and I didn't call him. I didn't call him and I kept not calling him because I wanted it all to work out before I did. I wanted to be able to say, "I told you it would be all right" to him.

I wasn't the only one in my family struggling; twisting, bending, reshaping our minds to cope with our love and fear for Linc. Hazel took to attacking and scolding me, insisting I wasn't handling things properly. Research was her forte and her bed was strewn with medical texts she had taken from the library. I didn't know how she read all this and studied her regular coursework as well. She tossed out books like life rafts to everyone in her troubled ocean, never minding that only she knew how to swim with them.

"You're enabling Linc," she said to me one day as I packed a dinner for yet another nightly search for our brother. "He's a crackhead and he's gonna stay a crackhead because you're helping him do it."

"I don't care. Somebody's got to keep talking to him. He's got to know that he's still connected to us." I felt the edge in my voice, nervous and shrill. I had heard it for days, but couldn't calm myself enough to smooth out the sound. "Do those books say anything about love, Miss Smarty Pants?"

"As a matter of fact they do. They talk about tough love—cutting off all contact, letting the asshole hit bottom, making him realize how serious we are."

"Linc already knows all that—you think he doesn't? Hazel, you haven't seen him like I've seen him."

Hazel rolled her eyes, threw up her hands, and started to walk away.

"Hazel, no, listen—he knows he's screwed up. Linc is so depressed I don't think he can stand to have daylight touch him, let alone one of us. He hates himself like you wouldn't believe. That's why somebody's got to keep talking to him."

She looked at me with a mixture of disgust and pity. "Who's going to talk to us, Crita? Who's gonna help Mama and Daddy through this shit?"

I stared at her a moment and went on packing the brown paper bag. "I don't know."

"Yeah, right. I didn't think so." Hazel walked out and left me alone.

The depth and darkness of Hazel's words didn't reach me until the day Mama came into my room. I remember the skin of her hands felt rough and dry as she took my hands and pressed a ball of rolled-up bills into them.

"Take this," she whispered. "Use it for your brother. Don't tell nobody where you got it from."

The gray in Mama's hair seemed more pronounced and I could see circles under her eyes beneath her glasses.

"Mama, where did you get this?" I counted out the bills and found $250. At first she just looked at me. She opened her mouth, closed it again, and said nothing.

"Mama!"

"I took it from the Sunday School fund at church. They just use it to buy cookies and juice for those kids, they won't miss it."

"But Mama . . ."

She shook her head and raised her hand. She was testifying, her eyes filling with tears. "I've just been praying and praying and I can't pray anymore, Crita. God won't help any other way. So I'm gonna make Him help by doing this. God don't need this money."

"Mama, this isn't the way." I pushed the money back into her hands, then took her face in mine. "You have to put this money back, okay?" I held my mother, her frame seeming so small next to mine. I wondered how I had missed the moment when I had outgrown her. That night I drove her to the church myself. We returned the money, in secret, together.

On another night I found Daddy's chair in the living room empty at a time when he was usually watching a rerun of *Sanford and Son* on TV. "Where's Daddy?" I asked Ella, who was standing at the stove heating up a straightening comb. Never one to be caught with any nappiness, she wanted to touch up her roots before her date with yet another of her nameless beaus. Ella insisted on life going on despite Linc, and for her that meant dating.

"He's outside with those damn cards, trying to see the future," she said.

I went out into the yard and found Daddy sitting at his card table underneath the catalpa tree and looking out over the evening sky that glowed red with the sulfurous fires of the steel mills. He pulled out the cards for seeing, not playing, and only when something troubled him. I knew it had to be Linc because that night he worried those cards, flipping them out of the deck and onto the table over and over again.

"I'm trying to get something out of these here cards," he said when he heard me come up next to him. "I'm thinking they might tell me something."

"Daddy, Linc will be all right. We'll get him some help." But Daddy just kept on flipping the cards. "Daddy, what are you looking for?" I insisted.

He picked up the cards, shuffled them again, cut them, then put the deck together and drew out a card and laid it on the table. He sat back in his chair, pulled out a cigarette, and lit it.

"Don't have to look for nothing," he said, taking a long draw and exhaling. "That card keeps coming up again and again."

I looked at the table and saw the jack of clubs faceup, a card I never liked as a child because of its evil profile and the sinister curve of the jack's mustache.

"That card there is Lincoln," Daddy said. "That's trouble there. That's death."

I sat down on the grass and leaned my head on Daddy's knee. "Daddy, Linc will be all right," I said again, only quieter this time because I knew the words were hollow and useless. "We'll get him some help."

The call from a hospital had come all too soon and I wasn't ready. Even though I hadn't heard from Linc in weeks and expected the worst, I had stubbornly refused to prepare myself for tragedy. I picked up the phone on the first ring and a concerned, informative voice on the other end told me to come right away to the emergency room. Mama was standing in the doorway of the kitchen looking at me, but I wouldn't answer the question her eyes were asking. In all the time since I had torn up my college applications, she had never said "I told you so" and yet I feared it and read it in her weathered face every day. I left the house without telling her anything. "I'll call you when I know something," I said.

The emergency room of Lorain Community Hospital smelled sterile and sickly. People rushed past me, but a nurse whose blonde hair I recognized from Linc's high-school yearbook waved me over to a space blocked off by a lime green curtain. Linc was behind the fabric. He was bent over slightly from the waist, his shoulders hunched, his arms wrapped tightly around himself as he sat on the edge of an examining table. His face was contorted, his eyes darting past me, around me, through me. A voice in my head said, *Lay hands on him,* and I did so, trying to get him to lie down. His rumpled black slacks reeked of urine and his body felt stiff to my touch. It was like laying down an ironing board. When his wild eyes fell on mine, I saw nothing but emptiness in them. Whatever he was seeing was not in the room but in his head, a tiny war exploding in each fiber of his brain.

Later he would tell me that he couldn't see me for the lights, the lights that were flashing before him in bright reds, purples, and oranges, the most beautiful he'd ever seen.

He looked through me and screamed, "Stop the lights! Make them leave me alone. Stop the lights!" He started pulling at his hair, then gripping his skull with desperate hands as though he were trying to hold the pieces of it together. The doctors whirled in and pulled me away. They laid hands on Linc, prying his fingers from his head. "Mr. Carter, please, can you tell us what you took?"

Then, as though he was possessed by the frenzy of a dozen tortured souls, Linc's body reared up and straightened like a ramrod. His eyes rolled back in the sockets, glowing with their whiteness, as he exhaled a forceful cry and threw himself from the table. He fell with a terrible crash and lay there thrashing and twitching in a horrid mass. *No,* I told myself. No.

"Seizure!" somebody screamed. "Grand mal!" Linc lay there trembling while a doctor held his head and another shoved his fingers into Linc's mouth, trying to grab his tongue. I fell to my knees. My brother was dying.

Whose hands they were I do not remember. They were there, on my shoulders, pulling me up and moving me, pushing me, propelling me into a room of chairs and more people. The hands pushed again and made my body fold and I sat down.

Later they told me Linc was still alive. The doctor who came to me, who pushed away the fog, took my hands, and pulled me back into the moment was named Leeper. He had dirty blond hair, a pudgy nose, and bird blue eyes that made him seem very young. But his voice was deeper and, while not old, it was older than mine. It held authority and I was willing to listen, especially when he told me that Linc was still alive. "His brain is trying to reestablish control," Dr. Leeper said. "It will take a few days. He won't remember any of this. Not for some time, anyway."

I nodded.

"This isn't the first time your brother has been here. Did you know that?"

I sat back in my chair, released a slow breath, and shook my head. "No, I didn't."

"We got him into detox once, but he left after a couple of

days. The other two times he was gone before anyone knew it. I'm hoping that since we were able to contact his family this time that things might be different."

I nodded. "I've wanted him to get help for a long time. Tell me what to do. None of our family . . ." I could feel my voice trailing off. "We just don't know what to do," I whispered.

"Miss Carter, if you can bring the rest of your family down here, we can help you stage an intervention. That's where you confront him, let him know how his behavior has hurt all of you."

"Yes, I know." Another of Hazel's terms.

"Then this will be your next step."

I looked past the doctor and scratched my scalp, trying to release the tension in my body. I wasn't sure if Mama and Daddy should see Linc like he was, translucent and frail, with tubes running out of his body. But then, I wondered, could the sum of us, the gathering of all our family power, be enough to push Linc beyond himself and into a realm of more control? And was the effort worth the risk?

"Miss Carter, I'm concerned your brother might be a terminal addict," Dr. Leeper went on. "He's traveling a downward spiral where there are times when he's sober, but he can't hold onto it. He's filled with self-loathing and it gets worse every time he backslides. In the end, with this kind of addiction, the addict either overdoses or he kills himself some other way."

"You think that's what Linc is? A terminal addict?"

"You tell me."

I thought of the times Linc seemed semicoherent, when I would show him pictures of Savannah and he would ask about her schoolwork. He must have been sober, or close to it, then. Those instances weren't as frequent as they once were, and had disappeared altogether in recent months.

"His case is bad. I'd even go so far as to call it malignant. I can tell your brother is educated, he must have had a good job once. There are no calluses on his hands. He must have fallen pretty far."

"Yes, he did."

"It's harder for someone like him to come back. It'll be a rough battle." He shook his head and stood. "You let me know when your family is ready to see him."

When I got home I took one of Hazel's books and sat down at the kitchen table. I looked up "terminal addiction." The pages foretold the same future Daddy had seen, but this time it did so well enough and clearly enough for me to believe it; that the addict would be dead inside of a year, maybe two. I heard the shuffling of Mama's soft-soled bedroom slippers in the hall and in another moment she was sitting down next to me, her tired eyes quiet and filled with expectation. I put my head down on the table and she stroked my hair as though I were six years old and she was comforting me from a bad dream. I sighed the whole of my life into her. "Oh, Mama."

Twenty-one

That evening I sat with my parents and explained in detail what Dr. Leeper had told me. It was like all those times in childhood, telling them about something I needed to do for school and the directions from a teacher or principal. Mama sat on the couch, her legs crossed at the ankles, listening and waiting to hear what Daddy had to say. Daddy rested his elbows on his knees, looking straight ahead as though down a tunnel, wondering when a devastating train would come. At times during my recital my voice would clog with the tears I restrained and his eyes would flick toward me, alert and concerned. He absorbed all the information into the thickness of his sixty-nine-year-old body, then lifted himself up straight in his chair as though he were testing the weight of the burden.

I waited to hear his voice. I wanted him to speak his commanding tones, the ones that moved the world, telling me to go on up to that there hospital and tell so-and-so that Henry Carter said to do such-and-such and everything would be just fine, and don't mess with him because he would come up there himself and kick some ass if they didn't do exactly what he told them to. But that voice never came. Instead Daddy sat back in his chair, laced his fingers together, and looked up at me with a question.

"Well, then, Crita, what must we do?"

I remember feeling the consequence of his query, looming large with tremendous inevitability like a tidal wave threatening to sweep me into a dark and forbidding sea. Daddy never asked frivolous questions. They were a waste of time in his book, especially when, in his illiterate life, he depended on asking correct, informed questions to get him through his everyday existence. Frivolous questions could display your ignorance. A smart question was always intelligent. And he knew, in this situation with his son, he needed to be as smart as he could be. If he had to ask me, "what must we do?", he truly didn't know. I understood the sense of such candor, but it still scared me. Suddenly I was a child standing in front of my parents, my father, really, and he was asking me which way to go. The world was upside down and I wanted to be afraid, but I could see what it is that adults like Daddy do see: that there was no time, no room, and no space for me to be afraid. A person puts aside the emotions that, as children, we didn't even know were luxuries. I wanted to be afraid. The needs of my parents required me to be otherwise.

"We'll go to the hospital, Daddy. We'll confront Linc like the doctor says we should."

The next day it felt like before, when Chandra was in the hospital having Savannah. There we all were, Daddy, Mama, Ella, Hazel, and I, all in the car and driving to the hospital. Only this time there were no giggles, no twinges of anticipation, no excited glances tossed back and forth between me and my sisters. There was instead a desperate silence clinging to our skins, deafening our ears and polarizing us so badly that we could no longer stand to look at each other. Ella and Hazel hunched themselves closer to their respective doors, arms crossed and staring out of their windows. I sat in the middle and glared straight ahead, feeling with each shift of their bodies how far apart the continents were where we dwelled in this part of the world. Every so often Ella would sigh, a sound so deep and lonely it could float into the blue notes of a Billie Holiday tune. She had gone out a lot in recent weeks, staying out of the house as much as possible. This was how she coped best, but the effects of this strategy had left her drifting too far from where the rest of us were. Out of the corner of my eye I could see her thumbnail, its silvertone polish chipped, and her similarly neglected forefinger picking at the color's flaking remains. I would have thrown her a line if I only knew which way to send it.

Hazel hated the whole idea of an intervention. She had protested to Daddy, who looked at her like Hazel had two heads and was talking to him backwards as in a dream. He didn't know what to make of her.

"What's the matter with you, girl? You don't want to help out with your brother?"

"Daddy, I'm more concerned with what this could do to you and Mama. There's gonna be a lot of stress involved with confronting Linc and that's no good for either of you. I've read all about this stuff, Daddy, and I'm just weighing the risk here for what we're liable to get out of it. I don't see it as helping all that much, so why bother?"

"You bother because I'm telling you to. You let me worry about me and your mama and get your ass in that car so we can get on down to that hospital. There's too little for us to do here as it is, like we're gonna throw away the one thing we can do because your ass thinks somebody's gonna get sick. Somebody's already sick! Your brother's sick! And we're gonna go down there and see if we can do something about it. Now am I right or wrong?"

Hazel mumbled, "You're right."

"What'd you say?"

"I said you're right, Daddy."

"I thought so. Nettie, gimme my damn keys and let's get the hell on out of here."

In the car, Hazel still bore the face of a child scolded. Though she was seventeen years old, her instinct made her scrunch up her forehead, her eyes dark with disgust. Only vigilant attention to her mouth kept the lips from slipping into a baby-faced pout. I knew she thought this was all my fault, and I dared not touch her for fear of setting spark to the vitriol rushing through her veins.

I was nervous. A summer wind, hot and airless, blew through the car and I felt as though I had to remind myself to breathe. Daddy was fierce and silent. Mama was silent and afraid. What would Linc think of seeing us all there at once? I hoped the enormity of us banded together would have some effect on him but then, at worst, he might not recognize us at all. How horrible would that be? Seeing Linc, his eyes glazed and empty, looking through the bigness that was our father and seeing nothing there? And what would Daddy say to that? What could he do? I tried to hush the anxieties, reaching deep inside my being to center myself. I closed my eyes, focusing on the motion of the station wagon flying down the street, and resolved to dream a dream of solitude that would settle my jangled nerves.

I kept thinking of Chandra. I had wanted her to be there with us. I had gone to her that morning and found her and Tree packing up the contents of the Oberlin Hill house. My heart sunk as I perceived the symbols of our loss strewn all over the driveway, echoing rumbles of the disaster that had placed them there. There were the boxes, stuffed to bursting with Linc and Chandra's old dreams, and Tree standing among them. I saw the anger in his eyes and understood why he went into the house as I got out of my car. He would rather not talk to me than raise his voice, which I'm sure he would have ended up doing had he heard what it was I desired. Chandra went on carrying boxes, placing them in the back of a moving truck she and Tree had rented.

I stuffed my hands in the pockets of my jeans and approached her with no salutation. "We're staging an intervention," I told her. "At Lorain Community Hospital this afternoon."

Chandra nodded and hoisted another box into the truck's cargo bay. "Fine. Good luck with it. I hope it turns out the way you want it."

"What I want, Chandra, is for you to come with us. His doctor says we all have to tell Linc what his addiction has done to us. He needs to hear from you what it's done to you and Savannah."

"What? Like he doesn't already know?" She motioned to the black and gold FOR SALE sign in her yard where a real estate agent had pounded it into the ground. "All he has to do is come here and see that sign on this lawn and see this house is empty for him to know what he's done to us."

"Chandra, please."

"Crita, don't 'please' me, honey. I mean what I say. I'm not coming anymore. I have to think about putting my life back together and making a good home for my daughter."

"What are you saying? You don't care about him anymore? I don't believe that!"

She kicked a box and swept a hand through her ponytailed hair in frustration. "No, I do care. What I'm saying is that I have three extra shifts to work this week and a house to empty and put on the market so I'll have some money to buy Savannah new school clothes in the fall." She stopped and sighed, a brief look of pity washing across her face as she saw how dejected I was. She put her hands on my shoulders. Though I had grown a full two inches since we first met, she could still tower over me and stare down into my frightened eyes.

"Crita, your brother knows who I am and where I am. I'm not reaching out anymore. If he wants us, if he wants me, he'll have to find his own way back to us. I can't do any more for him."

"Will you do one thing for me?"

"What's that?"

"Tell Tree I'm sorry."

She picked up a big-handled tape dispenser and started slapping long brown strips across the remaining boxes in the driveway. "I'll do that. You go on home now, honey," she said. "Give your mama my regards." I found myself staring at the faded fabric of her blue jeans and thinking of Angela Robinson, Linc's first girlfriend. No, I said to myself. Love does not last forever. As I walked away from Chandra I was certain we would never be close again.

We must have been a formidable gang, the Carters, filling that hospital hallway. Daddy barreled down in front and we were next to him, but one step behind. My sisters must have felt it as well because we all walked taller and straighter behind our father, our cheekbones held high and scraping the air with the ferocity of our grandmother. We were the purveyors of centuries of strength and impregnable constitution. Dr. Leeper, who saw us coming, must have felt our power because I could see how he drew himself up, shuffling papers in his anxiety and preparing to talk business with people who meant business. I could tell the very look of Daddy made him feel as unsure as a first-year intern.

"Mr. Carter," he said, then cleared his throat. "Your son isn't here. You . . . wouldn't . . . happen . . . to know . . . where he is? You . . . haven't . . . heard . . . from . . . him?" He spoke his questions slowly, with much embarrassment, as though he had misplaced Linc himself.

"What the hell are you talking about?" Daddy's voice thundered down the hall.

Dr. Leeper stammered, "He's gone, Mr. Carter. He didn't check himself out, he just left. Walked out. None of our staff saw him go."

We stared at each other, totally defused. Daddy moved his head and shoulders back and forth, trying to see into the rooms on the ward as though he wanted to tear down the green curtains in all the rooms until he was certain his boy was behind none of them. We floated in that nothingness for some moments with Dr. Leeper muttering apologies and Daddy, his hands on his hips, saying, "What kind of place you people running down here?" until I grabbed Daddy's arm and dragged us back to earth. I was insistent and pleading. "Daddy, take us home. Right now, Daddy, please? Let me get my car and I'll go look for him."

Daddy looked at me, his face tired and deflated, and started walking back in the direction we came. He shook his head and waved me off of him.

"Girl, we've done enough for that boy. Nothing else we can do now."

"Yes, there is, Daddy. We can find him. We can get him back here where people can help him."

He kept walking. "I feel bad about this, Crita. Real bad. There's something gonna happen and it ain't good. Just like it said in them cards. Ain't nothing we can do about it."

By the time we got back downstairs, our fullness had shrunk to half the size of what it had been before. Daddy didn't say any more. He never told me, "Don't go," but I knew by his silence he didn't want me to. But he was going home anyway; he had to take us home. What I did after that he could not control. I would do what I would do. I didn't even go in the house. I stepped from Daddy's car into mine and pulled out of the driveway again.

Twenty-two

I drove back to the hospital and began my search. Linc had to have fled on foot, I reasoned, so he couldn't have gotten that far, not in his condition. My palms were sweaty on the steering wheel and perspiration seeped through my T-shirt, smelling ripe with fear. I searched in ever-widening circles, spiraling outward block by block with the hospital as my center. Past the pink storefront of Miss Vivien's Beauty Emporium, where I'd had my hair straightened in my youth; past the Broad Street Episcopal Church with the bright red door and a bell tower so dark and forbidding I once thought vampires lived there; past the huge empty windows of the VFW local where tattooed veterans, their necks burnt by the sun, sat in metal folding chairs outside on the sidewalk, smoking Marlboros and damning the layoffs that left them marooned there because they couldn't bear to be at home with their wives and mothers during the day. I rolled down both windows in the Jeep and let the car slide down the street slowly like an open trap seeking out its prey.

I found Linc on Broadway, in front of Bob's Donuts. His presence, in his condition, in a place so familiar to both of us, stung me. I couldn't believe I was seeing him. His pants, already dirty, were now blackened in the rear with soot and tar from his sitting on the pavement. For a shirt he wore a doctor's scrub that he must have taken from a laundry bin, its torso stained with dried blood and tissue. He was standing outside, looking around like he wanted to hail a taxi but he had no money on him. Some gracious soul had given him a cup of coffee and he had it cupped in both hands sipping it and shifting his weight from one foot to the other as though he were trying to keep warm. It was sunny and eighty degrees that day.

When Linc saw me he threw the cup to the ground and marched toward the car. He slammed his hand on the passenger side door, reached in and unlocked it, and let himself in. His eyes burned hot and bright.

"Damn it, bitch, where you been?" He still smelled of hospital alcohol. There were dots of dried blood on his arms where he had ripped out his intravenous tubes. "I called you hours ago." I pushed down on the gas, eager to get us moving. The name he had called me throttled my heart and threatened to suck away my focus, but I steeled myself against it. It would be better not to respond to him on that level, I thought.

"You didn't call me," I said flatly.

"YOU CALLIN' ME A LIAR?"

I cringed, but kept on driving. In my head I calculated the miles between there and the hospital. As I passed vacant lots and abandoned buildings I felt as though I were driving through a war zone. The ground underneath me was mined, and a live bomb sat in the seat next to me. I wanted to reach out to Linc, to touch him so he could feel the sameness of our skin and know that within the fretful fever that held him, here was something safe and familiar that told him home was not far away. But I feared the strangeness of the electricity I could sense buzzing over the surface of Linc's body. My mouth went numb with the sensation, an explosion imminent in every passing moment. He shivered.

"Damn, what you got on you? Ten? Twenty?"

"We're going back to the hospital, Linc. You don't need any money there."

"The hell I am!" He seized the door handle and moved as though he would jump out of the moving Jeep. I grabbed his shirt by the back of its neck, pulling him toward me. Then, looking both ways, I drove through a stop sign.

"Okay, okay!"

He sat back, kicking the dashboard with his foot. Some miracle of Detroit engineering kept the plastic from shattering.

"Linc, where are you staying? I'll take you there."

He was silent for a moment. "I'm staying with a friend. But we have to go find him. I don't have the keys."

"All right. Just tell me which way to go."

There are no rules when the danger sits on your very shoulder. If there were, I would have followed each one to the letter and insisted that such diligence allow me to deliver my brother back to the hospital. But as surely as the heat rises from the pavement in the summer sun, there are no such rules. I navigated by the inner stars that light the darkness of our beings. And when you travel in that fashion only God can see where you're going. Now, with the benefit of hindsight, I see that at that moment I should have lied to him—told him "okay" in the sisterly voice most familiar to him, then drove like a madwoman to the hospital's emergency room bay where the ambulances go. Crashing the car through the doors would have been a perfectly acceptable option. Instead I moved as a censored child, going along with his directions and hoping an opportunity for escape—to talk him into his senses—would present itself.

He directed me down street after street until we were in Southie, but in a complex I didn't know. This was a place of rundown apartment buildings, where people hung out on the street and at the nearby playground because being inside their dank and dirty apartments would be too horrible a reality to face on a bright summer day. In the playground the desperation reared up through the cracked blacktop and killed all the grass and scented the air so deadly that children knew instinctively not to dwell there. Linc ignored a noisy basketball game going on and walked over to another part of a the park toward a baseball diamond grown over with weeds. I saw a man standing alone behind the batting cage who looked through the chain links as though he were imagining a game going on in the field. I looked in the same direction, thinking maybe it was just me who couldn't see the players, like in that movie, *Field of Dreams*. He wore black track pants unzipped at the ankles so his blue and white Nikes, the kind Bo Jackson wore and un-sullied by dirt, were fully displayed. When we got to within a few feet of him, Linc stopped me. He tucked his bloody shirt into his pants like it would make any difference in his pitiful appearance.

"Stay right here," he instructed. "Let me do the talking."

Linc moved toward the man and as they met, I watched them closely, trying to fill in the snippets I could hear with words from reading their lips. They seemed to be arguing. Ignoring Linc's instructions, I walked toward them, determined to talk my brother back into the car. Suddenly the faces of Linc and the stranger burst into surprise and shock, their eyes reeled to the road bypassing the diamond. I turned to see what had captivated them and saw a white Nissan with black tinted windows cruising by. When the barrel of the gun was thrust through the open window it seemed everything was moving in slow motion and I thought it all looked stupid and fake, like a bad movie. I heard someone scream. When I recall the sound now I can only think that it must have been me.

Linc ran. In the flash of sun blinding my eyes as I fell to the dirt I thought I could see Linc running on his high-school track team again. He looked beautiful. His stride was wide and his rhythm strong, his feet hitting the ground in perfect sync with the thud of my heart pumping the blood through the holes in my body.

Hitting the ground made the daydream real and my first thought was to call out to Linc and ask him where he was going. "Take me with you," I said inside, because when I tried to speak out loud, a gurgling sound rushed over my words. I felt as though I were drowning. I fought the sensation, fought the hands of the strangers who pressed down on me and begged me to keep still. But I struggled, crying out and looking in their eyes and throughout their beings and trying to comprehend why none of them were my brother. Why wasn't he there? *Why didn't he protect me?* An ambulance's siren wail washed the sounds of my own voice from my ears. Still, the pain of his desertion overwhelmed the pain of my wounds and it made me shriek myself senseless, preferring the void of unconsciousness to the lack of my brother's arms.

I cannot remember when I first heard her voice. Sometime after a mask covered my face and someone's hands lifted me up and sent me floating in transport—somewhere in there was her voice. It was low and comforting like a lullaby and laced with honey, flowing through my being like a prayer.

"Protect the child," it said.

I wanted to look around and see where the voice was coming from, but all of a sudden it seemed I had no head, no body to turn, and no sense of direction or even understanding as to what a turn was. Everything was around me and in me all at once. Then there were the names floating in the pink and yellow haze in which I existed.

William. Earline. Jade. Buford. Della. James. Vinola.

Vinola.

Grandmama?

"Protect the child."

I saw nothing, sensed everything, while the spirits of my dead ancestors engulfed me. As the names chanted on they were no longer familiar and yet their ancient tones held the substance of something I recognized as the essence of all the people I ever loved: Mama, Daddy, Aunt Mary, Granddaddy. On and on they spoke, whispering their names to me as the only comfort they could give. I can only think they must have carried my soul, passing it hand over hand through each of them, making certain I did not fall into the abyss that I skirted so precariously. My grandmother directed them and, in the growing drone of voices, hers echoed firm above them. I yearned to see her face, but didn't know how to look for her.

"Protect the child."

I don't know how long I lingered there, cradled in exquisite love. I do know I was completely without pain, without fear, totally content to give myself up to the sustenance as easily as a babe to the breast.

Semiramis. Priam. BoyBoy. Frances. Virgil. Bessie Mae. Sela. Sojourner. Cassius. Peaches. Vassal.

Suddenly, I fell no more. From that depth I was rising, rising as though from something more than darkness, more than ashes, more than the depth that man tries to imagine but can hardly conjure. When I surfaced and felt the breath of my body once more, I awoke to my father's face hovering in concern above me.

"Crystal," he said, and in doing so he christened me again as he had when I was newborn and crying in his arms. Though I wasn't certain I had been dead, I knew then that I was alive and whole and supported by his earthly love.

"Nettie, get that nurse to get a doctor in here. Tell 'em this girl done woke up. I told you she was coming 'round."

I could hear what I knew were my mother's crocheting needles fall and clink to the floor.

The story of those days came to me in pieces. And when I could, I told them what had happened to me, but only in pieces. I didn't tell anyone Linc had been there. Everyone assumed I had been looking for him and simply found myself in the wrong place at the wrong time. One bullet exploded through my hip. Another pierced my side, just missing the spinal column as it zinged to the other side of my torso. When I finally arrived at the hospital I had lost so much blood I was barely alive. I slipped the rest of the way on the table and I died. "Sweet Jesus," someone would say whenever this story was retold and Mama or Daddy or whoever was doing the telling got to this part. "Sweet Jesus."

Daddy relocated his life to my hospital room. The overstuffed high-backed visitor's chair covered in turquoise vinyl was just sturdy enough and big enough to stand in for his recliner at home. On a nearby table he kept his own hospital pitcher of water, the remote to the television, a deck of cards, and a pad of paper. He made every doctor or nurse who so much as stuck their head in the door to look at me and write down their name and shift time so he could say, even though he couldn't read the names, "Nobody looked in on this child since four o'clock" or two-thirty or last night's shift change, whenever it was.

When the candy striper brought the daily newspaper he would go through the grocery ads, the only part he ever looked at, because he could comment on the prices. As I improved he would show me the listings.

"Does that there say 'eggs,' Crita?"

"Yes, Daddy," I'd say, raising my head and peering at the bold black print.

"On sale for eighty-nine cents. Have to go by and pick some up."

"Uh-huh."

When I look back on that time I realize this was Daddy's

way of monitoring my progress. I could see, I could read, I could comment with reason. After a while he must have been satisfied that I was in my right mind, because he kept the prices to himself and let me zone out in the hum of the afternoon news on the TV.

Sometimes Mama was there, talking about what was going on at her church—what the preacher had said and who was praying for me and who made the best apple pie for the fellowship luncheon. My sisters would drive my parents there and hover in the room. We would talk a little, but Daddy would scold if he thought they talked too much or I looked too tired.

I could see sadness in Daddy's being, in the curve of his massive shoulders and in the heaviness in the back of his neck from having his head hang so low as he dozed in his chair. I worried about him.

"Mama, why is Daddy doing this?" I asked in a rare moment when she and I were alone.

"I told you before, you're a caretaker and your father is the same. He knows his own."

That was all she would say. The rest I had to build on my own and as I lay there and watched him day after day this is what I would come to understand: He would be more than a parent to me in this. In that room we were no longer father and daughter. We were caretakers. And in his sorrow and guilt he hoped to repair one like himself that he had sent out too soon. If it was possible to stand on equal ground with him, I did so then. I felt it then. In all the years I had never conceived of myself as anything other than a beloved daughter in my father's eyes. I didn't ask for more, didn't need anything else other than to know he would always look out for me. I never thought he would have a vision of me that saw deep into my construction, my abilities and possibilities as a human being, the picture of a dream of what I would become. Now, in that setting, I could see how he saw me. I was the one most like him. I was the caretaker, just like Mama had said. But never before had I known how deeply Daddy felt that. He saw our similarities much more keenly. Like him, I didn't stand out from my siblings. I wasn't blessed with the flash of my brother or the gorgeous fireworks that were my sisters. Yet I would be the one, as he was when his own mother lay bleeding on the floor, to make everything all right. Now I knew why he didn't resist when I moved in with Linc and Chandra. He had sent me like a talisman to follow my brother into the abyss, knowing his son needed a protection he could no longer provide. The guilt ran like an undercurrent in the flow of his words and actions.

I didn't see Linc. I was told he visited, but only in the middle of the night, when I was out cold with painkillers. But in my waking hours he stayed away, slinking under whatever burden he'd deemed right to place on himself. One night when I was nauseous from the morphine and falling in and out of a fitful rest, I thought I saw him there. He sat in the dark, in Daddy's chair, and breathed with the percussive sounds of a battered sinus. I didn't try to talk to him and pretended I was not aware. I had no words for him. I didn't know what shape he was in, whether or not he was high. I do remember thinking for the very first time—I didn't care. There was a deadness in me that went so deep it felt like a weed firmly rooted in my soul.

My world dried up and turned desert then. My heart heaved in its thirst and I had no love, no sustenance with which to cool it. It had run through my hands like so much water and I had no idea where it had gone. Nothing grew in the drought; nothing but my anger which burned relentless and hot in my soul. If I had been well and walking around the heat, slow and engulfing like volcanic magma, surely would have consumed me. The morphine helped. At the press of a button it cooled my disillusion, making me dwell in dewy fields of nausea. Besides, there was no place for this anger to go. When I wanted to lash out at Linc he was not there. Then the heat would attack inward and I would blame myself for all my stupid actions; for thinking I could help him in the way I had tried to help him. All senseless. Fruitless. How could I have been so dumb? But, I thought, where was Linc's blame in this? *Why didn't he protect me?* When the pain of the thoughts became too much, I'd press the button and medicate myself back to the beginning of the cycle. One night I dreamed I was sleeping on the dirt in a forest and a bear found me there and clawed out my heart.

Tree could see it in my eyes. The one time he came to visit me I could see his feet stick to the floor and his body stiffen when he met my gaze. That was exactly what I wanted. I didn't have to say a word to him, but he heard me without mistake: *Do not cross that line. Do not touch me. Do not come near.*

"Good morning, Mr. Carter."

Daddy looked at Tree over the tops of his glasses and nodded. "Boy, I didn't see you come in. Crita, how come you didn't speak?"

That's when I knew every spark in me was truly gone. A question like that from my father would usually make me snap to—"Yes sir," I was supposed to be saying, "Hey Tree." But nothing was happening—not the urge, not the interest. It was like someone had cut that nerve and now all I could do was look at them like strangers addressing me on the street—I wasn't obligated to answer.

I could now understand my grandmother Vinola. Something as traumatic as a gunshot wound brings to the fore more of what you really are. That is the part that takes over. I thought I had grown some of her strength, but where hers made her stay put, mine made me move. I was unwilling to resist it. After I had gone home and then, weeks later, was done with the wordless afternoons Daddy and I had passed in front of a television in the living room, I made my plan. The moment it was deemed safe for me to be on my own, I gathered the pieces of my shattered self, the one the doctors could not heal, and left home for New York City.

I remember Daddy not arguing with me when I told him I had to go. He probably thought he couldn't make the case pleading for my safety when I had been no safer at home. I still found it hard to face Mama, knowing full well why I should have made the trip a long time ago. Most of all I felt dead inside. Just dead. I wasn't sure what would happen to Linc, but the only thing I could think about was what if he died and the feeling had to stay in me forever?

When I first arrived in the city, after an eight-hour drive, I stayed in a women's dormitory on West Thirteenth Street in Greenwich Village. That night I slid my boxes under a bunk bed and listened to the restless movements of a woman who was not one of my sisters in the bed above. I listened to the foreign traffic noise and the styled desperation of a crazy young man bellowing "Stella" at the top of his lungs in the street. I covered myself with a sheet and sighed. The emptiness engulfing me felt too permanent, too complete. I worried I had strayed too far from the sound of my father's voice and the feel of my mother's hands in my hair.

Twenty-three

I watch my mother carefully over these days. I cannot fathom how I would ever let go of a husband the way she must do with hers, and Mama seems to know that this is one thing that only she can teach me and my sisters. If she cries, she doesn't do so in our presence. And though she is quiet and moves, with her age, very slowly, I can see by the way she looks at my father and by the low but urgent tones in which she reads to him from the Bible that Mama is very busy with a sort of leave-taking.

"Mama, do you want to take a break?" Ella asks. "You can't wear yourself out like this."

"That's all right. I must see to him first," she says. "I will see to myself later. There'll be all the time in the world for that then."

Chandra brings Savannah to say good-bye. She raises the little girl up to kiss her grandfather and, once set free, Savannah scrambles into Linc's lap where he sits in the corner of the room. She seems glad to have her father back and cuddles and whispers to him as much as Chandra will allow, which seems to be quite a bit as time goes on.

Everyone is praying, in one way or another—together or alone—and I feel a bit estranged from this. I do not pray often.

The practice does not come naturally to me and I am particularly suspicious of the idea of people praying with prayers prewritten by someone else. How deeply can you feel it when the words aren't even your own?

But when I do pray, I pray in thanks of whatever force it was that sends me back to Daddy's hospital room just at the right time. Hazel is there with Mama. Since our fight she has not disappeared, but we haven't spoken of it, either. The eyes she shows me look afraid and tired, but I don't want to address them. I kiss my mother's cheek and nod when she says, "Good evening, baby." Then I position myself in a corner chair covered in teal green vinyl and watch my father's motionless body until I fall asleep.

In the ether of my dreams, I am wading with Daddy in the waters of Lakeview Beach. He's holding my hand and in the distance we can see a family of dolphins leaping out of the water and joyously calling to each other. Their gray bodies, the skin thick and luxurious, sparkle in the sun. Of course we know these creatures aren't supposed to be in Lake Erie, but we watch and laugh and Daddy is so mesmerized he tries to wade further out toward them. He slips and falls into the water. I gasp, even though the water is not deep. My father has always feared drowning, even hates the feel of water on his face. I reach down to help him up and I fear he will be angry or afraid. But as he wipes the water from his face I see he is smiling. He looks out again at the dolphins and then he looks at me. He says nothing, but I know what he is telling me. It is a good sign, a prosperous sign. Everything will be all right. I smile back at him. "Yes, Daddy."

In this fog I am still murmuring and, half awake, I become aware of people moving in and out of the room. Mama's face, big and sad, materializes before my eyes. She is patting my hands. "Come on, baby doll, wake up now. The doctor says your daddy is about to pass on."

Oh, no.

Linc is standing at the foot of Daddy's bed. He has both hands on the end rail and he's leaning against it like he would fall down if he didn't. He is already crying, the tears falling in big drops down his cheeks. Hazel sits on the bed, her back to our brother, holding one of Daddy's massive hands in both of her own. I can hear Ella pacing outside with Forrest. She cannot bring herself to come in.

I go to the other side of the bed and take possession of Daddy's other hand. I bend over it, pressing his fingers onto my face. *Don't go.* I whisper into his skin. *Please don't go.*

But my Mama is kissing Daddy's face, and the gesture is fearless and full of an old love well spent. With that certainty, it is as though she is saying, so casual and sure, *Good night. I will see you in the morning.*

How long we all stayed that way, I do not know. But when Daddy dies, when the beeping monitors begin to whine and tell us he is gone, I run. I am running down the hall past nurses, past windows, past doors. I go faster and faster until I am outside, faster through the parking lot as though I can catch up with his spirit as it speeds toward the sky. I can almost feel him pulling up and away, so very far away, and my lips cry out and utter the impossible: *"Daddy! Take me with you."*

After some minutes of hearing nothing but traffic noise and my father's voice in none of it, I go back into the hospital. My heart is still beating hard from the running and I feel supercharged with a hyperclarity that makes me see as I have never seen before. I hold my hands in fists to keep them from shaking. I don't know where this energy will take me. My mother, my sisters, and Forrest are sitting in the waiting area, as though they are hoping someone will come and tell them where to go next. When they turn to look at me, their heads seem to grow until they are nothing but faces, round and glowing like a set of full moons. Suddenly they are so clear that I can read them like I have not before, and in that instant I capture and understand for the first time something I have always thought of as "The Look." It's that expression, always fleeting and barely there, that sweeps over my mother and sisters' faces whenever they initially see me. A mixture of awe and fear, The Look freezes their sculptured cheekbones for just a fraction of a second before a full and natural recognition of me flows into their eyes. I have seen it so many times, especially in these weeks since I came back from New York, but before it always fled like a fly too swift for my grasp whenever I tried to take hold of it.

But now, in my wash of hypersensitivity, I could see it all, read it all: I was something of a miracle to them—Lazarus come back from the dead—and they didn't quite know what to make of me. In those moments years ago when I myself had lain on a hospital gurney lifeless, I had slipped their existence and gone down into the valley of shadows, into the place our church teachings had prepared us for; the place whose true nature the preachers could only hint at but which they promised with a fervor hot enough to support the congregants' tired lives. I had gone down into the valley of shadows and walked among the peoples of the past, but instead of staying there in the bosom of our ancestors, instead of becoming the set of memories my family had already been fiercely constructing to comfort their souls, I had returned. What's more, I lived among them as before, their daughter, their sister, and one would think that life would go on unquestioning. But they could hardly see it that way, not when now, as I walked among them, they saw me swollen—filled to bursting with the answers to questions they dared not ask because they didn't quite know how to do so.

And because they didn't ask, I had told no one of the journey that had blistered my soul. I offered it to none of them. The decision wasn't a conscious one. Something in me protected that part of my being without my realizing, as though it knew I had already given away too much that was too precious to me. Any more and the world would want it all and they would want it for free. No. This I would not give away. If someone wanted that piece of my being, they would have to ask for it. Only then could I see what it was I that I would say.

And now, tonight especially, I see how they see me. They want to know where Daddy has gone and what else is there— all useless questions to me because I know I cannot grant their deepest, most impossible desire: I cannot go there, like some new Orpheus, and bring him back again. And he will not come again. *Where did you go? What was it like? Who did you see?*

My mind goes on processing in the hyperclarity. I see the gray in Mama's hair glide in clouds across her head. The white crisp cuffs of Ella's shirt glow like snowcaps peaking from the arms of her blueberry cashmere sweater. The hair on my forearms bristle. I cannot face them and the stare of their moon-round eyes. I cannot go forward and chase down Daddy's spirit in its newborn world. I can only take myself to where it once was. I go back to his room.

I pause at the door, fearful of confronting a corpse underneath a bare white sheet. It would be a thing so massive yet so empty that I fear the very paradox of it may drive me mad. The stainless steel of the door's handplate feels cold beneath my fingers. The chill crawls up my arm and I shudder, which makes me sob as I push into the room at last.

Linc is there. Daddy's bed is now empty, but Linc is there, sitting in the vinyl chair I had been sleeping in not too long before, and when he looks at me, it is with eyes that are earthbound and bereft of joy. I feel they must mirror my own.

"I want him to yell at me one more time," he says.

Just then a feeling wells up in me that I can only describe as primal—as instinctive as fear, as necessary as hunger. It drops like a weight into my being and brings me down to the floor in front of my brother. I rest my head against his knees. I start to cry. And then, as though Linc has silently given me permission to do so, I wail. I wail as though my heart has been irretrievably broken, as though I would shake the hospital apart with my grief, as though I have never had good reason to cry in my life before. This devastation I would take hold of as my very own.

Linc's hands stroke the back of my head and I feel that I am liquid—letting go of everything in me that feels hard and resistant and painful, I flow down into myself and am spreading across the floor. And Linc is accepting it all, gathering me up as though he were drawing water from a well, taking on what I can no longer bear myself.

I believe it is for those moments that I had betrayed my sisters, why I had brought Linc back into our presence and gone against our hard-drawn pact. I must have known I would need him, that only he could comfort me in this. But I had no way of knowing he would come through—that he would, as he did now, put his hands in my hair and hold me to him as though he would hold me together or that, after all this time, he would even remember how.

I can only guess that something inside me knew I had to take that risk—that what I needed far surpassed any disappointment or danger that could spring from the decision. The void Daddy leaves behind is so huge, so deafening in its roar that I cannot understand how he has passed away without the whole world not being compelled to feel it and comment on it, if only to say, "Did you feel something?" And what they had felt, that unnamed presence that had brushed by them like a thought on the wind, represented such a tiny fraction of the total pain and loss we were experiencing. Our root is gone and I, toddling around without a foundation, don't know how I will ever push my feet into the earth again.

Now I feel crazy and wild. I could, in that hour after my father's death, move to a commune, shave my head bald, and set fire to the great monuments of the world. It didn't matter because the one person I felt I had to answer to, who would weightily take me to task for doing these things, was gone. What came next would be of my own making, things brought about for me and no one else. And yet I didn't know where to begin. Daddy had been my lead and my inspiration. Would anything I did matter now if he wasn't there to see it, whether to praise or criticize? I would forever seek his face in the face of every one of our relatives, and be forever disappointed when I could not find him.

But Linc held on to me, taming the wild urges that surged throughout my soul. It is some time before I realize there are words falling from his lips, so many words, over and over again.

"I am here," he is saying. "Crita, I am right here."

I shake my head and the words that come out of me have nothing to do with Daddy. "But you weren't before! You weren't!" This is the way it should have been on that play-ground. I can almost see before me not hospital floor tiles, but the spot where I had fallen, and I'm surprised to see no traces of my blood in the dirt. I thought the earth would soak it up and the stains would be permanent, as they seemed to be on my heart. I whisper to Linc, "You left me there to die, you bastard."

"Yeah, I did. I left you there to die. You think I don't still live that? Do you know, Crita, how much it pains me to see you here, alive, walking around, and know that it's no thanks to me? I could say that I was just high and didn't know what I was doing, but that wouldn't be right. It wasn't the coke that put you in that situation. I put you there, on that ground. I left you. I'm sorry, okay? I am so sorry.

"And I know that's not enough," Linc went on. "It can never be enough because I betrayed everything we were taught to believe about our family. Crita, you gotta believe I know that, I know what I did. And I promise you I will spend the rest of my life making it up to everyone, especially you. Most of all you. Because you believed in me the most. Out of all of them, you loved me the best. And I hurt you the worst."

I grabbed him into my arms then, hugging him as though I would squeeze out the awfulness between us. Suddenly for the first time in a long time I felt warm. I kept crying, letting the tears wash through my system, thawing out all that I had kept frozen. *"I will make this up to you. I know what I did before, I know what I did. And I promise you I will spend the rest of my life making it up to everyone, especially you. Most of all you. Because you believed in me the most. Because you loved me the best, and I hurt you the worst."*

How long have I been waiting to hear these words?

We stay that way until an orderly comes in to clear the room. When we leave I am holding his hand. Already I am calculating: how long can I hold on to this feeling of comfort? To love Linc, once again, unconditionally? Because it was this for which my body and soul starved—my love for my brother. My anger, my fear, my indignity had displaced the food on which my soul fed ever since I was a child. And it didn't seem right to take it back, not when I still felt so hurt by him. How could I have known, enshrouded in simplicity as all answers are, that putting the anger and hurt behind would make the rest come easier?

"Who are you?" Linc once asked of me in one of his stupors.

"I am your sister," I had whispered in his ear, the better to make him focus on the words. "The one who loves you

always—fully, madly, childishly—because it is my distinct priv-
ilege to do so."

"Yeah," Linc would say, his teeth faking an unfettered smile.
"The good one."

And I believed that to be true. Not that Ella and Hazel didn't
love Linc—they just didn't, as I did, so completely avail themselves of the prerogative. No one—no wife, no mother—has
the right to have such a hold, so powerful in its purity, that a
sister may have on her brother. They can't take such wild joy
or bathe in the intense happiness of the connection. There
would be something unseemly about it. It wouldn't be
grounded in the deep attachment of having come forth from
the same womb, of years of protecting each other in childhood
because instinct would allow us to do nothing less.

That's brotherly love, as Mama once said. It sure is.

When Mama and everyone else see us, I know they cannot
believe their eyes and I don't care. When we climb into our
assorted cars to go home, Linc drives mine and I ride with
him. I'll answer to my sisters later if I have to. I am sure,
grieved and tired as we all are, they are willing to wait until
then. At the same time there's this tiny flame inside of me and
I'm trying to figure out how to fan it so it will grow into a
blaze passionate enough to keep me this warm all the time so
I can live my own life once again.

Back at home, Linc helps me from the car as though he were
lifting me from a crib. With an arm around my shoulders, he
walks me down the driveway, past Hazel's car, because they
have arrived before us, and into the house. It is cool from air-
conditioning and still holds the peppered flour smell of the fried
chicken Ella had cooked earlier in the day.

I want to run through the house and hide under the covers
of my bed, afraid to feel Daddy's absence. But before I can

break from Linc's arms I see Tree. He is standing there, near the entrance to the kitchen, with his hands in his pockets and looking sad and unsure of what to say.

"Your mom told me," he says.

Linc takes me over to him. "Take care of her," he tells Tree.

"Yeah," Tree says. "I sure will."

"I haven't been too good about that. You do a better job, okay?"

I can tell Tree is confused, but he responds. "Okay."

Twenty-four

In the darkness I dream again of my father. It was night and Daddy, wearing his favorite candy apple red robe, was standing out in the front yard, surveying the wear on the house, the indifferent rubbish on the scruffy lawn, and the Christmas lights still in the trees. A Jack Russell terrier, filthy with mud and tied to the cherry tree, barked insistently like he was trying to say something and just knew that if he kept on yapping, some English would eventually spill out. Daddy's eyes flashed brown and yellow with agitation. I felt a familiar churn of acid in my stomach and thought for sure I was in for a whippin'.

"Crita, this house is a goddamn mess. What have you been doin' around here, sittin' on your ass all day?" His hands, balled into fists, rested on his hips and as his voice cut through my brain he seemed so much bigger and taller than I remembered him. "Girl, I told you, we own this house, ain't nobody rentin' here. You better clean this mess up."

"Yes, Daddy," I said, looking around, my arms flapping aimlessly at my sides, unsure of where to start. I seemed small, toddler-size even, and the yard and the mess spread about me was the breadth of a football field.

"And take that dog into the house. That barkin's makin' me tired."

"Yes, sir."

"You hear me, girl?!"

"Yes, sir!"

I awake with the affirmation on my lips. It is morning. As I turn over and try to shake the remnants of the dream from my brain, I find Tree awake and watching me. He's not in the bed, there's no room for him, but he's sitting on the side of it, leaning back against the headboard. He's wearing the same red T-shirt and jeans from the day before so I'm sure he's been there all night.

"What are you still doing here?"

"Crita, why would I be anyplace else?"

I shake my head, lean back in the pillows, and smile slightly. " 'Natural concern,' that's what Talane said."

"I told her she had no right to go to you like that."

"She wanted an even playing field. You can't blame her for that. Fighting history, ghosts, that's rough stuff."

"Yeah, but you're not history and you damn sure are no ghost. You're right here, right now. Talane knew what she was getting into."

"And what was that?"

"She and I are friends, Crita. She wanted that to be something more and for the longest time I wouldn't let it. But after a while I agreed to try. And I did."

"You were probably doing fine until I showed up, right?"

Tree's hand, large and warm, is now on my forehead and as he moves it up over my hair, smoothing the curls away from my face, I close my eyes. "Part of it was okay," he says. "A bigger part of it wasn't. I said I would try, but there are certain things in a relationship that you shouldn't have to try so much on. Things you and I never had to try on."

"That's not a fair comparison. Not fair to her."

"No, but it's the way I felt. Crita, if you hadn't come back

I would've been up in that city looking for you inside of a month."

My eyes are open now and I'm trying to focus. "You would?"

"Yeah, because I couldn't stand it anymore. Even if I couldn't get you to come back, I still needed to know. I was gonna make you tell me."

"Tell you what?"

"Why you left. Why you let us go the way you did."

I'm searching his face because I can't believe he doesn't have that information already deep in the marrow of his bones. I thought I had given it to him, if not with words then with energy, with actions. But I don't see a thing in his eyes that would prove to me that was the case. "Oh God," I say. "And here all this time I thought you had read my mind that day— that day you came to see me in the hospital."

"What I remember is that you looked like a cat that day, a cat that had been beaten pretty bad. You were just lying there, but your eyes were frozen on me, hard as ice."

"Yeah, and you didn't say much."

"Crita, what was there to say? I thought you would jump out of your skin and scratch my eyes out if I even breathed wrong. You weren't even connecting with your father. I was gonna come back and try again when you were better. Then suddenly you were up and gone without a word. Your mom told me you were leaving town, but I thought no way were you gonna go and not see me first. So I waited. I didn't want to push you, Crita. But I got no call, no nothing. What was up with that?"

"I couldn't face you, Tree. I couldn't face anyone. I was too sad, too ashamed."

"Ashamed of what? You got shot, that wasn't your fault."

"That's not it," I say, shaking my head. "Tree, I never told you, hell, I never told anyone about the day I got . . . the day it happened." My hands graze over my abdomen. "I still have this picture of Linc in my head. He's running, just running."

"Running?"

"Yeah. Away from me. We're on the playground, in that field and some guy—God, I never saw his face—this guy starts shooting. And I turn to Linc—I may have been shot by then, I don't know, and I'm thinking, 'He's gonna protect me, that's what we do, we protect each other.' That's what he's supposed to do, he's my brother, right? I used to have nightmares about some asshole gunning Linc down and I'm scared for both of us. But in those dreams, Tree, I wasn't there. Maybe I thought that would be the difference there on the playground—the nightmare was coming true, but I was there and that would make things turn out differently. We were together and everything would be all right. So I turn to Linc and all I see is the back of his head! He's running away and I wanted to call out to him. I wanted him to take my hand and take me with him, but I couldn't breathe. Then I was falling and I couldn't see him anymore."

"What has that got to do with you and me?"

I feel like I want to pull on something. I want to reach up and pull down the curtains because maybe that will bring more light in the room, help me shed light on Tree and me. "Don't you get it? I failed him and he failed me in the worst way possible. I had nothing to fall back on."

"You had me."

"I didn't trust that. I didn't let myself have you because I thought I didn't deserve it. Look at what I did. I didn't listen to Mama, didn't listen to you. Then I got shot and I didn't have any right to you because I did this to myself. I couldn't take care of things."

"And who was supposed to take care of you, Crita?"

Tree gets up, pulls the chair away from Ella's old vanity, and drops himself into it. "Someone who's actually out there DO-ING something, trying to make something happen, that's the person who needs care. That person needs help, support, rest, understanding so they can stay strong and keep doing what's necessary. That's all I wanted to do for you, Crita. You need that kind of care, but you would never let me give it to you. And you know what? I need that kind of care, too. You were supposed to bring that to the table. We're supposed to be a team, Crita, in this together. How come you made me part of the other side, huh? Why did you do that?"

"Tree, I didn't mean to. Remember how you used to ask me about our future. I said I didn't think about our future, but I did see it. Damn, I used to have this vision of us living in a house with a pool. You were teaching our children how to swim." I cover my face with my hands. "I used to want that so badly. I just thought I couldn't have it. I was too screwed up to have it."

"You never told me that."

"I never told you a lot of things. Like I never told you I loved you. Still love you. Do you get that?"

"Yeah." He's smiling at me now and I'm feeling more awake, like he's the sun coming through my window.

"Only you're gonna have to help me with this team thing, because I'm not too good at it. I get distracted. I don't work well with others. Hazel, Ella, they would say that in two seconds."

Tree laughs and I hang my head and smile a little. I would laugh, too, but my father is too recently dead. I'm going to have to learn how to do that again. Perhaps Tree will teach me.

"Oh, God, girl, you don't know, do you?" he finally says. "You really don't know."

"Know what?"

"How powerful you are? How powerful you really, truly,

are. Your mama knows. Your sisters know, that's why they're so jumpy they can't even sit in their own skins when you're around. You went to hell and back, almost literally, and they know. They could never do that. And you remind them of that, you put it all up in their face whenever they see you."

"I don't mean to."

"I know you don't. You can't help it—it's what you are. The history is in your hair, it's on your skin. Hell, I probably saw it too when I first met you."

"Then why don't I feel like I have any power?"

"Now that's not really true, is it?" He comes to me and touches a spot of furrowed skin at the center of my brow and traces a line down to the tip of my nose. "You're already different. I could see it in your eyes when you came in last night. What is that, Crita?"

"I don't know . . ." In my mind I am digging through the folds of my heart as though I'm searching for a sweater in a dresser drawer. It was here somewhere, I am thinking. "There was Linc . . ."

"What about him?"

"He's my brother . . . and I love him. I need to be able to love him." I give him the words quickly, before they can escape me again. "Tree, I can't live without that, I can't not let myself feel for him what I've always felt, even if it means forgiving him in a way he can't even ask me for."

"Okay." Tree puts his arms around me again as if he would quiet me. "Can you hold on to that? Because this all seems good. You seem good. Can you hold on to that?"

"Yes," I say as I inhale the musty scent of his warm skin. I feel as though I have given Tree something very precious that I want him to hold on to, and I know he will do so without asking. "For your sake . . . no." I look up into his eyes. "For my sake, I will try."

That day my siblings and I find ourselves in Mama's living room, alone together for the first time as adults. Chandra and Savannah have taken Mama to buy a dress for the funeral, and Forrest and Tree have gone for coffee and, no doubt, will end up having a look at some interesting properties Forrest has spied along the way. I used to think it would be a wonderful thing when my brother and sisters would be old enough to get together like this. We would compare memories and each memory would be different, because we are bound to remember things in our own ways. Those memories would be like each of us having different pieces of the same puzzle, and when we get together we would put the pieces together and marvel at the whole of what we are. But on this day, in this room, I can feel that we all dislike this particular completed picture of us.

Perhaps it is because we are there to talk about money. Linc, sitting in Daddy's well-worn chair with a pad of paper on his knee, says we need to work out how we will all support Mama financially. She will get, as Forrest has researched for us, about $600 a month in Social Security and the remnants of Daddy's pension, which won't be much because the payments for her health insurance premiums will be deducted directly from that check. Fortunately, the house is paid off.

He is talking and his eyes are clear and his clothes are clean and he is confident and I want to believe this picture will progress in the way it always should have, with Linc taking the lead and being the pillar our family now needs. But his words tell me otherwise. They put me on my guard.

"I'll move in here," Linc explains, "and send out the bills and keep an eye on Mama. Haze, since you're still in school, we won't expect you to contribute much, but Crita, Ella, and I will shoulder a lot of this in the beginning. If we each pitch in $150 a month, we can keep Mama pretty comfortable. Her needs are pretty simple."

"Where's your part coming from?" Hazel asks. She is sitting the farthest from Linc in a straight-back chair from the kitchen with her bare feet propped up on one arm of the sofa.

"What are you talking about?" he asks.

"I want to know how you plan to ante up $150 a month. Crita and Ella work for a living. What do you do?"

"Don't worry about my portion," he says. Linc is scribbling on the paper. He seems to be calculating numbers. "I'll come up with it."

"Yeah, how?" Hazel demands.

He looks up at her. "I said I will get it. Crita and Ella, you guys can send your checks to me."

"Say what?" Now it is Ella's turn. "Lincoln, what kind of fools do you take us for? Why would we send our hard-earned dollars to a drug addict? We may as well just throw it out the window and pray it lands in Mama's hands!"

"Stop it, stop it right there!" Linc points his pencil at Ella. "I'm talking about taking care of Mama. I said I will be here. Drugs don't have a part in it. You saying you don't wanna help Mama?"

The raw energy builds and I see what is happening. It forms a dark wave and I see it churning as it moves toward me. I do not know how I will respond when it arrives.

"That's not fair, Linc," I say. I look at my hands; I look at my sisters' faces, urgent and expectant. I cannot look at him. "You know what she's talking about. Don't try to manipulate this. You can't push us around." For as much as I love him, I tell myself, I know what I can and cannot do, or allow him to do, for that matter.

"I'm not trying to."

"Oh, yes, you are!" says Hazel. "You've been pushing us

around for weeks now, like we're all supposed to pretend you're all clean now and the drug stuff never happened."

"I didn't say any of that."

"Doesn't matter," says Ella. "Look, you can move in here and do what you're gonna do, but you're not getting dime one from us, is he, Crita?"

When she lays the question at my feet, I look at Linc and, for the first time in many years, I see him. I know I love him. I know he can't be trusted.

And this is how it will be, this dual world in which I bathe in the warmth of that love and comfort that is so uniquely ours—and I only let that affection go so far, not allowing me to color the truth in more acceptable tones. I don't know yet how I would make my way in that world, but my first step in it would be here.

Linc looks at me and as I read the separate emotions washing over him, I defend myself mentally from each one.

Betrayal. *I didn't do it.*

Disappointment. *That's not my fault.*

Frustration. *I will not go there.*

Sadness. *I am sorry for it.*

All is necessary.

I don't like Ella's style of fighting, forcing me to her side in this way, especially when I do agree with her. But perhaps this is my fault that she needed to do this. She had seen how close I was to Linc last night, and I had betrayed my sisters once before where he was concerned.

"No, I say, bowing my head into my chest. "No, he's not."

"Come on, Crita, how can you say that? What gives you the right?"

I want to think he should know the answer, but for both our sakes, it is safer not to assume anymore. I stand and glance at each of my siblings before I go right up to Linc and stand right in front of him. I am wearing a red T-shirt and my fingers grasp at the cotton as I pull it up over my torso. I stand so that Linc cannot escape the view of my scars. I want each one to explode into his face.

"These do," I say. "I love you, Linc, but these tell me that loving you is dangerous. You haven't done anything that makes me not want to listen to them anymore. If anything, I've ignored them for far too long."

His hands are on my waist. I close my eyes and Linc pushes me away. I don't open them again until I hear the door slam and the car engine start and I know Linc is far away from our house. Only then do I realize that I can still breathe. It is not as it has been before, when he has left and taken all the air out of the room, out of us. I look at Ella, Hazel, and myself as though we have formed some magic triangle that had brought this all about.

"I'm sorry," I say when he is gone.

"You're sorry!" Hazel kicks up her feet, leaves the chair, and throws herself onto the couch. "The hell you should be. You should have let me take care of him my way!"

Now Ella is sitting in Daddy's chair as though she has claimed it as her throne and she waves a hand at Hazel. "Child, stop talking that crazy talk. You're just perpetuating the cycle."

"What cycle?" I ask.

"The cycle of . . . oh, you know," Ella says. "The cycle of *him*. It's always been this way."

"Tell it like it is," says Hazel.

"We have not existed because of him," Ella goes on.

I want to protest at once, the words jumping up into my chest like a jack-in-the-box, but I press them down again. Something tells me that I need to listen to Ella, to understand her. I look into her velvet brown eyes, the part of her most familiar to me, and I tell myself this beautiful, regal woman is indeed my sister and means no harm.

"I know right certain you think that's impossible. After all, we are here, aren't we? We have memories. I remember the smell of that stuffy old feather mattress we used to sleep on. I remember walking down the aisles and grocery shopping with Mama at the Goldberg store. I remember the smell of the grass when Linc cut it every Saturday. There was you and me and Hazel, running barefoot and wild, playing in the streets and screaming like we had lost our minds. So I know we were here, we were living! But there were these times—and believe me, Crita, they hurt like hell—when we were invalidated because of him. Everything he did—running track, going to college. God, even his damn addiction! It all took precedence over us in our parents' minds. It always seemed like Daddy was thinking about Linc, talking about Linc, worrying about Linc. Where was there room for us? When did he think about us? I wanted his attention so bad. The only thing I could do that Linc couldn't was be pretty, so I did that."

She catches the edge of a smile that wants to form on my lips. She nods, as if in response. "I know, it sounds silly, doesn't it? All that makeup. All those clothes. Burning my scalp with straightening combs so my hair couldn't even dream about being nappy. All that just to get Daddy's attention."

"Well, you got it, didn't you?"

"Yeah, but I don't know if it was the kind of attention I wanted." Ella pauses and swallows the watery drop of a tear that has risen in her throat. "I still feel like he didn't give me the respect he gave you. I wasn't substantial. Don't you see? I may as well have been a magnolia in some swampy tree. Somebody here has to take me seriously. I need to be substantial. I don't want to feel that way anymore, like I don't exist."

"And Linc's doing that now? Making you feel disrespected?"

"Of course he is, honey. Coming in here with all his bluster, thinking that he can get what he wants just because he yells loud enough. And it's all happening again! Our Daddy is gone, and what are we doing? We're talking about Linc again! I don't want him to have that kind of power over us anymore. I will not let him act as though we don't exist. He has to answer to us." Ella frowns briefly, then puts her hands on her hips so famously round with love and sensuality and gets up to gaze out the front screen door. Her perfumed air seems to sedate us.

I turn to my younger sister. "What do you want from him, Haze?"

For a moment, she says nothing. She is staring at the ceiling. Ella lights a cigarette and blows smoke through the screen. Just when I think Hazel will remain mute, she whispers, and I realize she's crying. I can't understand her.

"What did you say?"

"BECAUSE HE KILLED THAT BOY!" Hazel is sobbing. I jump to my feet. It's a strange sight. She's babbling like some soul possessed.

"What are you talking about?" I ask, taking her by the shoulders.

"The boy that he was! The boy that I loved!" Suddenly Hazel seems very small to me, like a child, and I realize I am again holding on to the five-year-old version of her. I am remembering it clearly: We were all at the Amtrak station in Elyria and Linc, he was sixteen then, was getting on a train and going to a summer camp for football. I was nine and tasked with holding on to Hazel. She was crying wildly, inconsolably, because she mistakenly thought that Linc was going away forever.

As Linc walked away from us and down the long corridor to the train, Hazel was pulling at me with all her might. I complained to Mama, who told her, "All right, you can go kiss him one more time." I let go of Hazel and she shot away from me like a comet. I rushed after her, afraid she would get lost, afraid that Linc would be lost in the crowding bodies before we could reach him. But now that I think about it, I don't see how I could have lost Hazel. She was wailing Linc's name, her voice echoing throughout the station. People stared at her in fright, amazed that such a voice could come out of such a tiny child.

And Linc heard her. He stood until she got there, and lifted her up into his arms. He whispered in her ear, said things that made her stop crying. Within a minute she was giggling. Whatever he'd said promised enough to make her walk back to me satisfied, when she had obediently taken my hand.

That's the boy Hazel speaks of. The one that she remembers loving with all her soul, all her being—the very same one that we had all loved. Only the loss of that boy could trigger such anger, anger over losing that boy and that love.

I'm not sure if Hazel will believe me. I know what she feels, but my hurt isn't as hard and untended as hers has been all these years. But it's with some hope that I say to her, "He's not gone. He's here."

Hazel keeps crying and shakes her head. "I don't know that. I don't know anything about that."

"Yes, you do," I tell her. "Yes, you will."

"We have a choice, though, don't we?" Ella is stubbing out her cigarette in an ashtray, her face shining with this newborn thought.

I wipe Hazel's tears and we sit on the floor and make a new pact, this one for ourselves. Because, as Ella has pointed out, we do have a choice in how we each decide to love Linc and how much influence we allow that to wield over our individual lives. We vow to put ourselves first in the equation, as Hazel had not when she went out in the streets and bought cocaine; as I had not when I had been shot and strangling myself with despair ever afterward; as Ella had not when she thought ignoring him would make it all go away. This promise is different, one I know I can keep. We love Linc, but he is not our god and he is not our savior. He is our brother.

My father's body would lie in Brookdale cemetery, or Memorial Park, rather. The day we bury him I learn the difference, having no occasion for doing so before. Cemeteries are the Halloween scenes I knew as a child, where stone monoliths rise out of the ground engraved in stern capital letters spelling out the last name of the deceased. Big crosses grow there, as well as angels doomed to sit in deep contemplation, or stand with arms outstretched as though scattering seeds of grace upon the grave below. The whole place seems strangely like a party, a crowd of stone, the forms and figures chattering noisily at each other, too much so for anyone to rest in peace.

So it makes me glad when the line of vehicles carrying our assorted relatives snakes into Brookdale and there are no nattering stones to greet us. Instead the ground is blanketed in soft green grass and the tombstones are merely markers, flat rectangular tablets that lie quietly in the turf.

There are nine men, including Linc, acting as pallbearers. All of them stagger under the weight of Daddy's coffin. These men look like ants trying to carry his form, and I am amazed because so much of Daddy had wasted away with his illness.

I am holding Mari's hand as she tiptoes gingerly from the car over to the gravesite. Her spindly black heels keep sinking into the ground and her smile shines on me like a spotlight. I have missed her.

When Tree joins us, he puts a hand around my waist, but he allows his fingers to rub across the contours of the wounded skin he can feel under my black cotton shirt. He is still learning to read them. I think he believes that in the future they will help him uncover words that I may yet keep buried. As if there was anything left for me to hide from him now. But I am grateful for the touch, the seeking. A man wouldn't dig if he no longer cared about finding something.

I find the peacefulness of the park and the words of the minister comforting enough to allow me to listen to my heart. It tells me Daddy is not in the steel-framed casket they are lowering into the ground. What had been his flesh and blood is in there, yes, but what had been his spirit is not. I feel a kind of joy then, and all the notions I have been taught about Christ and faith and resurrection are, for one glorious, ecstatic moment, lovely and clear. It burns like an ember in the pit of my being and in that instant it singes away my grief and devastation.

A moment later, loneliness douses the flame. For as we turn away from the grave, I know that Daddy will not be seen on the face of the earth again, no matter how hard I will try to see his face in the visage of others who look nothing like him. He is nowhere and yet everywhere all at once. I will look for him always and never find him.

Not far from us, another funeral is in progress. There are the same black stretch limousines, the line of cars behind, each with a tiny flag of a white cross on a purple field with the words FUNERAL in purple block letters attached to the cars' antennae. Black women are dressed in black, shoulders hunched over, shaking their heads. Black men in suits stand tall as the backbone of the procession, moving the grief along.

Then I see the orderly presence of Mr. Calvin Hayes, proprietor of the Hayes Funeral Home. He is the reason everything is the same. He's handling Daddy's funeral, too; indeed he engineers the grieving process for nearly every black family in the community. He stands at a slight distance, his job nearly done, as the minister is finishing the final prayer over the coffin, this one plain and unadorned, not like Daddy's shiny silver-toned version. Mr. Hayes's smooth bronze skin on his balding crown shines; the fluffy white hair climbs down behind his ears and across the back of his skull; the crisp white shirt collar stands out from his neatly pleated black suit. His manicured hands are carefully folded in front of him and his head is slightly bowed, as though to say, "At your service." I find the stance ironic since he is being paid, however graciously he chooses to act like money isn't an issue.

As the flock of the bereaved begins to disperse Mr. Hayes lifts his eyes and sees me. I walk over to him, because, I tell Tree, I do not want him bothering Mama. "Sister Carter," he says as I approach. He addresses me as though we were in church, a habit I dislike since he is connected to no religion that I know of. He probably does it so he won't have to remember anyone's first name. I am pretty sure he doesn't know mine.

"Sister Carter, what a comforting sight you are. It does a heart good, especially on a day like today, to see our young people like yourself thriving and beautiful."

"Thank you," I say.

"You've laid your Daddy to rest, I see. Lord, I'll never forget that Henry Carter. He was something else."

"That he was."

"I've been meaning to drop by and visit your mama. How is she doing?"

"Fine, but you don't have to do that. We'll be by soon enough with the check for the services." That is true, but on the other hand, I am sure he knows something of the problems we've had in the past with Linc. I don't want him lurking around Mama's house like a vulture, waiting for his next payday.

The mourning bodies around the other new grave finally part and begin to move toward the cars. I notice a woman in the middle of the group, her head up and hips thrown back, walking with a weariness that seems to go far beyond that moment, that day. She is familiar, but in a way that I cannot place her immediately. I feel I should know her, but then I have the same feeling when I see soap opera actors on the streets of New York: faces that are so familiar and yet I don't really know them. But this woman looks different, probably because her face is so contorted with grief. When I try to see beyond her tears I realize I do know her, if only in passing.

"Is that Mrs. Warfield?" I check with Mr. Hayes. That would be Annie Pearl Warfield. I had gone to school with her son.

"Lord, yes, it is, God bless her. We buried her son Malcolm here today."

"Malcolm?" I say, not believing. "Not Malcolm?"

"It was a sad case," Mr. Hayes went on. "His family didn't even know he'd died. The hospital couldn't notify the family so he'd been buried in a pauper's grave these past eight months. They only found out he was dead because the Social Security people terminated his disability benefits and sent notice."

I feel my heart floating down into the depths where the Warfields grieve. I see Malcolm in his Cleveland Browns jersey; I think of the big dent in the side of his blue Dodge Omni. I think of his kindness in loaning it to me. As Malcolm's mother passes I reach out and touch the sleeve of her knitted black sweater. She stops and looks up at me. "Mrs. Warfield, I'm so sorry about your son." And I really am, in a way that one is sorry about lost opportunities, however unpromising they may have been.

"Crystal Carter," Mrs. Warfield says quietly. Then her eyes open wide, dark and empty. "Do you know what they did to my son?"

Her son Michael, whom I recognize from Hazel's class, interrupts her. "Hey, Crita," he says, putting an arm around his mother. "Come on, Mama, now is not the time for this."

She shakes off his arm and glares at him like a dog about to bite. "It will always be the time," she says. "From here on out, this time ain't gonna change. This will *be* the time forever. She should know. Everyone should know what they did. There will never be enough time to tell the story of my poor child. The time of my last breath on this earth will be the time to tell of my boy."

Michael backs off, fading four steps behind his mother. She takes my arm. "Come on, honey. Walk with me a little. Did you know my son?"

"Just a little. From school. We had the same classes."

"He was a good boy."

"Yes."

"He was lost for months, but nobody would help me find him. The police. Doctors. Nobody. I prayed night and day.

"When they found him and took him to the hospital, they should have known my son was respectable. They did not pick up a bum on the street. His dress was impeccable and his apartment was always neat. Crita, he was fussier than I was. They claimed he had been treated and released. It just eats me up that they threw him away like a piece of garbage."

We reach the Hayes limo and Michael hops in front of us to open the door, but Mrs. Warfield doesn't get in. She places a hand on the car and stands confused, as though she has forgotten how to climb in. "I dream about him sometimes," she goes on. "He comes to me in my sleep and says, 'Ma, how could they do that?' I tell him, 'I don't know, baby. I just don't know.'" She begins shaking her head and I know she is no longer aware of me. Tears roll down her brown weathered cheeks. "I wish I could've seen him one more time. I could've said good-bye. I could've been a mama to him one more time."

Michael takes his mother's hand and gives her a snowy white handkerchief. Slowly, he eases her into the car in which I can see the waiting faces of other female Warfields. The limo pulls away and Michael and I walk toward his car. "Malcolm was on heroin," he explains. "He'd been off and on for years. The only reason we didn't know he was missing right away was because he'd drop out of sight like that sometimes. He'd go to rehab, just check himself in." He stops and looks away, tears choking his throat. "They said he was HIV positive when he died."

"Michael, I'm sorry. I really am."

"I should've kept in touch with him, kept better track of his comings and goings." He pauses. "We're gonna sue. Nothing else we can do. Shit like this probably happens all the time and they don't do anything about it. We'll sue their asses."

He says it with resolution, as though a lawsuit would be the answer, the thing that would stop his hurting. I want to tell him he will not get what he wants from the proceeding, that his brother will still be gone and he will still feel the blame; that action can often mask a problem instead of solving it. But knowing how useless these words would be to him, I only say, "Good luck."

I watch the cars pull away, all of them weighed down by the might-have-beens and should-have-beens of the assorted bereaved. I didn't want me or Mama to be Mrs. Warfield, our hearts dressed in black for the rest of our lives. I didn't want to come back to Brookdale with Mr. Hayes organizing the pathos. My brother was not like Malcolm, decaying in some unmarked hole. He was alive. That meant there were still possibilities.

But what am I willing to do? I am willing to let Linc go. For as surely as I am the caretaker that my blood and my daddy raised me to be, I know I am not God. I am willing to focus on the things that are in the realm of my humanity—worry, sadness, sorrow. I am willing to say I have done all that I can do. I am willing to cry when the time comes. And, when I am ready, and if it is necessary, to walk away from his grave.

Daddy didn't worry. In those last days of precious consciousness, he never uttered the ugly words: drugs, cocaine, dope (a word I thought always sounded silly on his tongue), or regret. It had been enough for him to see Linc there, to believe he was once again that obedient son, brave and beautiful, who would bring him only pride. He believed it even though Linc, bloated and broken as he was, no longer looked that way.

I suppose I only needed to give Linc the chance to come into the room and fill it as he always has, to have his head reach the ceiling and the walls curve outward with the fullness of his personality. But this time he wouldn't have that much space to fill because the room would be nothing so cavernous, so empty, as I have built it to be in the past. The room would be my heart.

Whatever comes, I tell myself I will incorporate the conflict of Linc's addiction, and live whatever I do to the fullness of it with Tree and with my sisters and with the scars inside and outside of me that may or may never heal.

"Who was that?" Tree asks. He is leaning against the long black limo, and my mother, Hazel, Mari, Chandra, and Savannah wait inside.

"I'll tell you later," I say, and I kiss him on the cheek. "It's a sad story." *But it is not my story.* As he helps me into the car I realize we will go home again, to our home, wherever that may be, very soon and I am glad. Mari takes my hand and holds on to me, but in a way that tells me she knows—I will not be living in New York City again—not now that I know how to be at home.

Hazel has not cried since that day in the living room. She is talking to Mama in an absentminded way about returning to school in the fall, but I wonder if she will indeed go back anytime soon. I know her workroom in the shed and her dolls await her—and I know for certain that from now on, the windows of Mama's home will forever sparkle.

"Okay, baby," Mama tells her. "You do what you want to do." Then she closes her eyes tight like a child fervently wishing. "Praise the Lord," she says after some minutes, then she opens her eyes. "Amen."

"What is it, Mother Carter?" Chandra asks. Savannah is on her lap and asleep with her head on Chandra's shoulder.

"I'm just thanking God that I have all you children. And that I had your Daddy for as long as I did." The sun shines through the tinted windows and highlights the gray streaking through her hair.

"Amen," we all say. "Amen."

We go to the church for a potluck dinner of barbecued meats, corn on the cob, and apple pie. The voices filling the room are cheerful, glad to have the job of grieving done. Ella is over-seeing the tables and I love watching her. She can put down a plate of biscuits, turn and accept condolences, wipe away one beautiful, graceful tear, then turn around and get more food from the kitchen.

I am watching Tree as well. He's across the room, wearing the most beautiful black suit I have ever seen, made of silk, with perfect creases in the pant legs. He's also talking to Talane. Her hair is braided and wrapped around her head like a crown and her black dress looks vintage, with short sleeves, a flared skirt, and white piping. The little lines around her mouth bend into perfect parentheses as she sips from her glass.

Mari nudges me in the side. "My dear, are you keeping an eye on the competition? Though it doesn't look like you have much to worry about, I'll tell you that now."

"Be cool, Mari." I put my arm around her waist and kiss her lightly on her left temple. "She could be a friend."

"Oh, really?"

"Yes, really. We have something in common." I'm nodding towards Tree. "We both know what it is to lose him. I feel for her, Mari, I really do."

"You have a good heart, love." She sighs and shakes her head. "What am I ever going to do without you?"

"You will come see me and remind me of who I am," I tell her. "And of how I lived when I had forgotten that." She's looking around like she's casing the place. "All right, Mari, I give. Who are you looking for?"

"I was just wondering where that delicious brother of yours got to."

"If he feels half of what I do, he blew this joint long ago. I'm about done with all this for today."

As if he's read my mind, Tree comes to me. "What's up, babe? How you doing, Mari?"

I touch his arm. "I'm gonna go back to Mama's house for a bit, okay? I just wanna crash before everyone else comes home." I love him so much more than I did a few weeks ago, and I wonder how that could be possible.

"I'll come by later and check on you, okay?"

"Okay. Mari, I'll see you tomorrow?"

"Of course, dear. We'll talk about getting your apartment packed up and your stuff back here."

"Thank you." And I'm kissing Tree. "Good-night."

The house is quiet when I return. I am fearful of echoes, the sound of my father's voice too recent in my memory to silence it in this place he once filled. But I move through the rooms with acceptance—his voice will always be around me, I know that for certain. There is nothing to be afraid of. I only need time to become accustomed to it.

I decide to take a bath. I do not notice the crevice of light slicing across the floor of the hallway. I open the bathroom door and there, awash in fluorescent light, is Linc. He has a razor blade in his right hand and he is cutting cocaine on the porcelain edge of the bathroom sink. When he raises his flustered eyes to me they are filled with sadness and exhaustion. It is no wonder he can do nothing but shrug his shoulders. He gives me no excuses, no ably constructed apology.

I go to my brother with no more quickness or concern than I would have if I had come upon him in a garden weeding. I take the blade from him, slicing my right index finger. But I do not relinquish the metal. I take Kleenex from the counter and, surprised by my own calm and clarity, wrap it around my bleeding finger. Linc is silent as I wipe the sink clean of my blood and the drug. He leans his head against my hips as I work, and when I turn, I kiss him on the forehead between his remorseful eyes. The blade is in my hand. I prepare to do battle once more.

Epilogue

The streets of Lorain are in worse shape than they used to be. You used to be able to drive around a gaping pothole or finesse your way over the jagged cracks. Now there's no point. Left and right, all of the pavement lies deeply pocked and you may as well drive right on through. Was it this bad in New York? Hell if I know. I didn't drive enough then to notice.

I'm conscious of it now because I don't want to disturb my son as I rumble home from the grocery store; he has nodded off in his Dalmatian-speckled car seat and I am grateful for the silence.

No, no amount of asphalt will repair these roads, they've been too long neglected. There will always be another hole, another blemish. It's like that with Linc, I see that now. You don't avoid driving the roads, though, do you? So it is with my brother. I stay on the path.

Linc went into rehab the day after Daddy's funeral. And we were all there, visiting on a regular schedule. We were good at that kind of thing—of course Linc had taught us how. It took the counselors some time to understand that. They like for a person to be cut off for a while, but that's not how we wanted to do it. Daddy's loss was too new, the grief too fresh. None of us wanted Linc to mourn alone, not when we hadn't given him proper credit for his support throughout our father's illness.

Us. We. Our. I say those words with pride and relief. There's a lot I don't carry around anymore because I share it with Tree, with my sisters, my friends, with Chandra. And it's a good thing, too, because Linc's first go round with recovery didn't take. He fell off the wagon two more times, but loudly enough for us all to hear—for us to know when we had to go get him. When those calls came I would sit down and breathe. I asked Tree to hold my hands and I would tell him what I wanted to do. Once I didn't want to do anything and he said, "That's okay. I got this." I stayed at home and poured mulch over the roots of my hydrangeas and mixed acidic pellets into the earth so the hydrangeas would bloom with the deepest blues.

I love my brother, but I wonder if he did all that falling off on purpose, to test his safety net. Because it was like once he knew it was there and functioning properly he went on and started living a normal life, as though he were finally getting around to an errand he'd always meant to do. Now Linc works at a shiny car dealership in Westlake selling Lexuses, Mercedes, and BMWs. I don't understand who around here has that kind of money for such luxuries, but then perhaps Linc's success in this venture is just another testament to his God-given charm. He could sell swampland in New Jersey if he wanted to. I think that's why he and Chandra do the dance that they do. Neither of them has remarried, and they act like they aren't together, but I don't see them spending any brain cells on looking for other partners. Savannah is an easy excuse, especially now that she's entering those tricky adolescent years. I'm sure Chandra is still working on trusting Linc. I'm sure Linc is still working on proving himself to her. I can never know for certain. I stay out of their business now.

Because I have Tree I can leap out into the air and love Linc with all that girlish craziness my heart requires. Tree is my safety harness—he will not let me fall. So whenever I see Linc it's like Christmas and the face he sees from me is one shining with unconditional love and not cloudy with mistrust or disappointment. I don't know how much of what I do helps or harms him, but I can't be concerned with that—I know that road and it was nothing but a damn dead end.

Tree and I have been married for four years and our son is two. I named him Henry, after Daddy. Ella's daughter Hope is the same age as Henry. When Forrest and Ella bring her here for visits she makes me laugh because I can tell who her mother is. The child won't go near a sandbox and I would swear I've seen her trying to pick dirt out from under her tiny fingernails. We watch the little cousins with wonder. Hope is already two inches taller than Henry and when she runs I see the struggle to fold her limbs just so in order to keep her from getting tangled up in them. She will be a runner like her Uncle Linc. And my son?

"Goodness," Ella says. "There's so much of Daddy in little Henry."

It's true. He is watchful like Daddy. I see him practice climbing our stairs with Hope and he stays two steps behind her, his chin up, the cinnamon skin of his arm already rounded with mini-muscles just like Tree's and he keeps a hand raised and floating in the air to catch Hope if she tumbles back to him. I'm proud of him. But I want him to be a child for as long as possible.

"Mari, I'm serious, he mirrors every face I make! I don't want him to start making that little frown, deep between the eyes in the middle of his forehead like I do." Mari makes me laugh when we speak, almost weekly, on the phone. I promised myself I would laugh more often, especially now that Little Henry is here.

"Oh, my dear, of course you don't! He'll need Botox before he hits kindergarten!"

"God, I didn't think of that!"

"That's why I'm here to do this kind of thinking for you. It's very important."

Talane keeps me clear-eyed and grateful. Whenever she walks into our home, which is often, I can see how easily it could have been the other way around, with me knocking on her door and visiting a family consisting of her and Tree and creamy-skinned children with muddy brown hair. I share with her the extra plants when I divide my columbines, hosta, and black-eyed susans. Tree vets the occasional new boyfriend she will bring to dinner.

We live just off of West Erie Avenue, not far from Lakeview Park, in an old Victorian with a wide porch and white wooden posts that hold the roof above it. Sometimes I'll sit there on a summer evening watching the fireflies and smelling the catalpa blossoms and conjuring the feeling of Daddy. I miss him. Every so often I'll see him in my dreams and I'll tell him so. It's like he's right there with me, on the porch or sitting at my kitchen table eating buttered biscuits with hot coffee. I'm going on as though it's perfectly natural, and then I realize it's not real and I have just a flicker of a second to tell him I love him before he's gone again and I wake up with Tree softly breathing beside me.

There are days when I crank open the paned-glass windows that look out over our backyard and I can smell the water in the air and it's like the lake is calling me and I go. I might have Henry with me and Tree and we're all holding hands. I walk and think about how it's a funny world, this one, where the caretakers are now well cared for, and the ones we once looked over look after themselves. I'm sure Hazel is bewildered by how little Mama needs her. But Hazel is still so young, as Mama says to me one Sunday afternoon as she walks along Lakeview Beach with me. "That child needs to be out and about her own life," she says. "And I need to be out and about mine."

She is walking barefoot in ankle-deep water and holding her sandals by the heel-straps with her fingers. She stops and rests her hands on her thick hips. "Lord, this water feels good on these old bones."

Mama surprised us all. Nearly a year after Daddy died she put away her grief and changed her life as quietly as she would change clothes. *And she learned to drive.* None of us could believe it, and I know for certain that Hazel didn't realize what she was in for. She had asked Mama what she needed, that she'd help with anything. And Mama just said, straight and clear, "Take me downtown to get my learner's permit. Then I want you to sit down with me and teach me how to drive the station wagon."

Mama drives straight through the potholes. Gonna tear up the bottom of that poor old wagon one of these days, but hell, at least she gets to where she wants to go.

I'm smiling because I'm hearing all the colors of that old conversation she had with me long ago in her words about Hazel. "You'll set her straight, Mama," I say. Hazel would pay more attention than I ever did. Plus she has an interesting life and friends, especially good-looking boyfriends, to lure her elsewhere. "No way am I gonna worry about Hazel."

"No one said you had to, honey. Never do beyond your share. The Good Lord will do the rest. I know too many times I went farther than I needed to into a world of worry."

A world of worry. That was another place, so far away. And here we are now with the sun on my mother's worn leathered face and suddenly she's smiling at me, her cheekbones round and prominent and her eyes sparkling like a little girl about to tell a long-kept secret—and she does.

"But then you kids always did take care of yourselves."

I laugh and in that moment I, with my cheekbones high and my dimples deep, must look very much like her daughter.

"Yes, Mama."

READING GROUP GUIDE

ALL I NEED TO GET BY

1. Do you agree with Mama's assertion that the world is made up of caretakers and those who are cared for? If not, why? Is it true for her family? Why or why not?

2. Why are the stories of their grandmother and Daddy's childhood so important to the Carter siblings? Do you have similar family stories that you consider important or inspiring? What are they?

3. What makes it so hard for Crita to go home again? Is it one issue (Linc) or many?

4. The theme of family and what is expected of a family member shows up repeatedly in the book. Crita and Tree argue over it as well. How far does one go to help family? Who in the book went too far? Who didn't go far enough?

5. In many ways Daddy seems both powerful and powerless when it comes to his children's lives. Is he an effective father? Why or why not?

6. How is Crita's story different from those usually written about African-American families? How is it similar?

7. How does Crita have to change so that she can find her way back to Tree?

8. What aspects, if any, in Crita and Linc's relationship do you see in your own with your siblings?

9. Linc grew up with a love and support that some young black men don't have. Why wasn't it enough for him? Do you blame him for his fall?

10. What role do dreams play in the book?

11. How does the family change as Daddy deteriorates?

12. If you were Crita, what would you have done differently when you learned of Linc's drug use?

For more reading group suggestions visit
www.stmartins.com

Get a
Griffin 🕊 St. Martin's Griffin